ELITE: RECLAMATION

by
Drew Wagar

Published by Fantastic Books Publishing
Cover design by Heather Murphy

ISBN: 978-1-522819-01-1

Based on the space trading game
Elite: Dangerous by Frontier Developments.

Elite: Dangerous © 2014 Frontier Developments plc. All rights reserved

© 2014 Fantastic Books Publishing

Elite: Dangerous © 2014 Frontier Developments plc. All rights reserved.

The right of Drew Wagar to be identified as the author of this book has been asserted by him in accordance with the Copyright, Designs and Patent Act 1998.

CREATESPACE EDITION

All rights reserved.

All rights reserved. No part of this publication may be reproduced, stored in or introduced into a retrieval system or transmitted, in any form, or by any means (electronic, mechanical, photocopying, recording or otherwise) without the prior written permission of the publisher or unless such copying is done under a current Copyright Licensing Agency license. Any person who does any unauthorised act in relation to this publication may be liable to criminal prosecution and civil claims for damages.

'Elite', the Elite logo, the Elite: Dangerous logo, 'Frontier' and the Frontier logo are registered trademarks of Frontier Developments plc. All rights reserved. All other trademarks and copyright are acknowledged as the property of their respective owners.

This book is dedicated to Hiram Holroyd Wagar, 1942–2013

It was my father who first kindled my interest in Astronomy and Computing. 'Thanks for showing me the "Frontier", Dad.'

Thanks to:

As you might expect, a vast number of people deserve credit for bringing *Elite: Reclamation* into existence. First and foremost, thanks must go to my wife Anita and sons, Mark and Joshua, for their enthusiastic support, uncounted cups of tea, chocolate, biscuits and generously allowing me to have the time required to write a book of this type.

Martin Gisle deserves the next mention for his now infamous joke on the Oolite forums – 'Maybe you could start a Kickstarter Campaign to fund your £4,500 pledge!' That truly was the genesis of this book.

John Hoggard, also from the world of Oolite, has been a staunch supporter throughout and has been a steadying influence particularly at the beginning of the project.

Griff, for the loan of his amazing Cobra Mark 3 model, for use in some of the promotional videos and assistance in getting it to 'fly'.

Dave Hughes, for bravely attempting to reconcile the backstories and history of the Elite universe. It's gratifying to see his work recognised in the official timeline. Oh, and the man hug.

Grant 'Psykokow', for just being a most unique individual and a huge source of encouragement and fun throughout.

Jason Hall, for a thorough proofread and valuable suggestions on the closing Chapters.

Michael Brookes at Frontier, for sheer hard work in dealing with his day job as producer, managing the authors and their insatiable desire for detail and writing a book at the same time. How does he do that?

Daniel Grubb, my publisher, for being the most professional and enthusiastic supporter of the project from the beginning. Probably the most positive, if occasionally unhinged, person I've ever met in my life. I couldn't have found a better person to encourage me along.

Mae, my editor, for invaluable suggestions on the manuscript. This story is far better as a result of her attention to detail and sage advice.

The 'Lave Radio' crew: Chris Forrester; Chris Jarvis; John Stabler; and Allen Stroud, for their amazing podcast and unfailing support of all the authors.

Allen deserves a special mention for his efforts in making all the fiction as consistent as possible.

Darren Grey, for his 'Comms from the Frontier' podcast. Ditto John Harper. Good luck with your books, gents.

Kate Russell, from BBC Click, for being such a good sport and siding with me in the 'dumping radioactive waste' affair.

Marko and Ulla Susimetsa, for waving their swords around. I think you'll both like my heroine.

To all those who followed my blog and website throughout, offering support and valuable suggestions during the tough process of writing the story.

Everyone at LaveCon who told me, 'No, you are doing an audiobook.' You got your wish.

The members of the Oolite forum themselves, for 'carrying the torch' for Elite through these many years. Zaqueesoan Evil Juices are on me, Commanders.

Thanks must also go to each and every person who pledged against my Kickstarter in late 2012 and via paypal over the following year. Without their financial help, this project would never have even started. That 465 people were prepared to back me, particularly when most didn't know me, was a very humbling experience indeed.

Credits

Those folk who pledged to my Kickstarter at the £25 or above had the opportunity to have their names mentioned here. Thank you for your generosity and helping to bring *Elite: Reclamation* to life.

Adam Mellor; Adrian; Aidan Thomson; Alex GS; Alexander R. Jenner; Anders Svensson; Andre Czausov; Andy 'Above Average' Smith; Andy Monks; Anis El-Mariesh; Anita Wagar; Austin Goudge; Ben 'MonkeyMan' Thwaites; Ben Staton; Brad Roberts; Chand Svare Ghei; Chonty; Chris Brind; Chris 'Crispy Leper' Lepley; cim; ClymAngus; Cmdr Ricardo 'Tricky' Harrison; Colin Barker; Commander Kevin Jameson; Commander McLane; CptSparky; Cristari; Cute Rabbit of the Obsidian Order; cuteLittleRabbit; Dale Thatcher; Dan Pehrsson; Darren Hill; Dave 'Selezen' Hughes; Dave Vint; David Pratt; David 'Saint' Bodger; David Wilkinson; Dean Crawford; Dennis Thony Pedersen; Denver Giles; deusx_ophc; Duncan Bell; Elkie; freuyh; Frog's Friend; Gary Edwards; Gerrit Ludwig; Gimi; Grand Admiral Scott; Griff; Håvard Sunnset; Howard S; Iain M. Norman; Ian Crawford; Jacqui Wagar; James Doyle; James O'Shea; James Weir; Jay; Jaymes Sattler; Jerry George; Jesse Lim; Jim Collins; John Darsley; John Hoggard; John Whitehouse; Jon Metcalf; Jonathan Hammond; Julian Crisp; Karl Matz; Maik Schulz s.p.; Majogu; Mark; Mark Bull; Matthew Benson; Michael Midura; MichaelT; Milton Stephenson; Mochyn Daear; MonkeyMan; Nat Saiger; Neil Lambeth; Neil Smith; Oliver Borchers; Paul Cook; Paul Maunders; Pekka Timonen; Peter Augustin; Peter K. Campbell; Phil Cherry; PrintsAhoy; psema4; purplepete; Ray Watkinson; Roland; Rorschach; Sam Stanley; Scott Conlan-Jackson; Sean A. Curtin; Shaun Chadwick; Shaun Gibson; Simon J. Peacock; Solids2go; Steffan Westcott; Stephen Varey; Steve Trumm; Steve Wyeth; Terry Walker; TFG; Thargoid; Tomduril; Tormod Guldvog; V3teran; Victor Tombs; Vincent Ecuyer and xzanfr.

Author's Note

In 1984 I was a young, slightly autistic, socially awkward boy with a penchant for computers. Space itself, adventure, exploration and the first faint flushes of romance were the storytelling I loved. I lost myself in the novelisations of *Star Wars*, the works of Arthur C. Clarke, Edgar Rice Burroughs and Anne McCaffrey.

Computer games were primitive and simplistic in those days. Insert coin. Left, right, up, down, shoot. Beat the high score, gain an extra life, last a little longer, die and try again. No story, no background, just pixels. It was all very predictable. I remember asking myself why there wasn't a 'Peace Treaty' button in 'Space Invaders'. Imagine that. Those games were fun, but you had no 'choice' as to what you did. Despite orders of magnitude improvement in their graphics, most games today have the same limitations.

Into all this came a game that was nothing short of a revolution, a game which broke the rules, tore them up and threw them away. A game you could play for months, not minutes: a game that had no ultimate goal or even a score, but a game that pitted you against the universe, ill-equipped, with just your wits to save you. Its name? Elite.

The graphics and gameplay were advanced for the time, but by modern standards, laughably primitive. Much can, and has, been written about the three-dimensional graphics and procedural generation that Elite utilised. Clever for sure, but for me, a focus on the technology misses the truly dramatic impact of this game on my generation.

This was the first game that started with a story.

The late Robert Holdstock wrote a novella to go with it: *The Dark Wheel*. A tragic loss, a shadowy villain, a quest for revenge, mixed with a smattering of romance. Derivative stuff perhaps, but new territory for a computer game. I can directly trace my own writing career back to this story. It inspired me to start writing. Thank you for that, Robert. Writing has given me immense joy over the years.

The game fostered immersion in its own self-contained universe. There were huge gaps in the experience of playing, which were impossible to avoid given the limited technology of the time.

Those gaps were filled over and over by the imagination of fertile young minds. Those weren't just ships on the screen, they were pirates and bounty hunters, crews with a mission, going somewhere, doing something. It left a profound impact on my friends and I, and hundreds more fans I've come to know in recent months and years. It changed us, became part of our culture; a shared formative experience with an effect that has lasted decades.

Thirty years has passed since the original game. No longer a child; I'm a husband, a father, a manager of people. Elite was a fond piece of nostalgia from my youth, wistfully remembered on rare occasions. There have been fan-remake games along the way, such as the wonderful 'Oolite' and 'Pioneer', supported by a vibrant community with their own unique flavours.

Yet in all that time there was almost total silence regarding an official sequel. I considered it highly unlikely that it would ever be written. I thought too much time had passed.

I was proven wrong on Tuesday, 6 November 2012.

Aiming for an astonishing funding target of £1.25 million, Elite abruptly reappeared on my radar as a 'Kickstarter', a new game called 'Elite: Dangerous'. I had no idea what a Kickstarter was, but it didn't take long to establish it was a crowd-funding initiative. £200,000 was pledged within the first day, it looked like a foregone conclusion.

I sent an email to the Frontier crew, asking whether they were considering a sequel to *The Dark Wheel* and whether or not there was a possibility to 'audition' to write it. There was no response. I guess they were pretty busy at the time.

Shortly afterwards a new pledge award appeared. It was for a 'Writer's Pack', allowing anyone to write an officially licensed book within the Elite universe. Frontier themselves would provide background detail on the game, privileged information, graphics, logos and even help with promoting the resultant story. Fabulous!

There was a downside though; the 'Writer's Pack' pledge level cost £4,500.

My initial reaction to that was 'Game Over, Commander'. Not many people have £4,500 to indulge on a speculative venture of this type, and I was no exception. It was far beyond anything I could finance with no surety that I'd be able to make the money back. Contrary to some perceptions, writing is not a lucrative career for the majority of authors. It wasn't clear at the time that the 'Elite: Dangerous' Kickstarter would succeed or not. Financially it was simply too much and too risky. I pledged £40 for the game and a 'non-player character' name – a little immortality in the game – and left it there.

And then a friend made a joke. 'You could always start a Kickstarter to fund the Kickstarter.'

It was a stupid idea. It obviously wouldn't work. It probably wasn't even allowed. We all had a good laugh about it. And then somebody asked the obvious question. 'So, why wouldn't that work?'

There was silence.

Research began. It wasn't against the Kickstarter rules as far as I could determine. I had written books before, so I knew what I was doing. I was confident I could write a book in that timescale. I even had some previously published work to point to as examples, I had a track record. I thought about pledge rewards; characters, dialogue, a copy of the finished work. Perhaps it could work, but would Frontier allow this approach? I summarised my intentions to them and sent another email. Would they respond this time?

The answer was prompt and from David himself – 'Yes, that's fine. And good luck!'

The only question left in my mind at that point was would the Elite fan community be prepared to fund £4,500 for a relatively unknown author based on little more than a page on the internet. Would it work? Frankly, I suspected it would crash and burn, but I knew I had to try or forever live with the knowledge that I might have missed my own personal 'Signing the Beatles' moment.

Feedback from the fan community, if the Kickstarter comments page was anything to go by, was mixed. Some folks thought it was a great idea, others (with various levels of ire) were much less enthusiastic, accusing me of 'cashing in' and trying to derail the 'Elite: Dangerous' Kickstarter itself. I got some quite unsavoury emails during that time, some laced with anonymous unimaginative profanity, some even accusing me of being a crook. Clearly it was a controversial idea.

My pitch was that I was a fan myself. I tried to indicate this with my videos and text for the Kickstarter project. I hoped to appeal to the nostalgia, allay fears and show that I merely wanted to fulfil an ambition, but also come across as a serious contender.

I launched my own Kickstarter at 9am on 21 November 2012.

Immediate friends, family and internet buddies pitched in on the first day as you might expect, but overnight on the first day a serious pledge came in, £500 in one fell swoop. One-third of the target had been reached. It was at that point I begin to believe it was actually possible.

Then the press coverage started.

A few internet articles may not sound like a big deal, but when it's directly about you and what you're doing it seems like a pretty intense spotlight. The controversy that had appeared in nascent form on the Kickstarter comments page, now raged across major gaming websites. On balance most of the coverage was on the negative side. There was lots of derogatory talk of pyramid and Ponzi scheming, even though I'd been very clear (I thought) as to what I was trying to do. I was after something very concrete – an official license. Many folks seemed to be under the impression that I was just grabbing money. The potential for people to misunderstand intentions, read in their own bias and attack something because it's already under attack was reaffirmed. Change is difficult and crowds are fickle things.

But some articles were positive. A number of internet stalwarts bravely defended me, a growing list of backers on my own Kickstarter indicated I'd done something right and, I'm told, there's no such thing as bad publicity. I persevered, trying to answer the detractors with rational explanations, reassuring people as to my intentions. The naysayers grew fewer in number (and some, all credit to them, converted to the cause) as the funding levels grew. Clearly it was working.

We hit the target a mere nine days later. It was 13:39 on 30 November 2012. Ultimately a total of £7,000 was provided mostly by strangers; fans of the game that wanted to see what I could come up with. I could hardly believe what had happened.

I had the privilege of taking the first 'Writer's Pack' and contributing that £4,500 into the 'Elite: Dangerous' Kickstarter. That pledge pushed the 'Elite: Dangerous' Kickstarter past its halfway point. David Braben posted a hearty congratulations. It was a welcome shot in the arm for the game, as it had been languishing a little in the middle of its own Kickstarter process.

Other Kickstarters followed, more books arrived, some funded to even faster and to higher levels than mine. The Elite community solidified behind the idea, more chunky pledges rolled in as a result. The 'Elite: Dangerous' Kickstarter exceeded its own target and went on to provide stretch goals.

I'm not saying the writers saved the 'Elite: Dangerous' Kickstarter itself, but we certainly helped turn the tide and raised the profile. Twenty-five thousand fans did the rest.

That's more than a year ago now. I've written the book, conscious throughout of the fan community that gave me this opportunity. I'll be forever in their debt; those who backed me, those who defended me, those who encouraged me along the way. To them I can only say a heartfelt thank you.

Elite: Reclamation is my contribution to the canon of this amazing game, this amazing adventure, thirty years in the making. This story has been crafted with much care, energy, enthusiasm and not a little heartache. It had its genesis in controversy and clamour. It's by a fan, for the fans. I hope you enjoy it.

Right on, Commanders.

Drew Wagar,
January 2014.

AD 3297
Prologue

The light of the Prism sun faded rapidly, a band of darkness sweeping in from the east like a thin ethereal shroud, the sky darkening from a bright azure to an inky blackness. The gas giant Mestra, though only a point of light, outshone every star in the sky and cast a shadow in the gloom.

Daedalion, far closer than that distant world, blazed like an immense ring of blue fire in the sky, its atmosphere illuminated from behind as the Prism sun was swiftly obscured. A multitude of stars sprung into the sky as darkness fell, glittering in Chione's cooling atmosphere. The wildlife fell silent; the daily eclipse had begun.

Chira was late; she sighed at herself for not setting off home earlier. The alignment of the three other stars in the system wasn't favourable this season; it was properly dark now. There were few lights ahead of them; the philosophy of the colony had always been to avoid the energy excess that plagued more 'advanced' worlds. Chira had often heard tell of worlds lost in a smog of noxious pollution where generations had grown up without ever seeing a star.

'Stay close, my dears. Tread carefully.'

She squinted into the dark and pulled her two charges close in beside her, grasping their hands firmly as she led them on. They were hurrying up a path that led from the coast back to the city; a steep climb away from the sea and then a walk along the cliffs before striking inland for the last few kilometres. She cursed under her breath, lamenting her advancing years. Had she been younger the walk up from the sea would not have taken so long. Both children were tired, having been fishing most of the day. Ahead, the dark bulk of the nearest series of dwellings could just be seen in the gloom, beyond a low rise. The pinnacle that marked the centre of the city was the only building that was conspicuously illuminated, glowing like a splinter of crystal thrust up from the ground. It wasn't far now, but somehow it looked further in the dark.

'What's that?'

Chira felt a yank on her arm as the small boy she was leading on her left stopped. 'Not now, Tomsh. We need to …'

'But, it's red. Pretty red. Why's it red?'

'Never you mind,' Chira admonished, pulling on the young boy's arm. He looked up at her with a frown. Just like the one his father used to wear at this age. Chira smiled at him fondly.

'Come now, or your father will want to know why.'

Tomsh and his sister Tarna were the children of a wealthy council member in Leeson City. Chira could see him in her mind's eye, impatiently awaiting their arrival on the steps of the administrative centre. They should have been back already.

Chira was a nanny; a task she found increasingly tiring each year. This was the third generation of children she'd brought up, and she very much thought it would be her last. A small but cosy cottage in the foothills beyond the city awaited her in a few short months where she could live out the rest of her days in peace and quiet.

'He's right, look!' the girl on her right added, turning around and letting go of Chira's hand in the process.

'Tarna, you should know better than to encourage him, it's time to …'

Tarna was the eldest of the pair and, if it were possible, even more inquisitive. She was nine to her brother's five years of age; a tall lanky girl, taking after her father's beanpole frame. She had bushy blonde hair that defied Chira's attempts to comb it under control.

A faint rumble interrupted her admonishment, a double roll of distant thunder. Chira straightened and turned, her back complaining with the effort. She squinted into the pale sky, annoyed at the intrusion.

She gasped in dismay.

Above there were streams of glowing smoke, radiating outwards as if from Daedalion itself, spreading like an ever widening fan. Each trail was headed by a flaming sphere of bright red fire, rolling and boiling across the sky. Shadows flickered uncertainly across the ground as if unsure which way to cast themselves.

Chira saw Tarna and Tomsh's faces eerily lit by the glow as the streams passed overhead. The streams were descending, slowing, yet the reverberation of their passing grew stronger all the time.

PROLOGUE

Crackles of thunder from high up in the sky echoed dully around them as they stared upwards in trepidation.

'What are they?' Tarna gasped, shouting to be heard above the rising din.

Chira firmly grabbed their hands. 'Nothing good, that's for sure. Come, quickly now.'

As they turned and began to run towards the city a stiff breeze arose, knocking them backwards, gasping for breath. The grass around them bent in the wind, trees creaked and birds rose squawking into the air.

Ahead, over the city, a dazzling but silent light broke out, white and pure. The children stumbled ahead of her, hands going up to shield their eyes from the intense glare. For a moment Chira saw the whole landscape in front of her lit up as if by the midday sun. She blinked, afterglow colours flashing in her eyes, half blinded by the brightness.

She heard Tarna scream and lost hold of Tomsh's hand. 'Tomsh!'

Then, without respite, came the blast.

Such a noise had never been heard on Chione in living memory. Wildlife around them scattered in panic, the ground trembled and shook. Tarna continued to scream, but her thin voice was swept away by the cataclysmic detonation. Chira was cast backwards to lie on her back prone on the ground, her mind shattered into panic by the reverberating clamour. The noise faded abruptly into silence punctuated only by a steady ringing in her ears. Her eyes caught sight of Tarna, looking down at her, eyes wide with horror, hands pressed against ears that were thick with dark red blood. Above her terrified face the sky was now bright with many streams of fire: red, orange and white, cascading downwards.

Fire arose. Chira saw Tarna's blonde hair consumed in a moment of agonising ignition. The sky blackened with soot. Pain and despair mixed in a final moment of lucidity. Tarna's immolated body was swept away in a shower of sparks.

Then, mercifully, consciousness was extinguished too.

* * *

The main planet of the Mithra system was, in Tenim Neseva's not so humble opinion, one of the best resort planets for those who valued doing as little as possible on vacation. Orbiting close to a red dwarf the planet was tidally locked, the large warm sun stayed permanently in place above the sunbather, preventing any need for them to tediously rearrange their recliner to ensure uninterrupted enjoyment throughout the day. The climate was constant all year round and here, in the temperate zone, cloud cover was negligible. Being a red dwarf there was no trouble with the inconvenient ultra-violet radiation that plagued the pleasure of hotter stars. One could find one's spot and, with the provision of food and beverages, enjoy it pretty much forever. That was certainly Tenim's plan.

A commissioner with responsibility for a small local group of star systems, his job had become routine, quiet and trouble free. The worlds were stable nowadays, unlike earlier times he recalled, with a shiver, when some tedious rebellion or uprising seemed to be happening almost every week. Back then he'd had to be in the office almost every day. He wondered how he'd tolerated it. At least now he could enjoy the fruits of his labours.

He sucked down another mouthful of his Zaqueesoan Evil Juice, a curious purple-coloured beverage. It was allegedly brewed from beetles, so the story went, somewhere down in the old worlds region. Tenim had meant to visit those systems once, all so rich in ancient history; Lave, Diso, Leesti and the rest, perhaps a spin across to the Tionisla Orbital Graveyard. Maybe next year, it was an awfully long way. Space travel remained something of an acquired taste.

A faint musical melody gently started playing, and the words 'Incoming call – Urgent' softly faded into his line of sight. He blinked in surprise and annoyance. The office calling him, and at drink time too?

The accompanying video was of an attractive middle-aged brunette with bright green eyes and a mischievous looking smile. He relaxed a little. Jenu was his secretary. She organised his life for him and undertook a number of other pleasurable, but surreptitious, duties too. Perhaps she'd organised one of their accidental, yet curiously fortuitous, meetings.

'Jenu,' Tenim said, with his best air of nonchalance, 'unless you are offering to come down here and rub Tionislan grub oil into my back for the next hour I can't see any possible reason why you'd feel justified in interrupting me.'

PROLOGUE

Jenu's next sentence, bereft of their usual banter, was short and to the point. 'There's been an attack, casualties …'

Tenim leapt to his feet, his glass of Evil Juice dropping from his fingers, smashing on the ground and splattering his feet with shards of glass and thick purple liquid. Tenim spluttered in response.

'Are you sure?'

'We've got footage bounced from a comms satellite. See for yourself.'

Jenu's image shifted right and a glowing rectangle appeared in the vacated space. It quickly resolved into a second video feed. It was decidedly poor quality with a low frame rate, but Tenim could easily make out the dark surface of a world, with faint lights from a small city on the surface. A tactical overlay identified a number of swiftly moving objects descending towards it.

'Where's this?'

'Chione.'

'Which is?' Tenim demanded, unable to recall the name.

'Moon of Daedalion.' Jenu waited for acknowledgement and when it didn't come she added, 'Second planet in the Prism system? It's on the edge of our jurisdiction.'

'Oh yes. I remember. Prism system, of course.'

'Of course.' Jenu's voice sounded appropriately demure.

A flash of white light sparked on the video, whiting out the camera for a moment as it struggled to adjust its exposure. Once it had cleared, the area could be seen to be aflame; the city obscured by smoke, the countryside around it burning fiercely.

'Simple airburst by the look of it,' Jenu said dispassionately. 'Enough to kill most, but leave a lot of the infrastructure intact.'

'Randomius! Who the …?'

'Hyperspace diagnostics record multiple targets arriving. I've already worked the tracks back to the Haoria system, there's no doubt about it.' Jenu was nothing if not efficient.

Tenim straightened. 'I thought those Imperial 'stards had been unusually quiet of late. Survivors?'

'Unknown. Won't be many by the looks of it.'

'Any clues on why they've done this?' Jenu's face registered confusion.

'That's the bit that doesn't make sense. There's nothing of value there as far as we know. It's just a far flung small-scaled settlement. No appreciable trade. Gross planetary product is well below tax thresholds. Nothing that warrants all this.'

'We'd better assemble the heads of staff, arrange rescue convoys and put the navy on standby.'

'Already done, boss.'

Tenim rolled his eyes and allowed himself a faint smile.

'Good girl, pull everything we have on this ... what was it again?'

'Chione,' Jenu replied.

'Chione, yeah.' Tenim grinned. 'I'm heading back to the office now. I want all the data in an hour.'

'No problem.'

'And get me their smarmy excuse for an ambassador, now.'

* * *

The Imperial ambassador to the Prism system was, as usual, fashionably late; a calculated insult aimed at enraging his Federation counterpart. Twelve minutes seemed to be the delay that the Imperials thought provided the greatest frustration value; long enough to be infuriating, short enough that nothing much could really be done with the wasted time.

The holofac system indicated a connection was being made and Tenim watched as the form of his counterpart, Imperial Ambassador Cuthrick Delaney, took shape, flanked by two of his aides, apparently sitting at the far end of the table despite actually being several light years away. As usual they were bedecked in their finery; flowing robes of rich colours, thick and heavy medallions and, new this time, what appeared to be jewel encrusted tiaras. Imperial fashion was fleeting, but always ostentatious.

They appeared deep in conversation as their images materialised, a show of indifference also calculated to offend in the politest way possible. After a few moments they looked up as if bemused to find themselves in the holofac conference. Tenim had long ago become immune to their machinations.

'Commissioner Neseva,' Cuthrick began, with a small incline of his head which his aides copied like marionettes. 'My apologies for our tardiness.

PROLOGUE

Such an unscheduled communication caused much consternation to our administrators. So many important meetings were moved so that we might accommodate you. Pray, how can we be of assistance?'

Tenim leant back in his chair with an air of nonchalance. He deliberately took his eyes off Cuthrick, looked around the room as if thinking for a moment and then locked eyes with him again.

'Why did you just bomb the crap out of one of my moons?'

One of the aides actually gasped in horror, a look of consternation crossing his face. Tenim smiled inwardly. Failing to acknowledge Cuthrick's title and lineage, and accord him the appropriate respect his lofty rank demanded was a breach of protocol that might have started a war in more fraught times.

Cuthrick made a subtle movement with his hand; the aide subsided. He would rise above this crude and uncivilised behaviour, thus demonstrating his own comprehensive and gracious grasp of etiquette.

Initial insults successfully exchanged and a confrontational agenda acknowledged. The meeting could now commence.

'To which moon are you referring?' Cuthrick asked, with polite disinterest.

'The one with the capital city full of dead people,' Tenim said, remaining deliberately antagonistic and uncouth. 'The one with the fires burning and Imperial ships huddled in orbit around it. Does that help narrow it down?'

Tenim flicked his fingers forwards and the satellite video feed Jenu had previously shown him appeared between them. Cuthrick studied it for a few brief moments and then consulted with one of his aides.

'Ah yes,' Cuthrick acknowledged. 'Perhaps you're referring to the Prism system.' Tenim nodded along gamely.

'That's the one.'

Cuthrick allowed the faint trace of a carefully prepared frown to cross his features. He looked up at Tenim as if about to speak and then turned back to his other aide as if to confirm something. Then his face cleared and he nodded as if in appreciative understanding.

'I believe I understand the confusion,' Cuthrick said. 'If I might explain …'

A text message flashed up in Tenim's line of sight, visible only to him. It was from Jenu. 'I'd be delighted to hear it,' Tenim interrupted, holding up his hand. 'A moment please.'

This time the other aide gasped and looked furious at another deliberate slight to his ambassador. Tenim acknowledged Jenu's message and requested the detail.

It's Tantalum! They're after the Tantalum. Big deposits apparently. It's for the new hyperdrive systems.

That would undoubtedly explain the sudden interest. Tantalum, already a relatively exotic metal, had seen its price increase by two orders of magnitude in recent months. New legislation and the decommissioning of old hyperspace technology had been on the priority agenda for a while now. Every jump capable ship needed a new drive and each new drive needed Tantalum …

Tenim faked listening to some conversation out of the line of sight of the holofac, nodding with an air of consternation before turning back to the Imperials.

'It may interest you to know,' he began, 'that I've just been informed that our navy will be conducting a battle drill shortly, all routine of course.'

'Of course,' Cuthrick nodded. 'If you feel your navy is out of practice that seems only prudent.'

Tenim smiled in response. 'By a curious coincidence it appears we've selected the Prism system as the zone in which to conduct our drills. It would be unfortunate if we weren't able to resolve this little matter beforehand. I'm sure we'd both agree that any potential misunderstandings are best avoided.'

'I completely concur,' Cuthrick replied.

'So might I humbly suggest that you withdraw your forces from our moon and consider compensation for your unprovoked and hostile actions?'

'In the interests of interstellar peace and cooperation,' Cuthrick began smoothly, 'we'd naturally want to comply assiduously. Unhappily, there is a legal matter that prevents us from so doing.'

Tenim's eyes narrowed. 'A legal matter?'

Cuthrick nodded with an unconvincing sympathetic frown. 'Indeed. Without wishing to impugn your records, it would appear that your assertion that this moon is "yours", that is to say it lies within the jurisdiction of the venerated Federation, is, in a word …' Cuthrick paused, as if considering the precise word to use, 'erroneous.'

Tenim was taken aback. This was not what he'd expected.

PROLOGUE

'It's been settled for over thirty-five years. We colonised it back in 3260. What are you talking about? It's never been an Imperial system.'

Cuthrick now looked distinctly smug.

'Without wishing to indelicately contradict your statement, it transpires that it is and has been for some time.'

'Nonsense!'

Cuthrick flicked his own fingers forward, with a little extra flourish for dramatic flair. A long legal document scrolled rapidly upwards between them, the text rolling past at a dazzling speed. As they watched, it slowed and a particular passage was brought into focus, zooming in and becoming highlighted.

'Mining rights to the systems were granted to the Empire in 3225,' Cuthrick noted in an offhand manner. 'Notwithstanding, notice of our intention to deal with the illegal occupation was vouchsafed on a number of occasions within various communiques, but alas, it appears the Federation have overlooked them.'

'I saw no communiques …' Tenim fumed, before realising he was playing straight into the Imperials' hands. The first aide gestured quickly and a series of date-stamped and detailed text messages appeared beside the legal document. Tenim had no doubt they contained the appropriate notifications, buried in obtuse and obfuscating language, couched in terms that no one would notice and almost impossible to spot.

'Given the dearth of response we felt we had no recourse but to exercise our rights under section …'

Cuthrick turned to one of his aides, who whispered something at him.

'… under Section 48, Subsection 2, Paragraph 3, Point 11. The forcible eviction of illegal occupiers …'

'Let me see that.' Tenim gestured towards the document and quickly submitted it for verification. To his dismay his own systems quickly came back with the words 'Authentication Confirmed' in glowing green text.

Tenim sighed.

'On a more positive note, ' Cuthrick continued, 'we have no intention of seeking recompense for the costs incurred in the eviction, or even for distress caused by the many decades of illegal occupation of our sovereign territory.'

'Most generous of you,' Tenim growled.

'However, might I humbly suggest that you find an alternative venue for your practice drill?' The echo of Tenim's previous words was a subtle, but effective, move.

'I'll take the matter under advisement.'

Cuthrick smiled thinly and courteously, inclining his head in the same infuriating fashion. 'Then, if we have no other business?'

'None whatsoever,' Tenim ground out. 'A pleasure then, until the next time.'

Tenim gestured for the holofac transmission to end. Cuthrick and his aides vanished in a glimmer of light. He sat still for a moment, allowing his frustration to ebb.

Various ideas formed in his head, each one quickly discarded in favour of the next, until he came up with a scheme he felt had merit. Then he contacted Jenu.

'Mobilise the navy?' she asked immediately.

'No,' Tenim replied.

'No? After what they did?'

'Not our moon after all apparently,' Tenim replied, offhand. 'The Tantalum belongs to them, there's no doubt about it. We're on the back foot too; they'll have an effective blockade already. Penetrating that from a tactically inferior position would be too expensive. They have the high ground.'

'We're just going to let them waltz in and appropriate it? Them?' Her mouth curved in distaste. 'What about the colonists?'

Tenim shrugged. 'Complete outrage of course. Mercy missions, emergency medical envoys, I'll demand everything. I'll also lodge a number of strenuously worded official protestations of complaint, naturally. Every possible and appropriate action will be taken.'

'Short of actually doing something you mean.' Jenu clicked her tongue in disapproval and shook her head slightly. 'And what about the Tantalum?'

Tenim stroked his beard carefully. 'Dangerous business, mining. Digging into the ground, extracting the ore, refining it. Just when you think you've got it home and docked you find your freighters ambushed by pirates and you've lost the lot. I imagine it's going to be tough keeping a supply line open to such a remote system. Piracy's a curse.'

'But there isn't any piracy in the Prism system,' Jenu countered. Tenim looked across at her and raised his eyebrows.

'Not yet, no.'

AD 3300
Chapter One

Grim laughter, raucous but coordinated singing, simple but emotive chants; the solidarity of workers standing together to assert their rights. Crudely made banners held high in grubby roughened hands. Defiance, anger and resolve. Women and children marching alongside their menfolk in defiance of curfew, claiming ground, demanding to be heard. Flags waving, feet stamping; a crowd seeking confrontation.

The protest had been watched for some time. It gathered strength, firebrand agitators whipping the crowd to a fury. A number of independent protests merged and converged towards the Loren Piazza, the ornate gardens that now surrounded the administrative centre of Leeson City. They were off limits to all but Imperial citizens, patrolled by guards. Military forces were brought to guard the administrative buildings, but the perimeter of the Piazza was too expansive to be adequately defended. The chants were predictable, the cry of the overworked and underfed. Even slaves had rights; rights that were being abused.

Thousands had come, thousands who knew their actions could result in the legal deaths of both themselves and their families. Thousands who felt they had little to lose.

The crowd stepped up to the edge of the Piazza where a single Captain of the Guard stood facing them, backed up by a phalanx of armed men, automatic rifles held ready. The captain's arm was outstretched, palm facing outwards.

'Who speaks for you?' the captain demanded.

A man pushed through the crowd. Bearded and unkempt he nonetheless carried an air of authority and stood tall, his bearing strong and erect despite shabby clothes. He stepped a few paces forward from the now silent crowd.

'I do.'

Both men looked each other over carefully. Each assessed and measured; sizing up and evaluating the other.

'Rieger,' the captain said, with a brief nod.

'Captain Dufus,' Rieger acknowledged, with a correspondingly faint smile.

'You will disperse and return to your work,' the captain said, raising his voice to the crowd and casting a look towards them over Rieger's shoulder. 'If you do this immediately, this infringement of curfew will go unpunished.'

Rieger turned, sweeping his arms wide to take in the crowd, who remained unmoved. He spun back around to Dufus with a laugh.

'I don't think you've convinced them, Dufus.'

Dufus stepped forward, motioning to Rieger. Rieger stepped forward. The two men spoke in hushed tones.

'Where's this going, Rieger?'

'We want relaxed working hours, three meals a day, a place by the sea and a holiday off-world. First-class hotel passes, our own private transport system and a nice hot shower.'

'Anything else?' Dufus prompted, deadpan.

'And I want to personally fuck all three of the Senator's daughters.'

Dufus smirked. 'Don't we all. And what will you settle for?'

'Just the older two, not so bothered about the dark-haired freak.'

Dufus stifled a laugh. 'I meant on behalf of your protest.'

'Our working hours as they would be in the core of the Empire. Medical supplies, food and drink, accommodation that's not full of shit and bugs. You know our demands, we want our rights, that's all. We're Imperial slaves, not vagabonds. A decree from the Senator that this will be done, signed by the Patrons.'

'And if you don't receive this?'

'Tantalite mining stops. Maybe Senator Algreb loses his head. Feelings are running high, Dufus. We can't keep a lid on this forever. The Senator's madness must be dealt with ...'

'He'll order you starved out, you know that.'

Rieger laughed. 'Think we haven't planned this? We can last far longer on what we've stashed away than Algreb can whilst trying to placate his buyers without having a product to sell. We know the situation, we've got off-world contacts. Buyers will go elsewhere for Tantalum if they need to.'

'If the buyers go, we all lose.'

Rieger grinned. 'Unlike you with your very fine uniform and fancy food,

CHAPTER ONE

we ain't got that much to lose, if you take the time to notice, begging your pardon. We figure Algreb has more at stake than we do. All we're asking for is our rights.'

Dufus nodded. 'Let me send that in.'

'You do that.'

Rieger stepped back a pace. Dufus turned and walked a few steps across the Piazza, touching a finger to his ear and beginning a conversation with a third party. He turned to look at Rieger, part-way through the conversation. Rieger stood, awaiting the outcome.

Dufus frowned. Rieger caught a little of what he said. '… not necessary, we can handle …'

A cry of dismay went up from the crowd. Armed personnel carriers and assault vehicles appeared from behind the administrative buildings. Even from hundreds of metres away it was obvious they were bristling with dark and forbidding weapons; heavy calibre chain guns, rocket and incendiary launchers. They hovered, turning towards the crowd.

Dufus turned, holding both hands up in a clear message.

Hold your fire!

A sharp crack echoed across the Piazza.

Dufus spun around, stumbling to his knees, a bright red stain spreading across his tunic. Rieger stepped back in alarm and surprise, arms held up in a gesture of innocence. Dufus fell, full length on the floor. The guards surged forwards towards Rieger, rifles at the ready.

As they did so, there came a deafening explosion from across the Piazza. The right side of the administrative building collapsed in a shower of debris and flame. The guards were sprawled to the floor by the air blast as it whipped past. Massive chunks of masonry spun through the air and landed across the Piazza, shattering into boulders and dust as they did so. Another, flung upwards into the sky, smashed into one of the personnel carriers, crushing the stabiliser at the rear and spinning it out of control. Men and equipment tumbled out to be dashed to fragments on the ground. The carrier itself careened across the sky, trailing smoke and debris, before spiralling into the terrified crowd in a whirling maelstrom of disintegrating metal. People screamed and surged backwards as rubble rained down.

The guards struggled back to their feet, catching Rieger as they did so. Rieger disappeared under the mass of bodies.

'Not us! Not us!' he was yelling as rifle butts descended. His voice was lost as a roar of noise descended from above. The armed vehicles tilted forward and accelerated towards the panicking crowd.

The sharp bark of weapons fire reverberated across the gardens. Tracer fire split the air, shattering pavements, ornamental statues and marble colonnades. Rockets streaked with ear-splitting shrieks, terminating their flights in lurid flashes of colour and destruction.

Then the rapacious fire found softer targets: skin, flesh and bone. Dozens of slaves were cut down, many trampled underfoot as those that had yet to be hit stumbled away in blind fear. This was no orderly retreat; men, women and children fought wildly to escape in the dreadful rout.

The lethal barrage continued, indiscriminately targeting the slaves as they tried to flee; ripped banners, shredded flags and bloodied bodies littered the edge of the Piazza, yet still the onslaught continued. One wretched family cowered in front of blazing guns as they tracked around. They were caught in the firing line and slain as they huddled in terror; the parents first and then their child thrown through the air to join the wretched mass of bodies …

'Stop. Enough.'

The vehicles froze motionless. The people stopped moving, some of them in the act of falling to the ground. Bullets hovered mysteriously in mid-air. The sound was abruptly silenced.

'Dufus was a good man, I knew him from childhood. He deserved better than to die in this manner, for a mere slave revolt.' A wispy silver-haired, elderly gentleman stepped carelessly through the holofac recording making it blur and flicker, unaffected by the frozen carnage around him. He was thin almost to the point of emaciation, his pale flesh and skin seeming to barely hide the skeleton within. His cream and gold braided toga swept past the crushed and bloodied bodies unstained. A pair of optical enhancers perched precariously on his nose, looking remarkably like a pair of spectacles from ancient days.

'Patron Zyair, I think you can see from this footage that the slave revolt is incidental. If there is blame, it lies elsewhere. The slaves have no access to

CHAPTER ONE

explosives of that magnitude. That was clearly technology from off-world. The Federation is behind this, supporting these Reclamist rebels.'

The second voice was owned by an exceedingly large gentleman, also wrapped in copious quantities of fine linen. Despite this, his girth was barely constrained. He reclined in an ornately wrought chaise longue, lazily consuming fruit from a nearby bowl, belching on occasion in appreciation and then wiping his lips with the back of his hand. An immaculately trimmed goatee beard completed the visage, adequately concealing a series of flabby chins. Gerrun was no beauty, but a fierce intellect resided within the vastness of unappealing flesh.

'And what do these confounded Reclamists want, Patron Gerrun?'

'They've made no formal demands,' Gerrun replied. 'Remnants of the original colonists, we suspect. Those that didn't have the decency to perish three years ago when we reclaimed this moon. They leave their usual calling card, an anonymous text transfer moments before …'

'Reclaiming what is ours,' Zyair nodded as he quoted from memory. 'I've seen it. Needlessly melodramatic.'

'One assumes they regard this moon as theirs,' Gerrun added. 'It's difficult to convince those who lack an appreciation of the law.'

'Perhaps they are unhappy with how the law was applied.' A third voice spoke from the back of the room. Zyair turned with a glare, but Gerrun raised his hand in greeting, before adjusting his position and resuming his consumption of fruit.

'Ah, Patron Dalk.'

'They could have been evacuated rather than murdered,' Dalk finished. He was a tall man, bald and tanned with an erect, almost military, bearing. He held his head high, with what most considered was a haughty and arrogant look. His dress was in sharp contrast to the other Patrons, a thick and heavy dark grey trench coat that gave the suggestion it concealed more than it revealed. The skin of his face was leathery; clearly a man who'd lived much of his life outdoors. His hands remained gloved despite the warmth inside the presentation room.

'Patron Dalk,' Zyair acknowledged with a faint measure of distaste. His eyes narrowed. 'You don't claim that these Reclamists have a genuine grievance, surely?'

'Not in the slightest,' Dalk replied smoothly. 'Yet, we should not underestimate them. We know they are backed by the Federation and it would seem their leader has a measure of tactical ability.'

'The mysterious Vargo and his wizard Solanac,' Gerrun mused. 'Both seem persons of some means; our spies reveal nothing of value about them other than the names. Those that get close are executed rather efficiently.'

'The Reclamists are well organised as a result,' Dalk added. 'They appear to be well versed in our capabilities. Spies undoubtedly.'

'You seem impressed by them,' Zyair said.

Dalk shrugged. 'I merely reiterate that we could have avoided this problem by a less confrontational approach. A pattern that is playing out once again.' He gestured at the bloodshed portrayed before him.

'What do you mean?' Zyair snapped.

'In much the same way as Senator Algreb sanctioned the original appropriation of this moon, he also directly instructed the military to undertake this disagreeable episode by personal command. Sympathy for the Reclamists runs high amongst the slaves now. They could overrun the military right now if they knew how weak our forces were. Fortunately at this point they do not.'

Gerrun looked around and stroked his beard thoughtfully. 'I feared as much. The Senator's actions grow increasingly erratic. Perhaps …'

'We should not be having this conversation, Patrons,' Zyair said, cutting across him. 'We have pledged our support. To consider any other course of action …'

'Should matters continue as they have we risk inviting attention of the most unwanted variety,' Dalk said. 'Our position is tenuous. A review of alternatives is only proper.'

'Dalk is right. The Senator's actions are destabilising the situation,' Gerrun said. 'Slaves slaughtered by whim in the midst of a protest? If word gets off-world, we risk an inspection from the Emperor's agents. If the Reclamists gain the upper hand or the slaves discover they are in a position of even greater power … well, I humbly submit this is not in our best interests.'

'I've supported Senator Algreb for forty years …' Zyair blustered.

'Then perhaps a change is in order?' Gerrun remarked.

CHAPTER ONE

'And this is the answer is it, Patron Dalk? Disenfranchise ourselves from the Loren family?'

'Dalk didn't say remove our support from the Loren family,' Gerrun observed, shrewdly.

Dalk inclined his head appreciatively. 'Indeed.'

'Then …' Zyair spluttered, 'you're not suggesting his daughters, surely? This is madness! None of them are fit to be a Senator! The very thought of youthful exuberance being allowed access to power. It will be mayhem and carnage within days.'

'As opposed to the mayhem and carnage of the last few days, you mean?' Gerrun gestured to the frozen tableau of slaughter behind them. Dalk nodded.

'I'll admit that Algreb is increasingly overzealous in his application of the law,' Zyair spluttered.

'An interesting definition of overzealous …' Gerrun commented, holding up his hands and looking from one to the other as if puzzled. 'I always get those two mixed up, overzealous and genocide; genocide, overzealous …'

'They're only slaves, that's hardly grounds for considering …'

'Speculating,' Gerrun said, 'not considering; merely debating a hypothetical solution to an intractable problem. There's no question of anything but unfailing support for the Senator.'

'The room isn't bugged,' Dalk said, 'I've checked.'

Gerrun laughed. 'Old habits die hard, my friend.'

'And which one of the Senator's glorious offspring are you considering, pray tell?' Zyair raged, raising his hands and waving them in frustration. 'Corine, whose greatest ever concern has been the precise arrangement of her hair and the cut of her dress? Tala, whose greatest asset is that she has so little personality that none of the nobles find her in anyway objectionable? They're not even vaguely credible.'

'There is a third, as I recall,' Gerrun prompted, with a mischievous grin.

Zyair stopped in mid-flow. 'Not Kahina. Please, anything but Kahina. I cannot abide that objectionable young woman.'

'She has the virtue of intelligence,' Dalk added.

'Tactless, antagonising, self-assured, rude, arrogant, proud, scheming …'

'A perfect Imperial daughter, one could argue cogently,' Gerrun pointed out. 'I'd imagine she could be housebroken, trained perhaps.'

'Tempered and moulded ...' Dalk added.

'Someone we could instruct and guide, influence and persuade,' Gerrun mused.

'In the best interests of stability and efficiency, naturally,' Dalk replied.

'Upholding the everlasting Imperial values. Peace and tranquillity. Don't you agree?' Gerrun completed with a wry grin.

'I do not!' Zyair was not amused. 'Tell me you're not taking this seriously ...'

'Our situation is grave. Perhaps graver than we realise,' Dalk said.

'And what of the Senator himself?' Zyair said. 'What do you intend to do about him?'

'Why, nothing at all,' Dalk replied. 'Our patronage remains loyal as it ever has. There's no question of our unfailing support.'

'Then what was this conversation about?' Zyair demanded.

'The Reclamists of course,' Dalk replied, looking over to Gerrun.

'They grow bolder every day,' Gerrun said. 'They've struck in the city, perhaps they might even strike at the Senator's family. That would be truly tragic.'

'Tragic indeed,' Dalk agreed. 'We must do everything to ensure the Loren Lineage is protected.'

Zyair frowned as he looked from one to the other. Then his eyes widened in appreciation. 'Ah ...'

* * *

The Imperial Palace, home of the Loren Family, had arguably the best view on the entire surface of Chione. It had been deliberately sited on the island of New Ithaca, itself part of an archipelago of islands in the otherwise empty Garian Sea. Its tropical latitude in the southern hemisphere of Chione afforded it a warm and pleasant climate at all times, with only occasional rainfall to mar the spectacle. Unlike the distant seas of old Earth, the water in the oceans was fresh and pure. Chione had been originally settled for its pastoral beauty and the aesthetics were not lost on the denizens of the Empire.

CHAPTER ONE

Low in the northern sky, forever hanging in full view, its reflection sparkling in the bay, was the enormous blue orb of Daedalion, the ocean world. It was an enormous planet, with seas a hundred kilometres deep. It hosted, so rumour had it, marine life of extraordinary size and might. Chione was Daedalion's only moon, forever locked to its parent, always facing it. The sun came and went, but Daedalion remained, marking the passage of time by its changing phases, going from crescent to full, back to crescent over the course of the day.

Daedalion grew to its maximum brightness in the middle of the night, its full globe reflecting light back onto Chione, bathing the bay, plains and mountains in a fresh azure glow. Thus it was never truly dark, a feature that both entertained and confused visitors. It was a perfect setting for the frequent soirees organised by the Loren Lineage. Having one of the most stunning backdrops in the known galaxy ensured their gatherings were well attended by the cream of Imperial society should they so wish it.

The palace and its gardens had been specifically designed to cater for this view and to augment it as effectively as possible. The palace was oriented north, directly towards Daedalion, with the gardens dropping through tiers downwards towards the beach that edged the bay. There were no roads or access routes; the island was entirely unspoilt; supplies and visitors typically arrived at a small airport on the far side of the island directly from the mainland and were then taken via an underground transport link to the palace.

Unseen to the casual observer the island was defended by a perimeter of anti-craft batteries and surface-to-air missile launchers alongside a variety of shield technologies. Squadrons of defence craft were stationed on nearby islands just out of sight of New Ithaca, ready to scramble at a moment's notice. The island was, in the eyes of the military, somewhat over protected; particularly as their resources were stretched thin trying to keep a handle on rising piracy and the activities of the Reclamists. The Senator had commanded it however, so it was done without question.

All this had been built in a scant couple of years following the appropriation of the system and the expulsion of the original settlers. The Lorens were nothing if not efficient.

The head of the family, Senator Algreb Loren, had inherited his grandfather's vast fortune at an early age, after the suspicious death of his father. Algreb's father had, by most accounts, been something of a fool and a popinjay. Many suspected wider interests had intervened to ensure the succession. In their quest to ensure that family lineage and purity continued untainted, much care had to be given to the choice of marriage partner. Genetic engineering ensured the worst anomalies were avoided, but it wasn't possible to avoid them all.

Algreb, through uncertain means, shrewdly invested and enhanced his grandfather's legacy, the family's money continued to be made through mining of rare and exotic materials extracted with cheap labour. It had given him much scope for influence and put enormous power in his grasp. With the capability and the experience, the opportunity provided by Chione given the sudden and unprecedented demand for Tantalite had been one for which Algreb had been perfectly placed to take advantage.

The entire household had moved to Chione: wife and mistresses (all discreetly housed in the remoter parts of the palace), his three daughters, their tutors and a small army of guards, musicians, servants and staff. Everything the Imperial family had enjoyed back in the Empire they enjoyed here, no compromise was accepted. This was often complemented by frequent visitors from the lesser noble families on the mainland and visitors from the Empire itself.

A young woman entered through the grand foyer of the Imperial Palace and strode purposefully towards the dark panelled doors that formed the threshold of the reception hall. She knocked three times, quickly and sharply, in accordance with tradition.

There was no immediate response. The woman waited, her arms folded impatiently, glaring at the closed doors. Her fingers tapped against her forearms.

She was dressed simply, in a loosely flowing pale green robe that fell to her ankles. Her hair, straight, dark and cut at shoulder length, was braided by a thin crystal tiara. Her eyes were grey with a hint of blue, her skin pale and only lightly adorned with colour. Her stance was erect and commanding, her expression cool and aloof.

Two guards on the inside slowly pulled the doors inwards. The woman abased herself reverently, but kept her head up, with her expression unchanged.

'Approach,' a deep and melancholy voice intoned. It was only just audible from the opposite end of the hall.

CHAPTER ONE

The woman resumed her stance and walked forward, conscious of her footsteps echoing on the mosaic floor. She kept her eyes locked ahead, only peripherally noticing the murals, images and stories passing beneath her feet; tales of conquest, resistance, victories, defeats and famous last stands.

She arrived at the foot of the dais and curtseyed, reluctantly lowering her head down. 'You summoned me, pater?'

'Arise.'

The woman stood up and looked directly at the owner of the voice. Steel grey eyes stared back at her. Senator Algreb Loren was still an imposing figure. Age had robbed him of some of his strength, but his stature and bearing were as intimidating as always. His face was lined and careworn, his eyes dark under heavy eyebrows. His expression was as inscrutable as it had ever been.

'You remain a disappointment to me, my gloomily haired daughter.' Algreb's voice was indifferent and unconcerned. 'I fear Chancellor T'Clow Guntat is less than enamoured with you. He claims that he fears an impure bloodline given your deformity ...'

The woman unconsciously ran her hand through her dark hair; it was in sharp contrast to Algreb's platinum blonde locks.

'Yet your lack of charm and grace are doubtless the real reasons for declining the match. Your worth is less with each suitor we try. Fortunately I have other daughters ...'

'My impression of him is even less flattering,' the woman replied, her voice sharp. 'Would you like to hear it?'

'Your impressions are of no concern to me whatsoever, Kahina,' Algreb continued, his voice still monotonic. 'You have but a single purpose, to fulfil your duty in promoting the interests of the lineage by an appropriate match.'

'Find a match for me then.' Kahina's voice was insolent and challenging, her own gaze unflinching. 'All you've found so far are fools, lackeys and inbred idiots.'

'The cream of Imperial families we'd do well to associate ourselves with ...'

Kahina shook her head. 'My description is more accurate.'

'Must I punish you once more?' The Senator's eyes flashed angrily. 'Compliance is all I seek. Would that you had a use like your amiable sisters. They understand their place.'

'Punish me all you like,' Kahina replied, unable to repress a shiver. 'It won't work. You won't change me.'

'That remains to be seen. I will consider the matter. Perhaps there is still some minor contribution you can make to our advancement. In the meantime, take this to Corine. She will succeed with T'Clow Guntat where you have failed.'

Senator Algreb handed out a commtab. Kahina snatched it from his hand.

'Thank you for the privilege of carrying your messages,' she said flatly. 'The opportunity to serve gives me much honour.'

Algreb bristled, but Kahina's words gave him no excuse to retort. 'You will leave,' he replied. 'Your very presence distresses me.'

'Your pleasure and mine, pater,' Kahina replied.

She curtseyed once more and turned smartly on her heel. Her finely wrought shoes clicked loudly on the marble flagstones of the hall as she walked away. She turned at the threshold, looking back and catching her father's eye.

Algreb waited for the customary and required nod of respect.

Kahina's eyes narrowed and she whirled on her feet, walking away as the doors to the hall were closed by the guards. Algreb's fists clenched. He initiated a holofac call. A tall bald man appeared before him, turning around to face him and then bowing immediately. The hologram flickered for a moment before stabilising.

'Senator, a pleasure. How might I serve?'

'Patron Dalk, I have a task for you. My daughter Kahina is sick once more.'

Dalk's eyes narrowed briefly. 'I'm sorry to hear that, Senator.'

'She needs ... treatment. I'm sure you understand.'

'Indeed, Senator. I will be there as soon as I can.'

Algreb nodded and closed the link, settling back in his plush chair, surveying the hall with a satisfied sigh.

* * *

The maid ducked as a further piece of crockery smashed into the wall beside her. She stepped neatly to the side and waited patiently. The broken pieces tumbled to the floor, joining several more that were already lying there.

CHAPTER ONE

'I said cream drapes, not tan drapes!' a high pitched voice yelled from across the room. It was accompanied by a fierce glare and a flick of long blonde hair.

'Do I have to repeat myself?'

Corine Loren was not an easy mistress to work for. The eldest of the Senator's daughters, she was dazzlingly beautiful, with a perfect complexion, immaculate hair and manicured nails. She had impeccable taste in clothing, style and jewellery. At every social event she always impressed and startled the men, whilst dominating and intimidating the women. She could be charming, sophisticated, elegant and debonair.

Often she was quite the reverse.

The maid sighed. It had been tan drapes when she'd set out to complete the instructions issued by her mistress this morning. Clearly Corine had changed her mind in the interim … again. It wouldn't do to point this out.

'Surely not, ma'am.'

'And is my dress ready yet, Marie?'

'We only gave the designs to the tailors at the midday meal, ma'am,' Marie said cautiously. 'I'm sure they will be working …'

'The soirée is this evening. I need time to get ready, Daedalion is already waxing. How long does it take? Do you expect me to wear rags?'

'No, ma'am.'

Marie didn't smile, she knew what would happen if she did. The last maid to have made that mistake was now working in the sewers beneath the palace. Pointing out that Corine had somewhere in the order of two thousand other alternative gowns would probably not help either.

'Do you have the dinner layout ready?' Corine snapped.

Marie handed her a commtab with the information she requested. Corine scanned it carefully. 'Viceroy Guwat can't come in after Chancellor Loquet. What were you thinking? He'll interpret it as a snub! Put Madam Veilla between them and change it around. Did you arrange for hot red wine? What about the fish? You remember Admiral Tvan hates fish? He's got to have fish after that insulting comment at the last concert.'

Marie acknowledged the changes.

'Now, about my entrance … grand staircase or front hall?'

'Staircase surely, ma'am,' Marie answered dutifully. Corine always came

- 23 -

down the staircase; she loved watching the sea of faces arranged below in the vaulted foyer turn to look at her as she affected unconcern and surprise at their presence.

'I think you're right,' Corine replied, as if thinking it through. 'Music. You've got the East Coast Orchestra haven't you?'

'Yes, ma'am. They cancelled their arrangements at your request.'

'Tianvian old age or Sotiquan Jazz?'

'Old age I think, most of the guests will be expecting old age music. Some absolutely hate the modern …'

'No, I don't think so. It's my evening. Instruct them to play jazz.'

'Yes, ma'am,' Marie sighed. Unlike her more artistic sister Tala, Corine had little time for music. It was a tool to entertain and delight, or to annoy and infuriate.

The entrance bells tolled; a gentle harmonious collection of notes. Someone had approached Corine's own personal wing of the palace.

'Now what?' Corine exclaimed. 'Can I never have a moment's peace?'

Marie hesitated. 'Ma'am?'

'Well don't just stand there, go and answer it. Or do you expect me to do it myself?'

'No, ma'am, of course not …'

'Stop blathering then. Go!'

Marie found Corine's youngest sister awaiting her. Marie had felt sorry for Kahina in the past; it was no secret that she was the least favoured of the three daughters on account of her dark hair. Loren tradition held that this was a sign of impurity, of weakness and poor character. Unfortunately Kahina did herself no favours by being deliberately awkward and antagonistic to all, regardless of whether they had any sympathy for her or not.

'Corine is not well disposed today,' Marie whispered, with a raised eyebrow.

Kahina rolled her eyes. 'Is anything else worthy of news?'

'She may not receive you.'

'I bring instructions direct from our exalted father, she has no choice.'

Marie's eyes widened in astonishment. 'The Senator? Has he decided …'

Kahina glared. 'You over reach yourself, maid. This message is for Corine's ears only.'

CHAPTER ONE

The maid bowed, her sympathy for Kahina eroded further. She turned and led her up to Corine's chambers. She knocked gently.

'Who is it?'

'Your sister, Kahina, with a missive from the Senator, ma'am.'

There was a pause. Corine was clearly wondering the same thing as Marie was.

'Send her in.'

Marie opened the door and showed Kahina in. She curtseyed low and awaited a signal from Corine.

'You may rise, sister,' Corine pronounced.

'Most gracious of you, sister,' Kahina replied, tartly.

Marie, satisfied that protocol had been observed, made to leave and went to close the door behind her. Corine signalled her to remain.

Kahina half turned aside.

'My instructions were to give this message to you alone,' she said.

'Marie is my trusted servant,' Corine replied.

'Nevertheless, my instructions ...' Kahina argued.

'Are you suggesting I cannot choose trustworthy servants?' Corine retorted immediately. 'Unlike you, I treat mine well and retain their services over a considerable period.'

'Honoured sister, I would not dare to judge such ...' Kahina's words were correct, but her tone was taciturn.

'Then don't. What is this message our father sees fit to send me at this ungodly hour?'

Kahina turned around the commtab she'd been given, taking her time to access the information contained within.

'I bring a missive from Senator Algreb,' she began.

'I already know that,' Corine hissed. 'Don't waste my valuable time, sister.'

Kahina read from the transcript.

'The Senator demands your presence in the main hall at sundown today, there to discuss the arrangements for the long awaited alliance with the representatives of the much honoured Rebian family ...'

'What?' Corine shouted out immediately, making Marie flinch. 'What about my soirée? I have three hundred dignitaries en route!'

'This appears to be the wrong season for soirées,' Kahina replied waspishly, with just the right amount of mirth.

Corine threw a vase at her. Kahina was able to sidestep it; she knew her sister's tantrums well. 'How dare you bring me this news?' Corine demanded.

'I am merely the humble messenger, exalted and much favoured sister,' Kahina crowed. 'The vessel into which our honourable father pours the fruits of his deliberations ...'

'How am I supposed to rearrange my soirée now? Tell me that!'

'Surely my exalted sister isn't suggesting that we put our own entertainment before the needs of state?' Kahina said, tilting her head to one side.

It was a clever riposte. Corine clearly had no choice but to do the Senator's bidding, so she changed tack.

'And for what? Some fool from Rebia? We hate the Rebians! Why does father need me anyway?'

'Perhaps the rest of the missive will further enlighten my exalted sister?' Kahina was clearly enjoying herself.

Corine scowled at her and gestured for Kahina to continue.

'"... there to discuss the arrangements for the long awaited truce with the exalted representative of Rebia, the most eminent T'Clow Guntat, emissary and head of the Lineage of Rebia, thrice decorated commander of the legions of Coran, being in truth the betrothal, nuptials and tithes appropriate for the joining of two such honourable houses to prevent further bloodshed ...'

'Stop!' Corine yelled, outraged. 'What did you say?'

Kahina smiled innocently, took a deep breath and started again. 'There to discuss the arrangements ...'

'Not that!' Corine snapped. 'The last bit, you dark haired imbecile.'

'Being in truth the betrothal, nuptials and ...'

'What does that mean?' Corine shouted at Kahina.

Kahina made a show of reading the missive again as if trying to interpret it. 'I believe, my exalted sister, you're about to be married. Congratulations.' Kahina looked up vindictively.

Corine was aghast. 'No. He can't do this. It's not fair. How dare he? I'm not some lackey he can dispose of at a whim for some cheap political game. I'm ...'

CHAPTER ONE

'A pure and virtuous golden haired daughter of the esteemed Loren Lineage,' Kahina said smugly.

Corine glared. 'This was supposed to be you, wasn't it? You were supposed to marry him. But he couldn't stomach your ugliness and your foul hair, could he? You've forced this upon me, you scheming bitch. This was your plan all along.'

Kahina's face was a mask of maliciousness. 'Enjoy T'Clow Guntat, he's agreeable enough to look at, if you squint a bit.'

'You're a disgrace to us all. They call you the freak, did you know that?' Corine fired at her. 'The undesirable one, heartless, cold and proud. You'll never find a match, you'll die a lonely bent old spinster, you know that?'

'By your leave, exalted sister,' Kahina said, curtseying once more.

'I will see you punished for your part in this. A marriage to T'Clow Guntat will give me power to dispose of who I choose!'

'Do what you will,' Kahina replied, offhand. 'I care not.' Another vase shattered against the wall.

Kahina turned and stalked out. Marie glared at her as she left and then closed the door quietly behind her, before turning back to her mistress.

Corine collapsed on her bed, a low keening wail escaping her.

Marie went to her side, torn with worry. Corine looked up, her face streaked, her make up smudged and stained. In all these years Marie had never seen her mistress shedding real tears.

* * *

On the outskirts of Leeson City were a ruined collection of burnt out, shattered and barely habitable buildings. The slaves were housed further in towards the centre, in purpose built, simple but functional accommodation. They were taken to the mines by a dedicated transport link, tagged going in and out.

Out here lived those who operated beyond the law, beyond surveillance. It was a dangerous place; none lived here who had a choice. Purges by the Imperials were regular, but they might as well have tried to exterminate rats; the ruins were a maze, the broken remains of the original settlers dwellings, firebombed three years before, after the 'Appropriation' of Chione by the Loren family and their lackeys.

Around one of the ruined buildings, a series of cheap but effective motion detectors alerted their owner deep inside that somebody had passed the perimeter. Miniaturised camera drones surged to the location, quickly assessing the intruder. Cowled and cloaked, the individual's particulars adhered to previous stored scans and the drones switched to a quiescent mode after relaying the information.

In the basement, a small collection of individuals regarded each other warily. They were all dressed in tired military fatigues; grey and dusty. The bare walls ran with damp, the occupants huddled in battered chairs around a rough metal table on which lay a crumpled map.

'Here, here and here,' said one of them, a big, strongly muscled man, with a crew cut hairstyle and thinning bronze hair. He jabbed at the map with grimy hands and split fingernails. 'The next logical targets.'

Murmurs of appreciation rose from around the table. The man continued. 'We should continue to spread fear and doubt. Now that the slaves have fallen victim to the Senator's madness we ...'

'You lack ambition, Mitchell.'

Faces turned to regard another figure. He reclined carelessly in his seat, not looking at the rest of them. He seemed unaware that the purple birthmark that reached from his left cheek across his ear always drew a second glance. He seemed concerned more with the gun he was cleaning than the audience he addressed.

'We blew up one of their administrative buildings, in the heart of the city,' Mitchell said in a rough gravelly voice, suggesting damage to his vocal cords. 'They fear us now, Vargo.'

'And are we closer to achieving our goal?' Vargo spared him a disinterested glance. 'No. This is the time to strike, and strike hard. We need to push our advantage, not fall back.'

The murmurs now took on a tone of uneasiness; muted discussions sprang up as the two Reclamists studied each other.

'And what do you suggest?' Mitchell folded his arms and leant back a touch.

'The Loren's are vulnerable. The slaves are ready to revolt at a moment's notice. The buyers are nervous. There is dissension in the military at being posted to this distant system with insufficient resources. The Senator's madness

CHAPTER ONE

grows, even the Imperials acknowledge this, many would rather return to the Empire.'

'So?' Mitchell demanded.

Vargo rolled his eyes in an exaggerated fashion. 'We give the Imperial 'stards all the encouragement they need. Let them all burn.'

'We're already over extended. Pushing further when our supplies our low ...'

'The Imperials have far worse problems than we do. The next shipment of Federation weaponry is due from Octavia in just a few days. We'll have the advantage. You'd throw that away?'

Mitchell bristled. 'Careful, Vargo ...'

'Still debating the next move?' A third voice interrupted the debate and its owner stepped forward into the light. All eyes turned to regard the cowled figure. The voice was clipped and sharp, with a mechanical undertone, as if muffled by some technology.

'Ah, Solanac,' Vargo said, turning to face the newcomer and then winking at Mitchell. 'Glad you could make it. Your advice would be much appreciated. Mitchell here thinks we've done enough and should creep away for fear of discovery. I say we press our advantage while the Imperials cower in their refuge. You?'

'I suggest you all consider your next move very carefully indeed,' Solanac replied with a trace of mirth.

Mitchell scoffed and turned aside. Vargo acknowledged his frustration. 'Yes, I was counting on a little more than that ...'

'We must stake our claim,' Solanac said. 'We cannot wait for the Federation.'

'The Federation has and will continue to help us ...' Mitchell began.

'The Federation desires only that the Empire is frustrated,' Solanac interrupted. 'They never defended this system when they had the choice, what makes you think they will in the future? Tantalum is what they all want. Everything else is irrelevant.'

'Listen to him,' Vargo said, with a nod of approval.

'The Federation and the Imperials have no real interest in our world, they want only a reliable supply of Tantalum. The Federation is currently denied this, the Imperials fear it will be disrupted by the Senator's behaviour. If another government was formed that could broker a deal ...'

'Deal with the Imperials and the Federation?' Mitchell said in surprise, unfolding his arms and placing his hands on his hips.

'Run the mines for both powers, ensure the trade is equitable. We mine, they protect the access,' Vargo said, with a grin.

'You think the Imperials will go for it?' Mitchell looked sceptical.

'Reliable supply coupled with no longer having to defend this system, so far from their worlds?' Solanac asked. 'Peaceful co-operation with the Federation rather than this endless terrorism? Their cost savings would be dramatic. They know the Federation is funding us and backing the pirates. With that obstacle removed all parties would benefit. It is only the Loren's effective dictatorship and the position of the Senator that prevents it.'

'And how would we pull off this amazing coup?' Mitchell demanded. 'You've just said the Federation will not help us directly.'

Vargo turned to Solanac. 'I assume you have some new information?'

Solanac nodded. 'The Senator's eldest daughter, Corine Loren, is due to be married in a few short weeks. The Loren family will all be in the Imperial Palace, on full display. Security will be tight, but not impregnable. With the Imperials suitably informed, the Senator and his family could be, how shall we say, encouraged to retire early?'

'And then?' Mitchell queried.

'The mining rights are owned by the Lorens,' Vargo said, excitedly. 'If the Lorens are no more, their claim dies with them. The Imperials have no other rights to the system. Chione would belong to us once more. Our claim as settlers becomes legal. The Federation and the Empire would be forced to negotiate with us!'

'Assassinate the entire family?' Mitchell said, startled by the audacity of the plan.

'It must be done in Imperial fashion, honourably and with care,' Solanac said. 'Or we would fail to gain the necessary Imperial support.'

'Can it be done?' Mitchell demanded.

'Is Chione ours?' Vargo fired back. 'Do we want it back? Are we prepared to fight for it?'

Mitchell glared at Vargo from across the table. Silence descended on the room, broken only by the faint sounds of breathing from the rest of the Reclamists. Vargo and Mitchell continued to confront each other.

CHAPTER ONE

'All right,' Mitchell said, slowly. 'I'll have a few extra special items for Octavia to deliver.'

Vargo grinned. 'Name them, I'll get them.'

Mitchell nodded. 'I'm in, assuming …' he looked at Solanac. 'We can trust this information?'

'Have I ever let you down?' Solanac replied.

'Looking forward to the day you do,' Mitchell replied, straightening once more.

'Enough,' Vargo snapped. 'Chione will be ours again.'

He looked around at the rest of the Reclamists. 'Chione is ours. Chione is ours!'

The cry was taken up. The Reclamists, led by Vargo, chorused it again and again, rising to a crescendo. Eyes blazed with zeal, fists punched the air. The decision was made.

* * *

Patron Dalk Torgen arrived at the Imperial Palace later that day, taking a swift airship from the continent. Favoured by the Senator, he was entitled to land the small vessel on the private landing area immediately below the palace grounds. From there he strode up through the ornamental gardens and on to the wide gravelled colonnade that led to the palace. Dalk, surprised as always at how the imposing building rose above him, cast an appraising eye over it once more. It was classic in the manner of Imperial fashion, with a mix of baroque spinnerets and sweeping buttresses. The palace was clad in white marble, but reinforced with various alloys for strength. It could easily serve as a fortress.

Dalk proceeded up the colonnade to the main entrance, an enormous arch of obsidian fashioned to resemble the entrance to the Hall of Martyrs on distant Achenar. Dalk smiled inwardly; Senator Algreb's desire for immortality was plain to see. Two flamewood doors, secured with bright steel reinforcements barred the way, but slowly and silently swung outwards as Dalk approached. There were no guards in evidence, but all movements were being watched. Dalk could sense them, appropriately concealed, but poised to act at a moment's notice.

The Senator's youngest daughter was waiting for him in the vaulted foyer, standing on the bottom step of the wide and imposing staircase that led to the upper levels, her features illuminated by the bright sunshine streaming through the entrance.

Without a word Dalk turned and walked to the right and down a flight of stairs. Kahina followed him without question.

'You have displeased the Senator once again,' Dalk said. It wasn't a question.

'He has displeased me.'

'You seem to believe your opinion has some merit. You are unrepentant. This is not acceptable. You bring these punishments upon yourself.'

'They are mine to bear,' Kahina replied. 'I will not comply with his wishes.'

'We shall see about that.'

Dalk led her downwards into the depths of the palace. They reached a door which responded to Dalk's palm against its face by opening inwards. Dalk gestured to Kahina and she stepped inside.

No tapestries adorned the walls that rose, bright white, from the polished wooden floor. Instead, weaponry surrounded them; primitive knives, whips and chains; gleaming sword blades; pistols and automatic rifles. Dalk closed the door behind him and turned to face Kahina. A faint grin crossed his face.

'Alone now and away from prying eyes and ears.' Kahina stepped back a pace, swallowing hard. Dalk loosened the clasps on his trench coat, revealing a leather tunic and breeches beneath. A thick belt girded his waist, from which hung an ornate scabbard. From it he drew a thin sword, embellished with filigree of high craftsmanship. Light from the overhead illumination flickered from it as he brandished it with a small flourish. Kahina's eyes followed the sword warily.

'Your father insists you need treatment for your illness,' Dalk said, stepping aside and sweeping the sword in a downwards arc.

'And yet I stand here full of vigour,' Kahina countered and moved to keep the same distance between them.

Dalk smiled. 'A sickness of the mind perhaps?'

'A disobedient daughter is the curse of many a father.'

'A euphemism for torture then, to convince you to change your ways,' Dalk said, regarding her carefully. She matched his footwork step for step.

CHAPTER ONE

'My ways will never change.'

'Fighting talk from a mere girl with no rank.'

'Cowardice from an old man armed with a sword against an undefended lady.'

Dalk scoffed. 'A lady? Without the Loren locks of gold and clear blue eyes?'

'Is there some rule that states a woman must be blonde to be considered worthy?' Kahina returned.

Dalk grinned and gestured to the walls. 'Let's find out.'

Kahina walked across to the nearest side and retrieved a sword, her eyes never leaving Dalk's. She returned to the centre of the room and then without warning, lunged at Dalk, sword point aimed directly at his heart. Dalk turned aside in a flash, parrying the strike with his own sword. Sparks flew from the blades as they clashed. A flick of his wrist and Kahina was pushed back. Both dropped into a ready stance, slowly circling each other.

'I'm gratified to see you've not forgotten your last lesson,' Dalk observed.

'I learn fast and practice daily,' Kahina said, lunging forward again. A rapid series of strikes and parries followed. Dalk turned her sword once again, sending her reeling off balance. She spun to face him again.

'Much still to learn,' he said.

'I'll have you one day, old man,' she fired back.

Kahina struck a third time. This time Dalk deftly twisted his wrist and Kahina's sword clattered across the floor. His blade swung rapidly, stopping just short of her neck.

'But not this day,' Dalk commented. 'You're dead once more.'

Kahina grabbed his wrist in her hands, twisted violently and his sword fell from his grasp. She bent his arm backwards at the shoulder, pulling him off balance.

'You taught me never to stop fighting until I could fight no more,' she said, bending his arm cruelly, hoping to see a flicker of pain on his face. She was disappointed.

Instead Dalk dropped to his knees, spun and abruptly rotated his hips. Kahina was flung over him to land with a heavy thud on the floor behind him. She gasped in surprise and pain, the breath knocked from her. A fist had stopped just short of her nose.

'A lesson you've yet to completely appreciate,' he said with a nod, before opening his hand and helping her to her feet.

Kahina winced as her strained muscles protested. Dalk studied her for a moment. The girl showed occasional flashes of skill with both the blade and her unarmed technique, but she never quite seemed to manage a strong level of consistency.

But she's learnt enough; enough to survive.

'Why do you do this, Dalk?' she whispered. 'You disobey my father's wishes. The risk …'

'I do not agree with torturing innocent women,' he responded. 'You've committed no crime other than knowing your own mind. You deserve more than your station allows.'

'Could you torture me, should you wish to?'

Dalk fixed her with a stare. 'Why do you think your father chose me?'

'I imagine you've done worse in your time,' Kahina said, shrewdly.

'You imagine correctly.'

'You fought for the independent worlds, so it's told. Your prowess speaks for itself …'

'I've fought for them all, but that was a long time ago,' Dalk interrupted. 'My place is here, serving the Loren family.'

'You serve my father, no?' Kahina teased.

'Indeed. But we must all look to the future. Your father will not be Senator forever.'

'Some might say those are the words of a traitor, Patron Dalk.' Kahina's eyes flashed with amusement.

'Mere fact, nothing else.' Dalk dismissed her with a wave of his hand. 'Age takes us all in time. Nothing remains constant.'

Kahina laughed. 'I will puncture your composure one day, trust me.'

Dalk grew more serious. 'Perhaps the Reclamists will succeed in their aims. Perhaps the slaves will revolt and overrun the administration. Perhaps the Empire will intervene.'

'A catalogue of possible woes.'

Dalk looked at her carefully. 'Or perhaps another Senator may emerge from the esteemed Loren Lineage. Whosoever they might be, they must be prepared for the task ahead. Strong, sound of mind and purpose; would you not agree?'

Kahina made a dismissive sound. 'I have not the tact for politics.'

CHAPTER ONE

'You did well in diverting that Rebian wastrel, but take care not to antagonise others unless unavoidable. Cultivate allies as well as enemies and perhaps you may find yourself in a position of opportunity.'

'I'm in debt to your guidance, wise old man,' Kahina said, raising an eyebrow. 'Will you always guide me?'

Dalk looked at her appraisingly and then picked up her sword, tossing it towards her. Kahina caught it expertly by the hilt and spun her wrist around with a quick circular movement, before dropping into a ready stance.

'More bruises?' she enquired.

'Your treatment must look compelling,' Dalk replied. 'I have a reputation to maintain.'

'Come and get me, old man.'

Their swords clashed again, sparks flew.

Chapter Two

Sushil jumped the gate and then leant back on it, admiring the view of the family agri-site from the summit of the low hill. Below, rolling green planes dotted with deciduous woods divided by the sinuous run of a river. The water flickered and sparkled in the bright light of twin stars. Nicknamed 'niece' and 'nephew' for reasons long forgotten, each added a different hue to the vista: one a warm red, the other an actinic blue. Sushil loved the overlapping shadows cast by everything he could see.

Before him, looking incongruous parked adjacent to the tilled soil and neat rows of growing vegetation, sat a spacecraft. It was an old design, its hull a patchwork of tarnished duralium, with the occasional bright shiny repair panel secured in place. The ship was squat, short, but wide, reminiscent of an old atmospheric ship. Twin wing pods extended port and starboard, giving it a rakish profile. A single-man vessel based on the size of the cockpit, though Sushil knew it had been retrofitted with a second seat aboard.

Faint sounds of whirring could be heard, accompanied by brief flickers of light from the underside. Sushil grinned.

He'd found his brother.

He hurried down the hill, feeling the heat of the suns on his dark face. It was a relief to be in the shadows of the ship. Sushil found his brother working away with a welder, his face hidden behind a dark protective mask.

'Don't tell me, the undercarriage is stuck again. I thought you'd fixed that, bro.'

The welder fizzed and died. His brother sat back wearily and pulled the mask off his head. His face was drenched with sweat, his long black hair bedraggled and damp. Sushil saw him blow it out of his face. The simple motion took him back to their childhood. Hassan had always worn his hair long, much to the annoyance of his parents.

'Stupid piece of crap actuator blew again,' Hassan replied, giving the nearby landing strut a kick.

Sushil spared the ship a glance. Close up it was easy to see it was old and timeworn; the hull was pockmarked and tarnished. He saw evidence of cheap and less than perfect repairs; uneven welding lines, panels that didn't quite line up parallel to each other. The technology was basic even by the standards of the agri-site.

'Gramps always said this old bird was a deathtrap.' He smiled to himself at the reminiscence. It had to be twenty turns since their grandfather had flown this ship. His brother had been working on it for years, hoping to make it space worthy again.

'You here for a reason or just to bug me?'

Sushil grinned. 'Just checking up on you, little brother. Dad …'

'I know, chores. I'll do them, all right? It's not like the farm is going anywhere.'

Sushil hunkered down beside him. 'Done 'em for you. Figured you'd need the time.'

Hassan looked up in surprise and then held up his hand and Sushil grasped it, giving it a firm clasp.

'Means a lot to you this old piece of junk, doesn't it?' Sushil said.

'She's called the *Talon*, remember?' Hassan rocked on his backside, throwing his feet forward and stretching his legs out. 'I'm not a farmer, Sush.'

Sushil laughed. 'We figured that out a long time ago. Remember when you stuck that fork in your foot and you got a grub infection? I nearly died laughing.'

'I was in the fucking medbay for a week!'

'Was funny though. You with that stupid massive bandage around your foot. And just before your hot date, what was her name?'

Hassan grinned. 'Can't remember. Don't think she was all that impressed by the whole "infectious grub boy" look I had going.'

Sushil grew serious. 'I guessed you just wanted this old thing to get a little private time with the girls, didn't figure you as a spacer.'

Hassan smiled. 'Gramps' fault. Remember those bedtime stories? The theme park on Epsilon Eridani? The hall of ancients on Achenar. Earth … birthplace of humanity.'

Sushil shrugged. 'Different people, same old bureaucratic shit. That's why we came out here, to get away from that. Taxes, permits, tolls, papers … that

CHAPTER TWO

what you want? Gramps said it was murder nowadays, not like his good ol' times way back when.'

Hassan shook his head. 'I want to see it for myself. I want to get to the edge of the frontier. Find a new world, maybe get it named after me.'

Sushil looked around at the tatty old ship. 'And you think you can do it in this old wreck?'

'Don't be a stupe. This is just the start. Few trading runs, up the spec, trade her in for something better. Won't take me long.'

'Takes money, bro. It's dangerous up there. You know it is. Gramps said folks would sooner shoot you than shake your hand. I know you got good sim scores, but fighting a mech is one thing, real folks with real guns …'

'I can handle it.'

'Oh yeah? How's that then?' Sushil eyed his brother suspiciously.

'Got myself a plan.'

'You going to tell me?'

'I'm gonna apply to the guild.'

'The traders' guild?' Sushil replied. 'They don't take rookies.'

'I won't be a rookie.'

'You've got no rating. Harmless, isn't that what they call it?' Sushil caught his brother's knowing look. 'You'd better tell me the rest of your plan.'

'No,' Hassan replied. 'You'll only try to talk me out of it like you always do.'

'That's because your plans are always crazy and someone ends up getting hurt. Usually me.'

'Like when?'

'Like when we were kids, pretty much every rest day?' Hassan grinned.

'This one is going to work.'

'Fame and glory, eh?' Sushil put on an affected voice. 'Going to come back here in a few years with your kick-ass blinged up monster ship, smart off-world threads, back with the attitude, impressing all the pretty girls with the big man gait? Hassan Farrukh Sharma – all debonair and sophisticated? That the plan?'

'Something like that.' Hassan was subdued. 'I got to do this, Sush.'

Sushil looked at his younger brother for a long moment, before giving him a brief nod. He looked at the offending actuator on the landing strut.

'You can't weld for shit. Give me that. Might as well start with it looking neat and tidy.'

They set to work on the old ship, still jibing at each other. The bright flicker of the welder slowly growing stronger as the suns set behind the hills.

* * *

The wedding of T'Clow Guntat of the house of Rebia and Corine Tanja of the house of Loren was an ostentatious event, even by Imperial standards. Supplies, provisions and exotic victuals from across the galaxy were couriered in to the Imperial Palace on Chione for several months in advance.

Servants, maids and slaves worked tirelessly to prepare food, set tables and dress the hundreds of rooms within the palace. Plans were made for the arrival of distinguished guests from across Chione and the nearby systems. Invitations were checked and double checked, seating arrangements planned. Transport vessels were chartered. Everything was set to converge upon the day of the wedding.

A veritable cornucopia of exotic dishes from across the Imperial systems were arriving in specialist cuisine transport vessels. Many foods were selected on their ability to impress visually rather than for their taste and texture. There were colours from across the spectrum, including some unusual appetizers that were recommended to be eaten under ultraviolet light for maximum effect. There were morsels, aperitifs, hors d'oeuvres and selections of fine cuts aplenty, enough to cause even the fussiest gourmet to salivate in anticipation.

Accompanying this was a sophisticated selection of wines, some brewed traditionally from fruits and berries, others from more esoteric ingredients including grain, algae and even, in one case, live invertebrates.

A small army of consultants had been drafted in to write speeches, check protocol and co-ordinate the fashions worn by the guests. In some parts of the Empire your clothing wasn't simply for show; subtle messages could convey loyalty, disapproval and understated declarations of superiority. It was important that such messages were checked, balanced and made appropriate for the wedding. Hats were a particular problem. Fashion had drifted towards the excessive in recent years, with the size implying a degree of status. Exotic

CHAPTER TWO

materials were now being used to ensure the more flamboyant designs could survive the rigours of a social engagement.

Music was to be provided by the much respected East Coast Orchestra, a favourite of the Loren family. They'd followed the Loren's to Chione and set themselves up in a newly built and prestigious Musicians Hall in Leeson City. Fortunately Leeson City was eastwards of New Ithaca, so their name could be retained. As musicians they were unrivalled in Chione and their fame spread beyond the limits of the system, deep into Imperial worlds. They were set to play a series of especially commissioned pieces to mark the wedding, prior to the speeches and the banquet.

New furniture was acquired, the top table where the two families would be seated being the centre piece. At a price beyond sensible consideration, an elegant table first hewn from the wood of the famous towering pines of the Leestian rainforest, then diamond turned and polished with Lavian grub wax, had been imported and assembled in the great hall of the palace, dominating the hall. It stood upon a Sotiquan redweed plush-pile carpet, woven from strands of the famous plant. Still alive, it caressed and massaged the feet of those lucky enough to walk upon it.

The palace itself was dressed with kilometres of luxurious ribbons and lavish fabrics, accompanied by acres of vivid flowers in complex and colourful arrangements, all lit by strategically placed globes of soft light. These displays seemed to be aimed at challenging the display of fireworks that had been organised to light up the sky as the evening drew on. Musicians, artists and entertainers were stationed around the palace for the happy diversion of the guests, all individually hoping that some of the patrons, clients and citizens might notice and look favourably on them.

Tala was naturally chosen as the bridesmaid, and accorded all the honour and pomp that her position required. Dressmakers, hairstylists and body conditioning experts monopolised the time of both sisters ensuring their hair, faces, decoupage and any other visible flesh was seen to be as healthy and glowing as possible. Make up specialists from distant worlds were drafted in for mere minutes of attention. No expense was spared for Algreb's beautiful blonde daughters.

Kahina, by comparison, had very little to do. She'd been accorded no special duty given the animosity between her and Corine, coupled with T'Clow's disapproval. Had it been possible, Corine would have prevented her from coming at all, but that would have caused too many awkward questions to be asked and would have been considered bad form. Kahina was relegated to organising the maids and servants. This consisted of little more than keeping them moving as quickly as possible with a snap or a sharp word. Kahina rather enjoyed it.

She'd been assigned to sit at the top table with the rest of the family, but far off to one side, so that her dark hair did not detract from the regal blonde splendour of the rest of the family both on the Loren and the Rebian side. T'Clow had, so gossip suggested, had his own hair lightened in order to exactly match Corine's. Tala had tried to convince Kahina she should 'go blonde' as well, Kahina's refusal had banished her to the edge of the celebrations. To her sisters' disappointment, she seemed unfazed by the snub.

Kahina had done her best to avoid any interactions with the rest of her family, but it was impossible to maintain such distance entirely. She had hoped to spend some time talking to Dalk, but he'd been occupied with arrangements for the incoming transports and security concerns.

Kahina received a summons from Corine's maid Marie late in the afternoon, the day before the wedding. Dutifully she traipsed up to her sister's bedroom and awaited her pleasure.

Corine was surrounded by her legions of health and beauty professionals. The room was entirely full of expensive equipment all with the singular purpose of transforming an attractive young woman into a stunning glorious vision of beauty. Kahina had to admit it was impressive. Corine already looked dazzling and she wasn't even close to being 'finished'.

Marie led her in and told her to wait at the threshold. Corine ensured Kahina waited whilst she had a series of pointless and insignificant adjustments made to her hair before finally acknowledging her presence after a few minutes.

'Sister,' Corine smiled. 'How good of you to come.'

Kahina curtseyed. 'You wanted to see me, sister?'

'Yes indeed,' Corine enthused. 'A matter I'm sure has been on your mind for a while, doubtless your most important consideration in fact.'

Kahina fixed her with a quizzical look. 'And what might that be, sister?'

CHAPTER TWO

Corine looked surprised, as if amazed that Kahina wasn't aware of her thoughts. 'Why, your dress, of course. You must look the part for the wedding, no? Something appropriate for you as my revered younger sister.'

Kahina braced herself, but answered correctly. 'I'm sure you've chosen with your customary taste, style and elegance, sister.'

'Oh indeed,' Corine said. 'I have given the matter much thought. I have selected something that reflects your personality and standing, your dulcet tones and the close bond that has been forged between us over the years.' Corine's tone had a sharp and vindictive edge.

'I look forward to seeing it,' Kahina answered in a level tone.

'And there's no time like the present,' Corine said brightly. 'Marie, bring out Kahina's dress for her inspection.'

Marie glanced at Kahina with a brief self-satisfied look before moving to one of the huge wardrobes that lined Corine's bedroom. She took a moment to locate the garment and then pulled it out. Kahina heard a number of stifled sniggers of amusement as the dress came into view.

Taken in isolation it was a pleasant enough gown. It was simple and unadorned, in complete contrast to the ostentatious gowns being arranged for the honoured visitors and a world away from what Corine and Tala would be wearing. It was, however, completely at odds with current fashion. Where most modern gowns featured a plunging neckline, this was high necked; where sleeves were short and the overall length measured to the floor, this one was long in the arm and short to just below the knee. Kahina could see at a glance that it was at least one size too big.

'Your disagreeable hair gave us the most enormous difficulty,' Corine added, with a pained expression as if she'd spent hours agonising over the problem. 'But in the end we found a shade that complements you to best effect.'

The dress was a pale and light shade of mauve, again, not unpleasant in itself, but it was exactly the same shade as the functional dresses worn by the maids of the house. The snub was blatant, even by Imperial standards.

Kahina absorbed this in a moment. Mindful of Dalk's words she fixed her face in a demure smile, walked across and took the gown. Holding it against her and performing a small twirl as if to show how delighted she was with the choice.

'Why, sister, I'm overwhelmed with gratitude,' Kahina said. 'I will treasure it always. Is there anything else I can do for you?'

Her smile was sickly sweet.

Corine's nose wrinkled and her lips pursed. 'No, you've wasted quite enough of my time already.'

Kahina curtseyed and withdrew, ensuring that she dragged her new gown carelessly across the floor.

* * *

Kahina endured the surprised and haughty looks, the half-heard supercilious comments and the giggles of amusement at her attire. She played her part without complaint, curtseying and acknowledging the seemingly endless stream of guests as they arrived through the grand foyer. Many mistook her for a maid initially, which seemed to satisfy Corine greatly as Kahina was forced to acknowledge the confusion with a humiliated smile and demeaning shrug of acceptance.

Her only saving grace was that she wore one of the Loren family's ceremonial swords buckled at her hip, a weapon of some distinction. To one particularly obnoxious gentleman, she was able to demonstrate that she could not only draw it, but she knew how to use it as well. Nobody teased her after that.

The wedding ceremony itself took place in the west wing of the palace, where a series of rooms had been opened up to form a big enough space to accommodate the guests, the Loren and Rebian family entourages. Senator Algreb and Lord Guntat performed the ritual exchange of weapons (another pair of swords) before Algreb began a long recital from the last of six impressive looking leather bound volumes that had been reverently placed on a series of baroque stands as a centre point to the ceremony. These were a series of books which every Imperial family were encouraged to own and venerate – the collective history of the Duval Dynasty. Needless to say, the copies owned by the Lorens were sumptuous, opulent and immensely valuable.

'The strength and vitality of the Empire,' Algreb continued in his customary monotone, 'comes from the sweat and toil of our fathers, and their fathers and their fathers before them ...'

CHAPTER TWO

Eventually the vows began. Corine and T'Clow were ritually and symbolically linked by the act of a deep maroon cord being bound around their wrists. Then they exchanged various lies about their undying affection and commitment to each other. It seemed strange to Kahina how a simple alignment of family interests needed to be dressed up in so much pomp and ceremony, yet it was the Imperial way in all matters of any significance.

Trumpets signalled the successful conclusion of the formalities and Kahina followed the families out down a central aisle towards the grand hall where speeches, music and the banquet were being prepared. She trailed at the rear, just in front of the maids.

They walked directly into the great hall, taking their places at the top table. Corine and T'Clow sat in the centre, facing directly back into the hall, with Algreb and T'Clow's mother to one side, and Algreb's wife and T'Clow's father on the other. Tala was seated next to T'Clow's father and surrounded by a gushing collection of T'Clow's brothers all vying for her attention to her great delight. His sisters were seated on the other side, looking almost as bored as Kahina felt. Kahina herself was relegated to the edge of the table, in a darkened corner with the maids standing behind her. She tried her best to ignore their whispers and giggles, contenting herself with watching the amazing display of hats and outlandish fashions that paraded into the hall as the guests found their seats.

The centre of the room was reserved for the East Coast Orchestra themselves. Kahina was surprised that they didn't seem to have already prepared their instruments, but the troupe was known for being somewhat risqué with their performances, something that endeared them to Imperial audiences, who enjoyed the unexpected.

The doors to the great hall were closed by the servants and everyone took their seats.

The conductor, his back to the assembly, stood up and turned. The musicians sat still, still having not taken their instruments out in readiness. Kahina wondered if they were going to start with a vocal rendition. She hoped so; their harmonious singing was a glorious thing to behold.

'Senator,' the conductor said with a deep bow. Algreb acknowledged him with a nod.

'Lord and Lady Rebia,' the conductor continued, bowing once more. 'Esteemed family, Patrons, clients, citizens and honoured guests. It is our privilege to play for you this evening …'

Kahina stifled a yawn. Her feet ached from having been standing for so long and even her face ached as a result of the false smile she'd had to wear to greet the seemingly unending stream of guests throughout the day. The conductor continued with his narration.

'… to celebrate this auspicious event in the manner it deserves, we have put together an original work calling to mind the momentous history of the Loren family …'

'Just play,' Kahina muttered to herself and scowled at the conductor, as if trying to hurry him up by mental command.

'… the impressive achievements of our glorious Senator and his family. Especially commissioned in tribute to this celebrated legacy, we call this first piece "Retribution for the original settlers of Chione".'

There was a brief pause. Conversation, which until this point had been a faint muted buzz, now stopped abruptly. Kahina looked up in surprise.

What did he say?

The conductor raised his baton. The orchestra rose to its feet.

Somehow, instead of the finely crafted musical instruments expected, each member now bore a gun; some small, some larger, depending on the musical case from which the weapon had been drawn.

No one moved; all eyes were fixed on the orchestra. Somebody pointed and shouted. 'They've got guns!' The conductor dropped his baton.

Deafening weapons fire crashed through the great hall. The screams of women and the cries of men rose in the turmoil. Bullets flew; shredding tapestries and smashing delicate works of art. A series of busts of the Loren's ancestors were shattered.

Kahina reacted faster than most, at the first sound of gunfire she threw herself under the table. She could see that these people were aiming to frighten rather than kill. Clearly the attackers had a particular goal in mind. She had an unpleasant feeling she knew precisely what it was.

Abruptly the gunfire stopped.

Kahina heard a faint series of footsteps; then she heard the conductor's

CHAPTER TWO

voice speak out. 'Anyone who is not a member of the Loren family, I suggest you leave now.'

There was not the faintest hint of movement from anywhere. After a pause Kahina heard a gun discharge rapidly. Screams split the air, rapidly silenced. Then the voice came again, shouting loudly.

'Move!'

There were fresh shrieks of fear and terror punctuated by the rapid movement of people towards the main entrance to the great hall. The conductor discharged his gun a few more times to encourage them to move quicker.

From her crouched position Kahina saw T'Clow stumble to his feet. She heard Corine call out in alarm.

'T'Clow?'

'I'm not a member of the Loren family,' he stammered.

Kahina peeked forward and saw the conductor turn to face him. 'No, I suppose you're not.'

Despite Corine's outraged protests, T'Clow and the remainder of the Rebia family stepped away from the top table and hurriedly made their way out after the departed guests.

'You're all bloody cowards though,' the conductor added. He turned and fired. The shot was not aimed to kill but only to maim. The bullet tore into T'Clow's leg. He screamed in pain, but his family managed to pull him out of the hall as they fled.

The conductor turned back to the Loren family, now cornered by the armed musicians. He laughed at the tears coursing down Corine's face and pouted at her.

'You could do so much better, darling.'

'I demand to know who you are,' Algreb said, a tremble in his voice.

'Well I'd be disappointed if you didn't,' the conductor replied. 'But you'll have to wait your turn.'

'You defy the Senator of Chione?' Algreb said, rising to his full height.

The conductor reached up to his face and pulled off a tight fitting mask, discarding it to reveal a narrow drawn face underneath. Kahina gasped at the strange purple birthmark that stretched across the man's face.

'I do indeed.'

– 47 –

'Reclamists,' Kahina whispered to herself. 'Vargo …'

'This is my world, Senator. Time for you and yours to return it.'

'The Empire will not let this go unpunished …' Algreb began. 'Kill me and you sign your own death warrant.'

'A risk I'm happy to take.'

Vargo raised the gun and fired at the Senator. Algreb was flung backwards by the force of the blast, cannoning backwards into his chair. Vargo didn't stop, but kept firing again and again until the Senator's chest was a bloody mess of torn flesh and tattered clothing. He signalled with his other hand.

Silence fell again, punctuated only by the sobbing gasps of Algreb's wife. Her cries turned to hysteria and then a high pitched scream.

'Oh be quiet, woman …'

Vargo raised his gun and fired again. She joined her husband in oblivion.

This was too much for the maids behind Kahina. At least one of them panicked; screaming and running for the exit. Gunfire was the result. The first was slain and then the others were shot down in quick succession.

'Kill the rest of them!' Vargo shouted over the din.

'No!' Kahina leapt from under the table, pulling her ornamental sword from her waist and striking at the feet of the nearest Reclamist. Blood splashed, he yelled and went down hard, his foot severed at the ankle. Kahina grabbed his gun and struck him around the head, before turning the gun on the others. With the gun in her left hand and the sword in her right she pulled the trigger.

Noise and harshness of a type she'd never imagined rose around her. She'd never fired live rounds before. The gun was designed for two-handed hold and was almost wrenched from her grasp. Her aim was wild. It was enough though; the Reclamists dove for cover amidst the ornate dining tables. A chandelier shattered and fell, adding to the confusion.

Kahina motioned to her two sisters who ran behind her as she overturned tables and fled towards the rear of the room, where a smaller pair of doors led out to the foyer, all the time firing wildly with the gun.

'Stop them!' Vargo yelled.

Kahina reached the door, pushed Corine through it and fired again, causing her pursuers to dive to the floor once more. Tala was not far behind. Kahina saw one of the Reclamists aiming at them and turned her weapon on him.

CHAPTER TWO

The gun spat once and then stopped, clicking impotently. Kahina realised it was empty. She had no idea how to reload it. The Reclamists smiled, took aim and fired. Kahina instinctively pulled back as bullets splintered the panelling around the doorway. Tala screamed.

Kahina felt a splash of warmth across her face. Blood. For an instant she thought she'd been shot, but a ghastly gurgling noise from before her turned her attention to Tala. Blood was spurting and gushing from a horrifying wound in her neck. More bullets flew around Kahina, one slicing through the skin on her outstretched arm as she made a desperate grasp towards her sister. Tala collapsed to the floor, blood spurting from her lifeless body. The empty gun spun from Kahina's hand as bullets ricocheted off it.

The pain galvanised her to action and she fled, slamming the heavy doors closed behind her.

Bullets peppered the door, sending more splinters flying.

Corine was outside, standing still, her face shocked and blank, blood streaming from a myriad of small cuts.

'Run!' Kahina yelled. 'Upstairs!'

Corine didn't move, so Kahina grabbed her by the wrist and yanked her along up the grand staircase. They'd made the first balcony when the Reclamists emerged from the hall, looked quickly around and spotted them fleeing along the landing at the top of the stairs.

'Up there!'

Bullets cracked and shattered the delicately wrought marble balustrade and the window behind them, but Kahina, still pulling Corine behind her, managed to gain the safety of the passageway.

Corine stumbled and would have fallen, but Kahina did not let go of her, pulling her upright and down the passage at breakneck speed. They turned the corner as more bullets hissed through the air, running into the east wing of the palace. Kahina made a final turn into Corine's bedroom. She locked the door behind her and then ran to the windows.

'Who are they? Why are they doing this?' Corine's voice was shrill and high.

Kahina ignored her and then jumped onto the furniture below the window. She climbed up to grab the fastening, tightening her hold so she could crank it open.

It refused to move.

Kahina adjusted her grip and tried again.

The bedroom windows were locked and secured. Kahina battered against them impotently with the hilt of her sword, but the windows were blast shielded. They had never been locked before. Someone had planned this down to the last detail. There was no way out. The doors thumped, the Reclamists were on the other side.

'Get away from the door. Get behind me,' Kahina screeched, looking around and leaping down to the floor. She grabbed the sword whilst motioning at her sister.

Corine ran, but she had not completed more than two steps before the door exploded into fragments, showering them both with flying debris. Kahina shielded her face with an outstretched arm, just able to make out her older sister falling to the bed alongside her. Smoke billowed into the room, obscuring everything for long moments.

Then, aside from the faint clattering as broken wood, glass and metal fastenings fell to the floor, everything became silent.

The Reclamists walked into the bedroom, their footfalls heavy upon the wooden floor. There were three of them; Vargo in front with two behind, flanking him. One was tall and thin, the other thick limbed and stocky. Vargo had an unpleasant looking handgun clenched in his right hand. Kahina stepped back, looking briefly to each side. There was nowhere left to run.

Corine, still bleeding from multiple cuts on her face and arms, tried to stagger up from her position on the bed. Vargo raised his gun.

'No, please,' Corine cried. 'Don't! I'll do whatever you want, please don't ...'

The gun fired once, then again and a third time. It seemed curiously subdued and muffled now. Kahina only just registered the flash from the muzzle and saw the recoil of the mechanism with a strange detached interest. Corine's body was flung back abruptly to lie prone on the bed, more blood quickly seeping into her white dress. Her face locked in a look of terror.

'And the last.' Vargo made a show of reloading his gun as he looked at Kahina. Kahina heard the thick metallic clunk as the gun was primed once more. 'Still ready to fight I see.'

Kahina stood tall, her fists clenching with the effort of not trembling with

CHAPTER TWO

fear. Her heart hammered. Sweat drenched her, she felt it trickle down her chest and back, chilling her. She quickly tried to work out whether she could rush Vargo, but the distance was too far, she'd be cut down before she reached him. Better to die with grace.

'Kill me then, I am not afraid of you.'

She raised the sword she held and pointed the blade towards him.

Vargo chuckled and looked briefly over his shoulder. The taller Reclamist standing behind him was cowled, with his head bowed. 'You were right Solanac. She does have a modicum of honour. She's yours.'

Kahina glared as the cowled man stepped forward. She could see a scabbard buckled at his belt, it looked oddly familiar. She frowned, puzzled.

She looked upwards as the man pulled away the cowl revealing a tanned and hairless scalp. A moment later he pulled off a mask supplemented with some kind of mechanism. Thus revealed, the expression on the man's face was dark and foreboding, the eyes glinting with a deadly intent. Kahina almost dropped her sword in a mixture of bewilderment, betrayal and mounting fury.

Vargo and Mitchell were clearly bewildered too. 'A Patron …' Vargo managed.

'Dalk …' Kahina's anguished voice caught in her throat.

'No longer at your father's service, young Kahina,' Dalk replied, easily. 'And yes, Solanac was a convenient alter ego. I fear the Reclamists might not have been too keen to deal with a Patron from the off.'

Vargo's face was split by a wide grin of satisfaction.

Kahina cried out in fury, leapt forward and slashed clumsily at Dalk in rage. Vargo stumbled backwards out of range, surprised at her impressive turn of speed. Dalk easily deflected the blow and pushed her backwards. She stumbled back against the bed and her sister's dead body, almost losing her footing.

'Murderer!' she hissed, before coming back to the attack. 'So you are a traitor then!'

'I do only what is necessary,' Dalk replied, watching her carefully as she approached again.

This time her attack was more measured, her skill with the blade more evident. Dalk sidestepped and tried to twist her blade out of her hand, but she had remembered that trick from before. She swung around with a vicious strike that left both swords ringing and notched. Both stepped back and circled each other again.

'This was my home before it was yours,' Dalk said, with a deft lunge. Kahina batted his sword away. She struck back and Dalk parried. They resumed their deadly dance.

'Speak plainly, traitor,' Kahina snapped. 'You claimed to be a man of the Empire.'

'Three years ago, your family attacked this moon, wiping out the original settlers …'

'They were squatters,' Kahina fired back.

Dalk's eyes blazed with fury and he slashed at Kahina. She only managed to block the initial blow and had to duck the second, her wrist twisted painfully by the force of the first blow.

'They were innocents,' Dalk seethed. 'Burnt at your father's command. Destroyed by your fleet of warships!'

'We had a claim,' Kahina's voice was uncertain, defensive. 'It was legal, they …'

'They died because of your father's lust for money, for a simple grey metal you can dig out of the ground on a hundred other worlds,' Dalk retorted. Their blades clashed again, the ringing sound of their impact echoing back from the panelled walls. Kahina came face to face with Dalk's angry visage.

'Just commoners,' Kahina shouted back. 'What did you care for them?'

'They were my people,' Dalk said softly, leaning in closely. 'Simple peace loving folk wanting to be left alone; my friends and my family. And your father butchered them …'

Kahina's eyes widened in shock at his words, for a moment she felt a pang of sympathy. In that moment Dalk's blade slipped under her guard, sliding softly through fabric and skin; then past bone. Kahina gave out a short sharp gasp.

'Full circle,' Dalk intoned. For a moment, all was still.

Kahina's own sword dropped from her fingers with a crash upon the wooden floor. Burning pain flooded through her chest. She looked down to see the hilt of Dalk's sword only inches from her breast. After an agonising moment he withdrew the sword. Pain convulsed her and she sank to her knees, only dimly conscious of Dalk kneeling down in front of her and taking her roughly by the throat in his other hand.

CHAPTER TWO

'It's better this way,' he whispered. She looked up briefly, uncomprehending. Then he let her go.

Blackness crashed in around her vision, she dimly heard laughter, saw the ground tilt upwards and felt the curiously numb impact as she fell sideways, sprawled on the floor.

Then the darkness took her and she knew no more.

* * *

Dalk wiped the bloodied sword on the edge of his cloak, before carefully returning the blade to its scabbard. Vargo stepped forward and pushed the young woman's body over with his foot. She rolled onto her back, lifeless, her still open eyes now staring upwards at the ceiling, her expression a frozen tableau of shock and betrayal. A little blood stained her dress, but the wound was small and precise.

'So falls the last of the Lorens,' Vargo said. 'A good death. She retained her honour as you said she would.'

'They value their tradition most highly,' Dalk admitted.

'Still counting yourself as one of them?' Vargo asked, with a wry grin.

Dalk turned to regard him. 'I was never one of them. I served them for the purpose of gaining a position whereby I could seek to undermine them. That is all.'

'And undermine them you did,' Vargo said, grabbing his arm firmly to congratulate him. 'There's a certain charm to this Imperial tradition I'll admit. Her end will be a story worth telling.'

'A pointless display of antique weaponry,' Mitchell sneered. 'We're wasting time.'

'We have a system to claim,' Vargo acknowledged with a nod.

'Leave me for a moment,' Dalk said, turning to face them. 'I'll join you shortly.'

'Why?' Vargo queried.

'I taught this one,' Dalk said, with obvious regret as he regarded Kahina's body. 'She was my novice in many ways. In another place and time she would have grown to be a great leader. Alas …'

'Going soft on us?' Mitchell jeered. 'She was the flux-stained offspring of an insane old 'stard.'

Dalk stiffened, but Vargo held up his hand. 'Dalk is a traditionalist. We have won, Mitchell. She died well. Let him mark her passing in his own way. He's earned that.'

Dalk remained motionless as the other two left the shattered bedroom. He stood there, immobile, regarding the cooling bodies of the two sisters. The sounds of Vargo and Mitchell's footsteps faded out of earshot.

Satisfied they were gone, Dalk knelt down and placed a small rectangular black tab on Kahina's forehead. As it came in contact with her skin, tiny lights flickered in an ordered sequence upon it, as if calculating some arrangement or taking a measurement. Then they became steady, with the exception of a small number which pulsed in a regular fashion. Dalk straightened and touched a finger to his ear. He looked up as his call was acknowledged.

'East wing, the eldest daughter's bedroom. You have only minutes, be quick.' His message delivered, Dalk swiftly left the ruined bedroom.

* * *

Ships belonging to the wedding guests were fleeing the palace in a panic. News of the assassination was already hitting the moon-side newsfeeds and would quickly be disseminated across the surrounding systems.

One ship, a smart Imperial vessel that had unloaded a cargo of foodstuffs earlier that afternoon, was parked towards the rear of the palace. A capsule, carried in the manner of a coffin with some difficulty by six Imperial Guards, was being taken aboard via the vessel's stern boarding ramp. The ramp retracted moments after they were all inside and, with a faint whine, the vessel's drives ignited. It lifted off gracefully, extending its twin engine nacelles into flight configuration and angling itself upwards into the heavens.

As it rose above the palace, two small fighter craft of similar design swooped in from behind the nearby mountains and arranged themselves alongside, accompanying it as it thrust upwards with ever increasing speed. Within seconds all three ships were dwindling dots in the sky, leaving Chione far behind.

Chapter Three

The Imperial Cutter *Caduceus* continued its flight outbound from Chione. The moon had already receded to a thin crescent on the aft display, accompanied by its parent, Daedalion. From this vantage point they looked like a double planet, their water-dominated surfaces casting a bright blue glow through space.

Retaining their tight escort formation, the two Imperial fighters were just visible through the port and starboard observation windows, their sensors keeping a close watch for any unexpected heat signatures. There was no sign of pursuit. Traffic ought to have been light out here; most of the ships in the Prism system were freighters and their escorts, concerned only with docking alongside the orbital space station and ore processing facility, *Hiram's Anchorage*. Efficiency and a quick turnaround meant that most ships hyperspaced out as soon as they cleared the immediate navigation space of the station and Chione's gravity well.

The *Caduceus'* captain had deliberately taken the decision to drive his ship deep into interplanetary space using its frame-shift drive. He was wary of being followed. With the right equipment, savvy pursuers could 'hitch' onto your hyperspace entry point, potentially arriving at your destination before you did. That always led to an unpleasant reception. Better to make sure no one was following you before you jumped.

'Secure drives,' he ordered. The helm officer responded with a quick series of finger gestures. The faint hint of acceleration abruptly faded away. The captain, satisfied that all was in order, called up the visual cue for his seat to release him.

It was an experience he'd never really acclimatised to. A viscous gel-like fluid, eased away from his extremities, returning to storage in the base of the chair. It left no moisture behind, but the sensation was as if hundreds of groping and invasive fingertips had run themselves over the length of his body. He was unable to prevent his customary shudder.

His boots activated a moment later, clamping themselves to the floor. He stood up, grasping an overhead railing and surveying the small bridge.

'All hands, observe zero-G protocol. We jump in fifteen minutes.'

The navigation officer, seated next to the helm officer, turned around. 'All sensors dark sir, no signs of pursuit.'

The captain nodded. 'Plot the jump for Haoria, let me know when we're ready. I'll be in the cargo bay. Babysitting detail.'

The navigation officer grinned and turned back to his work. The captain turned and made his way to the rear of the bridge. A series of recessed hand and foot grips led downward to a lower level, but he ignored them, simply pushing gently and allowing himself to float to the deck below. His boots clamped on once more and he strode rearwards.

* * *

The *Caduceus*' cargo bay was not usually pressurised; there was no point. Automechs loaded and unloaded the large cargo canisters from the hold without supervision and any perishable materials were handled in self-contained systems, bringing their life support or temperature compensations along with them.

This trip was an exception. The captain unlocked the bulkhead door, stepped through and secured it behind him, taking a moment to appreciate the internal size of the bay. It was a rare opportunity to see his vessel from this perspective. Pods were stacked in orderly rows and columns; he knew more than two hundred of them were secured aboard.

The cargo bay was functional of course, its designers mindful that it would be seldom seen. It was efficiently and flexibly laid out, but the captain, with a small smile of recognition, spotted the designers' nods to Imperial mores; a hint of baroque decoration here, straps with buckles wrought as claws and hands, subtle use of Imperial colours to enhance the sense of grandeur.

The captain stepped towards the centre rear of the bay, where a space had been reserved for the special cargo. It had been loaded into a standard trading canister for safe keeping, stored horizontally. The canister was currently open at the far end. The captain stepped around and ventured in. Inside was a curiously small pod. It was an unusual design, with a suggestion of more sophisticated technology, its exterior an untarnished bright white, without the

CHAPTER THREE

scrapes and dents that typically marked freight containers. It was suspended at waist height, securely held in place in the midst of the canister. A man was standing next to it. He looked up as the captain approached.

'Ah, Captain,' the man said. 'Have you finished shaking us around?'

The captain didn't respond to the jibe. 'Smooth as silk from here on out, Doctor. How's our patient?'

'Still dead, I imagine,' the Doctor replied, brusquely. 'We don't have much time.'

The Doctor stroked his hand through his thick grey beard and then tapped out a series of patterns on the surface of the pod. White light flashed beneath his fingertips and then pulsed green. The pod hissed and opened, both men stepping back as the cover lifted and a thin white mist rolled out.

Inside, supine in more of the same viscous gel the captain had recently experienced, was the body of a young woman. She was entirely naked, save for a small black tab on her forehead; her skin pale and her eyes closed. She was unnaturally still, her arms at her side. The captain could see tiny needles puncturing the skin of her arms and legs. The Doctor gestured with his fingers and the gel seeped away.

The captain swept his eyes up and down. The Doctor cast a disapproving glance in his direction.

'Don't get any funny ideas.'

The needles retracted as the gel exposed them, neatly folding back into their housings around the edge of the pod's interior. The Doctor continued to work and an intricate set of glass-like fibres emerged from the pod's roof, growing organically and descending towards the woman's body.

The fibres gently probed her chest, where the captain could see a small wound; a neat diagonal cut about two inches wide. As he watched, the glass-like fibres pulled the wound gently apart and ventured inside the woman's body, throbbing and pulsing. As they did so, holofac images of internal organs appeared in the space above her body. The Doctor observed and guided, the images adjusted themselves. Light flickered bright on the images, accompanied by faint glows from within the woman's body.

Brief minutes later the glass fibres emerged, retracting. As they did so, intense actinic light flickered over the wound, sealing it. The faintest of scars was all that remained. The Doctor touched the black tab on the woman's forehead and inspected the configuration of lights that it displayed. Satisfied all was in order he gestured for the pod to close. Gel surged up around the woman and the pod locked itself in place again.

'That's it?' the captain asked as they both stepped outside the canister. The Doctor bashed the locking mechanism and the hatch hissed closed.

'Back from the dead in eighteen hours,' he replied. 'The physiological stuff is simple. Ensuring her memory and personality is intact takes longer. Though with this one, rumour has it, a new personality might not be a bad thing.'

'I'm impressed.'

'You should be. That pod cost more than you'll earn in the next decade.'

'She's worth that?'

The Doctor tapped the side of the canister with his fingers. 'To someone she is, yes.'

* * *

Six ships hung in the darkness between worlds, starlight flickering sporadically off pitted and radiation scarred hulls. A quick glance at the vessels would give a seasoned star traveller a sense of wariness. The ships were battered and well used, with all the signs of a hard life. Heat-tarnished weapons jutted out from the hulls in an ugly but functional way. They might have once been honest trading vessels, but no longer; their pilots turning to a less admirable vocation in pursuit of cold hard cash.

Clustered here in a dark system they played a waiting game, holding station at a waypoint on one of the many hyperspace routes. For passers-by these systems were a place to pause, check navigation, recharge their jump drive and then proceed onwards …

… For pirates it was the ideal place to stage an ambush.

The major routes were patrolled; squadrons of Vipers would roam the flight corridors on the busy tracks, keeping an eye out for illegal activity. But that was in the core systems; out here coverage was sparse. You brought along your own protection, prayed to whatever deity you thought took an interest and hoped you'd brought along a surfeit of guns.

CHAPTER THREE

'Due in one minute.'

Aboard the *Talon*, Hassan heard the narrowband comm transmission from the lead ship. He could see it half a kilometre in front of him, a seriously modified Asp heavy fighter gently adjusting its position with brief flashes of thruster fire. Flanking it were four Sidewinders, basic but dependable ships. His own vessel, an old Eagle Mark 1, was bringing up the rear. He gripped the flight controls to stop his hands from shaking.

My first heist!

He checked his weapons load-out. He'd already done it countless times, but it kept him occupied during the interminable wait. Twin rapid fire pulse lasers, a rack of guided small missiles and a decent set of shield generators. It didn't sound bad when recited like that, but despite his best efforts his ship was by far the least potent of the six vessels.

Trading between worlds was an established career path to fame and riches, but like any profession, it often required patience and planning. Lone wolf traders like Hassan often struggled, particularly early on. Joining a Guild was the ideal way to gain some protection but the Guilds could afford to be picky, there were always more candidates than places.

His brother had been right, the Guild didn't take rookies. They'd turned him down. But after this, he'd be no rookie.

'Fifteen seconds. Standby to attack.'

And my last ...

He felt sweat drip from his forehead.

The captain felt his muscles tense. He was aware of his two Imperial escorts docking with *Caduceus* as it spooled up its hyperspace drive. The fighters couldn't jump themselves, they had to be carried through. Hyperspace was one of those things that never became routine. The moment of sending hundreds of tons of ship and personnel through an infinitesimally small multi-dimensional compression, crossing light years of real space in a fraction of a second ...

Best not to think about it too much. 'Jump ready,' the helm officer called out.

The captain nodded. 'Execute.'

Stars leapt towards them, dust and nebulous gas streaming past the ship at speeds beyond imagination. It was all over in seconds, accompanied by a faint surge of deceleration. It would take the on board systems a few moments to catch up and confirm their location. Meanwhile the drive would suck power as it spooled up again, ready to perform the next jump of the sequence.

'Jump secure,' the navigation officer said.

That was welcome news. Occasionally ships might suffer a failed jump and re-emerge ... somewhere else. You never found out where; they never came back to tell.

'Spool up for the next jump,' the captain ordered. 'Passive scans?'

'Receiving,' the navigation officer said, squinting at his instruments. The captain could see him rechecking something.

'Problem?'

'Faint heat signature, sir. Difficult to read, can't localise it, nothing visual.'

The captain leant forward to examine the readouts himself. There were plenty of mundane reasons for heat signatures out here. A powered vessel would typically be easy to spot, so it was probably just a rock, warm through the decay of radioactive elements and glowing softly in the infra-red, but it paid to be cautious. Dark systems were well named; far away from the glow of a sun, waypoints between the inhabited worlds, with maybe a frozen asteroid or dwarf planet to be used as a convenient marker, otherwise lost forever in the vastness of the cosmos.

The captain considered a quick active scan. That would positively identify the signature. It would also broadcast his exact position to anyone hereabouts who happened to be looking. He decided against it.

'Could just be a sensor ghost,' the navigation officer volunteered. He didn't sound convinced. The captain straightened. 'Well, they say witchspace is haunted.'

The navigation officer grinned. 'Witchspace? You sound like my grandmother. The ghosts of the early ships that went out here and didn't come back again ...'

'Enough of that. Deploy the fighters and get them to run a sweep while we're prepping. Eyes sharp.'

'Aye sir.'

After terse instructions, the two small fighter craft undocked from the *Caduceus* and broke off in opposite directions, thrusting to the limits of the *Caduceus*' effective scanner range in order to extend the range of the

CHAPTER THREE

sweep, searching for any trouble that might be lurking. The navigation officer could just see them faintly on the edge of his scanner, dull red heat signatures slowly circling the perimeter. Nothing else appeared to be in range.

The scanner crackled with static momentarily, the holofac displays flickering uncertainly. The navigation officer frowned and ran a diagnostic; no errors appeared.

'Still not happy?' The captain queried, still standing behind him.

The helm officer shook his head. 'Just picking up some static, probably a gamma ray burst or something.'

The captain tweaked a few settings on the scanner. 'More likely we got short-changed on the last maintenance stop,' he muttered.

The dull red glow of the starboard fighter flared. As the captain stared, it became a red stain on the scanner as it broke from its patrol pattern, hurtling towards them at flank speed.

'What's he doing?' the captain demanded. 'Call him up.'

'Flight One from *Caduceus*. Explain deviation from flight path.'

A crackle of static erupted from the narrowband channel then faded to a low buzz that drowned everything else.

'Impedance on all narrowband comms, sir. Communication bandwidth just dropped to zero.'

Shock coursed through the captain's body. Jammed! 'Sound general quarters! All weapons hot. Shields to full power.'

He raced to secure himself in his flight chair, aware of the other two bridge officers scrambling to get back to theirs before the deadly effects of inertia at battle stations crushed the life from them all. Whirring mechanical thumps echoed through the hull as weapons emerged from their storage pods and locked into place on the hull of the ship.

Six fighters burst out of the darkness. They were small. An Asp, an Eagle and a troop of Sidewinders; classic fighting machines. Neither as quick nor manoeuvrable as the Imperial fighters, but they had the advantage of surprise and carried enormous firepower.

The *Caduceus*' targeting computers locked onto the closest attacker and the autocannon weapons began their staccato fire. The incoming fighters scattered.

'All ships! Break and defend. I repeat. Break and defend,' the captain yelled into the narrowband comms as his seat enveloped him.

He stared in disbelief. The Imperial fighter still flanking the *Caduceus* seemed oblivious to the danger. The attackers were close, too close.

He can't hear us and hasn't seen them.

Missiles flickered on the threat warning indicators. Electronic counter measure systems activated immediately. That got everybody's attention; astrogation consoles lit up like solstice celebrations.

The missiles came on, two apiece, indefatigable. The attackers were taking no chances. The ECM aboard the *Caduceus* spun out its charged energy halo in vain. Hard-head missiles, expensive, but effective.

The captain watched in despair as the missiles impacted on the *Caduceus*' shields, splashing debris across space, fire blossoming briefly in the cold void before being extinguished.

Laser fire raked across the *Caduceus*' shields a moment later, with a faint thrum of energy. The shields flared in response, protecting the ship. The Sidewinders jinked past, threading a course through the defensive flak-fire spraying from the beleaguered Imperial vessel.

Hassan saw one of the two Imperial fighters drawing a bead on his companion's Sidewinder. A fierce red beam of light leapt out, shredding the Sidewinder's port upper hull plate. Plasma, fuel and coolant leaked into the void, streaming behind the mortally wounded vessel. Hassan heard a brief scream on the narrowband before the ship disintegrated.

He wrenched his ship around, trying to concentrate on the wildly twisting Imperial fighter rather than the dizzying whirl of motion that the star field backdrop had become. His Eagle's own pulse lasers struck out, flaring brightly in the faint wisps of dust and gas through which the battle raged. The beams sliced neatly across the Imperial fighter's starboard engine nacelle, completely severing it. The fighter spun up like an out of control centrifuge and broke apart.

'I got one!' Hassan yelled.

'All escorts down. Concentrate fire on the target's rear shield generators.' The voice of the lead pirate was matter of fact. 'Watch the flak. Missiles for the drives; disable only. Too much damage and we don't get paid.'

CHAPTER THREE

The five remaining ships spread out in a loose formation and formed up behind the besieged Imperial Cutter.

* * *

The *Caduceus* jolted severely. There was a hideous cracking sound followed by the terrifying hiss of escaping air.

Canopy breach!

The room filled with streams of condensation, the ventilation system unable to compensate for the pressure drop. The hiss grew to a wail and then a shriek. The navigation officer turned to see the captain had been thrown from his chair, the mechanism damaged.

'Captain? Captain!'

The captain, blood drenching his face and uniform, managed to get to his feet and stagger back.

'I'm all right. Shields?'

'Rear shields gone, sir! Forward shields holding at thirty-six per cent. Weapons offline.'

'What about the hyperspace drive?'

'Still spooling, sir. Thirty seconds …'

A missile slammed into the unprotected ship's starboard engine nacelle. The nacelle cracked and shattered, partly detaching from the main body of the ship, sending the *Caduceus* into a brain jarring spin. Unprotected from the inertia the captain was flung across the bridge, smashing into the far bulkhead with a sickening thud, his body pinned as the ship helplessly gyrated. The bulkhead came apart with the strain. The navigation officer had a brief glimpse of the captain's body being ripped apart as both he and the bulkhead were explosively ejected into space. Then, in abrupt silence, the vacuum took the rest of them.

* * *

Hassan saw the bridge depressurise and bodies eject silently into the void with tiny fragments of debris. From his vantage point he couldn't tell if the

Imperial crew had remlok masks. It didn't matter much, they were dead anyway, no one was going to rescue them out here. Survival gear was only going to prolong the inevitable. He wished he hadn't seen the bodies. It made the nagging guilt worse. People had just died. He was an accomplice in an illegal act of piracy.

'Just this once …' he murmured to himself.

'Ship is ours,' the lead pirate acknowledged. 'Secure it and take it in tow.'

Hassan stabilised his own vessel and slotted in behind the other pirates. Two of the Sidewinders cautiously fired grappling pitons that dug into the hull of the rotating Imperial Cutter, taking care to avoid the clouds of debris that now accompanied it. It was a delicate operation, but the pirates had long experience of such manoeuvres. With deft thrusts and careful vectoring they brought the rotation under control.

A course was set and the wreck of the *Caduceus* was towed away.

* * *

'Must we go through with this?'

Patron Zyair looked pained. Gerrun smiled reassuringly.

'My friend, politics was ever thus. We must play our parts as the scene dictates. Representatives of the Imperial Senate we remain.'

The two men stood outside the Imperial Palace, surveying the tarnished glory of the entrance foyer. The dust had settled, but the beautiful interior still bore the marks of weapons fire. Tapestries were ripped and torn, delicately wrought masonry chipped and smashed, statues defaced and walls marked with crudely drawn slogans.

Zyair allowed his optical enhancers to slip down to the end of his nose. He peered over them with a stern, almost academic, look as he studied his companion.

'You seem awfully accepting of this. Need I remind you that these, these … barbarians have just murdered our senator and his entire family?'

Zyair's eyes drifted briefly to the dark smears that still stained the floor. The doors to the hall were riddled with bullet holes and hanging loosely from their damaged mountings.

CHAPTER THREE

'Almost his entire family,' Gerrun replied. 'Alas, the abuse of power rarely occurs without consequences.'

The doors creaked and a man emerged. The two men recognised him immediately.

'Patron Dalk,' Zyair said, favouring Dalk with a slight bow. 'Or should I call you revolutionary Dalk now?'

'Dalk is sufficient.'

'Or traitor Dalk?' Zyair continued. 'That has a ring to it I feel.'

Dalk ignored him and turned to Gerrun. 'I trust our ships are safely en route?'

Gerrun nodded. 'They broke orbit and made the jump to hyperspace without intervention. They should arrive at Haoria within twenty hours.'

'Then our duty to the Loren Lineage remains assured,' Dalk replied. 'Gentlemen, I must crave your indulgence further. Power must now be ceded and you must do the ceding.'

'Another punishment we are forced to bear?' Zyair added with a heavy sigh. 'We suffer for your intrigue, Dalk.'

'There is worse to come,' Dalk added.

'In what way?' Zyair asked.

'I fear a rather demeaning experience awaits us,' Gerrun said. 'We must appear servile, meek and deferential; lest we offend the new owner of this little world.'

'Obsequious even,' Dalk said, with a grin.

'I will not bow and scrape to an upstart criminal.'

'I suggest you do,' Gerrun said. 'Your life may very well depend upon it.'

'I dislike this more every single day …'

'You have the documents?' Dalk talked across him.

'Of course we have the damn documents. Do you think us fools? More importantly, can these ruffians actually read?'

'The deeds themselves are sufficient,' Dalk said. 'Their value to the Reclamists is, shall we say, symbolic.'

'And what is to stop these thugs from slitting our throats once they have what they want?' Zyair demanded.

'Dalk will have persuaded them that peaceful co-existence with the representatives of the Empire is in their best interest,' Gerrun said, looking to Dalk for confirmation.

Dalk nodded.

'You play a dangerous game, Dalk.'

'All worthwhile games are dangerous, Zyair. Follow me.'

'And to the victor, the spoils,' Gerrun added, under his breath.

Dalk led them into the hall, which was still strewn with the debris from the interrupted wedding feast. Tables remained overturned. Zyair and Gerrun were led across the floor, stepping carefully around the shattered decorations, fallen chandeliers and furniture. Both gasped in dismay to find that the Senator's body and that of his wife, family and staff remained where they had fallen, their blood-stained corpses a testament to their gory end.

Next to them, reclining in a chair with his feet propped up level with his head, was the leader of the Reclamists, Vargo. He held the Senator's sceptre, the mark of his office, a highly valuable staff decorated with many centuries of family history and other heraldry. Vargo tapped the sceptre lightly against his hand.

Dalk stepped forward.

'May I present Patrons Zyair and Gerrun,' Dalk began. 'Servants of the Empire and here to …'

'Imperial dogs will bow in the presence of the Master of Chione,' Vargo interrupted, not even looking at them.

Zyair and Gerrun exchanged a glance. Dalk nodded at them, almost imperceptibly. Zyair and Gerrun bowed to the knee, their heads lowered. Vargo could not see Zyair's flushed face.

Vargo swung his legs around and stood up.

'So this is the best of what's left of the Imperial hierarchy is it?' Vargo crowed. 'A corpulent lackey and a timeworn minion. They should distribute Imperial rations more evenly I feel. This one gorges himself fit to burst whilst this one wastes away. And I thought you told me the Imperials valued egalitarianism, Dalk.'

Zyair and Gerrun remained bowed. 'No system is perfect,' Dalk replied.

'You don't say.' Vargo strode up to the duo of Patrons. 'Words that seem confirmed by the presence of these two less than inspiring examples of Imperial might and splendour.'

Vargo stepped directly in front of them. 'Stand up, sycophants.'

CHAPTER THREE

Zyair and Gerrun climbed slowly to their feet, one troubled by his age, the other by his weight.

Vargo stared at them closely.

'You supported Senator Algreb, did you not?'

Zyair and Gerrun nodded slowly.

Vargo gestured to the pale bloodstained body of the Senator.

'I have ... usurped his position.' Vargo strolled around the pair, continuing to tap the sceptre in his hand. 'What does your mighty Imperium make of that?'

'There are those,' Gerrun began, 'ourselves amongst them, who considered the erstwhile Senator had rather exceeded his mandate ...'

'Acting without the greater consent and accord of wider Imperial interests,' Zyair continued, his voice rapid and stuttering.

'The outrageous murder of innocents and the subjugation of an entire world,' Vargo mused. 'Is it such a little thing in your Empire?'

'An atrocious crime,' Gerrun hastened to reassure him. 'Egregious in the extreme ...'

'Debauched and base,' Zyair added. 'To be deplored utterly.'

'You did not approve of your Senator's actions then?'

'It has never been the place of a Patron to question a Senator,' Gerrun answered, carefully. 'Suffice to say, our support of the Loren Lineage is at an end.'

'The Loren Lineage is no more.' Vargo raised his voice. 'They are slain along with their hated progeny. This is my world now.'

Zyair and Gerrun nodded dutifully.

'If it please you, Master of Chione,' Zyair managed to grate out, holding up a sealed tube. 'We have prepared a revised deed of tenure, pursuant to your rise to eminence; setting out the rights and entitlements previously accorded to the Loren Lineage. With their demise, such rights both legal and temporal belong to ...'

'The surviving settlers who escaped Imperial carnage,' Vargo said, snatching the tube and tapping its side. A holofac representation of a document appeared, projected by the tube. Vargo scanned it briefly and then pocketed it.

'It also contains an Imperial mandate, promising no further interference in the government of this world,' Gerrun explained. 'In exchange for ...'

'Exchange? You're in no position to bargain.'

Gerrun bowed again, gesturing wide with his arms. 'The Empire is a mighty force, Master of Chione. The Loren's may have overstepped the boundaries of decent conduct, but the reasons for their interest remain as cogent as before.'

'What is it you ask for?'

'Merely a reliable and regular shipment of Tantalum.'

'At what price?'

'We are prepared to pay the market rate plus a consideration for your favour.'

Vargo straightened.

'A consideration?' he said, slowly. 'I'll give you something to consider, lackeys. We are backed by the Federation. A task force is already assembling. The Imperial vessels in this system will leave within a single week or they will be destroyed. Your illegal occupation of this world is at an end. If you wish to be considered for a trade franchise in the future I suggest you come up with a more compelling offer.'

'You'd defy the Empire?' Zyair said, a twitch in his cheek.

Vargo laughed and gestured to the bodies of the Loren's behind him.

'You know, I do believe I would.' His short laugh fell into an aggressive sneer. 'Now get out of my sight and take your trash with you when you leave. Dalk, see to it that these cronies are encouraged to depart.'

Vargo turned and strode away, leaving Zyair and Gerrun with Dalk. Dalk waited until the doors to the hall had closed behind him. 'Admirable restraint, my friends,' Dalk said. 'I congratulate you.'

'I'll be sure to attend his execution. To treat representatives of the Empire with such disregard ...'

'I thought you made a magnificent toad, Zyair,' Gerrun said. 'You seem to have a natural talent for grovelling.'

Dalk laughed. Zyair shot him an unfriendly glance.

'And you're prepared to work with him, Dalk? I grow less convinced of your loyalties, daily.'

'I do not expect to have the pleasure of his acquaintance for an extended period,' Dalk replied. 'The Empire will not have long to wait.'

'We will take our leave,' Zyair said. 'We will arrange for the bodies to be given appropriate Imperial honours.'

CHAPTER THREE

'I shall ensure that appropriate respect is given,' Dalk replied.

'Respect,' Zyair almost spat. 'These Reclamists don't know the meaning of the word.'

Chapter Four

Starlight glimmered faintly from darkened hulls as the phalanx of pirate vessels, accompanied by the shattered bulk of another ship, slowed their approach. Thrusters fired in a coordinated sequence, the vessels' velocity reduced to a mere drift. Ahead, a minimum of navigation lights could be seen shining out from a huge, slowly rotating silhouette hanging against the starry backdrop. Gantries and docking ports jutted out into space, as if to snare unwary vessels. Behind it, a rocky dwarf planet split the ghostly light of the Milky Way in two, slowly turning on its own cratered axis.

A searchlight blazed out from the sombre black shadow, brightly illuminating the lead Asp. Unseen to the approaching ships a dozen heavy ballistic turrets swung around, their computers calculating targets, vectors and trajectories for the entire group of vessels. Assured destruction was awaited at the whim of the operators within.

The narrowband comms crackled and a rough, deep voice spoke. 'Identify.'

'Commander of the *Malcontent*,' the lead pirate answered. 'With clan *Tiber*, here with salvage. Open the gates, *Basilica*.'

The search light flickered rapidly between the five vessels, with the battered *Caduceus* held immobile in their midst.

The convoy of vessels briefly fired retro-thrusters, now coming to a complete halt relative to the enormous facility before them. For a long moment there was no response.

Light cracked out from an opening, bathing the convoy in radiance. The pilots squinted into it, trying to make out the various docking bays they knew were housed within. As their eyes adjusted they could make out the immense locking mechanism that protected the *Basilica*; a series of interlocking panels that dwarfed the vessels waiting outside; huge constructs of metal a hundred metres thick. Inside, a cylindrical void was revealed, lit by a fierce electric-blue glare. Picked out at intervals across its surface were the gaping dark mouths of docking ports, each one numbered, looking small and insignificant at this distance despite easily being able to accommodate a vessel apiece.

'*Basilica* to *Malcontent* and convoy. Proceed. Docking in berths eighteen to thirty.'

The convoy proceeded inwards. The escorting ships peeled off to the respective docking bays, airtight doors closing in sequence as they entered. Those ships still towing the silent bulk of the *Caduceus* carefully arranged themselves in order to allow the damaged vessel to coast into another bay, releasing their grappling hooks in a practiced efficient sequence, easing it into the bay. It was a tricky manoeuvre. From the centre of the cylindrical void, every direction was down. The ships grappled with the increasing coriolis force as they lowered themselves and their prey into the bay, compensating by matching the rotation as they descended.

Hassan watched the operation silently, impressed despite himself. The procedure was accomplished without fuss or error. To their rear, the heavy gates slowly wound themselves back in, stars eclipsed from view as they cycled closed. Hassan braced himself for a heavy thump as the massive parts interlocked, but there was nothing to be heard in the vacuum.

He followed the towing ships, gently thrusting his small vessel neatly in behind as they came to rest on the floor of the bay. From his perspective the floor was a 'wall', with the *Caduceus* and its captors perched precariously against it as if they were mounted trophies. Choosing your frame of reference was better done before starting a manoeuvre, not during one. Space sickness could be very unpleasant. Hassan made a quick mental adjustment and the 'wall' became the floor.

That was all very well, but now his vessel was pointing directly downwards and hanging above the ground. Quickly he adjusted his ship's attitude by ninety degrees, triggered the undercarriage and allowed his vessel to descend. The docking bay closed above him, now serving as the 'roof'. A gentle nudge indicated his vessel had come to rest. Magnetic clamps secured the ship in the bay. He felt the gentle tug of artificial gravity and a slight sensation of nausea before he acclimatised. He powered down the drives, power plants and avionics, looking out of the forward view to where the *Caduceus* lay, canted slightly to the right on its damaged nacelle, directly ahead of him. He could already see the pirate leader standing defensively beyond the ship, arranging for the docking bay to be opened.

CHAPTER FOUR

Now comes the hard part.

The internal doors from the bay into the interior of the *Basilica* remained closed. The pirate leader and his two most trusted accomplices gathered at the bow of the *Caduceus*, weapons drawn. Each acknowledged the other's arrival with a brief nod, but nothing more. The remaining pirates, Hassan amongst them, had been instructed to remain aboard their ships for the time being. The finer points of negotiating the illegal tended to go more smoothly if fewer guns were present.

'Good luck with the "Vice", boss,' one accomplice said.

The pirate leader nodded grimly. This was an unusual mission for a customer with a fearsome reputation. He wasn't aware of how she'd come by her nickname, maybe it was for the stranglehold she had on the trading in this group of systems. Nothing went through this region of space without her taking an interest and, more often than not, a cut.

The internal doors clunked, hissed and then snapped back into the adjacent bulkheads. Three people walked into the dimly lit bay. The pirate leader quickly sized up the two flanking men. They were tough no nonsense bodyguards, armed with semi-automatic pressurised rifles; guns that worked in a vacuum. They were dressed in dark grey fibre-reinforced fatigues; material that was pretty much impermeable. Theirs looked smart and new, suggesting a well-heeled operation.

But it was the woman standing at the centre that commanded everyone's attention. The pirate leader swallowed before stepping forward, raising his hand in acknowledgement. The woman was tall, as tall as her guards, with an athletic build framed by a smartly tailored maroon gown embroidered with gold embossing that fell elegantly from her shoulders. Blonde hair streamed backwards from a face that would have been beautiful but for the penetrating stare and harsh set of the firm mouth. Her chin was ever so slightly raised, giving her an authoritative stance, which was further enhanced by a fashionably chrome-plated and heeled set of magnetic boots which glittered and clicked noisily as she strode forward into the bay.

She stretched out her arms slightly, pointing a finger of both hands outwards with a subtle sideways twist of her head. The gown parted, revealing a trim but voluptuous figure. A sidearm was secured at her left side. The pirate leader recognised it as a Lance and Ferman Widowmaker. An old-fashioned weapon, inaccurate at range; lethal, messy and brutal close up.

Her guards snapped to attention and stood stock still.

Octavia Quinton.

Owner and boss of *Basilica*, a decommissioned military installation, now appropriated for more clandestine, but no less violent, operations. Her minions called her 'Domina', a word of honour from some ancient language. Only up close could signs of her age be seen; skin that was no longer firm and wrinkles across her face. She glanced around at the motley collection of pirate vessels, her eyes then sweeping across the forlorn Imperial Cutter and then finally to the pirate leader.

Her pace didn't slacken. She walked straight past him and on under the battle-scarred lower hull of the *Caduceus*. After a moment, he turned to follow her, hurrying to keep up.

'You weren't followed?' She wasted no time in getting down to business. Her accent was curious, a mix of exotic Alliance tones with a slight Federation cadence.

'All the escorts were destroyed, no escape pods were released.' The pirate leader didn't use her assumed title.

'You know I'll be reviewing the flight footage to check,' she said.

The pirate leader smiled by return. 'I thought you might. I'll have it prepped.'

'Any survivors?'

'Hull's blown. We spotted a couple of Imperial goons getting spaced. We've not been aboard to look.'

The line of her mouth hardened. 'Then I suggest you check.'

They'd reached the rear of the *Caduceus*. The docking bay ramp, though slightly buckled from the fight, had lowered into place.

'Ladies first?' The pirate leader asked. 'Men just before,' Octavia replied.

He stepped up onto the ramp, pulling out his own sidearm and ventured inside. After a moment, Octavia followed.

The inside of the bay remained more or less intact. A couple of the cargo canisters had dislodged slightly; the starboard side of the ship had taken the most damage and one of the internal structural bulkheads had been breached. Cracks in the overhead conduits signalled a major repair job would be required

CHAPTER FOUR

before the ship might be flight worthy again. Crushed against the bulkhead near the breach was a body. The pirate leader holstered his sidearm and turned the body over with his foot. It was an older man, with a heavy grey beard. His face was pale, his lips blue and his eyes bloodshot. His hands were locked at his throat, his tongue protruding.

'Must have been in the bay when it blew,' he said.

Octavia gestured for him to step back. Quickly she searched the man's uniform, pulling out an identity tag. She queried it.

'Doctor Rafe Reinhardt,' she said. 'Looks like you got the right ship. Congratulations. Find the pod.'

It didn't take them long. A horizontally stored canister in the centre of the bay had the correct ID code. It had been carefully stored, giving it maximum protection.

'This is what you wanted?' He looked at the pod, baffled as to what it might be. 'What's in it?'

'Just a little piece of Imperial decor to adorn my chambers,' Octavia said, with a faint grin. 'Rather exceptional and difficult to come by.' She looked up. 'You'll want paying, I suppose? What did we arrange?'

'Two hundred thousand credits,' he responded immediately.

'One hundred and fifty is what we agreed. Even that sounds exceedingly generous for a tatty old wreck such as this.'

'The ship was heavily defended,' the pirate leader responded. 'I lost a ship.'

'The battle is not my concern; you should have paid for better pilots. I agreed to a salvageable vessel and its cargo,' Octavia replied easily. 'Does this look salvageable to you? The hull's blown, the cargo bay is compromised and I'd take a guess that you've written off that starboard drive given it's hanging by only a couple of conduits. It will cost me a fortune to make this serviceable again.'

She gestured to the shattered bulkhead where the Doctor's corpse lay. The structure had partially collapsed under its own weight.

The pirate didn't answer, he just went for his gun. He pulled it in a smooth and practised motion.

'Two hundred thousand,' he repeated. 'The cargo's what you were after. I know that much.' To his surprise Octavia didn't respond in kind or even flinch backwards.

'You're going to kill me? Do you really think that's wise? Here in the midst of my stronghold? Do you think you'd get out alive?'

'I'm guessing you want to live just as much as I do. I just want my price. No one needs to end up shot.' The pirate tightened his grip a little. 'My price, lady.'

Octavia looked him up and down briefly and then raised her hands slowly in submission. 'You're right about the cargo.' She shrugged. 'Shall we shake on it?' She lowered her hands and held her right one out towards him. It was empty.

The pirate leader hesitated. Too easy. The hairs on the back of his neck rose. Nothing seemed amiss. Maybe she wasn't as fearsome as he'd been led to believe, just a carefully crafted reputation. She was unarmed, he had the upper hand. Satisfied, he holstered his weapon.

'Two hundred thousand,' he confirmed. 'No cuts, no tax. Net, not gross.' Octavia nodded, her hand still outstretched. 'Net, not gross.'

The pirate leader took her hand. She had a firm grip for a woman. No, she had a firm grip for a man …

Shit!

'I'm surprised at your ill-advised audacity, trying to renegotiate with me,' Octavia said, mildly. 'I suggest you don't do that again.'

Agony jolted up his arm. He yelled as the sound of cracking bones rang out from his hand. 'Fuck you,' the pirate leader said, pulling his other arm back to swing at her.

Octavia twisted his hand back and sideways, jolting the pirate leader's wrist. He was flung over on his side, his hand still locked in her grip, falling heavily on the corrugated floor of the cargo bay.

'Let go of me you fucking bitch!'

'One hundred and fifty thousand, yes?' she asked, her voice still sweet and light.

Her grip tightened, more cracks; blood seeped through her fingers as bone fragments pierced skin from the inside out. The pirate leader shrieked and yelled, battering at her arm with his other hand to no avail. She continued to mash his hand, it was as if it were being crushed in a …

Vice!

CHAPTER FOUR

Fear coursed through him. He'd underestimated her. No telling what else she might be capable of.

'All right! One fifty!'

He felt her pressure go, replaced by pain. He yelled again as blood spurted from his ruined fingers. By the time he was able to look up she was standing over him, looking down with contempt. She was clenching and unclenching her right hand, rubbing her thumb against fingers that were slick with blood; his blood.

'The money will be deposited immediately,' Octavia said. 'I suggest you get that seen to.' She gestured to the cargo bay ramp.

You'll pay for that, you smug bitch.

Pain-fuelled anger surged through him. No woman was going to humiliate him like this. He swung a punch at her with his good arm.

Octavia grabbed his fist easily, turned the wrist, grabbed his elbow and threw him sideways. As the pirate dropped to the floor she rotated her grip in a practised move. He felt his body spin out of control in a whirl of motion before a yell of agony was ripped out of him. She'd dislocated his shoulder. A moment later he felt his body slam into the ground with a stunning thump. She still held his outstretched wrist. Pressure. More pain. He heard a sickening crunch as she broke bones. Screams; his own screams.

He felt his head yanked roughly up by the hair.

'You just killed your men, too,' she whispered in his ear. Panic now. He had to move.

His voice gurgled out something unintelligible. Octavia ignored it. She grasped his head firmly in her hands and gave one final sharp twist before dropping it back, lifeless, to the floor.

She stood up, sending a message to her guards.

'Negotiations complete. They were generous enough to give us the ship for free. Anything of value?'

'The lead ship is worth a handful of creds,' a voice replied in her ear. 'Nothing else but cheap junk. There's even a Mark 1 Eagle. Not seen one of them in years.'

'That's because they're utterly useless,' Octavia replied, dismissively. 'Invite the rest aboard, get them drunk and dispose of them quietly. Choose one to spread the news. The owner of that Eagle will do. Take the other ships. Make preparations for unloading the cargo, I want this all shipped back out within the day.'

'It shall be done, Domina.'

She looked down at the pirate leader's bloodied body. 'Oh, and somebody needs to do some housekeeping.' Octavia cancelled the call with a brief flick of her eyes.

She walked back to the canister, pushing the hatch release mechanism. The hatch hissed open, allowing her inside. She smiled as she saw the unblemished pod, running her hands over its smooth surface. A series of illuminated displays appeared on its shiny exterior. Quickly she located the command sequence to open the pod. She touched it, confirming her request.

One message flashed in red; urgent and demanding attention.

Psychometric profile restoration in progress, interrupting this process may cause memory corruption. Confirm?

'I only want your body, sweetness …'

She touched on a green circle, indicating in the affirmative. The displays faded into the translucent surface of the pod.

There was a click and a faint hiss of equalising pressure. The top of the pod opened and folded back. Octavia peered over and smiled in satisfaction, taking a long look at the supine body that lay within.

She walked a few steps down to the end of the pod, turned and then languidly traced a finger up the girl's body, starting at her toes and up her shins, walking slowly back the way she had come. Two fingers were placed across her thigh, rising up to her pelvis, teasingly skirting the dark triangle of hair. Octavia ran her fingertips across the girl's stomach, her hand reversing to gently caress the breast nearest to her before tracing the outline of the girl's chin, lips, nose and forehead.

Octavia reached in and pulled the small black tab off the girl's forehead. It beeped in complaint and then fell silent. Octavia carefully pocketed it.

'Yes, my Imperial beauty. You are most suitable; most suitable indeed.'

* * *

CHAPTER FOUR

Hassan watched, peering over the flight deck of his ship, as the intimidating woman and the pirate leader entered the battered rear cargo hold of the *Caduceus*. Neither of them emerged. Negotiations seemed to be on-going.

After a few minutes he watched as the rest of the pirates gathered in a small group outside the ships, talking with the guards. Faces seemed relaxed and friendly. Not always a good sign, but reassuring for now. Hassan saw one of the pirates point in the direction of Hassan's ship. One of the guards headed in his direction.

Shortly afterwards there was a bang on the lower exit hatch. Hassan flipped the latches and unwound the vacuum seal. The hatch dropped downwards, revealing the floor of the hangar beneath his ship. The guard was looking up at him.

'You're invited aboard,' he announced. 'Word is Domina is happy with the shipment. They're just scanning the fine detail. Beers are cool, you coming?'

'Got some repairs to make first,' Hassan replied. 'Scanner shorted out in the battle, took a hit on the dorsal plate. Can't fight what I can't see.'

'Want my techs to take a look at it?'

'At your hourly rates?' Hassan fired back. 'No thanks.'

The guard grinned. 'You've got to try.' He looked appraisingly at the tarnished hull of the old Eagle. 'Haven't seen one of these in a while.'

'She ain't much,' Hassan replied with a sigh, looking around at his tatty vessel.

'Had one of these when I was a kid,' the guard said. 'They're not so bad. They keep going and going. Don't buy the Mark 2, yeah?'

'With the dodgy retros? Yeah, I read about them …'

Hassan paused. The guard looked aside, towards the entrance doors to the hangar. He nodded, clearly hearing something through his comm link. Hassan could see all the other pirates had left.

The guard looked back up. 'You got a minute?'

Hassan nodded and the guard gestured for Hassan to follow him. The guard walked across to the *Caduceus* and up the boarding ramp. Hassan followed him inside. As they turned a corner Hassan caught sight of the bloodied body of the pirate leader.

'Shit!' Hassan made to run for it, but the guard stopped him with a firm shove.

'Relax, kid. Your boss just made a stupid mistake asking for more cash. Kinda …' the guard shrugged and clicked his tongue, 'career limiting, if you know what I mean. Smart money is on getting out of here sharpish. Domina will make sure you're paid up, she's good like that. But you ain't gonna see your buddies again. You following my navplan?' He raised his eyebrows. 'Make yourself scarce.'

'You mean they're …' Hassan was still looking down at the body on the floor.

'Yeah. Or worse. Depends on her mood. Worse, I'd guess.'

'You guys play rough. Who's your boss, anyway? Who's this Domina?'

The guard scoffed. 'You don't know?'

Hassan shrugged. 'I'm just the gun for hire in this posse.'

'You've heard of Octavia Quinton, right?'

Hassan stopped and stared. 'Octavia … Quinton?'

The guard grinned at him. 'Now you get it.'

'Can … can you send me down a fuel canister?' Hassan stammered. 'Then I don't need to top up the tanks.'

'Sure thing, kid.'

The guard walked off, leaving Hassan staring after him, nonplussed. He heard the whirring noise as the automech unloaders formed up and headed for the wreck of the *Caduceus*.

Octavia Quinton! If I can pull this off…

It was now or never.

* * *

Octavia returned to her sumptuous suite aboard the *Basilica*. It straddled the main width of the facility with rooms overlooking the interior docking void on one side and the vista of infinite space on the other. The view of the stars rotated slowly as she watched it for a moment, taking time to pick out the various star systems that she controlled and influenced. It took her a while.

The rooms were dimly lit by cunningly concealed lighting, Imperial style, but with modern hi-tech touches that Imperial tastes would have shunned. Food outlets, complex restorative cleanliness units and washing facilities integrated astutely with a panoply of mirrors; some discreet, others full length

CHAPTER FOUR

and obvious. Servants waited in the recesses and adjoining rooms ready to spring into action at a moment's notice, supplying any dish from across the known worlds. Holofac displays were much in evidence; statistics, graphs, monitors, vid-feeds. It was clear this wasn't just a place to relax; it was a nerve centre of operations.

Octavia dismissed her staff with a sharp command and walked into one of the bedrooms, quickly washing her hands. She flexed her right hand as the dried blood was carried away by the cleansing water, examining it absentmindedly. The skin was a perfect match for her arm, few knew her secret. She liked it that way.

She changed, slipping into a demure flowing gown and dropping her stained garments to the floor. They would be returned, cleaned and pressed, to her wardrobe within minutes.

An antique brush was employed to adjust her hair; blonde, with the merest hint of added colour to hide the advancing years. Hard grey eyes stared back at her as she looked in the mirror, only a slight sheen of make up lifted the skin of her face.

Satisfied, she walked back out into the suite, settling in a luxurious leather chair facing the view into the galaxy. A brief gesture caused walls to slide into place around her, sealing her in a conveniently private room. The walls were unadorned, giving no hint as to her location.

A circular table in front of her glowed, initiating a holofac transmission. A moment later a ream of technical information streamed rapidly up before her. It had to be a secure call, routed in several redundant directions, encrypted and obfuscated, its origin impossible to trace. Security was everything to an operation like this.

The text slowed. *Connection Established.* 'Ms. Quinton.'

A figure appeared, apparently seated in the chair opposite. It was a comfortable illusion. 'Commissioner Neseva,' Octavia acknowledged with a nod. 'I trust I've not caught you at an inconvenient time?'

'Of course not, my dear woman,' he replied smoothly. 'I was hoping you might call.'

'Really?' Octavia feigned interest. 'And why might that be?'

'A small matter in the grand scheme of things,' Tenim replied, examining his finger tips with interest. 'I hear there has been some disturbance in the Prism system. The Imperials appear to have a little difficulty on their hands.'

He looked up and grinned broadly. 'Most unfortunate for them.'

'It appears a disastrous coup has taken place,' Tenim said. 'The Imperial family has been wiped out and the Chione moon now lies in the hands of a sordid group of revolutionaries.'

'How distressing.' Octavia raised her eyebrows.

'Yes. It appears they were supplied with illegal shipments of stolen federation weaponry. Absolutely shocking.'

Octavia smiled herself. 'Which reminds me, you've yet to pay for that last operation.'

'Details, my dear.' Tenim waved his hand towards her. 'The tally will be reconciled by month end as always.'

'It had better be,' Octavia added, leaning forward ever so slightly.

Tenim seemed unfazed. 'We do feel somewhat responsible for the situation. We've extended every sympathy to the Imperials, but they've yet to take us up on any offer of help.'

'How ungrateful of them.'

'The bastards squirmed like Zaoncian blood worms. They couldn't pin it on us in the slightest.' Tenim laughed and leant back in his chair.

'You say the entire Imperial family was wiped out? I assume you're referring to the Loren Lineage?'

'Every last one. Those peasants even slaughtered the servants and slaves apparently. Shot them dead. Quite a bloody mess. Serves them right for invading our moon in the first place.'

'Interesting.' Octavia looked away from Tenim, letting her eyes wander around the featureless interior of the temporary room.

Tenim frowned, folding his hands together and leaning forward himself. 'How so?'

'Interesting … in that I have a member of the Loren Lineage aboard right now.'

Tenim stopped abruptly. 'That's impossible. All the bodies were accounted for …'

Octavia gestured to an auxiliary display and with a deft flick of her fingers sent a small image of the Imperial girl's supine form into the holofac display.

CHAPTER FOUR

'Who is …'

'She is Lady Kahina Tijani Loren,' Octavia replied. 'Third daughter of Algreb Loren and sole survivor of that unfortunate coup you mentioned.'

'But …'

'Someone went to a lot of trouble to ensure she survived the assassination. The Imperials were smuggling her out.'

Tenim stared at the screen, his face a mask of fury.

'Oh, you didn't know?' Octavia asked. 'I take an interest in these little affairs. It's the detail that counts …'

'Kill her now,' Tenim demanded. 'If the Imperials …'

Octavia crossed her legs, relaxing into her chair. 'Now why would I do that? I dare say the Imperials will be quite concerned that their own little machination has gone awry. They might make me a compelling offer.'

Tenim sighed and considered for a long moment. 'How much do you want?'

Octavia smiled. 'She's not for sale. Not yet, anyway.'

'What do you intend to do with her?'

'She's a pretty thing, don't you think? My doctors tell me that the unit in which she is contained allows her memory to be restored. It even allows for that memory to be tweaked, her personality to be shaped and moulded, inclinations and preferences to be made … compatible.'

Octavia placed a finger on her lips and gently sucked the tip.

'You want an Imperial whore? I can have a dozen with you inside a day.'

'You can be so indelicate at times, Commissioner. My needs are rather more subtle than you might imagine.'

'You need to kill her. If the Imperials get hold of her …'

Octavia leant forward. 'If she's that valuable, you'd better come up with an offer I can't refuse before they do, hadn't you?'

Tenim was about to reply, but Octavia cut him off, cancelling the call. The walls around her folded back and she stood up and stretched, enjoying the view of thousands of faint remote stars. She ran a hand across herself, shivering with anticipation.

* * *

Hassan watched the automechs mindlessly carrying out their tasks. They'd obviously been instructed to begin unloading the beleaguered Imperial ship almost immediately. As usual they carried out their tasks without supervision. They trundled up the cargo bay loading ramp in pairs, arranging themselves inside and then returned carrying out the large canisters. Each was stacked in a neat hexagonal configuration whereby further sets of the automech would carry them off.

Whilst waiting for the fuel to arrive Hassan had been watching the growing stack of cargo being pilfered from the *Caduceus* wondering what was contained within them. He selected one at random and pointed a small device at it. A single beep was emitted. On the device a coded number appeared. Hassan grinned to himself.

He didn't have to wait long. Two automechs lowered a fuel canister into position outside his vessel and proceeded towards him. As they did so he pulled the small device out of his pocket again.

'Let's see if you were worth it,' he muttered to himself, pointing it towards the fuel canister. The device beeped twice, another code was displayed. Quickly he pointed the device back at the canister he'd selected and was rewarded with a further double beep. The automechs approached.

'Specify the required destination of canister 45/DMJA/3327,' the first machine stated, tonelessly.

'Just load it into the cargo bay,' Hassan replied.

The automechs spun around on their articulated wheels and trundled back down the loading ramp to the fuel canister they'd just deposited. They moved as if to secure it and then stopped. One stayed motionless, but the other turned around and moved back towards Hassan.

'What's up?' Hassan asked innocently.

'Specify location of canister 45/DMJA/3327,' the machine queried.

Hassan gestured to the growing pile of canisters. 'I think you'll find it's over there somewhere. Hurry up, I need to get going.'

The automech descended the ramp and rattled across the floor of the bay towards the growing stack of canisters, accompanied by its counterpart. Both moved around briefly until they located the canister Hassan had pointed at. Without thought or consideration they hefted it between them and brought it back to Hassan's ship, depositing it in the cargo bay.

CHAPTER FOUR

In the meantime Hassan had transferred the identity of the newly acquired canister to the fuel canister still residing outside his ship. The other automechs dutifully came and retrieved it, placing it with the others from the *Caduceus*.

Hassan shook his head with a rueful grin. Artificial Intelligence was dumb, automechs especially so. There was some law about keeping it that way that he vaguely recalled from simschool. The cargo decrypter had cost him several months hard trading, but it had worked.

Now to get out of here.

Octavia arranged for the canister with the Imperial girl in it to be separated from the rest of the cargo stolen from the *Caduceus*. The remaining canisters were quickly loaded aboard other vessels ready to be fenced off to other systems at inflated prices. There had been an eclectic mix of foodstuffs and luxuries aboard, spares for the Loren's lavish celebration. They would fetch a tidy profit. Her two primary guards stood awaiting her arrival.

'Cargo is unloaded, Domina,' the senior guard said as she arrived. 'The pirates have been … entertained. The lone ship will carry your message as requested. He's just made the jump-out …'

'Excellent,' Octavia nodded and then gestured at the remaining canister. 'Open it and take the pod to my chambers.'

The guard nodded and stepped up to the canister, prodding the hatch release. It swung back with a hiss.

Inside were tightly packed tubular metal bottles all bearing a common warning. *Caution. Liquidised Hydrogen. Observe Safety Protocol 26645/5a.*

The guard quickly ran an identity scan of the canister, turning to face Octavia in complete bewilderment.

'Where is my pod?' Octavia asked, her voice icy. 'I don't understand …'

Octavia stepped up to inspect the interior of the canister, her fingers clenching into fists. 'Where did this fuel come from? There was none on the manifest. It was foodstuffs and luxuries.'

'I …' the guard stuttered.

Octavia whirled on him. 'Yes?'

'The Commander of the Eagle ordered fuel. But he couldn't have …'

'Swapped the ID codes? Clearly he could!' Octavia bellowed. 'You festering fool! Weren't you supervising the operation?'

'The automechs were …'

She grabbed him by the throat and propelled him backwards against the side of the canister. It rang with the impact.

'You let him steal from me? You let a flux-sucking low birth steal my prize?'

The guard struggled to say something but he was given no reprise. She pulled back, slamming his head against the canister again and again. Even up to the third time he tried to free himself. A stomach-turning wet crunch followed the fourth impact and his body went limp in her grasp. Eventually she threw the body to the floor in disgust and turned her attention to the second guard, who was still standing, pale-faced, behind her. He was watching the pool of dark red blood spreading from the mangled head of his erstwhile superior.

'Find that ship and bring it back intact,' Octavia howled. 'Immediately!' She had a crazed and haunted look in her eyes as her voice dropped to a whisper.

'And I want the pilot alive.'

Chapter Five

The three kilometre mass of *Hiram's Anchorage* swept past on the forward viewer. As usual the immense facility was surrounded by freighters either empty and inward bound, docked unloading Tantalite ore having risen from the surface of Chione or loading up with refined Tantalum ready to head back out of the system. From this vantage point in high orbit it was difficult to make out the mining operations on the northern hemisphere, they were obscured by the wispy cloud formations that drifted across the world.

Between the freighters a panoply of smaller ships zipped around; refuellers, small restaurant ships, advertising droid-boards and the freighters' fighter escorts. A salvage gang could be seen dismantling a series of old wrecks and breaking them for parts and alloys.

It was easy to tell the different factions apart based on their design. Imperial ships with smooth organic lines and flowing curves, Federation ships with bold, stark and functional form. The Alliance vessels were a blend of the two, resulting in some oddly configured vessels.

Dalk left the docking arrangements to the autopilot as he continued to watch the vista unfolding before him. He looked past *Hiram's Anchorage* with a grim expression on his face. The big station was functional, a mining and refining platform custom-built by the Mastopolis Mining Corporation and brought in by the Imperials three years before. Even their designers had been unable to tame its aesthetics to something pleasing. There was only so much you could do with an industrial facility. Inside it was little different. Vast processing plants and power amenities composed the bulk of the interior with only a relatively small section reserved for recreation, food and lodging. The rest was taken up by docking facilities for the large number of ships the station handled on a daily basis.

It was also heavily defended. Mining operations were lucrative and whilst there had been no historic trouble in the Prism system, *Hiram's Anchorage* was more than capable of defending itself from any who had a desire to help themselves. A huge rotating habitat ring completed the monstrous facility.

One day the Tantalite will be exhausted, then things will change.

Dalk smiled to himself. If all went well, things would change far sooner than that.

The surface shuttle orientated itself towards a docking bay and flew inwards, latching into place with smooth precision. Dalk disembarked, quickly threading his way towards the rotating habitation levels of the station. Here, at least, life was reasonably luxurious.

His cabin featured a circular orifice that scrolled open to reveal a breathtaking view of Chione, slowing turning in the view with the rotation of the habitation ring. Daedalion could be seen slowly rising behind it, lightning crackling from a major storm raging in its atmosphere. Dalk had yet to take a trip to that massive world. Totally covered by endless ocean there was no great scenery to admire, but some of the animals that inhabited its almost unfathomable seas were magnificent beasts by all accounts. He'd a desire to take a classic old Moray sub-aqua vessel and go hunting, pitting his wits against those behemoths.

Perhaps one day.

Dalk surveyed Chione for a long moment. From this vantage point it looked unspoiled, virgin, very much as he remembered it back in the days before the Appropriation. The most pleasant parts of the world were in the southern hemisphere, where a series of archipelagos dotted the Garian Sea. He'd just come from one such series of islands, New Ithaca, the location of the Loren's now defiled Imperial Palace. The north was dominated by a large continent and a vast plateau thrust high above the surrounding land. It was dry and barren for the most part, bordered by steppes and then dry grasslands before a narrowing promontory of land at the equator provided enough moisture to support lush forests.

That plateau played host to the mining operation, conveniently far enough away from habitable areas so as not to be a source of irritation. It was, nonetheless, a scar on the surface.

A holofac transmitter in the suite chimed softly and illuminated. Dalk expected the call. He gestured in acknowledgement and turned to face his visitor as he materialised in the middle of the room.

Dalk bowed in the customary way, acknowledging the Imperial ambassador, Cuthrick Delaney.

CHAPTER FIVE

As usual he was decorated in his Imperial regalia, his tiara now even more flamboyant than before.

'Ambassador. I'm honoured to receive your communication, revered servant of the Empire,' Dalk said.

Cuthrick bowed, his bow just a fraction less low than Dalk's, an acknowledgement of their relative status in Imperial society. 'Patron Dalk, always a pleasure.'

'I trust all is well.'

Cuthrick straightened. 'Alas, it is not.'

Dalk looked up in surprise. 'What do you mean?'

'The *Caduceus* has not made its scheduled rendezvous here.'

Dalk's face fell. 'Not made …'

'Once it was overdue we sent out a scout to search for it, wideband communications being ill-advised.'

'And?'

'The scout has just reported back. Debris from Imperial fighters was located in a dark system en route. There was no sign of the *Caduceus* at all. It would appear your audacious plan has run into something of a set back.'

Dalk paced for a moment.

'Ambushed. It couldn't have been a chance encounter. Which dark system?'

Cuthrick gestured and the holofac before him expanded to create a three-dimensional map of the nearby systems.

'Wreckage was found here,' Cuthrick said, indicating a point about one-third of the way between Prism and Haoria.

Dalk thought hard. 'You say there was no sign of the *Caduceus*?'

'None that could be detected.'

Dalk rubbed his chin and turned back to the circular window, staring out at Chione.

'Without the girl our claim is legally unsupportable,' Cuthrick continued. 'A confrontation with the Federation will be unavoidable. We cannot afford to lose such a significant source of Tantalum. Our ambitions in this sector cannot be thwarted.'

Dalk turned back. 'How much time have I got?'

Cuthrick shrugged. 'Two weeks. It will require that long to arrange a force sufficient to overwhelm the Federation presence. You believe she's still alive?'

'You say the *Caduceus* wasn't found.' Dalk frowned, considering. 'It's been taken. This was no random strike of bad luck or lucky happenstance on behalf of a hapless pirate. Somebody knew what we were doing. Somebody with close ties to this system.'

'Federation spies are talented fiends.'

Dalk shook his head. 'Not the Federation, they believe they've killed her. It's not in their interest to keep her alive. Somebody else has her, somebody who …'

He looked back at the holofac system chart, his eyes tracing the route between the stars. Then he turned back to Cuthrick.

'I will leave immediately.'

Cuthrick nodded. 'Your plan?'

Dalk smiled grimly. 'Find her and bring her back, naturally. Re-establish the lineage.'

'And where do you intend to look? How would you find one girl amongst billions? Dozens of inhabited systems?'

'I've got a pretty shrewd idea where to start. There are few hereabouts who have the means and audacity to snatch an Imperial convoy out of space.'

Cuthrick nodded and bowed. Dalk acknowledged with a slightly lower bow.

'Two weeks, Patron Dalk. We cannot risk a delay. Chione must be ours again.'

The holofac communication ended, leaving Dalk alone. He slung on his thick leather travelling cloak and checked the holster for his Whittaker Twinlock before striding purposefully out of the suite and heading towards the docking levels.

* * *

Light crackled in the depths of empty space. A ship appeared for a brief moment before being lost to sight. Shrewd observers would have seen it reappear thousands of kilometres from its previous position. The process repeated a number of times, the ship tracking randomly across the vast expanses of emptiness, a faint glow emanating from its drives.

CHAPTER FIVE

Hassan had already shut down every non-essential system aboard his Eagle. Next came the drives, shields and the astrogation systems, even the navigation lights were extinguished. The heat vents cooled from a fiery orange, through cherry to deep mauve and then finally a dull grey. The ship drifted impotently in the deep void, unseen and virtually undetectable. With no discernible energy emission the Eagle wouldn't appear on a passive scan at all, even an active scan would show it as an inanimate object; a rock or other similar space debris. Hassan even let the ship tumble gently around its central axis to further support the illusion.

He sat and watched the passive scanners for almost an hour before he was satisfied he'd made good his escape. The cockpit cooled, condensation freezing on the inside of the canopy with a faint crackle.

He'd done it. He'd lifted contraband from the most feared crime boss in this part of space. Now he'd command respect with the Guild, for sure. He grinned and leant back in his flight chair, wistfully gazing out across the light years, hands behind his head, whistling jauntily.

He relaxed for a moment considering his position. He accessed the on board inventory systems, querying the hold and running a check on its contents.

The computer paused for a long moment before responding.

Hold Inventory: 1 Ton Capacity Canister. Contains 1x Saud Kruger ThruSpace Hermetic Bio Support Pod.

Hassan blinked at the display. He had no idea what the description meant. Saud Kruger was a high tech, high cost manufacturer of luxury items. He gestured for more information. The computer responded a second time.

Saud Kruger ThruSpace Hermetic Bio Support Pod. Manifest error: Internal cargo type unknown.

He'd have to set down in order have a look, it was too risky to open a cargo pod in zero-G if you didn't know what it contained. The system map indicated a small rocky planet not too far away; that would do. It wasn't inhabited; it was just used as a way marker for hyperspace navigation. He countered the rotation of his ship and nudged it in a new direction.

* * *

ELITE: RECLAMATION

The cargo bay of the *Talon* was nothing like the size of the one within the *Caduceus*. The Eagle was a small vessel; originally a single person multi-role ship aimed at the impecunious end of the market. They were no longer manufactured and were now very firmly in the 'not quite a classic' and 'a notch above an old wreck' category. They had three particular virtues: they were cheap, reliable and easy to repair. Hundreds of thousands of the things had been made, so parts were still readily available. It was outclassed by pretty much everything short of a Lifter, but at this price point, nothing could beat it.

The cargo bay was cramped, with space for only four of the standard issue freight canisters once all the necessary flight equipment took up its fair share of space. Yes, you could squeeze a little more in if you had to, but only a mad sadomasochist would venture into space without an autopilot and some form of weaponry.

The small cockpit of the ship naturally sat on the centreline of the vessel, but the interior was arranged such that the cargo bay was located towards the rear of the hull, with the rest of the space below the cockpit being assigned to a simple combined living, eating and sleeping area.

Hassan watched the rocky surface of the planet rise up towards him as he gently guided the ship downwards. The landing gear unfolded and extended, adjusting for the uneven terrain. A moment later the contact lights turned green and the ship settled amidst a brief flurry of dust. Hassan looked at the g-meter. It was reading zero point three. Enough to be useful. He cut power to the drives and the main power plant.

Hassan lowered himself from the cockpit into the living area, ignoring the ladder that led between the two levels. On connecting with the hull plates his boots clamped on to the floor, providing additional stability. Thus secured he made his way backwards through the ship until he reached the hatch to the cargo bay. He spun the vacuum seal open and proceeded in.

The pilfered canister remained where the automechs had stored it, bolted securely to the floor and vertical struts of the bay. He stomped his way across to inspect it. The canister seemed quite mundane, its exterior marked with dents and rust. Canisters were general purpose devices used for years and years before eventually being recycled. Hassan thumped the release with the back of his hand and the canister's hatch groaned and swung open.

CHAPTER FIVE

Inside, the canister was pretty much empty. Hassan felt a crushing disappointment. He'd hoped for exotic luxuries, maybe silks or spices given the nature of the Imperial ship he'd helped to ambush. Not that the cargo mattered as long as he could demonstrate the audacity of his heist, but if it was just an empty canister, there'd be nothing even to fence.

Then as his eyes adjusted, he saw the white pod. It lay secured in the very centre. He stepped closer. It was featureless and smooth surfaced, like nothing he'd seen before. There were no obvious control points or interface. After a brief inspection he ran his hands over the exterior.

As he did so, holofac displays appeared, providing a series of what looked to be medical diagnostic readouts. For the most part they appeared green, but two were showing red. They were complex and technical. Hassan had no idea what they might mean. One control was obvious though.

Open/Close. Obvious enough, let's see.

Hassan pointed his finger at it tentatively and then stood back. There was a brief hiss and then the pod split in two, the top folding back in a smooth ballet of sophisticated mechanical design. He looked in.

'Woah ...'

A naked woman lay there, shrouded in a thin mist of slowly rising vapour. Hassan peered over the edge of the pod in bemusement. She was entirely still save for the gentle rise and fall of her chest. After a moment he stretched out his arm and reached towards her. As he did so her eyes snapped open and she looked across at him. Her stare was feral, fierce and wild.

Hassan stumbled back as she emitted a blood curdling shriek.

Noise; the blistering discharge of weapons. The fear of capture; heart pumping with exertion. Running, fleeing, panic, desperation and despair. The possibility of reprieve cruelly dashed away. Confrontation, defiance. Pain; her chest on fire, metal against bone. Swirling darkness followed by nothing, until ...

An arm, reaching towards her out of the darkness. Fingers outstretched, grasping, reaching. She screamed in terror.

The arm disappeared out of her sight. Everything was blurred, she could see little but a white glow surrounding her with a small rectangle of darkness within which was the vague outline of an unfamiliar dark-skinned face. She screamed again, her body convulsing, contorting into a foetal position save for her arms which wildly thrashed about trying to find some purchase within the whiteness. Cold. So cold!

Her fingers found an edge and she pulled herself up only to overbalance and fall into a dizzying spin interrupted by a hard unforgiving surface. She could see dark rust-stained corrugated metal within the narrow limits of her vision. Bile rose in her throat and she vomited, acid burning her throat and mouth, retching hard, unable to control the spasms that jerked her body.

Ahead she could see a space. Somewhere to hide? She heard a sound, the stomp of a metal-plated boot adjusting its position. She rolled her head around. A figure stood over her. She heard a voice but the words were unintelligible and painful to her ears. She shrieked in defiance, squashing her hands to her head to block out the sound and the discomfort.

Stumbling to her feet she staggered away, tripping across the threshold of the darkness into a wider space. Lights were painfully bright and harsh. She squinted, seeing more clearly now. She recognised nothing, spinning around to try and get her bearings. The movement unbalanced her, sending her careening wildly about before succumbing to the inevitable and ending up sprawled across the floor again. It hurt, the pain overriding everything else.

* * *

Hassan had almost brained himself on the interior of the canister. Inside the confined space the woman's shriek had been deafening. He blundered backwards, falling against the inside, watching with shock as the woman raged madly, lurched up out of the pod and then fell with a yelp before heaving and spewing her guts out all over the floor. She jerked and shook as if having a seizure. Hassan instinctively moved towards her.

'Hold it! I'm only trying to help …'

At the sound of his voice she clasped her hands to her head and screeched even louder. Her voice a harpy-like rasp of sound that made him wince, his ears ringing painfully. She crawled forward, gathering momentum, and managed briefly to get to her feet before spinning around and collapsing full length on the floor of the cargo bay in a slow motion whirl of uncoordinated limbs.

The fall seemed to stun her. She lay, gasping for breath, prone and shaking

CHAPTER FIVE

upon the decking. Hassan slowly ventured around her, crouching down and not getting too close, hoping not to alarm her further by slowly moving into her field of view. He held his hand out, palm down, trying to reassure the strange woman.

'Hey … just take it easy.'

He saw her clench her eyes tight shut at the sound of his voice and lowered it further. Her left arm flailed about for a moment before seizing up. He could see the tendons and muscles taut against her skin.

'I'm not going to hurt you.'

Her body trembled from head to toe; he could see goose pimples rising across her skin. The cargo bay was cool, she must be freezing. She threw up again and rolled onto her side.

'Don't move, yeah? I'll get you something.'

* * *

She tried to move, but her muscles were knotted and locked. The face appeared again. The instinct to flee almost overpowered her again. She tried to move but nothing would respond. Dizziness came in an overwhelming rush, spinning, whirling and twisting, going round and round and …

Her stomach clenched. Bile rose, burning in her throat. Pain speared her midriff. Then the cold bit into her flesh. Freezing! Why? Where was she? What had happened? Thoughts flew into her head and dissolved before she caught them. Anger rose … turned to fear and evaporated into bewilderment. Answers danced just beyond her reach. She shrieked her frustration.

Something touched her and she jerked in fear. More words. The voice was back. This time it made a little sense.

'… Keep you warm.'

Something wrapped her. The cold faded away, save where she was in contact with the ground. It felt good, comforting. She slipped back, drifting towards unconsciousness. A panicked thought crossed her mind and she searched her memory in vain. She should remember. Why couldn't she remember? Anger and frustration boiled over and she screeched out her questions before yielding to the darkness rolling around her.

*   *   *

Hassan had retrieved a couple of insulating blankets from a storage locker. They hadn't been used in a long time and smelt stale, but they were better than nothing. Heating failures on ships weren't unknown and it was best to be prepared. He gently covered the woman with them, pulling them across her.

'Can you wrap them around you? They'll keep you warm.'

There was a flicker of recognition in her eyes this time and Hassan saw her relax a fraction. She grasped at the blankets clumsily, propping herself up. He saw her eyes flicker from one side to another in rapid succession. Then she looked straight at him and spoke for the first time, her voice full of anguish and misery, yet angry and demanding.

'Who am I?'

Hassan shook his head. 'Lady, you tell me.'

She tried to get to her feet, but she wasn't able to. 'I was … who … what is this place?'

'Take it easy.' He moved towards her.

She screeched again, flinching back. 'Don't … don't kill me … please …'

Her eyes suddenly rolled up in her head and she fainted, falling back against the decking.

Hassan surveyed her for a moment before shaking his head. There was nothing in the flight manual about dealing with insane naked women aboard your ship. None of this made sense. It was illegal to carry slaves in the local systems and slaves weren't carried in isolation anyway, it wasn't profitable. He had no idea who the woman might be.

One thing was clear enough though. She wasn't a nice straightforward cargo of luxuries he could sell at the next stopover for a fat profit.

She was trouble.

*   *   *

Octavia's newly promoted second in command guard hesitated briefly before asking permission to enter her suite aboard the *Basilica*.

CHAPTER FIVE

His predecessor had been clumsy and foolish, but trusting the automechs to do their job was a natural response to the need to quickly unload a large vessel when speed was of the essence. The cargo had to be moved and sold on before it could be logged as stolen. That meant hours rather than days. There was no time to perform a detailed inspection of every canister.

Clearly Octavia had some special interest in part of the haul. What that was, neither he nor his predecessor knew. The rest of the cargo was secondary. He'd not make the same mistake in determining her priorities.

Unfortunately he had only bad news to report, but he felt confident he'd done everything he could. Octavia should see things in the same manner. She'd always been a supremely effective leader, organised, her attention to detail almost legendary. She never suffered fools for long. Cold and unemotional, harsh but strong.

Yet in recent months …

Something was awry. He took a deep breath and announced his presence.

The door to the suite opened immediately. Octavia was waiting for him. She faced outwards, looking out of the composite windows to the distant stars. She turned as he entered, striding across to him.

'Progress?'

'We've been unable to locate the vessel,' he replied. 'The hyperspace trace was inconclusive by the time we reached the jump-out point.'

Octavia stiffened, but said nothing. He continued.

'I sent scouts to all the nearby jump points and systems. Active scans show no sign of the ship. None of our listening posts have seen any comm traffic or unauthorised travel. I've advised our contacts in all the major trading ports to watch for the ship.'

Octavia looked away for a moment, thinking it through. 'He's gone dark.'

'That would be my guess too, Domina. He could be nearby, but until he moves …'

'He can't hang out there indefinitely, but a small ship like that …'

'Might slip through our surveillance.' Octavia nodded. 'Who is he?'

The guard gestured and a holofac image of a young man with dark skin and long lanky hair appeared in the space between them.

'Hassan Farrukh Sharma,' the guard recited from memory. 'Reads as a simple trader. No previous. Basic ship, nothing special. Mostly harmless. An opportunist I'd say.'

'And just a boy,' Octavia murmured. 'The recklessness of youth. I want him found and brought back here.'

'I've taken the liberty of putting out a contract …'

'Bounty hunters?' Octavia said with distaste.

'It's the fastest way to find him.'

'Be clear that he must be alive and the cargo … unmolested,' Octavia said, her gaze intense.

'It might help if I knew what the cargo was.'

Octavia shook her head. 'It is valuable and it is mine. It is not to be touched. That is all that should concern you. Keep me informed.'

The guard retreated, relieved to still be in one piece. He was wise enough to know it would be a temporary state of affairs unless that canister and the boy were returned soon.

* * *

Hassan decided he couldn't just leave the woman in the cargo bay. She hadn't regained consciousness. She might be sick or dying. After some consideration he decided to move her to his quarters where there was some basic medical equipment.

It mostly went to plan. She might not weigh very much in such low gravity, but she still had mass; something he had never really appreciated before having to manhandle an unconscious body through his ship. It was not a graceful operation.

Having wrestled her into place on the spare bunk, he turned his attention to the on board medicomp. It was able to diagnose and treat a limited array of uniquely space oriented maladies. Radiation treatment was one, along with a series of wide-spectrum antibiotics, anti-nausea drugs and pain killers. He clipped the monitors on to the woman's finger tips and was rewarded with a display of diagnostic information on her health. It all looked pretty normal to him. He cleaned her face with antiseptic wipes and left her to the medicomp.

The machine ran an identity scan as a matter of course. Hassan waited for

CHAPTER FIVE

the results with interest, keen to know who his stowaway was and if she was ok.

Error! No tag, memrec or subcutaneous identity found. Warning! Biometric record not on file.

Warning! No Galstandard bio-immunity present.

Status. Vital signs nominal. Blood sugar and fluid levels low.

Hassan sat back and blew a long strand of hair out of his face. She was healthy enough, but this was a puzzle. No tag, no chip, not even standard bio immunity. If she were a slave, she'd have been tagged with her owner's identity, but he'd already guessed she wasn't a slave. And no chip meant she couldn't be a Federation or Imperial citizen, not an ordinary one at any rate. Alliance maybe? But no standard bio? All space travellers had the jab as a matter of routine. She wasn't a passenger, she wasn't a slave and this must be her first trip into space. Stowaways were an occasional fact of life, but he'd never heard of one who came with her own storage pod. Or for that matter, without clothes. Her hair was neatly trimmed, her skin soft with nails perfectly manicured. She was no stowaway.

Hassan patted the Cowell '55 at his side. Best to be prepared, she could be anyone.

He was spared any further speculation. She came to with a choking cough, her eyes opening and quickly latching onto him. This time the gaze from her grey eyes was steady. She stared at him for a long moment before looking around herself.

'It's ok,' Hassan said gently. 'Just take it slow, ok?' The woman seemed to recognise him from before.

'Where am I?' she demanded, fixing her eyes on him once more. This time he immediately noticed that her voice had a strong Imperial tone with its characteristic musical lilt. It was clipped, precise and tutored.

So much for the Alliance world.

'You're aboard the *Talon*,' he replied.

She looked around again, taking in the dingy cramped cabin.

'I was …' she shook her head, a frown creasing her forehead. 'A what? A *Talon*? What is a *Talon*?'

'It's a ship. You're on board a ship.'

'How did I get here?' Her face bore a completely innocent expression for a moment, but then distrust grew and spread across her features. 'A ship? What am I doing on a ship?'

Hassan shrugged. 'That ... is a very good question.'

'Who are you?'

'Name's Hassan. I'm the Commander ...'

'A Commander?' She looked unconvinced.

She sat up slowly and then became aware she wore nothing aside from the blankets that Hassan had covered her in.

'Where are my clothes?' she demanded, pulling her sole blanket up around herself and then glared accusingly at Hassan. 'What is this? How dare you ...'

'Nothing to do with me, lady.' Hassan grabbed a spare pair of flight overalls and chucked them in her direction. 'Here, knock yourself out.'

She took them, turning them around appraisingly for a moment. She gave them a cautious sniff and then wrinkled her nose in disgust.

'These are ... eugh! They won't do, find me something else.'

Hassan shrugged and folded his arms. 'It's all there is, make do.'

'I am not a servant that you can dress me in rags, you will find me appropriate attire ...'

'No, I won't.' Hassan was enjoying her discomfiture. 'Wear those or wear nothing. Either way works for me.'

She looked shocked. 'You dare speak to me in such a tone?'

'My ship, my rules, lady.'

The woman inspected the flight suit at arm's length with an expression of haughty distaste before looking up at him.

'I require privacy. You are dismissed.'

'Oh, I am, am I? Real generous of you.'

'Go.'

Hassan considered explaining how he'd had to manoeuvre her naked body across the deck but thought better of it. He left the living quarters, climbing back up into the cockpit. He gave her a couple of minutes and then returned. She was sitting on the edge of the bunk now wearing the overalls, looking around her. She sat straight, shoulders back and head erect.

CHAPTER FIVE

'So,' he said, sitting across from her on the opposite bunk. 'Just what are you doing on my ship, lady?'

She fixed him with an arrogant look and started speaking confidently in her haughty accent. 'You will address me in the proper manner. I am ...'

She faltered and a look of panic crossed her face before she looked down in puzzlement and tried again.

'I'm ...'

She looked back at him. 'I ... I can't remember.'

'Uh-huh,' Hassan said. 'And I'm guessing you don't know where you're from either.'

'Of course I do, I am not a fool.'

'Go on then.'

'I come from ...' She stopped again, anger rising in her voice. 'What's happening? Why can't I remember? What have you done to me? All this nonsense about being on a ship; you're lying! You've kidnapped me, you've ...'

She jumped to her feet and swung clumsily at him. Any doubts in Hassan's mind as to whether she'd really been off planet before were cleared aside. She lurched forward, overbalancing in the low gravity, trying to stop her forward motion before ending up sprawled at his feet after a slow bounce.

'That's not ...' She looked around her in bewilderment. Hassan laughed at her predicament. *Mass aint the same as weight, lady. How many times did they drum that into us in flight school?* Hassan held out a hand, aiming to steady her. She grasped it and then twisted instinctively.

Hassan found himself thrown back against the bulkhead wall, a blast of acute pain shooting up his arm. Before he could stop it her other hand raked across his face, nails gouging his skin. She made to escape, but miscalculated how quickly she could move; without gravity boots she had no purchase on the floor.

It was too much for Hassan. He punched her hard, sending her reeling back across the narrow space to fall back onto the bunk with a yelp. He pulled his 55 out and trained it on her.

'Shit, woman!' he yelled, dabbing at the traces of blood welling up from the cuts on his face, wincing at the throbbing pain in his right wrist. 'I should pitch you out the fucking airlock.'

'Let me go,' she answered, getting back unsteadily to her feet, warily watching the gun, a bruise already forming on her cheek.

'You can breathe in a vacuum, can you? Airlock's that way. Be my guest. It'll be nice and quick.'

She frowned, considering his words, looking around the cabin again. 'I'm really on a ship?'

'Yeah,' Hassan said, gesturing with his 55. 'My ship. If I could let you go I would, but there's no way out right now. Got it?'

'I get it.'

'And next time you try and attack me you get a whack upside your head, we clear?'

She nodded slowly, sitting back down on the bunk.

'Glad that's settled.' He reholstered the 55 and then wiped his face with one of the medipads, looking cautiously at her.

'Can we stop with the violence thing already? Bullets do bad things inside a ship.'

She nodded, rubbing her own cheek.

'I didn't mean … I just don't understand …' She looked lost and confused.

'All right. Sorry I hit you. We'll figure it out, yeah? One thing at a time.' He stretched out his hand.

'Pax?'

'Pax,' she answered uncertainly. They warily shook hands. He helped her to her feet and she took another look around at the stained and tired interior of the cabin.

Hassan took a pair of boots out of a locker. 'Here, put these on, they'll help.'

She took the proffered footwear. They were ungainly, heavy-looking items. As she slipped her feet into them they tightened and shrank. She placed her feet on the floor and the boots clicked into place.

'Magboots,' Hassan explained. 'Stops you floating off. Come on, this way.'

He led her to the rear hatch and they stepped through, ducking through the narrow egress. She looked quite comical as she struggled to adjust to the sharp clamp and reclamp of the boots on the metal flooring.

The hatchway led into the bay. He saw her stare around this larger space. She seemed unable to recognise what she saw. Imagining it through her

CHAPTER FIVE

eyes, he was struck by how grimy and timeworn it looked, full of tarnished machinery, pipes, connectors and all manner of controls decorated with the occasional light. He saw her react as the faint reverberating thrum of activity reached her ears. In front of her sat the massive container with a hatchway open at one end.

'Is this really what the inside of a spaceship looks like?' She sounded disappointed.

'This is a working ship, not a pleasure craft,' Hassan said in an aggrieved tone and then pointed around at various areas. 'Cargo bay. Cargo canister. Exit ramp and airlock. Do not touch when we're in space otherwise you die horribly. Any questions?'

She shook her head.

'Back the other way.' He turned on his heel.

She looked at him as he signalled for her to follow him back through the hatchway into the cabin. Once there he jumped onto the ladder, the only other way out of the room.

'Follow me. Do exactly what I do and take it slow. Any funny business and I brain you. Got it?'

She watched as Hassan slowly climbed up the ladder out of the living quarters. As his feet rose above her, he gestured for her to follow. She stepped onto the ladder and moved up behind him.

The ladder led up a short distance through another circular hatchway in to the rear of an even smaller space. As she climbed up she could see two complex metal chairs in front of her, bolted to the floor. They were positioned one behind the other. Hassan had already swung himself into the one at the front. Around the chairs the room was festooned with a bewildering array of instruments, displays and controls, backlit with a comforting soft orange glow. They framed a large canopy through which …

Oh … !

She stared, her mouth dropping open. She hadn't really believed it until now.

Beyond the window was a backdrop of absolute darkness, spangled with thousands upon thousands of tiny points of light, some bright and sharp, others faint and dim. It was crystal clear, without a hint of fuzziness. Each point was cold and hard, with not even the barest flicker. As she began to take it in she made out patches of faint colour, filaments of wisps of tenuous material between the stars.

Space. Infinite space. It was cold and harsh, but somehow mesmerising, enchanting, bewitching. Even the air in the cockpit was cool. She shivered.

As she stood up she could see the dim outline of a close rocky horizon, faintly illuminated by the light of the stars.

'I really am on a ship,' she said softly, still gazing out of the windows. Her expression was a mix of fear, awe and disconsolation.

Hassan pressed a control and his seat swung around one hundred and eighty degrees. He gestured to the other seat and guided her into it, showing her how to pull the straps in around her. Then he sat back and regarded her.

'So, lady,' he said, folding his arms. 'What were you doing in that pod?'

'Pod?'

'The pod you were in. Lying there like you was dead …'

A sword, striking forward abruptly; a roughened hand grasping a hilt; pain and blood …

She gasped, struggling to hold the faint flash of memory. She ran her hand against her chest inside the flight suit. Her fingers traced the faintest of scars on her skin; a small diagonal mark, almost undetectable.

'I can't remember,' she whispered.

'Well, that ain't good enough. You've stowed away on my ship, you've no ID, no memory and I'm in a shit load of trouble as a result.'

'Why? I've done nothing … have I?'

'Smuggling people is illegal round these parts! Your pod was inside the canister.' He groaned at her blank look. 'That big metal thing with the hatch in the cargo bay? I stole it, it was supposed to be something worth having, instead I got you.'

'Thank you for the compliment,' she snapped before her eyes widened in alarm. 'Stolen? You're a pirate?'

'No, I'm not a bloody pirate,' Hassan replied.

Maybe that's technically true, but I'm not doing it again so it doesn't count, does it?

'You just said you stole me. You are a pirate,' she repeated.

'I didn't know it was you, did I?' Hassan said. 'I didn't steal you on purpose.'

CHAPTER FIVE

'Where from? Tell me.'

Hassan rolled his eyes. 'Listen, it's complex ...'

'Tell me.' There was a fierce determination about her manner. Whoever she was, she was used to giving orders.

'I joined in an ambush on an Imperial ship, helped disable it,' Hassan explained.

'Imperial?'

'You know who the Imperials are, right? Strutting overdressed toadies, obsessed with appearance above everything ...' Belatedly he remembered her accent. 'No offence ...'

She glared at him. 'I know who the Imperials are, I was ...' She stopped again, groaning with frustration, pressing her hands against her head and squeezing her eyes shut for a moment. 'Why can't I remember? I almost ...' She opened her eyes and looked at him. 'Why in the void did you attack an Imperial ship?'

'I need a rep. I can't join the traders' Guild until I've got a rep. I didn't know you'd stowed away on board.'

'It was my ship? You attacked my ship?' she echoed in surprise. 'That's what it takes to get this "rep" of yours, is it?'

'No,' Hassan said. 'Listen. I needed to prove I could pull off something big. I figured if I could pinch some Imperial cargo I could fence it in Federation space. It would show the Guild I had the right stuff.'

'And?'

'There was a contract. Cash, no questions asked. I didn't know what the deal was. I just had to help with an ambush. I figured we'd just pinch the cargo and I'd help myself. But it ended up we only disabled your ship and towed it to some pirate base. The cargo was for someone else, someone else wanted the ship you were on.'

'So you deliberately ambushed my ship without even knowing why?'

'I didn't care.'

'So who did care?'

'Our customer,' Hassan gulped. 'A woman called Octavia Quinton.'

'And who is she?' The woman picked up his nervousness immediately.

'Pretty much the meanest, most ruthless crime boss in this whole sector. She controls pretty much everything hereabouts. The Guild was set up to counter her stranglehold on trade.'

The woman took a moment to assimilate that information.

'So how did we end up here?' she finally asked, looking out of the window at the bleak landscape outside.

'I stole a cargo canister from her, and you were in it.'

'You stole cargo from a ruthless crime boss?' Her voice was high with fear.

'The Guild hates her!' Hassan replied, waving his hands around. 'I couldn't leave empty handed, could I? I figured if I could swindle her the Guild would have to let me in.'

It makes sense, doesn't it?

'That's the most stupid plan I've ever heard in my life.' The woman's voice was now stiff with anger.

Hassan felt his stomach cramp in anxiety.

Maybe she's right.

'If I had a nice case of luxuries to trade rather than a crazy flux-stained woman with no ID I'd still have a plan! You're the one who's messed this up.'

'I've messed it up? You're the one who stole me from wherever I was going!'

Hassan thumped his chair in frustration, looking aside.

The woman looked at him expectantly. 'So this Octavia woman of yours is going to be looking for us then.'

'You think?' Hassan replied. 'Guess why we're hiding out here in the void. Maybe I should take you back, try to explain. She might understand … no, stupid idea.' He leant forward. 'So, come on, why the hell were you in that pod?'

'I don't know.'

'You must know. Think, for Randomius' sake. What do you remember before being here?'

'I told you, I can't remember anything!'

They were almost nose to nose, glaring at each other. 'Listen, lady …'

'Stop calling me lady. I have a name …' she paused, fighting back unexpected tears again, before dissolving into sobs of pure frustration. 'I had a name … I had a name!'

Hassan held up his hands. 'All right, all right. Time out. Let's figure this through. Better give you a name for starters.'

She shrugged, wiping at her eyes and regaining her composure. Hassan thought about it for a moment.

CHAPTER FIVE

'Got it,' he said after a moment. 'Salomé.'

'Sal-low-mee?' She experimented with the sound of the name, frowning and suspicious. 'Why? What does that mean?'

'My sister had a cat called Salomé,' Hassan answered, prodding his tender face. 'Proud, aloof, annoying and bloody sharp claws; suits you perfectly.'

Her lip curled in anger before a confused look crossed her face. 'What's a cat?'

He rolled his eyes. 'What's a … never mind the sodding cat.' He reached out and pressed a couple of buttons. 'We've got to figure out what the hell we're going to do.'

A holofac chart appeared between them.

'We're here,' he said, pointing to a glowing reference mark in the midst of the chart. Salomé could see a number of systems marked, connected to each other by faint green lines. 'You've got an Imperial accent, so I figure you come from the Empire.'

She nodded, that felt right. 'The Empire, yes. I'm sure of it.'

He waved at the chart and it moved. Systems drifted off to one side and disappeared, with fresh ones appearing on the other.

'This is Imperial space. Recognise anything?'

Salomé examined the chart carefully. It did seem vaguely familiar, but none of the system names jolted any memories.

'Where was my ship when you attacked it?'

Hassan waved the chart back again. 'Here.'

Salomé looked again, but shrugged hopelessly. 'It's meaningless.'

'Well, we've got to make ourselves scarce and soon,' Hassan said. 'Octavia'll expect us to dock someplace, probably got all the local systems marked already. We need to go somewhere busy and get lost in the background, somewhere she can't operate …'

He gestured to the chart and it shrank, zooming out to show a wider view of the surrounding systems.

'Imperial space?' Salomé asked.

'Octavia's no friend of the Empire. She works mostly for the Feds when it suits her. The Empire lays claim to most of this. She operates round the edge, giving the Feds inroads. We'll be safer in there. Closer to wherever you come from too, maybe we'll figure out who you are.'

She nodded in agreement.

Hassan pulled up the system catalogue, scanning down the list of systems.

'This looks good. Ferenchia. It's Independent, but friendly to the Empire. Busy trading hub, lots of imports and exports. Plenty of ships just like us. We can hide for a bit, snag the transponder and re-register, maybe even swap to another ship …'

'How long will that take?'

Hassan shook his head. 'Have to do it in stages. Don't worry, I've got a plan.'

Salomé leant back and folded her arms. 'Is it going to be better than your last plan?'

Hassan shot her an unfriendly look. The memory of his brother's face filtered into his mind.

That's because your plans are always crazy and someone ends up getting hurt.

'Still got that airlock. Don't you forget it.'

Chapter Six

Another vessel approached the *Basilica*, slowing to a drift. It was bigger than the previous set of fighters that had approached just a day before, but not as large as the Imperial Cutter they had ambushed. It was an Asp, a vessel capable of handling a sustained combat, small enough to evade turret fire yet big enough to pack a formidable array of ordnance.

Expert eyes would have seen that the ship was deployed in an 'interceptor' configuration. It could function equally well as a warship or in an anti-fighter role. This one featured a load-out aimed at taking down smaller ships. A bounty hunter.

Dalk eyed the dark bulk of the *Basilica* with a practised eye. Whilst he knew of Octavia by reputation, it would be interesting to meet her face to face. Given what she'd managed to amass in the last few decades it was clear that she wasn't to be underestimated. Her control of trade across the nearby systems was draconian, something that he'd used indirectly to his advantage in order to smuggle weapons to the Reclamists on Chione. She was the unofficial arm of the Federation in these parts, tacitly supporting them in undermining the interests of the Empire.

Dalk had a low opinion of the bounty hunter profession in general. He regarded them as opportunists, feeding off the misfortune of others, extending the cycle of revenge and retribution time and again. It was particularly galling to have to masquerade as one, but he had no other choice.

'*Coup de Grâce* to *Basilica*. Request docking clearance.'

A searchlight flashed out, illuminating Dalk's vessel for a few brief seconds. 'State your business *Coup de Grâce*,' came the brusque reply.

'Hoping to serve and assist with Auntie's family woes,' Dalk replied. There was a pause before the response came.

'*Basilica* to *Coup de Grâce*. Proceed. Docking in berth twenty-one.'

Dalk watched as the gated defences of the *Basilica* rolled aside, revealing the interior space. He couldn't see the multitude of weapons trained on his ship, but he knew they were there. It wouldn't do to discount them. He slowly guided his ship towards the selected bay, taking a good look around as he did so.

Octavia was already at the top of his list of suspects for having ambushed the *Caduceus* on its way out of Chione. That she'd issued a contract shortly afterwards seemed too much of a coincidence. It gave him a chance to have a poke around at the very least.

Most of the docking bays were empty, but a few were occupied. He could see flickering flashes of light coming from one bay and squinted at it. As he drew level he could see that automechs were working on repairing a ship. It had familiar lines, an Imperial Cutter with a damaged starboard nacelle.

Was it the *Caduceus*? He couldn't be sure, the hull plates were too small to resolve at this distance and he'd raise suspicions by triggering an active scan. If so, Octavia would know about Kahina. A high ranking member of an Imperial family would be a perfect bargaining chip with the Empire or command a high price as an object of ransom if sold to the Federation. But there'd been no ransom demand from her or the Federation. Either Octavia didn't appreciate yet what she had or something else had happened. Then there was the contract she'd issued. Dalk reviewed it again.

Missing person, much missed by Aunt and wider family. Last seen en route to Haoria. Only the best need apply. Top price paid for information leading to happy reunion.

Aunt was one of many curious pseudonyms that Octavia used; whoever had gone missing was clearly important. Was it related? Time would tell.

The *Coup de Grâce* nested down in the bay, its landing gear gracefully taking up the strain as the ship came to rest. Dalk powered down his ship and gestured at the controls. His pilot's chair descended through the base of the cockpit, lowering him into the bay. He stood up and stretched to his full height, his thick black trench coat wafting out around him as he strode forwards. His ship sealed and locked itself behind him.

Two guards with pressurised rifles were waiting to meet him. One gestured for him to follow and the other fell in behind. The synchronised footsteps of the guards clacked noisily on the panelled metal flooring. Parallel light bars flickered past Dalk's vision in a slow motion strobe as they walked deeper into the recesses of the station. They arrived at an internal lift. Dalk looked aside

CHAPTER SIX

at the guard behind him, but there was no response as the doors hissed open. The trio moved inside. Dalk felt his stomach drop as the lift rapidly descended. His feet were pressed harder, the simulated gravity growing strong. He leant slightly to one side to counter the faint coriolis force without even thinking about it, taking a moment to adjust his stance and prepare for the meeting. They were clearly heading towards the outside edge of the facility.

The doors snapped back and the three of them emerged into a wide, low-ceilinged room. A large holofac projection unit was mounted in the centre. Dalk recognised the room as an auxiliary command and control chamber. It would have been used extensively for battle planning and strategy in wartime, directing squadrons of fighters into battle.

A number of other individuals were already seated around the outside of the projector, a misfit collection of bounty hunters from across the sector. The two guards turned smartly on their heels and departed in the lift. The doors snapping closed behind them.

'What's your name, stranger?'

Dalk looked across and saw a tall woman observing him from across the room. It had to be Octavia herself.

'Harfitt,' Dalk replied, slurring his speech with a happy go lucky drawl. 'Simeon Harfitt.'

'Show us your ID,' Octavia said.

Dalk pulled a datatab out of his pocket and chucked it carelessly onto the projector table. A holofac representation of himself, his fake name, his ship and various biometric markers appeared, slowly rotating. His pilot's ranking appeared beneath them.

Elite.

A moment later the word 'Verified' appeared, glowing in green lettering. He looked over at her with a questioning glance and a slight bow.

'Sit down,' Octavia said. 'We're wasting time.'

Dalk settled himself beside one of the other bounty hunters, a grizzled looking fellow with a rather ornate handlebar moustache.

'Nice ship,' the grizzled fellow said.

'Thanks,' Dalk responded, not wanting to get distracted from Octavia as she walked around the back of the assembly.

'Just as well, she just spaced a guy for wasting her time. He turned up in an old Adder.'

Dalk scoffed. 'Chancers. If you can't take the heat …' He enjoyed playing the part of a relaxed and easy going professional.

'… stay out of the corona.'

Dalk turned his attention to Octavia.

'To business,' she said, leaning against the projector, hands outstretched, looking at each one of them in turn. 'This is what you're looking for.'

The schematics of an old Eagle fighter appeared on the holofac. Dalk recognised it as an original model. It was a simple old ship, easy and cheap to maintain. This one was pretty much an antique.

'Registration code is TY–198,' Octavia added. 'It's a standard model. Old ship. A few mods, nothing fancy.'

'Who's the pilot?' one of the others, a man with a red and white striped bandana, called out.

Octavia gestured to the display and an image of a young dark-skinned man with a flop of unruly black hair appeared. It wasn't a great picture, it must have been taken by a security camera from some distance.

'My nephew,' Octavia said, smiling and gesturing to the image. There was a general chuckle from around the room.

'Hassan Farrukh Sharma. Age twenty-eight. Mostly harmless. Last seen here eleven hours ago.'

'Any idea where he was heading?' This time it was a woman dressed in a skin-tight one-piece black outfit. The whites of her eyes seemed to glow in the gloom, standing out from her dark face. Her hair was arranged in a fashionable series of coloured spikes.

Octavia shook her head. 'Our guess is Federation space, though we believe he's gone dark for now. We've seen no activity in the immediate jump points or the local systems.'

Dalk nodded to himself. That was no surprise. Hyperspacing in consecutive jumps was a dead giveaway. Letting your trail go cold was a smart move. The youth had some nous at least. He wasn't convinced that a jump towards the Federation made sense, but he kept quiet.

'You want him back alive?' Skin-tight asked.

CHAPTER SIX

Octavia looked at her. 'I want him alive, I want the ship back and I want the cargo back.'

Dalk seized his chance. 'What's he carrying?'

Octavia looked around at him. 'Something of mine, that's all you need to know.'

Dalk shrugged. 'Count me out then. It can't be done.'

A surprised look crossed Octavia's face. 'What did you say?'

Dalk looked deliberately disinterested and spoke in his lazy accent. 'I'm guessing your nephew's not looking to be found. So, first thing he's gonna do is scrub his ship's identity. Next he's going to find himself a busy port and blend right in. We'd be looking for a cruddy old ship amongst a thousand others. Unless we know what's aboard we can't scan for it, can we? Can't work miracles.'

Skin-tight and Moustache were nodding in agreement. Bandana unfolded his arms and leant forward, listening intently.

Dalk looked around the room and then fixed her with a shrewd eye. 'And I'm figuring that it's the cargo you want back.'

Octavia glared at him for a moment before relenting.

'Very well. He's carrying contraband Imperial biotech in a specialised container. Here's the profile.'

Dalk schooled himself not to react when the schematic of a bio support pod appeared on the holofac. The youth had stolen Kahina! From under Octavia's nose, no wonder she was pissed. There was no mistaking the profile of the pod, it had been custom made and there wasn't another like it. His plan still had a chance.

'What's it do?' he asked, innocently.

'Specialist pod for conveying hazardous bio samples,' Octavia snapped. 'Don't be thinking of opening it. You'll be dead without the proper handling tech.'

'Just here for the money,' Dalk assured her.

Skin-tight nodded. 'Good call. How much you paying and how long have we got?'

'Fifty thousand and as long as it takes,' Octavia replied. 'For the cargo, the ship and the … my nephew. All intact and unmolested. Any questions?'

The bounty hunters looked at each other, but none spoke. It was a generous fee, you could buy a half decent ship for that.

'You've all got the profile,' Octavia concluded. 'Suggest you get moving.'

* * *

Dalk took a moment to think things through before he departed. Octavia had clearly figured out who Kahina was, hence her fear about the pod heading towards Federation space. It made sense that the youngster would head that way to get the highest price for her, but only if he knew what he was carrying. Dalk thought it more likely the youth was an opportunist and had only stumbled on the pod by blind chance. If so …

The Pod would remain secure assuming no one had tampered with it. Dalk felt the youth must be running scared. He'd go where Octavia would find it hard to follow. That meant the Empire and not the Federation.

There was a good chance Dalk's superior vessel could overhaul him, but that wasn't the problem. He had to put the other bounty hunters, and Octavia if possible, off the scent for long enough to find the youth and then escape with Kahina to the protection of Haoria. Once there they'd be safe, but there was little point finding the Eagle and then not being able to get away himself.

But why did Octavia intercept the pod in the first place?

He watched as two of the bounty hunters set off, triggering their hyperspace drives shortly after leaving the *Basilica*. Dalk instructed the computer to analyse their course. They'd taken Octavia's cue and headed towards Federation space.

The third bounty hunter remained docked. Dalk had a feeling the owner of that ship was waiting to see what he did. He didn't want a shadow following him.

He gestured for a narrowband comm link and was rewarded with a holofac of the dark woman with the skin-tight suit.

'Would ya believe it,' he drawled. 'Got some nav vectors all messed up. All fixed now.'

'Not good,' Skin-tight answered. 'These modern ships. Don't make them like they used to do they?'

CHAPTER SIX

Dalk grinned at her. 'Well, best o' luck.'

'You too.'

Dalk cancelled the link.

Definitely waiting for me.

He watched as her ship eased out of the dock and thrust rapidly away. It was a Viper, a tough modern fighting machine. She had money and the right instincts for the job. She'd most likely go 'dark' herself and wait for him outside. Well, she could try. He relaxed into his flight chair, waiting a few more minutes as he considered his strategy. Then he engaged the power systems, allowing the protective flight-gel to ease up around him.

He fired up the drives and accelerated out of the bay.

* * *

Hassan gave Salomé a series of sticky bars. She took one and nibbled on it tentatively, before hunger overtook her and she gulped it down. Feverously she grabbed more of them and pulled them out of their wrappers. She finished them off in short order.

'Woah, take it easy, those are supposed …' She looked up with a scowl.

'Ok, so you're hungry.'

He'd moved her into the forward pilot's chair to keep her out of the way with firm instructions not to touch anything. It still didn't make sense. Not a slave, not a passenger. What was she doing on that Imperial Cutter? He'd no idea where that ship had come from or was going to. The nearest major system to the ambush point was some obscure backwater mining outfit. How did that fit with her snobbish Imperial accent?

Somewhere along the line she'd been coached and tutored. He recognised the conceited tones of the Imperial privileged classes in her style of speech. That spoke of money and some level of status. If he could figure out who she was maybe that was an angle worth pursuing, somebody must have missed her. He'd check the lost and found postings when he got a chance.

Maybe the pod was some kind of medical device, transporting a sick patient? Physically the woman appeared to be fine but clearly she wasn't right in the head. But why an entire canister for just one person? And why not a medical ship? And why not sort her out on a planet with medical facilities? It didn't make any sense.

Maybe she was some kind of refugee? Maybe she was being covertly smuggled out-system, incognito. That might explain the whole veil of secrecy, the escorts and so on. Did Octavia know about that? Was that why there was an ambush? If so he might have wandered into some kind of big stakes political situation …

Not good … shit!

A cold sweat broke out on his forehead. He was in over his head. He took a deep breath and tried to stay focused. He had to get rid of her and soon. Maybe the airlock wasn't such a bad idea after all. She was so clueless about space operations he could probably con her inside without much trouble.

It would be quick.

She looked around at that moment, as if aware she was being scrutinised, before resuming her stare out of the cockpit windows. She wasn't a classic beauty, but she wasn't unpleasant to gaze upon. Hassan turned back to his work.

Killing in cold blood. He already knew he wasn't going to do that. It was one thing shooting down other ships at range. All pilots signed up to the danger and possibility of being spaced in combat. It was just a game; point, lock, shoot and *Right On, Commander*. It was quite another to push an innocent woman into an airlock and pull the release.

Innocent though. Really?

She seemed innocent. Had she really lost her memory like she said? She was a good actor if so, but if she was a politician she'd be accomplished at that. Maybe he was being played again. If she was acting she'd be trying to influence him, wouldn't she? Dropping in hints to go to this or that system maybe, or arguing over the destination.

Another thought occurred to him. Maybe she was a psycho, undergoing some expensive new mental treatment off-world. No telling what she might do if that was the case, some innocent gesture might set her off. She'd already demonstrated she knew something about hand to hand combat with that little trick with the wrist hold.

He puffed out his cheeks and primed the hyperspace system. His best bet was to make her somebody else's problem, and as quickly as possible.

CHAPTER SIX

'That's it, we're spooling,' he said, a little louder than he needed to. Salomé looked around. 'Spooling?'

'Hyperdrive is spooling up. I'm taking you to Ferenchia. We can get you set up there with a new ID, some emergency creds, maybe even find you some work.'

Salomé nodded absently. He'd have given a stash of credits to know what was going on behind her solemn grey eyes.

* * *

The *Coup de Grâce* launched from the *Basilica* towing a plume of hot plasma in its wake. Dalk pushed his vessel to maximum acceleration for a few seconds. The passive scanner was blank as he expected. If Skin-tight was waiting to see where he jumped to she wouldn't hang around making herself easy to spot. She'd be out of range, but close enough to sweep in once he'd jumped and analyse the resultant hyperspace cloud, figuring out his destination. It would be a simple matter to piggyback on his jump and follow him. His drive thrust would be lighting up her infrared sensors like a solstice celebration.

'Not going to happen,' he muttered to himself. 'Activate frameshift.'

On board automation acknowledged his command with a faint musical tone and the Asp leapt forward into the void. His scanner was still blank, but he was convinced that Skin-tight's ship was lurking behind him somewhere, waiting to follow him through hyperspace.

Dalk activated a secondary series of displays. The *Coup de Grâce* wasn't just well equipped with weaponry; Dalk had ensured that a number of stealth technologies had also been installed.

'Activate decoy drone.'

The displays showed a small device, mounted on the underside of the Asp, a sleek needle-like affair, hardly bigger than a mid-range missile. Status lights glowed orange and then flickered to green one by one.

Dalk grinned.

Bet you don't have the military contacts I do.

He turned the *Coup de Grâce* in a lazy arc back towards the *Basilica*. As the station swept back into range he cancelled the frameshift. The *Basilica* was a much larger source of heat than his ship. He switched off the power to his shields and pulled the throttles closed. His ship continued drifting towards the facility on a course that would take it just past the edge of the main hull.

'Spool up drone hyperdrive module,' he called out to the on board automation.

Skin-tight would have seen the turn and most likely slotted in behind him again. Without exhaust glow his ship would now be indistinguishable from the background glow of the station. He was invisible unless she went active. Bounty hunters never went active, it just wasn't *de rigueur*; an admittance of failure.

'Set drone hyperdrive target to Mithra,' he instructed. A faint chime sounded in acknowledgement.

'Standby to release drone, negative trajectory course, two hundred metres astern.'

This time the computer buzzed in response.

Drone subsystem: Course confirmed. Hyperspace destination confirmed.

'Acknowledged,' Dalk said, watching the approaching bulk of the *Basilica* sweeping toward him.

'Deploy drone and activate drone hyperspace countdown … now.'

There was the faintest of clunks as the drone detached from the hull of the *Coup de Grâce*. It slowly retreated behind the main ship until it was holding position as instructed.

The *Basilica* was close now. He had to time this perfectly. Too close and the jump would be jammed by the mass of the facility, too far and his plan wouldn't work.

Drone subsystem: Hyperspace Engaging.

There was a flicker of harsh light across the hull of the *Basilica*. Behind the *Coup de Grâce*, a flickering sphere of sparkling energy had formed. A hyperspace cloud; the telltale marker that meant a ship had jumped out …

But the *Coup de Grâce* hadn't jumped, only the drone.

The moment the cloud appeared, Dalk spun his ship around and nudged it behind the bulk of the *Basilica*, bringing it to a halt and then cutting power to all systems.

On the scanner a faint red mark appeared, rapidly closing on the flickering cloud. From his vantage point Dalk could just see Skin-tight's Viper. Right

CHAPTER SIX

about now she'd be scanning the cloud the drone had left. Advanced scanners could decode the destination ...

'Come on,' Dalk whispered to himself. 'Take the bait.'

A few moments passed and a second cloud appeared. Skin-tight had jumped. Dalk grinned, targeting his own scanners on it.

Destination coordinates: Mithra.

'Got you.'

The *Coup de Grâce* fired its drives back up and blasted away from the *Basilica*, its hyperdrive charging for its own jump, ready to head in the opposite direction.

'A wily one, that one,' the guard said, having observed the manoeuvre. 'Got to hand it to him though, clever move. Looks like the best of the lot. He's got the tech, the expertise and the contacts.'

Octavia nodded, but her expression was grim.

'I don't trust him. Do some digging. He was too smooth. He's covering something up. I reckon he plans on taking the cargo himself. He figured it was valuable.'

'Tricky to avoid revealing that. Why would anyone want a contract on some dumb kid and an old ship like that?'

Octavia pursed her lips and let out a sigh. 'You got homing tags on all of them?'

'All bolted up when they were docked. Telemetry too. We can track these low births anywhere in the galaxy. If they find him, we'll know.'

Octavia nodded.

'Get my ship prepped and ready to go immediately,' she ordered. 'It's going to be him. I want to be there when he tries to double-cross me. About time I had a little fun.'

* * *

Salomé pulled the straps about her, trying to stop herself from trembling. Hassan had directed her into the rear chair again and was busy adjusting the myriad switches and controls around the cockpit. A series of rising hums sounded around her as the ship readied itself.

She felt numb as she tried to piece together the fragments of memory that swirled around in her mind. They refused to coalesce. Every time she got close a headache would flash across her brow forcing her to stop. It was wearisome and maddening.

The faint recall of pain in her chest was a recurring theme. A sword, bright steel flashing before her eyes. Running, fleeing and panic. A shadow, a dark cloak twirling around a mysterious figure. Blood. Feelings of fear, defiance and betrayal. Blurred faces tantalised her, blending into a spinning maelstrom of out of focus faces. Voices that were achingly familiar but yet utterly unknown echoed around her, sometimes soft and reassuring, but more often tinged with warning, desperate calls and yells of anguish.

Then it was all gone again, infuriatingly ephemeral and elusive. The more she concentrated the more the memories receded from her. Her mind felt foggy, slow and unresponsive. She couldn't remember anything before seeing the young Commander who had woken her up. What had happened? Had he kidnapped her? Erased her memory? He wasn't to be trusted, that was for sure, yet he was the only person who knew anything about her. She was helpless.

If he hadn't done this who had? He'd said she was on board a ship. Why? He'd laughed at her inexperience with space flight, it seemed clear she'd never stepped foot onto a spacecraft before, so why had she been in one? Why had she been sealed in a pod? Who had done this? Why couldn't she remember? Was her memory permanently gone or would it return?

She'd heard her own voice as she spoke. She could speak. She had an Imperial accent. How did she know that? She remembered seeing the charts, the names, even the customs and clothes but the moment she tried to recall the detail …

… there was nothing. Did she have family? Parents? Siblings? A pet? She felt sick and confused. She stopped trying, concentrating on her breathing, hoping to settle her stomach and her fears.

What am I going to do?

The Commander didn't want her aboard; he was likely to abandon her at the first opportunity.

Then what? Despair clawed at her mind.

She trembled, pursing her lips and clenching her hands against the seat restraints. Something in her solidified. Anger rose. She'd not allow herself to

CHAPTER SIX

crumple, she was better than this. The strength of feeling surprised her. Pride and self-respect surged through her. She would find a way to understand and restore, no … reclaim her memory. No one would stand in her way. If someone was responsible, there would be retribution. She'd make sure of that.

Another memory flashed across her mind, unfamiliar, but yet well known. It prompted a strange ambivalence.

Never stop fighting until you can fight no more.

She let out her breath, aware she'd been holding it for some time. Where was that from? Beneath her the ship trembled and began to rise. Faint whirrings sounded through the hull; machinery performing its function as directed. She gripped the arms of her seat to steady herself.

Hassan chucked something back towards her. It was a plastic bag with some kind of face seal on it. She caught it.

'You'll need one of these,' he called out, still keeping his attention on the controls as the rocky landscape below dropped out of view.

'What's this?'

'Remlok. Some folks call it a barf-bag.'

'What's it for?'

'You'll see.'

Salomé felt something moving under her legs, her back and arms. Instinctively she jolted forward in her seat, but it was to no avail, the seat had moulded itself around her and was holding her in place in a strange gel-like substance.

Her short gasp of bewilderment was abruptly severed. The *Talon* lifted off and reached for the stars.

Chapter Seven

The *Coup de Grâce* gently coasted through the blackness, its immaculate time-stressed duralium reflecting starlight off its smooth tapered hull. It rolled to port, the pilot executing a smooth change of direction towards a dark planet, grey against the backdrop of bright stars.

Aboard, Dalk was scrutinising the passive scanner information being presented to him as his ship approached. It didn't take him long to find what he was looking for. The reading was subtle, but obvious to anyone who knew what to look for. The infrared scanner told a story; a faint red stain marked the surface of the planet, the telltale mark of residual heat. Another ship had recently passed this way.

Judging by the size of the reading the signal hadn't been left by a big vessel, it was right in the ball park for the Eagle. Dalk guided his ship downwards, confirming the strength and size. He had to know how far behind he was.

'Eight hours, give or take,' he said to himself with a satisfied sigh, before calling up the holofac chart of the nearby systems. He had already searched a number of the possible jump points the young pilot could have used. A few more hours and that trace would have faded away beyond detection.

The young man was reasonably canny. He could have easily kept jumping until he ran out of fuel and was forced to make a stop, but that sort of trail was easy to follow; the jump points were simple to read with enhanced scanners. By letting the record of his first jump decay into the darkness the pilot would have thrown many off his trail. Landing on the planet was another smart move. It was possible to see a ship against the darkness of space even with all power sources switched off, but hidden in the shadow of a deep crater it would be virtually undetectable.

Dalk's first hunch had paid off, now he had to strike lucky again.

The Eagle-class ships didn't have a huge hyperdrive range, so there were only limited locations available and it would need to refuel to make a further jump. If the pilot was sensible he'd avoid any official refuelling spots. That meant lesser known locations along the route. The Eagle didn't have a fuel scoop either, so he couldn't use a convenient gas giant.

But where?

Dalk studied the map. The pilot might make a detour to one of the many mining worlds in the sector to refuel. The *Zegami Foundry* wasn't too far away, a big metal refinery and fabrication plant, nicely off the beaten track.

Too much of a detour though …

Ferenchia seemed the most likely immediate destination. Even with the need to refuel the Eagle was still a long way ahead. Dalk couldn't arrive there ahead of his quarry, but with a bit of judicious plotting he could close the gap. He'd likely still have to locate them when he arrived. The system served as a major trading hub in this region. There was a lot of commerce, mostly provided by small time traders. It was the perfect place to hide a small ship.

'Set hyperdrive target to Ferenchia,' he called out. 'Spool and jump when ready.'

The computer emitted a double chime. Dalk settled back and waited as the rising hum signalled the power being bled into the core of the ship. With a brief flicker the *Coup de Grâce* disappeared from sight.

* * *

Jenu frowned at the communique that appeared in front of her. She was privy to most information that Tenim dealt with, but this particular item confused her. It was coded for Tenim directly and only his express permission had allowed her to view it. She replayed the short video. It was laced with static, as if it had been hastily recorded.

'… Where's the damn shipment?' Jenu recognised the disfigured face of Vargo, the Reclamist leader. She recoiled in distaste. 'We need those weapons and we need them now. What are you playing at?'

Some kind of explosion sounded in the background, static crashed across the display before the image stabilised again. Vargo was staring straight into the camera, leaning in close.

'The Imperials have sabotaged the mines, we're losing control of the slaves. Answer me for fuck's sake. You want your Tantalum? I want my weapons!'

Vargo moved away and the video cut out. Jenu leant back thoughtfully.

'And what do you make of that?' Tenim said, leaning across her and running

CHAPTER SEVEN

his hand carelessly up her body. She rolled over, stretching her arms up and wriggling closer, enjoying the warmth of their close embrace.

'It would seem our shipment has gone missing.'

Tenim pouted. 'My dear Jenu, I'm disappointed. Our shipment indeed.'

Jenu clicked her tongue. 'It was your idea.'

Tenim pulled a face of mock innocence. 'Me? How can you even think of such a thing? Is it my fault that pirates are making a profit out of the calamity that has befallen that system? Smugglers and brigands ferrying illegal weapons to revolutionaries? I would never countenance such behaviour.'

Jenu pushed him back down on the bed and rolled across him.

'Fine words to cover your nefarious plans,' she said, stopping his reply with a kiss. It was a moment before he was able to respond.

'Sometimes words are all we have.'

Jenu folded her arms and leant on his chest, looking into his eyes. Her relationship with Tenim had brought her financial independence, as much travel, responsibility and power as she had ever desired. All their other diversions had been most pleasurable. It had been a profitable association in every way except one; Jenu didn't trust him.

Part of her desired a simpler life away from all the intrigue and plotting endemic to Federation politics. She could be the wife of a better man, a man for whom lying was not as natural as breathing. Tenim would discard her the moment she was no longer useful. She'd hardened herself to these possibilities over the years, wondering how much of herself she'd compromised in the process. She was wise enough to know the intrigue and the danger excited her. Would she be bored by a more mundane existence?

It was all about timing your exit from the game. For now, Tenim still had much to offer her. 'Vargo is going to need more than words, I think.'

'Vargo who?'

Jenu laughed, despite herself. Tenim turned bare-faced lies into an art form.

Tenim stretched underneath her. 'It would seem that Octavia has decided to feed his battle, but starve his victory.'

'Surely it's in our interest to continue to help him?'

Tenim didn't answer. Jenu changed the subject.

'Do you think Octavia really has the Loren daughter?'

Tenim sighed. 'No doubt about it. Vargo and his cronies must have bungled their own assassination. Somehow the girl was spirited off planet into Octavia's waiting arms.'

'Does Vargo know?'

'I doubt it.'

'Shouldn't we let him know?'

Tenim smiled. 'Don't you think he's got enough to be worrying about?'

'What does Octavia want with her? She hates the Empire, I guess abducting a member of one of their high-ranking families counts for something. A bargaining chip?'

Tenim shook his head. 'That's not it. Octavia's no fool. She knows we'd pay a high price to get rid of the girl. She'd like nothing more than to humiliate the Imperials as well, so she won't turn the girl over to them either. She's stringing us all along.'

'So what is she trying to do?'

Tenim thought for a moment, looked aside and then looked back with a gleam in his eyes. 'She wants a war. The cunning bitch wants a full-scale war.'

Jenu recoiled. 'A war? Why?'

'Plenty of ways for her to profit,' Tenim replied. 'Selling arms to either side, information, spies, you name it. She's dangling the girl between us like a tasty morsel. The Imperials will be forced to defend their honour. With her, they have a legal claim to the system. We'll be forced to intervene to assert our claim and secure the Tantalum.'

'But the destruction, the waste …'

'Think about it. Octavia's militia is powerful, but there is no way she could challenge either us or the Imperials at present, but if a war is fought …'

'Both would be weakened.' Jenu whistled. 'Enough for her to assert her own claim and make it stick?'

'She already has most of the sector's trade in her pocket. A few bribes would bring the local independent traders along for the ride. Dish out a moon or a planet to a few big-time operators and you've got yourself an armada strong enough to take on anybody this far out. By the time the Federation or Empire could send reinforcements from the core worlds the battle would be over. Taking it back simply wouldn't be worth the investment.'

CHAPTER SEVEN

Jenu stretched. 'Wow, and I thought I was ambitious.'

'Octavia thinks she has the upper hand, that we'll be forced to invade because she's cutting off supplies to the Reclamists. She's trying to force our hand.'

'What are we going to do?'

'The idea of a full-scale war is less than appetising, either to ourselves or our Imperial counterparts. That leaves us with only one practical option.'

'Which is?'

Tenim drew in a deep breath and then let it out. He looked back at her. 'We'll have to deal with the Loren girl, and soon.'

'And Octavia?'

'She's going to end up like you,' Tenim said, a grin touching the edges of his mouth.

He rolled Jenu onto her back, caught her arms and moved across her, taking her with a practiced move of his hips.

'Oh yes?' she asked, demurely.

'Completely screwed,' he replied, his grin widening.

* * *

'Don't hold it so tight. Relax.'

Salomé loosened her grip on the flight yoke. The *Talon* jinked upwards and steadied out. At her request, Hassan had allowed her to try her hand at flying the ship while the hyperdrive was spooling up for another jump. She was seated in the forward pilot's chair, surrounded by all the instruments that marked the vitals of the vessel.

It had been overwhelming to start with, but it didn't take her long to realise that many controls and readouts around her were duplicated. Much of the ship was automatic. To fly the ship you could rely on various mechanisms to do their job. It was as close to being foolproof as it could be.

'All the flight assist computers are on,' Hassan said, when she queried some of the controls. 'You don't need to worry about most of it. Only the hardcore Elite pilots and the military switch them off.'

'Elite?'

Hassan scoffed. 'Don't worry, it's just bragging rights. Macho stuff, you know? I'm a better pilot than you.'

The flight controls were a surprise though, and nothing like she expected. They looked heavy and stiff, but even the lightest of touches moved the vessel around; it took a deft hand to be smooth with even the basic turns Hassan showed her.

'It's so quick,' she said, overcompensating in the opposite direction. The stars whirled around outside the windows. She felt her body jolt to one side as the turn came to a stop.

'It's a small ship,' Hassan replied. 'It was a half reasonable fighter craft when it was new. Centre the controls before you want to stop moving and it will glide to a stop.'

Salomé tried the technique and found she could anticipate when the ship would come to a halt. With a little practise she had it down to a fine art; rolling, pitching and yawing the ship around its centre axis with a great degree of precision.

Hassan watched as she rapidly improved. The girl's hand-eye co-ordination was pretty good; she would make a decent pilot given half a chance. She'd acclimatised to zero-G faster than most too. She'd looked a little grey for the last hour, but it no longer seemed to be bothering her. Some folks never got used to it.

Perhaps she might actually be useful.

With a fake ID he could sign her up as a co-pilot; he'd be able to jump further and faster with two pilots. He'd have to break with this part of space, maybe take a long haul to the Alliance worlds or take a chance out on the Frontier. It was better than losing out completely on this deal. Would she be up for that? One thing at a time.

'Now for the drives,' Hassan instructed. 'That lever on your right controls the main thrust. Notch it forward to the second stop. See that blue zone? Stick it there.'

She did as she was instructed and felt herself eased back into her seat as the *Talon* accelerated forwards. The ship reverberated with a turbine-like drone, rising in pitch, throbbing through the controls and making the hairs on the back of her neck rise in response.

CHAPTER SEVEN

You can feel the power!

'Try the turn now.'

Hassan watched as she gently moved the controls and saw her surprise when she found them reluctant to move, she had to push much harder than before. The *Talon* came about in a lazy arc to starboard.

'It's all stiff,' she complained.

'That's the ship letting you know how fast it's going. Tactile feedback. You can only pull as much of a turn as you can physically handle. Saves knocking yourself senseless halfway through a move.'

She pushed harder and Hassan braced himself as the *Talon* banked into a steeper turn. A firm pressure gripped their bodies, pushing at their chests and making it harder to breath. A flip to port gave them a brief respite before the G-forces pushed them in the opposite direction and the pressure returned.

'It's hard work,' she said, blowing her hair out of her face.

Hassan laughed. 'You've got to be fit and strong to fly a ship, especially in combat.'

'You've got weapons on board?' There was a hungry, excited tone in her voice.

Hassan looked at the scanner. There was nothing about, other than a few drifting rocks left over from a comet that had passed through a few months back.

'Sure thing. Flip those switches on the left bank.'

Salomé looked as Hassan indicated two small red hinged covers, which opened to reveal two switches. She pushed them both down. The illumination in the cockpit faded further and a quick rising hum resonated around them. Two gauges on the console moved up their dials. Salomé saw messages appear at the base of the console.

Pulse Lasers Deploying ... Shield generators online 100%.

An echoing clunk resonated through the hull. With a whine of servo motors Salomé saw a pair of complex contraptions rise from the forward hull and lock themselves into place. More screens flickered into life around her. A glowing representation of Hassan's ship appeared, surrounded by glowing cyan circles of light.

'Check the scanner,' Hassan instructed. 'Align the ship so the nearest blip is directly ahead.'

'What's out there?'

'Just rocks, see the colour coding? Rocks show up brown. If it's yellow it's a ship, if it's red it's a ship that's trying to kill you.'

'Oh.'

She brought the *Talon* around, noticing Hassan watching her as she slewed the ship with greater precision this time. As she looked up at the windows she caught sight of the orange holofac targeting display. In the centre was a complex cross-hair arrangement. It looked as if it were outside the ship, projected on the backdrop of space. It was an illusion, but very effective.

'That's where the gun is aimed,' Hassan said.

'Am I pointing in the right direction? I can't see any rock.'

'We're still kilometres away. You need to lock on the target. Just touch the blip on the console.' Hassan saw her stretch forward and select the target carefully. Ahead a series of triangles appeared, designating a patch of space. More information accompanied it; a distance indicator, slowly counting down.

'Line the ship up with the target and move in.'

Salomé pushed the throttle gently forward and banked the *Talon* upwards and starboard. The circles moved into the cross hairs. The reticule flickered for a brief moment, indicating a target lock.

Her reaction speed was impressive. Her fingers closed on the flight yoke trigger. A deep rumbling sound reverberated through the cockpit as the lasers discharged into space. Twin beams of coruscating light flashed out, lancing out into the distance before they flickered and died as she released the trigger.

'Your angle's wrong, you'll get an easier shot if you ...'

Salomé had already figured out her error. She moved the ship on a parallel course and then adjusted her angle of attack. The display locked on again and she squeezed the trigger. The rumble returned and a lance-like flash of light signalled the discharge of the lasers. A brief moment later she could see a rapidly expanding cloud of dust and debris which then slowly faded into the darkness.

The blip on the scanner faded away.

'I hit it!' Her excitement was palpable.

'Not bad,' Hassan acknowledged in surprise.

Wasn't expecting that.

CHAPTER SEVEN

She'd hit the rock from a three-kilometre range without the gimbals, eyeballs only, and on her second shot. He'd have bet good money she wouldn't have hit it at all. The girl had potential.

'Maybe you should try your hand at this.'

She closed the throttle, bringing the ship to a halt before spinning the pilot's chair around. 'Meaning what, exactly?'

Hassan smiled. 'I figure it this way. You've got no cash, no identity, no bio, no credit and no memory. I put you off at the next port and you'll be marooned. No telling what might happen to you. No one has much time for stowaways. Easy prey for a slaver crew maybe or a prostitution ring …'

Her eyes narrowed. 'Don't threaten me …'

'Easy, sister,' Hassan replied. 'You got to make money somehow. There's no free ride wherever you go. Not here, not out on the Frontier … especially not out on the Frontier.'

'Frontier? What's the Frontier?'

Hassan waved at the cockpit windows and sighed.

'Beyond the core worlds, beyond the trade routes. Out there. More worlds than you could ever count. Rich pickings if you find something worth having. Exploring where no one has gone …'

'Your point?'

'I have a proposal. You've got some skills. Why not ship in with me for a time?'

'With you?' Her voice had a strong note of disdain. 'Doing what, exactly?'

'This ain't a big ship, but it doesn't fly itself. With two pilots we could go further and faster. Trade on the longer runs, make more money. Run the ship, replace equipment, handle negotiations. Really set ourselves up properly. We could go exploring – the Frontier's the ideal place for folks who want to keep a low profile.'

'What's in it for me?'

'I'll get you ID, a credit account, a share in the profits. Teach you to fly. That will help you get started, maybe figure out who you are. After that, at least you'll have a trade, you can work your way on another ship if you want. Maybe find your way home.'

'What about this woman who is after you?'

Good question.

Hassan thought about it for a moment.

'We've got to keep moving. Octavia's influence only stretches so far, but she might have sent a bounty hunter after us. The independent worlds are our best bet. In the meantime we'll swap out the ship's transponder at the next base and recode it. That'll make us harder to track.'

'Is that legal?'

Hassan hesitated before responding. 'It's an old ship, stuff breaks. The transponder on this ship is decades old, probably about due to go pop.' He winked at her. 'You can't always get a new part.'

'So you'll take one from some other vessel.'

'I prefer to call it recycling.'

'And then what?'

'If we can make some lucrative runs we can trade in and swap to another ship. Then we're untraceable.'

Her face was uncertain. Hassan saw her eyes flicker from one side to another before she looked up.

'And how long do I have to work for you?'

Hassan grinned. 'Well let's see. Transport fees, rescue, medical care, not chucking you out of the airlock, putting up with the attitude, pilot's training ...'

'Don't forget compensation for shooting up my ship, kidnapping me and pointing a gun at my head,' she replied.

'How does six months sound? Thirty per cent of any profits, straight off the top. I'll even throw in your food.'

She pursed her lips. 'Thirty-five.'

'What makes you think you can negotiate? You've got nothing ...'

She grabbed his arm, turned it and pushed it back. He felt his bones click and his wrist lock in an uncomfortable position. She pushed slightly, a vengeful grin on her face. Pain jolted up his arm.

'Owww. Hey!'

'I might not remember,' she said softly. 'But whoever I am, I know how to fight. That's got to be worth something.'

He tried to pull his arm away but she just pushed the lock tighter. He yelled in surprise. It was a practised and effective move.

CHAPTER SEVEN

'All right, thirty-five it is. Let me go.' He rubbed his wrist after she released him. 'Gods, woman. What is that?'

She shrugged. 'Instinct maybe. It comes naturally.'

'You'll have to show me some time. Remind me to stay on your good side.'

'I want a bunk, as much privacy as is practical and in no way am I at your disposal for anything else. Clear?'

'Clear as the void, lady.' Hassan blinked in surprise at her business-like assertiveness.

'And you won't call me lady, either. Salomé's a ridiculous name, but it will do until I find out who I am. Are we agreed?'

She held out her hand towards him. He took it gingerly, but this time there was only a firm handshake.

'Six months, yeah?'

'Just remember,' she said. 'If you betray …'

Her eyes widened and the colour drained from her cheeks. Her hand went limp in his grasp. 'Hey, what's up? You remembering something?'

She sat stock still for a long moment before recovering and looking him in the eye. 'Don't think of double-crossing me, that's all.'

He had few doubts on that score. Whoever she was, she'd been thrown some serious flux before winding up on his ship. She was as tough as Duralium hull plating.

'A deal's a deal.' A buzzer went off.

'Hyperdrive is spooled,' Hassan announced, looking around at the indicators. 'Time for your next lesson. Want to try that?'

Salomé nodded and spun her pilot's chair around to face forwards once more.

'Disarm the weapons and shields … yeah that's it, flip the switches back up. The chart is over there, bring it up and tap the Ferenchia system. Got it?'

'Four light years,' Salomé read off the display. A whir and a mechanical thump signalled the weapons had been stowed.

'We've got a jump range of five. Just call up the jump control and we're set.'

'That's it?' She seemed surprised it was that easy.

'That's it. Just don't touch the flight controls. The ship can't be spinning when you jump.'

'Why not?'
'Because bad stuff happens if you do.'
'Bad stuff?' Salomé asked.
'Mis-jumps. Trust me, you don't want to know.'
Salomé touched the jump control. The *Talon* flickered and disappeared.

* * *

Plasma streaked past the cockpit windows, a burning hell of atoms ripped asunder by temperatures beyond imagination. Below the boiling maelstrom of sunspots and faculae rolled away, the surface of the star an almost infinite wall of emolliating fury. Ahead an incomprehensible arc of glowing fire curved up into space, magnetic field lines pulsing with more energy than a civilisation could consume in a thousand years; a solar flare a hundred thousand kilometres long.

Into this inferno flew the *Coup de Grâce*, its shields carving a flowing wake through the superheated gas. Heat shields strained at their limits, the cooling systems fighting a losing battle against the overwhelming rage of the star.

A trickle of sweat rolled down Dalk's forehead, but his grip on the flight controls never wavered. Fuel scooping in the atmosphere of a star was not for the faint hearted. Reckless in the extreme or the move of the desperate, it was a calculated chance to refuel sufficiently to intercept his quarry. To give him time to extract them before Octavia could find them.

Warning: Hull Temperature 125% of Tolerance. Abort manoeuvre!

Dalk had an experienced sixth sense for how much punishment his ship could take. He'd calculated his trajectory with utmost precision. Too deep and the *Coup de Grâce* would burn up in a flare of disintegrating plasma, lost in the blazing ferocity of the star's corona. Too shallow and the fuel scoop would pick up nothing of value.

Internal tanks full. Fuel scoop deactivated.

Dalk wrestled his ship upwards, gently pushing the drives to full power. The *Coup de Grâce* blasted away, its trajectory marked by a glowing stream of superheated solar atmosphere. The blackness of space beckoned.

A faint tinkling noise echoed through the ship as it cooled. Hull panels contracted as heat was radiated away into the void.

CHAPTER SEVEN

An audacious move, dangerous even. Danger was part of the job for any Elite combateer. High stakes and high risks for those that knew when to push and when to back off.

With the additional fuel Dalk could cut down his jump times dramatically. He was only two hours behind his quarry and gaining all the time. It wouldn't be long now.

The ship oriented itself … and jumped, leaving the blazing fury of the star light years behind.

* * *

The *Talon* materialised in the Ferenchia system. A series of quick transits pulled them into orbit space around the main planet. Known as the *aegis*, this area of space was supposedly a safe zone. Experience often taught otherwise.

Salomé could see a myriad of bright dots moving slowly against the background of stars. There were streams of lights in some places; queues of ships stacking up to dock or take a new course through the system. Ahead of them in the distance were bigger objects. Salomé glanced at the scanner, realising they were out of range. To be visible this far away …

'That's one of the main stations,' Hassan said, reading her thoughts. 'It's a beast, ten kilometres across at its widest point. Holds thousands of ships.'

Salomé blinked in surprise.

Ten kilometres?

'You should see the ones in the core worlds though,' Hassan said. 'There's one called Raymo's R & R & R, you wouldn't believe how big that is …'

'What about those others?' Salomé asked, gesturing at the other bright points of light.

'Those'll be friends of yours. His Majesty's Imperial Navy. They've usually got one of their flagships hereabouts. Reminds everyone how impressive they are.' The narrowband comm communication buzzed.

'Eagle Mark 1 *Talon*, this is approach control. State destination.'

Hassan toggled the comm and returned the call. 'Approach control. *Talon* receiving. Requesting clearance for surface approach. Spares and luxuries for sale planetside.'

'Standby, *Talon*.'

Salomé looked around. 'Problems?'

Hassan shook his head. 'They need to slot us into one of the traffic lanes. It's a busy system, that's a lot of work. Give 'em time.'

Ahead the space station grew larger. It was a vast wheel, turning slowly on a central axis where a large rectangular docking slit could be seen. The tiny lights of approaching ships could be seen in a series of parallel lines approaching the docking bay. To the rear was a separate section, which was stationary. Larger ships were docked nearby, connected to the hub of the station by various clamps and securing tethers.

'Eagle Mark 1 *Talon*. Vectors and descent profile are being sent now. Do not deviate from your assigned flight path.'

'Confirmed, approach control,' Hassan replied, 'and thanks.'

'Eagle Mark 1 *Talon*, handing off to port authority jurisdiction. Make contact after entry interface. Out.'

Hassan studied the data and configured the autopilot to manage the approach. The *Talon* banked around as he let the on board computers take control. Hassan frowned as he looked back at the series of Imperial ships that were holding in high orbit. One capital ship was fairly common, the Imperials liked to demonstrate their might to the outlying systems on regular occasions. Today there were a series of escort ships flanking the massive Interdictor battleship positioned adjacent to the station. Neat formations of fighter ships could just be made out escorting the mammoth vessels, alongside a menagerie of smaller frigates, destroyers and support vessels. This wasn't just the typical Imperial display. It was a task force.

It could just be an exercise, but Hassan had an uneasy feeling there was more to it than that. Moving an Imperial fleet through independent space was always going to raise a few eyebrows. He cast a glance across at Salomé.

Mysterious Imperial girl, mysterious Imperial ships.

It had to be a coincidence, she couldn't be that important could she? He scolded himself for being jumpy. A flagship like that meant a Senator of an entire system; it was nothing to do with his mysterious passenger. He needed to focus on the task in hand; a quick stopover to throw any pursuers off their tail.

CHAPTER SEVEN

The drives fired, nudging the *Talon* into a lower orbit and reducing its velocity relative to the planet. By silent autopilot command the ship flipped over and pitched up, angling itself for atmospheric entry.

'Gets a bit bumpy here,' he said. 'Make sure you're buckled up.'

Salomé had already done so. She was studying everything assiduously, filing the information away in her mind. Hassan watched her rehearsing what he'd already taught her. She was a quick learner, he'd not had to repeat a single instruction to her.

A few discreet enquiries via a few contacts might reveal who she was. Maybe there was a reward for her recovery, maybe he could even pull off a ransom? Somebody in Imperial space had to know who she was. He'd have to be careful about how he did that, assuming he wanted to keep his limbs intact. A shame in some ways, but less risky than keeping her aboard if she did have some kind of profile.

Ionised gas flickered around the cockpit windows as the ship entered the rarefied grasp of the upper atmosphere. Slight tremors caused the ship to vibrate and a distant roar signalled the growing density of the atmosphere.

It didn't last long. The stars above faded from sight as a pale azure glow surrounded them. The sense of deceleration was palpable. The streams of glowing gas faded away as the ship adjusted its configuration. Outside small flaps corrected the aerodynamic profile of the vessel, steering towards the correct approach for the city.

Hassan felt the increasing grip of gravity pulling at him. It was accompanied by a sense of unease. He didn't plan on this stopover being a lengthy one, but there was plenty to do.

Clouds whipped past the cockpit windows. A sizable storm was brewing to the west of the city. They could see lightning crackling around the towering white peaks as they flew across far above the clouds. Below it was pouring with torrential rain, yet up here the sun always shone.

'Eagle Mark 1 *Talon*, this is port authority. You are secure from ablative phase. Follow guidance beams. Landing confirmed at Bay 48, Plaza 16.'

Hassan thumbed the comms again. 'Port authority. Confirmed, 48, 16.'

The clouds disappeared astern. Salomé watched the approaching city through the cockpit window with wide eyes. The central buildings were dramatic. Lofty crystal spires speared the sky, rising kilometres above the surface. Delicate buttresses connected some of them, looking impossibly fragile at this distance, sparkling in the light of the system's bright star. Every one was designed with a variation on a smooth organic curve, blending into each other and sweeping out into smooth enormous arms at ground level, within which nestled beautifully manicured gardens and immaculate forested areas. Above them tiny transports zipped and turned in ordered procession. Salomé could just make out tiny figures moving in the wide streets. Larger spacecraft were arriving and departing all around them.

She sighed, puzzled at the way she felt. There was something captivating, even enthralling, about travelling between worlds. It had always sounded so mundane, but watching the sky brighten from the darkness of space, seeing the sun disappear behind a distant horizon, watching the planet rise up beneath you, seeing the city come into sight. There was beauty here, even poetry, something beyond just the mechanics of flying. She nodded to herself. Wonder, that's what it was; the call of exploration and the unknown. She felt it, pulling at her soul.

To take a ship, head out into the unknown ... what's out there?

She gasped involuntarily with the thought of it all.

The main city fell behind them and the *Talon* slowed, banking and descending. The buildings out here were less impressive and far less attractive. Blocky structures mixed with domes, towers and haphazardly planned expressways. As they continued to overfly the area Salomé could see a wide expanse, with hundreds of vessels clustered below. Hassan toggled a series of switches and a faint whirring announced the extension of the undercarriage. The ship came to a halt above an empty expanse where a large 48 could be seen marked on the ground. With a blast of thrusters the ship settled down with a light thump.

The narrowband comms buzzed.

'Eagle Mark 1 *Talon*. Welcome, Commander. The Landing fee of fifteen credits has been deducted from your account.'

Hassan shut down the *Talon*'s avionics and sprang up from his seat. 'Gets more expensive all the time,' he muttered. 'All set?'

CHAPTER SEVEN

'What, precisely, are we doing?' Salomé asked.

'I need to order some fuel, supplies, and sort out that transponder.'

'And what about me?'

'You're going to need a bio-check and immunity meds. Once that's done we'll see if we can get you that ID.'

Hassan led her down from the cockpit, through the living quarters and into the cargo bay. He punched a large control on the bulkhead. With a clunk and a hiss, the rear quarter of the bay folded outwards and a ramp lowered into position. A blast of humid hot air wafted into the bay. Salomé recoiled in surprise.

'It's hot!'

'Tropical latitude,' Hassan explained. 'We're not far from the equator.'

He walked down the ramp and stepped onto the smooth tarmac of the landing plaza. Salomé followed him out, hesitating as she took in the startling sight of huge vessels moving around above her. Some were leaving, some arriving just as they had. Others were loading or off-loading cargo using huge mechanised units. The tall buildings of the city could be seen far in the distance, framed by the thundery clouds they'd flown above on the way in. People shouted orders, gesturing above the din of noisy loaders, ship thrusters and the occasional roar of a vessel overhead.

I'm on another world.

'Over here!' Hassan called, grabbing her hand.

Salomé saw a small ground transport had arrived next to them. A door slid open and they climbed in. It was cool within, a welcome relief from the oppressive heat and humidity of the landing zone. The door slid shut and the transport whisked them towards the main transport hub at the centre of the spaceport. The ride was short; Salomé only had time to register the transport passing a wide selection of ships of all shapes, sizes and configurations. She'd never imagined a place could be so busy.

'Let me do the talking,' Hassan advised.

She looked across. 'Why?'

'Because you don't have an ID,' Hassan replied. 'Looks odd.'

'Odd?'

'Yeah, odd. If the border controls hear your accent they'll start asking questions. You're too posh. So unless you want them to stick probes in all of your holes – shut up. Got it? You're just any old ship-hand. Don't make eye contact.'

'What are you going to say?'

'Hopefully nothing. They don't really give a 'goid where you come from out here as long as you're clean. That's the problem. You're going to need the bio-checks. They'll pick up you've got no immuno.'

'So how do I ...'

'A brief stopover in the hospital. Don't worry, it's only a jab and a zap. I'll pick you up from the medbay in an hour or so; it don't take long.'

The transport came to a halt and slotted itself neatly into the wall of the transport hub. They exited and were quickly shepherded into a facility marked 'DeCom'. A number of folks in classic ostentatious Imperial attire were standing in a line as a team of medics, covered from head to toe in one-piece fitted outfits, scanned them with a variety of portable equipment and then guided them through an archway. A light signalled green for most of them.

A light flashed red and a buzzer sounded for one of the people in the queue and Salomé watched as they were diverted into a separate corridor.

'What do they do?' she whispered to Hassan.

'It's just medicine, everyone has it.' Hassan nudged her forward.

The queue moved further forward and Salomé found herself at the front. With a wave from one of the medics she stepped forward. Their portable scans seemed to go ok, but when she stepped through the arch the buzzer went off and the red lights flashed. She jumped and looked nervously back at Hassan. He stepped through with a green light.

'This way,' one of the medics instructed her.

'You'll pick me up?' she asked Hassan, ignoring the medic.

'Yes. It's routine, just go ...'

'Does it hurt?'

'No, not at all.'

Salomé's face dropped. 'That bad?'

'Stings like hell for a bit,' he grinned. 'See you in an hour.'

'Miss ...' the medic interrupted.

Salomé scowled, but allowed herself to be led away. She was escorted into an airlock of some sort. The door closed behind her.

CHAPTER SEVEN

'Please lie down on the floor,' an automated voice announced. 'Decontamination procedure is starting.'

The interior was small and featured a series of tiny vents and tiny bright blue lights. As she leant forward to inspect them, jets of chilly vapour surged out. She backed off, caught a whiff of the vapour and slumped to the floor in seconds.

* * *

Hassan hurried through the spaceport, taking a lift down to the lower levels of the building. These areas were mostly filled with machine shops, ship repair outfits, breakers and unofficial dealerships. It took him only a few minutes to locate what he was looking for: a less than salubrious looking parts store.

An extremely large woman was flopped behind the shop-front, her eyes glazed over as some soap opera played itself out in her vision. Hassan drummed his fingers on the scarred and dirty surface of the counter. The woman looked up in annoyance.

'Yeah?'

Hassan tried a friendly smile. It seemed to have no effect, the woman continued to glare at him, wiping spittle from her mouth with the back of her hand. A small pile of crumpled stim packets were carelessly discarded at her feet. Given the number she'd ingested he was lucky she was intelligible.

'Need a DB50 transponder.'

She eyed him suspiciously. 'You got paperwork?' Hassan tried the smile again. 'I've got cash.'

The woman's lips pursed in disapproval, but she slowly got to her feet. 'Five credit mark-up for cash. Transponder is thirty-five.'

'Done.'

The woman hobbled back into her store, muttering under her breath as she limped down an aisle crammed full of racks of various bits of junk and spare parts. She grabbed a small box with a thick conduit hanging off one side and limped back towards him, plonking it on the counter.

'Transponder.'

'Come with a new squawk?'

'Dunno,' she replied, eyeing him suspiciously. 'You're supposed to rekey it to the same squawk you had before. Law says so.'

Hassan nodded. She'd given him what he needed and covered her own backside. Hassan couldn't help but glance at her obese frame. Covering her backside was a considerable achievement.

He flipped the necessary credits onto the counter and the woman settled back down with a thick sigh.

No receipt, no trace. Cash is always king.

His next stop took him to a comm terminal. He locked himself inside the small cubicle and paid for an encrypted link, typing in a complex code. He sat back as the connection was made.

A thick jawed, heavy set face appeared, dotted with rough stubble. The man was chewing something as he looked around, spitting it out as he recognised Hassan's face. The background on the viewer was blurred, probably deliberately.

'Hey, if it isn't the cutest little trader in space. How you doing, Hassan? Still flying that flux-stained excuse for a ship?'

'Same old,' Hassan replied, 'and I thought you told me it was a fantastic craft for the discerning young buyer with high hopes and big dreams.'

'Time you traded up, fella. Successful young entrepreneur like you. Should be in a Viper by now. Got a couple in as it happens …'

'Not looking to buy. Looking to make a deal.'

Canos licked his lips.

'You're calling me crypto, got something interesting?'

'A couple of things as it happens.'

'Yeah?'

Hassan gestured at the screen and a schematic of Salomé's bio-pod appeared. Canos studied it carefully for a moment.

'Imperial shiny stuff. Classy. What is it? Bio-tech?'

'It's some kind of new cryo-system, diagnostics, body repair, genetics, memory mods – you name it.'

'Sounds expensive.'

'Guessing it is.'

'Where'd it come from?'

CHAPTER SEVEN

'It was just lying around.'

Canos laughed. 'Well, wasn't that just handy for you. Funny how careless some folks are, eh?'

'Like you wouldn't believe.'

'What you looking for?'

'I need a new ID, a cargo of luxuries and thirty light years' fuel.'

Canos frowned. 'ID? You thinking of changing your name?'

'It's not for me.'

Canos rubbed his stubble. 'You do live an interesting life, kid. Sounds like a story there.'

'Needs to be quick too.'

'Now there's a surprise,' Canos replied. 'Send over his profile and we'll sort it.'

'He is a she.'

Canos leant closer to the camera. 'Hey, you finally scored, kid? Or just kidnapped some pretty from a backwater for a bit of fun in the void?'

'She's a passenger needs ferrying, that's all.'

Canos winked. 'Gotcha. Let's have a look.'

Hassan sent Salomé's record across the link. A holofac representation of her appeared on the screen and rotated slowly. Canos studied the image for a moment.

'Not bad, fella. Not bad. I would too.'

Hassan figured it didn't matter what he said. Canos had already made up his mind as to his motives.

'She's …'

'No need to be embarrassed, kid. You'll need to bring her in for the bracelet, she with you?'

'Just getting her bio done.'

Canos nodded. 'Reckon we can deal. I'll arrange for the Imperial tech to be offloaded and we'll pack you full. Good?'

'Deal.'

The video link terminated.

'Stupid little shit,' Canos muttered, shaking his head.

He sat back, watching Salomé's rotating image. With a quick gesture he transferred the image to another projector and then let her now life-size image rotate around in front of him.

'But you on the other hand … your card is marked, sweetness. I was hoping you might turn up here.'

Chapter Eight

The *Coup de Grâce* arrived in the Ferenchia system. Dalk was faced with deciding on his next course of action. His quarry could be anywhere and he had to figure out where to start looking.

He was working on the assumption that the young man suspected he'd be followed and would be taking steps to be as elusive as possible. Dalk hoped the pilot would underestimate how quickly he'd caught up. By his calculations he was only half an hour behind by now. Kahina was somewhere close by.

The transponder was the key weakness. All the time a ship was active its transponder would, by law, respond to basic identification checks. Ship systems were always active when on the move, but crucially, they were also active when docked in stations. To power down the vessel, the young man would have had to have gone planetside. That narrowed down the options considerably.

Dalk sighed ruefully. Only an entire planet to search.

If he had the cash the young man might just buy a ship and make good his escape. It would be hard work to track him if he did so, Dalk would have to gain access to the official transfer records. Ownership transfer was heavily bureaucratic – mostly to stop folks from dodging fines and putting future owners at risk from bounty hunters.

And I hate paperwork.

Flying around in a battered old Eagle didn't scream plenty of cash; it seemed unlikely that the young man would have the funds.

But if he only intends to change the transponder.

The youth would have to go somewhere with a thriving black market, no reputable shipyard would swap a transponder out without rekeying it to the original code. That really only left the main city. It was the biggest and busiest planetside habitation in the system. There was plenty of scope for underhanded trading down there.

Dalk quickly requested the necessary orbital insertion and descent authorisation. With luck his chase would soon be over. The young man could fend for himself with Octavia. With Kahina aboard and a quick jump to Haoria they'd be out of her reach and he could reassert his plan for Chione.

Dalk eyed the Imperial capital ships, holding station in orbit. Time was running short; Imperial forces were already massing.

The *Coup de Grâce* blasted down through the atmosphere, switching to its atmospheric thrusters and extending flight panels as it hit the dense lower atmosphere. Dalk saw the city emerge through a bank of heavy thundery cloud, the dreamy spires visible even at dozens of kilometres out. He triggered a series of active scans as he passed over the various designated landing areas using the information Octavia had provided him. It didn't take long.

There were three Mark 1 Eagles docked around the city. One looked particularly tatty and battered. It closely matched the visual record Octavia had provided. Dalk smiled as his ship was routed to an adjacent landing bay just half a kilometre away.

'Got you.'

* * *

Salomé woke and found she was moving. Someone was pushing her along a clean white gently curving corridor in some kind of mobile chair. She shook her head to clear it.

She tried to sit up, but found she could hardly move. A feeling of nausea washed over her. She swallowed and tried to breathe deeply. Her arms and legs ached horribly.

'Don't try to move,' said a man's voice, cultured and educated. Salomé felt a hand on her shoulder. 'There's a restraining field to keep you safe. Some people don't react well to the drugs.'

Salomé remembered what Hassan had said about not talking too much and decided not to answer.

'Doctor Graham, by the way. Immuno hazard department. You've just had the full works. It's not safe to venture into space without proper meds.'

Salomé let out a breath, trying to ease the pain in her limbs. Her head was throbbing too. 'Head hurting?'

'Yes ...'

CHAPTER EIGHT

'That was your own fault,' the Doctor said. 'Didn't you hear the machine tell you to lie down? You knocked your head when the treatment started.'

'Oh, sorry. Doctor ...?'

There was something slightly unusual about the man, but she couldn't quite identify what it was. She wanted to turn around and have a look, but the seat prevented her. His voice was measured, refined and sophisticated, but he seemed slightly distracted and there was a subtle but distinctly odd pause each time he started speaking.

Almost as if ...

'Call me John,' he said, cutting across her thoughts. 'Don't worry, it'll pass. I assume you've never been off-world before?'

'Not that I can remember,' Salomé replied, truthfully.

That pause again ...

'You've had the full spectrum profile,' he said. 'Don't worry, the ache is temporary and you won't need another for two years.'

Salomé found herself wheeled into a wide room which featured a series of large windows along one side. It seemed to be a recovery ward. Through the window Salomé could make out immaculately manicured gardens framed with strange exotic plants. Huge leathery bird-like creatures circled them, occasionally swooping down through the gardens. Salomé watched them, fascinated.

Dotted around the room were a variety of medical stations, each featuring an array of monitoring equipment around a central couch. Some were occupied, but most were empty. It seemed to be mostly older folk. Unlike the faded ship's overalls that she wore, the others were dressed in flamboyant outfits with dramatic collars, frills and colourful dresses or pantaloons. The women, and some of the men, wore thick and heavy make up, making them look as extraordinary as the flora outside. It reminded her of something.

Hats ... something about hats ...

Salomé found herself reversed into one of the stations and then gently helped across into the couch. She settled down and felt the material around her adapt to her shape and posture. It was supremely comfortable. She stretched, adjusting her position and trying to relax.

'Stay still,' John said. 'You'll be weak for a bit, but you should be up and about in an hour at most. The re-vig will have kicked in by then. Try to get some rest. I'll be back to give you the booster and then you can go.'

Salomé nodded. It wouldn't be difficult to have a snooze, she felt exhausted. The Doctor left her and moved to the station next door. She watched him for a moment, trying to figure out what had made her feel ill at ease. Dark haired with just a trace of grey, middle-aged, of average height and build with a slightly jowly face, he looked fairly unassuming. Nothing seemed out of place, but she couldn't shake off the odd sense that she'd seen him somewhere before.

Salomé frowned and put it down to the drugs. She turned her attention to the birds for a few moments before she became aware of voices. The Doctor seemed to having a hard time placating the patient next to her. Salomé looked across and saw an old woman pointing an unsteady finger, scolding him.

'Don't you be telling me what I can and can't do,' the old woman said. Her voice was crotchety with a slight warble, but there was no doubting the determination in her eyes.

'You must rest, the treatment …'

'I didn't get to live to this age by sitting around on my backside wasting time,' the old woman said. 'I've been from one end of space to the other and I could tell you stories …'

'I know, I know,' the Doctor's voice was patronising.

The old woman was infuriated. 'I was an Elite combateer once you know. Time was when that commanded some respect …'

'That's lovely. Just lie back …'

'I don't want to lie back.' The old woman batted him away. 'Get on with treating some sick people and leave me be. You're not wiping the drool from my old grey lips. I can do that myself.'

'If you're sure you don't need …'

'I can manage!'

The old woman scowled and Salomé watched as the Doctor beat a hasty retreat, clearly glad to have an excuse to leave. The old woman settled back for a moment, closing her eyes and letting out a sigh of relief. Salomé watched for a while, puzzled. The woman's voice had an unusual twang; it certainly wasn't Imperial like her own.

'Useless flux-stain,' the woman muttered.

CHAPTER EIGHT

It was impossible to tell how old she was. Her face was lined and wrinkled. Her arms were thin and delicately boned, her skin pale with only a few age spots. Her hair was straight, grey for the most part and almost transparent at the ends, but it held just a faint hint of the brown that must have been the natural colour from her youth. It was simply brushed into two neat folds on either side of her head. The skin on her cheek was stretched slightly, revealing a thin, almost invisible, scar that looked like a knife wound from long ago. Unlike most of the other patients Salomé had seen she wore no make up, no jewellery or other adornment. She was dressed in a simple medical smock.

A frown crossed the woman's face and she opened her eyes, looking across at Salomé, as if aware she was being scrutinised.

'You got a problem, girl?' The woman asked. Salomé was confronted with a pair of deep brown eyes that still sparkled with fierce intelligence. There was something else there too; the gaze was hard and almost brutal.

Salomé tried a faint a smile. 'I've got a lot of problems.'

The woman cackled and her face relaxed. 'You and me both, sister. What you in for?'

'Immunisation.'

'Sucks doesn't it,' the woman replied. 'Really knocks the crap out of you. Better than dying out in the void though. There's enough out there trying to kill you from outside without worrying about what might be killing you from inside.'

'How about you?'

'Replacing this, replacing that,' the woman said with a grin. 'Not sure how much of me is original anymore.'

There was a flicker of light outside the windows and a ship flashed past, too quick to make out other than a blur of duralium hull. It had been surprisingly close to the ground. A moment later a faint rumble echoed through the building. The birds scattered and disappeared from view.

'Boy racers,' the woman tutted. 'I'd teach them a lesson. Flux-stains, the lot of them.'

'You fly?' Salomé asked.

The woman gave her a disparaging look.

'Now? Don't make me laugh. But I did. Oh I flew all right.' She paused for a moment as memories flooded through her mind. 'None of this namby pamby flight assist stuff they use now. Real flying. I was Elite, you know ...'

'I heard you say. What does that mean?' Salomé remembered the word from the argument with the Doctor and how disparaging Hassan had been about it.

'Deadly? Dangerous? Elite?' The woman rolled her eyes at Salomé's blank look. 'You've no idea what I'm talking about, have you?'

Salomé shook her head.

'Kids.' The woman waved her hand vaguely around her. 'They've mucked it up of course, fiddled with the ratings so much now that no one can figure it out. Used to be simple back in my day. You spaced a ship and you got a rating. The more you killed the more fearsome you became. Lots of folks got to be dangerous; you didn't last long if you weren't dangerous, you know.'

The woman paused for a moment chuckling to herself.

'A few got to be deadly, but Elite ... well, we were special. People respected us. Being Elite meant something out on the Frontier ...'

'You've been to the Frontier?'

'To it, through it, past it,' the woman smiled. 'Don't tell no one, but I got as far as the Formidine Rift, not many folks can say that! No one has gone past it and lived to tell the tale.'

'The Formid ...?'

'Edge of the galactic arm. Take a line from Reorte to Riedquat to the edge of the arm and ... keep going.' The woman grimaced. 'Stars thin out, you can see the whole galaxy just hanging there. I took a fancy to going exploring after I lost ...' she paused, a sadness creeping across her face, '... had some time to spare. Quiet for the most part, until ...'

'Until what?'

'Let's just say there was some serious shit out there, stuff you wouldn't believe. No really – no one believed me, said it was all a fabrication. I had no proof, you see, and they edited my memory afterwards. Ah, it'll all come back to bite them one day, it's all there in the Imperial databanks somewhere – and they thought the Thargoids were trouble ...'

The woman pointed a wavering finger at Salomé.

'Going out to the Frontier isn't for the faint hearted, you know. You have to

CHAPTER EIGHT

fight for it. I almost never made it back. You need a tough ship and more than enough talent behind the guns.'

'You flew a ship in combat too?' Salomé asked, in surprise.

The woman snorted. 'Girl, I took out an iron-assed Python on my twentieth birthday using nothing but a Sidewinder and pulse laser. I was born in space, a trading family for three generations. I was so hot I could shoot missiles down by hand – I had to, couldn't afford an ECM early on; bet you don't see that sort of flying nowadays.' The woman looked across with a flicker of excitement in her eyes. 'I don't suppose you've heard of the Tionisla system?'

Salomé shook her head as the woman continued reminiscing.

'Pity. It's a long way from here. Commissioner Hughes gave me the Crossed Dagger, you know, damn stupid ceremony that was. I shot down gangs of pirates, escaped bounty hunters. Even took on a Thargoid mothership once and I won ...'

She looked away, a sadness creeping into her voice.

'All ancient history now I guess. I had a rep in the old worlds, see. My ship was a real beauty. Damn, I miss that ship.'

The woman coughed briefly.

'What ship was it?' Salomé asked the obvious question.

'Cobra, you know, Mark 3 ...' Salomé didn't understand much of what the woman was talking about. '... with the outrigger thrusters? It was an Apocalypse engineering special. Hardly see them now ... proper old school ship ... wouldn't have slipped the bounty hunters without it ... not like these modern designs.'

Bounty hunters? Hassan said something about ...

'You escaped bounty hunters?' Salomé asked. 'How?'

The woman looked up with a mischievous grin. 'That was one of my better tricks, you know. He had a better ship, tougher even than mine. Couldn't outfight him, had to run. Shields were gone, laser overheated and the missile launchers had jammed. Hull was leaking plasma. It was a last resort, oh yes. Don't you be trying it. Not safe, not safe at all.'

'What did you do?'

'Mis-jumped!' the old woman cackled. 'Jammed a spoke in the drive and clear disappeared into witchspace. Bounty hunters track your hyperspace cloud, see? Figure out where you're going. But if you mis-jump they see you go one way, but you end up … somewhere else. Got away scot-free. Saved my life that day it did.'

'Mis-jumped,' Salomé said, thoughtfully. Hassan had said something about mis-jumps. 'But isn't that …'

'Dangerous? Sure as ships is ships, kid. Last resort of the desperate.' The woman settled back in her bed, her eyes drooping wearily. 'Those were the days,' she said, as if to herself, her voice softening.

'Sounds like it was fun,' Salomé said, with a faint smile.

'Right on,' the woman whispered, her eyes closing. 'Quite a saga it was. Life on the Frontier; not easy, but one hell of a ride. Elite combateers, we always … always made a difference …'

She was asleep, her frail body sinking back into the comfortable grasp of the medical couch.

The Frontier, everyone talks of the Frontier.

'Hey!' A fierce whisper came from the opposite direction.

Salomé turned to look and saw Hassan peering around the edge of the ward. On catching her attention he walked in.

'You ok?'

'I am now,' Salomé replied. 'It hurt like hell though. Did you get my ID?'

'It's arranged, but you need to come with me to get it set up. Let's get you out of here.'

He pressed some controls on the cubicle. The bed rose up, levering Salomé into a standing position.

'Wait,' Salomé whispered urgently. 'The Doctor said I needed a booster …'

'Only so they can charge more credits,' Hassan replied. 'You don't need it. Come on.'

He pulled her up and dragged her along behind him. She still felt a little stiff, but the pain had gone.

* * *

CHAPTER EIGHT

Dalk walked through the series of terminal buildings until he was standing adjacent to the Eagle. A brief inspection confirmed it was the right ship, and a few discreet checks showed it was currently unoccupied.

The Eagle was being loaded by automechs. A series of canisters were being crated aboard. It looked like the ship would soon be ready to depart.

The pilot would be somewhere nearby. All Dalk had to do was wait.

* * *

'He's back, boss.' One of Canos' bouncers leant into the room that served as the HQ for Canos' operation. It was a simple affair, a series of prefab constructions on the edge of the spaceport. There was storage for a dozen ships, some ready to go, some under repair. Basic medical facilities and cargo storage pens accounted for the rest of it. The centre of the complex was reserved for accommodation, which featured a brothel and an unlicensed 'recreational' area. Both were well attended by the local clientele.

Canos looked up, holding up a hand for silence. He turned his attention back to the holofac transmission still playing in the air above his desk, his fingers steepled in front of him as he reclined in his chair.

'He's here.'

'Is he alone?' a voice crackled back. It was clipped and transposed, classic hallmarks of a voice obfuscator.

'Nah. The girl is with him.'

'You understand about the girl? Good. Detain them both until I arrive. I'll be with you in an hour.'

'I'll want paying.'

'Hand the girl to me safe and sound and you'll be able to retire. Safe, sound and … unspoilt. Are we clear?'

'I get it.'

The holofac transmission flickered and shut itself down. Canos poured himself a tumbler of Anlian gin from an ornate glass carafe, taking a sip before beckoning to the bouncer.

'Danz, send 'em in.'

Hassan led Salomé through Canos' complex. It was dark inside, lit by strobing pulses of light and obscured by plumes of sweet-smelling intoxicating smoke. Loud and rhythmic music assaulted her ears. She watched, in surprise, the antics of scantily clad women and men performing strange feats of acrobatic prowess on small raised platforms for the delight of a noisily jeering crowd. Drinks, drugs and stims were being consumed with abandon all around her. As she watched, one large individual collapsed to the floor. His companions laughed uproariously.

'This way,' Hassan yelled at her, giving her arm a yank.

Salomé could see a large man waiting beside an unobtrusive doorway. He was huge, muscled and looking in their direction. As he caught sight of them he gestured briefly for them to follow him.

'Who's that?'

'His name's Danz.'

'And what does he do?'

'He ... keeps an eye on things. Remember, let me do the talking ...'

Salomé looked up at the man as they came close. He was a good half metre taller than her. He wore only a pair of loose fitting trousers and a T-shirt. A gun was strapped conspicuously by his side. He spared her a brief glance and then gestured for them to go through the door way. The door slid back and they moved inside. Salomé heard him step in behind them.

Hassan led her inside. A short corridor led to a bare and simple room containing a few unhealthy looking plants and a tired desk. Behind the desk a man sat, hands steepled in front of him, watching them as they entered. He wasn't as big as Danz, but he was bigger than Hassan. Thin greasy hair sat on a pale unhealthy looking pockmarked face that smiled a lot, but not often for the right reasons. Salomé was immediately on her guard.

She looked across at Hassan. He looked nervous. The man behind the desk saw it too and Salomé saw the brief impression of a smirk form on his features. She wondered if Hassan really knew what he was doing. If these men caused trouble there was no way he was going to be able to protect her. She saw him look briefly around, his gaze lingering on the holster at Danz's side. She saw

CHAPTER EIGHT

Danz look back, stretching to his full height. Hassan swallowed, nervously eyeing the bigger man's muscular arms and torso.

Salomé tensed. The man behind the desk was looking at her intently. She looked back at him, feeling his eyes scan up and down her body. Something about her intrigued him, she saw a flicker of puzzlement cross his face as he appraised her appearance. She stood up even straighter and returned his gaze without flinching. The man licked his lips.

'Canos,' Hassan said, by way of an introduction.

'Hassan, good to see you again so soon.'

'Got that ID for us?' Hassan asked.

Canos got to his feet. 'One thing at a time, my young friend. You're forgetting your manners. Aren't you going to introduce me to your delightful companion?'

Hassan sighed. 'Look we're in a hurry.'

Canos leant back in his chair, his voice firm. 'Indulge me.' Salomé looked across at Hassan, who nodded briefly.

'My name is Salomé,' she said.

She saw Canos' eyebrows rise as she spoke. Evidently he was surprised. Her tone of voice, perhaps? Hassan had said she sounded posh.

'Welcome to our humble abode, m'lady,' Canos said, waving his hands in a flowery manner and bowing his head. 'What can we do for you?'

'I need an ID.' She looked at Hassan. 'He says you can get me one. Is he right?'

Canos nodded. 'He is, sweetness, he is indeed. But fake IDs are illegal, how do I know this isn't some elaborate sting by the local enforcers? You don't sound like the sort of person who needs an ID. In fact, I can't help wondering why you need an ID at all.'

'That's none of your business,' Salomé replied.

'Maybe, maybe not,' Canos admitted, 'but you won't get one anywhere else around here, so you can humour me.'

Canos folded his arms and stretched back in his chair, propping his feet up on his desk. 'We don't want any trouble,' Hassan said.

'I'm not giving you any trouble, fella,' Canos said, picking up a small bracelet from a tray in front of him. 'Got your ID right here and a hundred credits to get her going. I just want to know where your little pretty here thinks she's going all dolled up in that fetching ship's onesie. She isn't a spacer, that much is clear.'

'I told you she's a passenger,' Hassan said.

'So where you going, pretty?' Canos asked, ignoring Hassan. Salomé didn't answer. Canos snorted. 'Where you come from? Can you tell me that? No?'

Hassan stepped forward. Salomé saw the bouncer move in behind him. 'Sale's been done. You've got the Imperial tech …'

'And you have your cargo as agreed. Deal's changed though, kid. You didn't level with me.'

'What are you talking about?' Hassan's voice shot up an octave.

Canos leant back. Salomé was aware his gaze rested on her for a moment.

'Your woman here is hot and not just as a piece of pretty. She's got an appointment with a very important person and I'm here to make sure she makes it.'

She saw Hassan's anger and frustration as he jumped forward, but he only made half a step before Danz grabbed him and swiftly immobilised him.

'We had a deal …'

'You messed with Octavia Quinton, kid,' Canos said with a shrug. 'That was a dumb call. You really thought you could take her for a ride and survive? There's Elite pilots out there that wouldn't face her down. Gotta admire your pluck, but she owns this entire sector and she's got deep pockets.'

'You're going to turn us over?'

Canos shrugged. 'You're catching on. She'll be here inside the hour. She'll have her fun with you, but you're not what she's after. Octavia wants something else. She wants …' Canos turned to look at Salomé, '… you.'

Salomé retreated a step. Hassan struggled, but Danz clamped down on him. Hassan yelped and relented.

Canos got to his feet and walked around his desk, pulling a gun and pointing it towards her.

'I thought you said we could trust him,' she snapped at Hassan, not taking her eyes off the gun.

'Business is always a fluid thing, pretty,' Canos replied. 'Turn around and put your hands behind your back.'

CHAPTER EIGHT

Salomé glared, but slowly turned around. Sound more than sight told her Canos had holstered his gun. She tipped her head and glimpsed a pair of wrist binders. She felt flesh as his hand closed round one of her wrists. His other hand snaked around her waist, giving a slight squeeze.

'Nice ...'

A red mist flooded her vision, anger coursing through her, burning hot. Another man trying to take advantage, using her for his own ends.

She spun, not thinking, just reacting. She grabbed his wrist with a deft twist of her own, stepping back and pulling him off balance. The binders flew across the room. Canos' yell choked as Salomé's fist crunched into his windpipe. He staggered back, gasping for air, stumbling across his desk. Salomé leapt forward to snatch the carafe, smashing the top. Liquid and glass sprayed in an arc around her.

Out of the corner of her eye she saw Danz push Hassan into the nearest wall and move to pull his gun on her, advancing rapidly.

With a sharp cry she drove the jagged shards of the carafe into Canos' chest. Blood soaked into his shirt and splashed across her face.

Danz's gun came up, she spun deftly around. Canos yelled and his body jerked spasmodically for a few moments before lying still. Whether it was the yell or her own blood-splattered visage that gave him pause she wasn't sure, but Danz hesitated for a brief moment ...

A kick sent the gun flying. Salomé raced forward, the bloodstained carafe still clenched in her hand. She struck. Danz tried to avoid it, raising an arm to protect himself. The jagged glass sliced deep. More blood. A yell of fear, anger and pain. He lashed back at her, a blow connecting with the side of her head, sending her reeling backwards.

She hit the floor hard. Pain jabbed across her ribs and back, knocking the breath from her. She had to move, there could be no respite. She saw Danz moving forward to finish her, blood gushing out of his lacerated arm. She cast around her, seeing his gun just out of arms' reach. She saw Danz aiming a brutal kick at her. She rolled aside, grabbing the gun and turning it on him. She fired, the gun jolting painfully in her hands, the noise shocking in the confined space. The bullet missed, ricocheting off the ceiling. His kick went wide as he ducked instinctively.

Danz had a moment to contemplate his own existence before it was snatched away. Salomé adjusted her aim and fired again. Danz was thrown backwards and still the shots came. Her lips curled back and with a sharp yell of anger and hate she kept firing until the gun clicked onto an empty cylinder. Danz slumped to the floor, his body a mess of ripped and bloodied flesh.

Salomé's cry petered out and she slowly lowered the gun.

In the sudden silence she got to her feet, her body trembling and her hands shaking. Her breath came in ragged gasps. A thin haze of smoke filled the room laced with a stench of strong liquor. The gun fell from her fingers and clattered to the deck. She looked across to Hassan, who was cowering in the corner, staring back at her with terror etched on his face.

'Who the fucking hell are you, lady?' he managed to croak.

'I didn't mean to kill …' Her voice was soft again, almost puzzled.

Salomé staggered to one side, stumbling over to the desk and falling to her knees beside it. Hassan got to his feet and pushed Canos' lifeless body to the floor. He picked up the ID bracelet, clipping it onto her arm. She was staring at the bloodied body in shock.

'Salomé? Salomé!'

She didn't respond. He wiped away the worst of the blood with his hand. She looked up. 'We got the ID. We've got to get out of here.'

He pulled her to her feet, dragging her out by the arm. 'Move!'

* * *

Dalk heard the sound of booted feet heading across the terminal floor. The rhythmic thumping making him turn his head. He saw a squad of local law enforcers heading past. He eyed them suspiciously; it didn't look routine. The number of people in the terminal was increasing as more ships landed. It was a busy time of day.

He strode up a wide flight of stairs to the higher shopping level, looking down across the massed ranks of visitors. There was still no sign of the pilot.

A bolt of lightning flickered across the sky, lighting up the interior of the terminal. The sun faded out behind the thick clouds as the storm moved across the city.

CHAPTER EIGHT

* * *

Salomé and Hassan ran around the back of Canos' complex. A series of service corridors led down through the rear section of the building, connecting the various rooms and allowing food, beverages and staff to move around without disturbing the guests. The corridors were a maze, with several routes leading in different directions.

'This way,' Hassan shouted, pulling Salomé behind him.

They ran onwards, finding a sealed doorway at the end of the corridor. They frantically unbolted it and stumbled out into the brightly lit flight terminal. The crowds had built up dramatically since they'd arrived. A dozen passenger vessels had disgorged their contents. The place was teeming with visitors.

'We've got to get to the ship,' Hassan said over the hubbub of noise. 'Somebody will find the bodies, we've got to move. We need to get that transponder swapped over so we can clear out of here.'

He pushed through the crowd, still dragging Salomé behind him. She seemed to be in a daze, stumbling along behind him. People glanced in their direction, eyeing Salomé's bloodstained clothes with surprise and consternation. Hassan continued pushing onwards.

'What, haven't you seen a nosebleed before?'

The crowd thickened as they crossed a queue. People jostled them, angry at being disturbed and defensively holding their place in the line-up. A large man turned and shoved at Hassan, he lost Salomé's hand in the crush.

'Salomé …'

He saw her a few metres away, getting back to her feet, trying to force her way towards him. 'Get to the ship,' she called. 'I'll catch you!'

Hassan nodded and pushed onwards.

* * *

Dalk saw the crowd of people grow denser about fifty metres further up the terminal. From his position he could see there was some kind of disturbance. He moved across a connecting bridge to get a better look. People were jostling in one of the bio-check queues. A man was lifting somebody off the floor. As he watched a woman's figure was revealed, clothed in a grubby spacers outfit, stained with something dark and red.

As she stood up she turned, looked around and stared straight at him.

* * *

Salomé had been knocked to the floor, the breath knocked out of her. 'Sorry luv, thought you were trying to jump t'queue.'

A big hand lifted her back to her feet. She brushed it off angrily, trying to see where Hassan had gone.

'Only tryin' t'help.'

Salomé spun around and looked up. The crowds parted for a moment. A darkly attired man was standing there on a gantry, looking down at her, his body silhouetted against the expansive windows. Salomé gasped. The black cloak in her memory solidified into a thick and heavy dark overcoat, the image of the man's face sending shivers of fear and fright through her. Her throat constricted and she struggled to draw breath, feeling her heart hammering in her chest. A voice echoed though her mind; dimly she recognised it as her own.

Murderer!

She was rooted to the spot, as more memories flooded back. The sword again, piercing her chest … a hand holding the hilt … an arm, a body cloaked … no not a cloak, an overcoat … a thick and heavy overcoat. His stance, stature and the expression on his face were suddenly familiar. She knew this man somehow. He had tried very hard to kill her. No, he had killed her!

A crackle of lightning flickered and smashed its way across the sky, startling her with its noise and ferocity. The echoing rumble of thunder battered at the terminal.

'You all right, luv?'

The man on the gantry raised his arm, pointing directly at her with some kind of gesture. She stumbled back a step. The man started after her immediately, running across the connecting bridge and heading down the nearest flight of stairs, closing the gap across the terminal. Salomé fled in panic, running as fast as she could in the opposite direction.

CHAPTER EIGHT

* * *

Dalk swore.

It's her, she's been revived!

He started after her immediately, running down the stairway onto the floor of the terminal. Immediately the crowd surged between them, slowing his progress. He roughly pushed people aside, forcing his way through with little concern for the consternation and anger he caused.

One man, shoved out of the way, turned and tried to hold Dalk back. The altercation was brief and meaningful. Dalk continued unhindered whilst the man writhed in a silent agony clutching a broken wrist. Folks began moving out of his way, reading the fierce determination etched on his face.

Salomé had run across the terminal, then right through the exit doors and out onto the flight apron, heedless of the danger of approaching ships. Rain was falling now. The old Eagle starship nestled amidst the larger vessels parked on the wet, glistening landing pad just a few hundred metres away. The crowd thinned, she wasn't far ahead. Dalk picked up his pace, striding rapidly towards the ship.

* * *

Rain hammered down in thick sheets, the sky darkening to a thick gloomy grey. Salomé was completely soaked by the time she reached the *Talon's* loading ramp. A bolt of lightning flashed, momentarily illuminating the landing apron around her with an intense glare and impenetrable shadows. The deep boom of thunder reverberated around her, instinctively causing her to flinch and duck. She sheltered herself as much as she could and ran up the loading ramp, checking behind her as she did so. Was the man still pursuing her? He must have seen where she'd gone. She turned and ran straight into Hassan who was bolting up the transponder.

'You made it, we'll be …'

'We've got to get out of here, now.' Salomé hit the control to seal the hold, shaking her head to clear the rain out of her eyes. The hydraulic struts whirred and began pulling up the loading ramp.

'We can't take off in a thunderstorm ...' Hassan began, hitting the opposing control. The hydraulics stopped, shuddered and then began hissing back down.

'He's here,' Salomé yelled, pushing past him. 'Bounty hunter! He's after me.'

'After you? Who's after you?'

Salomé reached out to press the close control again. Hassan grabbed her arm and pulled it aside. For a moment they struggled back and forth.

'He's going to kill me!'

'What the fuck are you talking about?'

The man appeared at the bottom of the ramp. He had drawn a gun. 'Shit ...'

Hassan backpedalled. Salomé reacted instinctively; somehow her body knew exactly what to do once more. She twisted Hassan's wrist around, dropping into a crouch and twisting her hips in a practiced motion. Hassan yelled in surprise as he was flung through the air and slid down the slick rain-swept loading ramp.

Lightning flashed again and the rain poured. Thunder made the ship vibrate.

Hassan bounced clumsily onto the tarmac, straight into the man at the bottom, knocking him backwards off his feet. Salomé hit the close button and retreated back as the ramp closed. She saw a hand grasp the frame of the ramp. The man had jumped up and caught it as it rose into place. He struggled to pull himself into the bay before the ramp closed. She caught his eye as he looked directly at her.

'Open the hatch, Kahina. Stop. Listen to me ...' His voice was deep and commanding.

The name struck dread into her, like a physical blow. She staggered backwards in shock.

Kahina? Kahina!

What did it mean?

'No,' she yelled. 'Go away. Leave me alone.'

Full circle.

More words pounded at her mind; more death and betrayal; a blonde woman's face, splattered in blood. She could remember his proud and haughty expression. She had known this man well. Was he responsible for what had happened to her? He'd stabbed her with a sword!

She cast around and caught sight of Hassan's gun next to the ramp controls.

CHAPTER EIGHT

She grabbed it, turning towards the man and squeezing the trigger. She saw his eyes widen. The gun spat fire and with a yell the man dropped out of sight in a shower of sparks. She didn't know whether she'd hit him or not. The hatch sealed and locked into place with a clunk and a hiss.

Salomé ran to the cockpit.

* * *

Dalk dropped heavily back to the floor of the pad, rolling in a practiced manner to absorb the impact. He got back to his feet in a smooth move. His shoulder hurt. A quick inspection showed that a bullet had clipped him. Lucky for him he'd never taught Kahina how to use a firearm properly.

He heard the sound of the young man getting to his feet and pulled out his own gun, training it on target without even looking.

'Don't move.'

The young man held up his hands immediately. Dalk looked down on him, the gun held in his right hand, pointing directly at the youth's head. The cascading rain flooded down, splashing off his clothing. He could feel it impacting on his head, heavy and thick. It was coming down so hard it was splashing back from the ground and his clothing.

'I didn't kidnap her, it was an accident,' the youth stuttered. 'She just stowed away, I was just bringing her back here for a medical, honest. I didn't hurt her or nothing. She's half out of her mind ...'

'Shut up.'

Dalk looked up as the whistle of the main drives started up above them. 'Shit. She's taking my fucking ship,' Hassan yelled. 'The bitch ...'

Dalk grabbed Hassan by the throat and pulled him off balance, teetering on tiptoe, water drenching him.

'Hey ...' Hassan grabbed Dalk's arm, struggling uselessly for a moment. 'You taught her to fly?' Dalk asked angrily.

'What?'

'Can she fly?'

Hassan gasped. 'I showed her the basics; orbital manoeuvres, drive trim. She was pretty good for a rookie ...'

'Does she know how to operate the hyperdrive?'

'I guess so …'

'You guess?' Dalk squeezed his fingers tighter.

'Ow! I showed her how it worked, so yeah.'

'What about the weapon systems?'

'She's fired the laser a couple of times.'

'Wonderful.'

Lightning crackled again followed by a distant boom. But it had competition now; above them the *Talon* rose on its thrusters. A blast of wind caused them both to stagger. Water swirled around them, whipped into a frenzy by the rising bulk and drive thrust from the ship. It continued to rise gracefully before angling itself upwards and moving away. The reverberation of its drives faded rapidly in the warm, humid air.

Dalk dropped Hassan back down, spun him around and then grabbed his collar. 'We've got to stop her. You're coming with me.'

The traffic control officer for the downtown launch corridor frowned at his readouts as a new entry appeared on the list, flashing red for his attention. It quickly began moving across the display.

He gestured for information and the flight specs of an old Eagle fighter appeared on the screen.

He quickly read and then thumbed the narrowband comms link.

'Eagle Mark 1 *Talon*. You are not cleared for launch, abort and return to base. Do you copy?' The blip on the screen continued moving, erratically weaving across the screen.

'Eagle Mark 1 *Talon*. Respond please.'

The track of the ship was going to intersect a major flight corridor in the next few minutes. He followed his procedures.

'Eagle Mark 1 *Talon*. Launching without permission incurs a hundred credit fine. Acknowledge and return to base. Do you copy?'

Only static returned across the link. The officer switched to wideband comms.

'All ships in the northeast corridor. We have an unresponsive vessel in the pattern. I repeat; we have an unresponsive vessel in the pattern. Target is an Eagle Mark 1 Fighter, ETA one minute. Adopt holding position and advise if you have contact.'

CHAPTER EIGHT

The blip continued moving, heading upwards. The officer tagged the vessel and applied the fine. Whoever they were they wouldn't be landing here again without spending a little time cooling down in the cells. He sat back, watching as the markers for the other vessels stopped their own descent and adjusted course. The flash of active scanner traces flickered across his display as all the ships in his airspace tried to locate the rogue ship.

He was just keying in the registration information so the ship could be intercepted by authorities in the surrounding systems when another blip appeared on the screen. He stared at the readouts in disbelief.

'What's going on out there?'

* * *

Salomé ignored the demands from the narrowband comm system. It made no difference to her whether a fine was incurred or not, escape was the only consideration. That man, it was him, the one who had stabbed her. His face was clear now, she could remember a fight, a duel with swords … and she'd lost. What happened after that? She was still alive somehow.

Kahina. Is that my name? My real name?

Sudden brightness forced her to squint and shield her eyes from the glare. The *Talon* had breached the top of the cloud layer.

The console beeped loudly in front of her. The ship lurched; she could see the speed was no longer rising. The throttles were set full forwards. Messages were scrolling up the display in the centre.

Warning! Undercarriage down. It may be damaged by micrometeorites.

She hunted for the controls she'd seen Hassan use on the approach and stabbed at them. With a whirr and a clunk the landing struts folded away and the ship blasted forwards again. The sky ahead slowly darkened from azure to mauve. Checking some of the other controls she flipped a series of switches and was gratified to see a message appear.

Hyperdrive subsystem, spooling.

She saw the scanner light up with a contact on the stern quarter. It immediately turned red and began flashing. She locked the computer on target as Hassan had shown her.

Target Locked. ID: Coup de Grâce, Class: Asp

Salomé remembered what Hassan had told her about the colour coding and shoved the flight controls downwards, dropping the *Talon* into a sharp dive.

* * *

Dalk pulled Hassan aboard his own ship and flung him bodily into the second pilot's chair, triggering the automated sequence for launching. The ship's system lit up and switched to a ready state in seconds.

'Buckle in and keep quiet. We're going after her. Any attempt to interfere and I will kill you. Understood?'

Hassan nodded, his eyes wide and his hands shaking.

Dalk expertly raised his ship and set off in pursuit of the fleeing Eagle. The narrowband comms flashed for attention.

'Asp *Coup de Grâce*. You are not cleared for launch, abort and return to base. Do you copy?'

Dalk acknowledged the call. 'Port authority, I am in pursuit of a dangerous political criminal. Please tag the Eagle fighter as fugitive and hold for further instructions. Clear the flight corridor around that vessel and do not engage.'

There was a pause on the other end of the line. '*Coup de Grâce*. Who the hell are you?'

'Authorisation Pi, Alpha, Delta, Niner, Zero. My ID is in your systems.'

An even longer pause followed, the voice subdued when it responded. 'Sir, you're cleared. All traffic will be rerouted.'

Hassan stared at Dalk. 'You can override traffic control? But only the military …'

Dalk ignored him, concentrating on pushing the *Coup de Grâce* forward through the atmosphere in pursuit of the *Talon*. It didn't take long for him to close the range. The Eagle was flying with its undercarriage down.

'Still a lot to learn,' Dalk mused, 'but she learns fast. She always did.'

'Who the hell is she?'

'Her name is Kahina Tijani Loren, daughter of Senator Algreb Loren, the last of her line,' Dalk replied, gliding his vessel onto an intercept course. 'She belongs to me.'

CHAPTER EIGHT

'Belongs to you? A Senator's daughter?'

The Imperials ships! A Senator!

'I saved her life.' Dalk looked across. 'She didn't recognise me. Why?'

Hassan looked bewildered. 'She doesn't know who she is. When she woke up on my ship she was all over the place. She's a crazy ninja woman. She went berserk and killed two guys back there! Her memory …'

'The pod was opened too early,' Dalk interrupted. 'No wonder she's …'

As they watched the undercarriage on the *Talon* finally retracted and the ship rocketed upwards. Dalk triggered the weapon deployment and Hassan watched as a pair of heavy duty looking gun implacements rose out of the forward hull of the Asp.

Rich ship … military laser and a rail gun!

Dalk locked the targeting computer onto the Eagle. Flickering triangles appeared around Hassan's ship, shrank and flashed red.

Target Locked.

The laser aboard the *Coup de Grâce* fired, the dynamo thrum of discharging power echoing through the hull. Laser beams streaked towards the *Talon*, narrowly missing as it twisted and turned ahead of them. It yawed sideways and abruptly dropped out of the sky like a stone, spinning out of control.

'You're going to kill her,' Hassan said, hands clenched in the co-pilot's chair.

'I'm not going to kill her. I'm going to bring her down.' Dalk nudged the controls and snaked his ship around, aiming to keep the Eagle in the cross-hairs. It was jinking erratically. Kahina had no grace whilst flying, but she was certainly unpredictable.

'And who the hell are you anyway?'

'I'm the one who's trying to save her from Octavia.'

'Octavia's here?' Hassan's face drained of colour.

'It's only a matter of time. She hired a pack of bounty hunters to come looking for you.'

'And you …?'

'Lucky for you I got here first. I only want the girl.' Dalk triggered the laser again. 'She's all that matters.'

The laser fire splashed across the *Talon*. Hassan saw the shields flicker and drain as they struggled to repel the fierce energy.

'That's my fucking ship!' Hassan yelled. 'It matters to me.' Dalk spared him a brief glance.

'Then let's hope I don't damage it too much.'

* * *

Salomé didn't immediately recognise the laser fire. She belatedly looked at the scanner and the rear-view display. The *Coup de Grâce* was firing on her! As she watched another fierce beam flashed out; searing red in the atmosphere. The man was trying to kill her again. She flung the controls hard over and the Eagle yawed into a stomach lurching flat spin, dropping precipitately.

Salomé felt the seat material push back hard against her as the world outside whirled around. When she could stand it no longer she pulled the controls back. The Eagle's nose twisted back, the drives hammering back to full power. The atmosphere faded away, stars shone in the darkness ahead.

The rear-view screen was empty for a few moments before the other ship drifted back into the frame. Laser fire flickered towards her again, this time splashing across the rear shields. She saw the shield indicators flicker from a healthy cyan to dim red. A moment later the cockpit displays blinked and signalled more bad news.

Shields failed!

* * *

Another laser discharge from the *Coup de Grâce* finally penetrated the rear shields of the *Talon*. Hassan saw the shields on his ship sputter and collapse. A cooling vent took the brunt of the remaining undeflected beam, glowing white hot before melting, disintegrating and breaking off from the dorsal hull plates.

'For fuck's sake be careful!' Hassan yelled as he saw his ship stream a shower of sparks. 'She's old, she won't take any more punishment.'

Dalk continued to close the range. He disarmed the laser, switching instead to his secondary weapon, a rail gun. With the shields now gone, his next hit needed to be precise and surgical. Too much and the *Talon* might break up,

CHAPTER EIGHT

too little and Kahina would escape. The ship had to be crippled before she could activate the hyperdrive or the shields managed to recharge.

'No ... are you mad? You can't shoot my ship with ...'

Dalk's hand closed on the trigger and a single blast of intense energy surged across the gap between the two ships. Hassan watched the track expecting to see his ship disintegrate in a fiery inferno. Dalk's aim was perfect. The rail gun discharge hit the *Talon's* starboard drive, shattering its inner workings and sending the ship into a spin. The on board computers automatically shut the other drive down to compensate.

Hassan looked astonished. '... that,' he finished.

'We'll lock on and board your ship,' Dalk interrupted. 'Help me get the girl safely aboard and I'll tow you back to the station and pay for repairs. Acceptable?'

Hassan nodded. 'Er, yeah ... Whatever you say.'

The scanner beeped and then emitted a pulsing warning klaxon. Dalk looked at in surprise whilst Hassan stared out of the cockpit windows.

'What the hell is ...?' Hassan said, open mouthed and pointing.

Dalk saw the predatory lines of a massive Anaconda-class vessel bearing down on them. It had simply appeared on the scanner. It must have coasted in, drives dead, cold and dark. Silent running.

He grabbed the flight controls and brought the *Coup de Grâce* around, arming the laser again. 'Octavia Quinton,' he said.

'Oh shit ... no,' Hassan cried. 'Not now ... gods, look at that thing! We are so screwed ...'

* * *

Octavia watched the approaching *Coup de Grâce* with amusement. It was a tough little ship, but it was severely outgunned in this contest. With his focus diverted by the fleeing Eagle, Dalk had been unable to see Octavia's vessel drifting inwards, the sun behind it and drives off, stealthily closing the range.

Firing up the drives had triggered a response of course, but it was too late. The *Retribution* was an Anaconda-class ship, heavily customised and packing heavy ordnance.

'Are we charged?'

'Forward array is ready, Domina.'

Octavia grinned. The shield protecting the *Retribution* flashed and sprayed scintillating light under the fierce assault of a military laser. Ahead missiles streaked in the darkness. The *Retribution* shuddered, but was otherwise unaffected.

'So, comrade Harfitt. Let's see how you cope with this.' Octavia glanced at the console.

Plasma Accelerator 100% Charged.

'Forward weapons array. Open fire!'

* * *

The pilot's chair had been wrenched from its mountings, but was still just attached. Salomé pulled herself out of it painfully, gasping as she struggled to move. That last jolt had almost knocked her out. She had no idea what had happened to her ship, but it was clearly bad. Redness tinged the edges of her vision and she blinked, trying to steady herself. Something felt sticky on her face and she wiped a hand across it. She looked in surprise at a bright red bloody smear.

Red lights flashed in various sequences of failure, alarm and emergency across the console. The displays were flickering, some showing nothing but static. There was a faint smell of hot metal wafting through the air supply. Staggering upwards she grasped one of the handholds and turned herself around to see out of the small rear windows of the cockpit.

She saw two ships. One was the *Coup de Grâce*. The other was bigger, it hadn't been there a moment before. Laser fire blazed in the darkness and two missiles streaked out from the *Coup de Grâce*, impacting violently on the bigger ship. She squinted and shielded her eyes from the twin explosions. The ship seemed unaffected.

A glaring beam of intense white energy lanced out, impaling the *Coup de Grâce* across its flank. Electrical discharges crackled across the beleaguered vessel, ripping through hull plating and interior componentry, leaving the ship a smoking burnt out husk.

CHAPTER EIGHT

The beam of light faded, evaporating into the darkness. The big ship turned, facing her. Was she going to be obliterated too?

Salomé watched in apprehension as grappling pitons fired from the ship. Two missed, but one slammed into the unprotected hull of the *Talon*. Another alarm sounded.

Warning! Hull penetration in section 7! Leak suppression system in operation.

The *Talon* jolted and spun around underneath her, twisting helplessly like a hooked fish. Debris spiralled around the two ships. A second piton fired and hit with a resounding thump. The *Talon* steadied and hung impotently in the darkness. Salomé pulled herself back up and looked around.

Caught. They're reeling me in!

She spun back to the console, seeking anything that she could do. Her eyes fastened on the only control that showed a green light.

Hyperspace subsystem: Spooled and ready.

She pulled herself back down, hitting the controls to activate the hyperspace systems. The console buzzed angrily.

Error : No Hyperspace Coordinates Set.

Salomé pulled up the chart and selected a system at random, desperately jabbing the controls again. The console buzzed a second time.

'No …'

She tried again with the same result before she squinted at the error display.

Warning : Mass-locked. Powered ships within range. Hyperdrive inoperative.

There was nothing she could do.

* * *

Dalk found himself pinned against the roof of his own cockpit. The *Coup de Grâce* was spinning out of control, the stars whirling past the viewer. As he watched, the arc of the planet slid into view causing him to squint in the sudden brightness.

Canopy Breach!

He could see Hassan slumped in the co-pilot's chair. Around him the cockpit was in disarray. Instruments either dark or flashing red status. A large crack ran across one of the windows. Air was hissing out into the void. Dalk levered himself around, grabbing a pair of remlok masks from their holders, strapping one across his face before slowly making his way across to Hassan to repeat the process.

He punched out some commands on the console, using the few systems that remained operational. The ship was crippled. He'd never been on the receiving end of a plasma accelerator. It was amazing he was still here to be worrying about it. It couldn't have been a direct hit.

His thoughts were awhirl. How had Octavia found him so fast? He'd been jumping as fast as was practically possible and his ship was state of the art, almost impossible to catch. Somehow Octavia had to have known where he was going.

He cursed.

Some kind of homing device? Should have seen that coming.

A frantic scan of the console showed the main drive was gone, as were most of the manoeuvring jets. Only the basic emergency attitude thrusters responded to his frantic diagnostic commands. The *Coup de Grâce*, blackened and burnt out but somehow still in one piece, sluggishly came to a halt and then turned to face the *Retribution*.

Dalk took in the situation in a single glance. The *Talon* had been caught and impaled. Two cables were being reeled back towards the *Retribution*. Octavia had her prize.

None of his weapons were working. The shields had failed.

He was dead in space.

Almost.

There was only one move left. If Kahina couldn't be his ... He hit the thruster control.

* * *

Salomé stared in horror as the *Coup de Grâce* lurched towards her. She watched it, terrified and unable to move as it barrelled in, spinning, apparently out of control. As it closed she could see it was angled a little way aside, it wasn't going to hit ...

It's aiming at the other ship!

CHAPTER EIGHT

Belatedly those aboard realised the intention. The big ship reversed course, pulling back out of the way, the *Talon* jolting along behind it. The *Coup de Grâce* couldn't alter course sufficiently. Instead of hitting the ship it sliced into the cables near to the *Talon*. They whipped back, cutting vicious gashes across the hull of the *Coup de Grâce* and that of the other ship. The *Talon* lurched and spun away. The jolt almost tore the flight controls out of Salomé hands.

Salomé tried to steady her ship, but nothing would respond. She caught a glimpse of the battle and watched in detached fascination as the *Coup de Grâce* began to disintegrate from the shock of impact. She saw the starboard hull section twist, fold and detach from the rest of the vessel. Debris sprayed out in a spinning plume as electrical discharges crackled through the remains of the structure. The battle spun out of her field of view, still receding as the *Talon* spun away.

The console beeped and a siren sounded. Salomé looked down at it, trying to determine what had caused it. A series of diagnostic errors flooded the console, scrolling up faster than she could read. A hum rose around her. She recognised it from before.

Mass-lock cleared. Engaging hyperspace subsystem in 10 ... 9 ... 8 ...

She stared for a moment, incredulous, before scrambling back into the co-pilot's chair, pulling straps around her and grabbing the controls as the hum rose to a crescendo; a high pitched scream which was suddenly cut short.

Wait. The ship's still spinning ... Can't stop it! 4 ... 3 ...

Spinning is bad for hyperspace. What was it that old woman said? 2 ... 1 ...

She called it something ... a mis-jump!

Salomé reached out for the controls. It was too late.

Hyperspace engaged.

The *Talon* flickered, crackled ... and disappeared.

Chapter Nine

Gerrun joined Zyair on the expansive boarding ramp of the Imperial transport *Aegidian*, turning to look back on the damaged and war-torn buildings of Leeson City. The Capital of Chione had been scarred by the aftermath of the assassination of the Senator Algreb.

'Seen enough?' Zyair asked. 'The other Imperial vessels have departed. We're the last.'

Gerrun looked at the horizon. 'All given over to the wise auspices of our revolutionary friend, the self-styled Master of Chione. Everything has been ceded to him as requested, including the slaves.'

'Curious how revolutionary ideals of freedom and self-determination are so easily cast aside once power and money creep into the equation,' Zyair said. 'Aren't revolutionaries supposed to free the oppressed? I feel I should be waving a flag and singing. Am I becoming a hopeless romantic?'

Gerrun smiled. 'My friend, no one would dare insult you thus. Though I imagine those slaves who revolted under the Senator are finding their new master's sense of justice and equality rather eye opening.'

'I will take great delight in bringing Vargo and his men to trial after this affair. It wouldn't even need to be rigged.'

'Filtered and calibrated for justice, I think you mean,' Gerrun replied.

'I know what I mean,' Zyair grumbled.

The faint boom of a distant explosion rumbled across the sky. Shortly afterwards a plume of smoke could be seen rising from another building.

'It would appear that the Master is struggling to assert his mastery.' Gerrun smiled to see their ingenious plan coming to fruition, knowing Zyair had thought it too risky from the off. But they'd succeeded. They'd allowed the Reclamists to win and wear themselves out with the victory.

'Now they're exhausted,' he said, 'we can deliver the heir to the Loren family and reclaim this little moon once more.'

'That's all very well but our claim depends on the Loren daughter and if we can't produce her on schedule ...'

'I'm sure Dalk has it in hand.'

'You are, are you? I remain unconvinced. Why has he not been in contact? If he's lost her, then what?'

Gerrun shrugged. 'Without the girl we have no claim, my good patron. The family line we followed is, alas, extinguished and we, loyal subjects of the Empire as we are, must find another Senator to serve.'

'The Empire won't give up this moon. You know that. A fleet is already massing.'

'As are counterparts from the Federation. Is there an appetite for war? Threats and stratagems, perhaps the odd minor skirmish I will give you. But war, for one little moon? I think not. It's too expensive.'

'Let's hope the diplomats' wits are as sharp as you hope.'

'I'm sure a mutually acceptable agreement will, in time, present itself.'

Zyair snorted. 'You're an optimist. The Federation undermined the operation here covertly by supporting these Reclamists. And yet …'

Gerrun nodded. 'They seem curiously reluctant to supply Vargo and his men with sufficient weaponry to effectively subdue the population. They wait for something too.'

'Perhaps they fear what he would do given that kind of firepower. An unexpected flash of wisdom?'

'All intentions are yet to be made clear. In the meantime we must continue to be patient. It's appropriate that we leave now. The situation will deteriorate further before it improves.'

'And what of Dalk?' Zyair asked.

A faint frown crossed Gerrun's features. 'I am concerned at his lack of communication, but we must trust he has matters under control. He knows what needs to be done and what the stakes are.'

Zyair signalled to the captain of the *Aegidian* and the boarding ramp closed. Both patrons retired within the luxurious vessel. As they walked towards the take-off lounge, Zyair sighed deeply.

'Time grows short.'

* * *

CHAPTER NINE

Consciousness returned and with it, pain. Dalk struggled to remember what had gone before. His head throbbed and something was bound tightly across his eyes. More pain registered, his arms were pulled above his head and his legs were bound. He twisted his wrists, attempting to free them. At once a burning haze of agony and cramp flashed down his arms. For a moment he panicked, biting down on instinct that surged in revulsion at being restrained. The bonds were tight, he was going nowhere. He relented for a moment, concentrating on his other senses.

The faint hum of the life support systems whirred above him. A faint smell of dampness and sweat reached his nostrils, mixed with grease and a metallic tang that eluded him. Whatever he was bound to creaked slightly when he moved. The air around him was warm and humid; his clothing was damp, soaked in sweat.

Gravity too, something near one-G. They must be planetside or aboard a sizable station. Still in the Ferenchia system or not? Where were they now?

His movement caused another nearby. Dalk felt someone stir beside him.

'Who's there?' a voice called, tremulously. 'Who is it? Talk to me damn it.' Dalk could almost smell the fear. He recognised the voice of the youth he'd snatched aboard his ship.

'Quiet,' he said, sharply.

'That you, bounty hunter? What happened? Where are we?'

The sound of a door opening, footsteps clinked on flooring. Dalk raised his head, focusing his attention in the direction of the sound.

He sniffed. A waft of perfume drifted on the air. It was subtle, feminine, expensive, and, if he wasn't mistaken, laced with pheromones. He felt his body react to it despite his best efforts to remain stoic.

That answered where he was.

His head was jerked roughly backwards, the device in his mouth removed. A hand slipped under the material bound across his eyes, pulling it free.

Bright light dazzled his vision, forcing him to squint. For a moment he could see nothing but vague figures standing in front of him. Slowly they resolved into people. He heard a shriek from beside him.

'Get your hands off me ... oh god, oh god ... shit ... no.'

'Welcome aboard the *Retribution*, gentlemen.' Octavia's voice was sure and steady, with a hint of amusement. She stood languidly, flanked by two of her guards. Dalk recognised one from the briefing he'd attended. He was wearing an unpleasant grin.

'You will become ...' Octavia smiled demurely and paused for a moment, '... intimately familiar with the name of my vessel. It was named for a reason, to carry a message to those who ought to know better.'

Octavia stepped aside, turning her back on the two helpless men. Dalk could make out that he was bound against a side bulkhead in an otherwise featureless chamber. It looked like a hold compartment originally designed for carrying small merchandise, packages and mail. Hassan was bound beside him.

Dalk quickly looked around, his eyes adjusting to focus on the other side of the room. The metallic tang was explained. Blood had pooled on the floor. Above the stain hung a body, no ... the carcass of some unlucky individual. The body hung by only one arm, soaked in sweat and partly congealed blood. The other arm was severed, but still chained at the wrist, bone and ragged flesh hanging from it, ripped and torn. It looked to have been a woman given a dark streak of long hair, but it was otherwise difficult to tell. Dalk was no stranger to the sight of a mutilated body, but this wasn't a time of war. It was pure sadism. He felt his lips tighten.

Hassan was also staring at the body. Dalk could just see his gaping mouth open, his head shaking from side to side in rapid twitching motions.

Octavia, dressed in flight overalls, walked across Hassan's line of sight, her heels clicking sharply on the flooring.

'You've seen my previous guest. Her name was Melissa. She thought she could renege on a deal. She was wrong.'

Dalk saw Hassan try to speak, but only a brief moan escaped him.

'I explained the situation to her,' Octavia went on. 'A lesson had to be learnt and a message needed to be sent. Sadly, she died before either was achieved ...'

She smiled and looked at Hassan. He recoiled.

'... so I'm sending her back to her family instead. Communication has to be clear and precise, wouldn't you say? People might doubt my reputation. Business might suffer. That is not acceptable. Which brings me to you.'

She moved closer to Hassan. Dalk felt him shiver beside him.

CHAPTER NINE

'You stole from me,' Octavia said, frowning as if only mildly puzzled. 'Audacious, but foolhardy. You must learn not to do that. Nobody steals from me. That is not how things work.'

'What do you want? I'll do it, anything you ask,' Hassan's voice stuttered out. Dalk closed his eyes for a moment. 'Be quiet,' he whispered, 'don't give ...'

Octavia moved up close to Hassan, now mere inches away, pouting in mock sympathy. 'You'll do anything? How sweet you are, little boy. What would you do for me?'

Dalk watched as Octavia looked down on him, clearly enjoying her height advantage. She raised a hand to Hassan's face, stroking his cheek, enjoying the fierce trembles that wracked his body as she did so.

'Anything ...' Hassan managed to whisper, from between cracked and parched lips.

'You don't have anything I want, little boy,' Octavia said, her mouth curving into a grimace. 'Except your screams perhaps ...'

She punched him in the stomach. Hassan yelled and lurched against his restraints. '... or your tears.'

Another blow, this time to the face. Hassan was flung back, his head smacking against the pole.

He collapsed, flopping forward, shrieking with pain. Octavia pushed his head back up.

'I like blood too,' she said, wiping her finger across his forehead. She pulled it back revealing a fingertip stained with red. Her voice dropped just above a whisper. 'Ancient holy books say that without the shedding of blood, there is no forgiveness. Blood purifies us all. We can learn much from old customs I think.'

She smiled for a brief moment then her face became cold and callous. 'Forgiveness takes time ... and sometimes the blood runs too quickly ...'

'Please ...' Hassan managed.

'Theft, sweet little boy,' Octavia said, gently stroking his hair. 'Wrong acts cannot go unpunished. Justice must be served. Don't you agree?'

Hassan crumpled, sobbing, his chest heaving.

'No? You stole from me. I must take something from you. Then order is restored and all is right with the void.'

She pulled a dagger from a clip in her waistband. Hassan's eyes focused on it as she turned it slowly around. He panicked, bucking against his restraints, but powerless to escape.

'An eye for starters perhaps,' Octavia mused holding the dagger before his face, 'or a finger. A soupçon of retribution to be going on with. They used to cut off the hands of thieves so it's said.'

With a fast strike she jammed the dagger towards him. He yelled, clenching his eyes closed as he anticipated the impact, but she hadn't stabbed him. Dalk saw him open his eyes to stare at where the dagger stuck point first in the bulkhead between them, its jewelled hilt glinting in the lights of the compartment just inches from his head. Dalk saw his fellow captive's eyes were wide with terror, his face grey.

Octavia pulled Hassan's head around and looked straight into his eyes.

'You'll decide what you will sacrifice by when next I return. Choose well little boy.'

Hassan's face crumpled into a whimper. Octavia let him go with disgust and turned to Dalk. He was taller than her, so she stepped back half a metre, crossed her arms and regarded him.

'You're so taciturn, bounty hunter.' Her voice was no longer teasing, but firmly business-like. 'You can drop that stupid drawl. Simeon Harfitt isn't your real name. It was a convincing ID. Somebody did their work well.'

Dalk looked at her and then looked up at his restraints.

'Not the hospitality I'm accustomed to,' he said, giving the restraints a tentative pull. 'Your standards seem to have slipped.'

Octavia smiled. 'I have various classes of accommodation. Some are better than others.'

Dalk nodded. 'You know, I expected to be paid rather than shackled. Unless this is how people are rewarded in your organisation? Slightly kinky, I'll admit.'

'I reward those who do as I bid.'

'I found your cargo, I was in the process of retrieving it …'

Octavia stepped in and slapped him around the face. It was a firm blow. Dalk took it, surprised at the power it contained, her hand felt like a club. The woman certainly knew how to hit.

'You take me for a fool?' Octavia said, quickfire. 'Your hyperdrive was locked

CHAPTER NINE

on Haoria. You had no intention of returning the girl to me, which means you knew who she was all along. You're a liar and a thief, and mostly likely an Imperial lackey. Would she have earned you a fortune in ransom? Was that your plan?'

Dalk tasted blood on his lips but smiled anyway.

'You don't have her, do you?' he asked. 'She got away.'

'Your little stunt allowed her ship to jump-out, it won't take long to …' Octavia's eyes narrowed. 'She means something to you. You care … What are you? Her protector? Mentor? Guardian?'

Dalk gestured to the restraints. 'Release me and we'll talk.'

Octavia closed angrily and hit him again. The force of the blow knocked his head back against the bulkhead, pain lanced through his neck. Blood on his lips … swelling …

'Make no demands, bounty hunter,' she said. 'I will find the girl, with or without your assistance. Do not doubt that. I will hear your unspoken truths.'

She pulled the dagger out of the bulkhead wall, turned on her heel and strode purposely away, gesturing to her two guards to follow. They stepped in smartly behind her. The bulkhead door slid shut and locked into place with a dull clank.

Then it was silent save for Hassan's piteous cries.

* * *

Noise.

The relentless shriek of a siren roused her to consciousness. Salomé raised her head, struggling to make sense of what she could see. She was slumped in the dislocated pilot's chair. Before her, the arc of a planet rolled around in the view. She caught a brief glimpse of a red-tinged mountainous landscape before it spun away. She could feel the ship rotating and tumbling.

She shook her head to clear it, clamping down on the bile rising in her throat. Where was she?

The hyperspace jump.

The siren intruded into her consciousness, stopping her from thinking. She batted at the controls, silencing it. Only then did she look at the console. Most of the status indicators were flashing red. One was particularly insistent.

Warning! Descent vector incorrect. Adjust. Warning! Life Support failure in ten minutes.

The planet rolled into view again, it seemed closer. A thin curving arc of magenta light above the planet's surface signalled some kind of atmosphere. The *Talon* was going down. It didn't matter how she'd got here; she was here and she was going to crash if she didn't do something about it.

She wrestled the flight controls around. The ship responded sluggishly, but she managed to counter the spin and the yaw with some trial and error. The planet was definitely larger now, she could see those mountains far more clearly. The ship was coming in too fast.

She remembered how Hassan had adjusted course. It was all done by autopilot. She had to engage it. She hunted around for the right controls.

Warning! Descent vector incorrect. Adjust.

Salomé could see the flight direction on the console. It was indicating that the *Talon* was going to intersect the planet. Uncorrected, the ship would slam into the ground at several kilometres per second, assuming it survived the entry into the atmosphere and didn't simply burn up. She had to slow down.

She found the autopilot controls and switched them on. More red lights flickered across the console. She selected a spot away from the mountains and locked on. More messages.

Warning! Main drive malfunction! Warning! Lateral thruster damage! Warning! Undercarriage malfunction! Warning! Hull integrity 47%!

She pressed the activate control and felt the ship rock in response.

Warning! Rerouting to retro-thrusters.

She was flung forward in her seat, which tilted precipitately. She grimaced as the straps dug into her shoulders. Forces ripped her around, a sickening twisted pain burned in her neck.

No protective gel! Wasn't it supposed to …

Vibration distorted her vision; she couldn't see. She tried desperately to breathe, flailing in a vain attempt to relieve the pressure from the straps. A shuddering violent jolt, even worse than before. Blood on her shoulders, the straps cutting flesh.

CHAPTER NINE

… stop? Oh god.

Intense light burst around her, forcing her to clamp her eyes closed.

Abruptly the deceleration stopped and the flare faded. Gasping for breath she looked up to see the arc of the planet flattening out below her. Before she had time to move, flickers of ionising gas pulsed over the nose of the ship and a thin scream of superheated air thrummed through the superstructure. She was mashed forward in her seat again and cried out as the pain seared through her.

Warning! Heat shield damage! Warning! Hull integrity 34%
Warning! Excessive yaw. Adjusting trim.
Warning! Lateral hull temperature sensors off-scale!

An acrid smell assaulted her nostrils. Hot metal, a definite tang of something electrical overheating and burning out. She heard a brief groan, twist and a loud thump. Bits of the ship were breaking off. The *Talon* rocked and dropped with a horrendous mechanical moan. The planet had disappeared from view, now all she could see were flames. The temperature was rising fast, heat prickled her skin. She screamed, helpless, as the instinctive urge to flee overcame her. Burning death, incinerated …

She could see parts of the hull from the cockpit windows; they were glowing red hot, heating swiftly to amber. Even the struts holding the cockpit together were beginning to glow. Smoke wafted around her, causing her to cough. It was bitter, burning in her throat and on her tongue.

The ship was dying around her. She was going to burn alive.

More status indicators failed. The external hull indicators were now showing nothing at all, maybe the sensors had already burnt away with large parts of the external plating, probably floating around in the *Talon*'s wake, several hundred kilometres behind.

The deceleration faded. Salomé could see a mauve sky.

Warning! Autopilot failure! Switching to manual control.

The *Talon* rolled sideways. Salomé grabbed the controls and managed to hold the ship out of a spin. She yelped in pain, the control was burning hot in her hand. The nose of the vessel dropped, trailing a plume of smoke.

Wisps of high altitude cloud tore past as the ship plummeted downwards. Salomé could see a thin band of cloud ahead, obscuring the surface of the planet. She desperately wrestled with the controls trying to decrease the negative pitch of the ship.

'Up!' she yelled.' Up!'

Visibility dropped to zero as *Talon* dropped into the cloud bank.

For a moment everything was peaceful. All sense of motion faded away. Salomé could hear her own heart thumping fast in her chest, painfully conscious of her life and how fragile it had become. Blood pounded in her ears and she heard herself gasp, the air rough in her lungs.

The ship dropped out of the cloud bank and the surface revealed itself. Vast swathes of sand dunes stretched out as far as she could see, rapidly rising to meet the ship and tearing past at terrifying speed. The mountains formed a distant misty backdrop in the thickening air. Lightning flickered around the ship as it emerged from the clouds.

She pulled one last time on the controls. They barely responded. The ship lurched back upwards, as if trying desperately to return to its home amongst the stars.

It was all in vain.

Salomé was crushed into her seat as *Talon's* lower hull clipped the tallest dune. She felt the ship tilt forwards and down. The sounds of crunching impacts echoed through the hull. Salomé was buffeted around violently, still desperately clinging on to the flight controls. She got one last view of the sand dunes rising around her as the ship made firm contact with the ground.

Terrifying crashes and bangs echoed from below and behind her as something big smashed around in the cargo bay. She felt the ship slew sideways as it lost velocity. Unidentifiable debris spun in a maelstrom outside the cockpit canopy. She was flung sideways. The noise stopped abruptly.

Sand, sky, sand, sky …

Another impact. Salomé was flung forward as the deceleration gripped her one last time, desperately trying to shield herself from the spinning tumult of debris that was now all that was left of the cockpit. The canopy smashed, showering her in a rain of sharp splinters.

With a screech of tortured and mangled metal, the *Talon* finally came to a halt, paused for a moment and then settled to one side, metal crackling as it

CHAPTER NINE

cooled. It lay wrecked in the barren wilderness of a lonely desert, thick dark smoke billowing up into the still dry air.

* * *

Octavia sat alone in her stateroom, staring at her reflection in a mirror fixed to the bulkhead. A Carreenian tortoise hairbrush, with a jewel encrusted handle was held loosely in her hand and she drew it slowly through her hair, gazing all the while on her own face.

Treatments, rejuvenation clinics, drugs; the best the Empire could provide, she'd indulged in them all. Her body was augmented in many ways, some legal, others less so. Each had served a particular purpose, allowing her to achieve a goal, defeat an opponent, realise a crucial business transaction. The financial cost was immense, but that concerned her little. She had more money than she could ever realistically use.

Her drive and ambition had come at a much greater cost; things she had once dismissed in youth now seemed far more desirable in older age. To be young again; an elusive dream that tantalised many.

Yet, unlike them, I have a way to realise that dream.

She knew the technology existed. Deep in the empire there were laboratories that worked on many advanced avenues of research. Some were twisted and perverted, others dubious and immoral, still more would terrify and alarm even the most blasé technologist. There were hidden research projects that touched on the very limits of human ingenuity and beyond.

She'd come to hear of some of them and how they were occasionally put to use. Planning her heist had cost her far more in spies and information than the simple execution of the plan itself.

It might have been completed by now, save for the intervention of the hapless pilot. He would pay dearly for her inconvenience.

The Imperial girl had to be found.

Her hands clenched, with an almost imperceptible mechanical whir. She looked down at them, hating them for what she'd done to them. Choices she had made, decisions she could no longer undo. Her body could not be changed back.

She would have shed a tear, but her optical enhancements no longer required that to be necessary. She had to content herself with a blink.

'It is prepared, Domina.'

She turned to see her personal med-tech. He bowed low and gestured to the other end of the room. Octavia nodded and stood up, walking across. The viewing platform windows dominated this side of the ship, with the view across the beautiful, but deadly poisonous surface of a desolate moon serving as a backdrop. Purple mountains set against a green-hued sky lent an unearthly ambiance to the moment. Before the windows, Salomé's pod stood, open and supported on a delicate framework of struts.

'If you would care to enter, Domina.'

The med-tech gestured to the pod. Octavia slipped off her robe and carefully arranged herself within the pod.

'It should take only moments.'

Octavia nodded. 'Proceed.'

The roof of the pod closed down above her, she held her breath for a moment, fending off a brief moment of claustrophobia. Faint lights illuminated the interior. A deep pulsing hum resonated through her. Brief pain registered in her head, like a headache, but mobile, as if something inside her was probing her brain and seeking release. She closed her eyes and waited.

The sensation subsided and with a faint hiss, the pod crackled open again. The med-tech was looking anxiously down at her.

'A moment, Domina, I must store it.'

He attached a small black tab to her forehead. After a moment she heard it beep. The med-tech studied it and then gently peeled the tab away, stepping back and nodding to her.

'It is done, Domina. The match is confirmed.'

He handed her the robe and she climbed out of the pod, swinging the robe around herself. 'The trace?'

'All stored,' the med-tech confirmed, handing her the tab. 'It can be used at your convenience.'

'It's definitely compatible?'

The med-tech nodded. 'Absolutely, Domina. There is no doubt at all.'

CHAPTER NINE

Octavia looked at the small black device. It was such a tiny thing, yet it held all her remaining hopes and dreams.

Once the girl had been found.

* * *

Salomé's next sensation was of heat and dryness. She coughed and spluttered, feeling a burning sensation on her face. For a moment she panicked, struggling to rise. She could hear a strange keening noise. It took her a moment to recognise the sound of wind whistling through the damaged ship.

She struggled to sit up, finding herself half submerged in the tumble of debris from the wreckage of the cockpit. The canopy above her had totally caved in and sand, blown by the wind, was pouring in. It was rising fast around her. A few minutes more and she'd have been buried.

Overhead the sky was a uniform mauve, a clear but unfamiliar colour. A pale white sun lit the scene from a low angle. It was barely more than a point of white and it hurt to look at it. The gravity was low. She couldn't tell how long she'd been unconscious.

She looked around her. The cockpit was a virtually unrecognisable jumble of debris, consoles blackened, instruments smashed, supporting struts and exposed conduits dangling everywhere. She undid the seat buckles and staggered up out of the pilot's chair, dislodging the sand in which she was half buried, shaking her head to clear it. The sand slipped smoothly like a liquid into the gap she vacated and continued to rise.

She clambered up onto the remains of the cockpit canopy and managed to peer over the nose of the ship. It was still a long way from the ground. The prow of the ship was hanging over the drop created by the tip of a dune. No longer protected by the cockpit, gusts of wind threatened to blow her off the slick duralium hull.

The vista before her made her heart drop. There was no sign of anything other than endless rolling dunes that faded out of sight in the remote distance. She could see no vegetation, no animals or any suggestion of civilisation or habitation. Only the far-off mountains gave any suggestion of possible shelter.

She retreated inside, giving the few remaining instruments a quick prod. None of the holofac screens appeared, there was no power at all. She'd hoped to at least identify where she was and perhaps call for help. She moved further backwards.

The ship jolted underneath her. She stood stock still for a moment. The motion came again. The ship was sinking, tilting back as it settled into the soft sand. She looked back at the desert outside. Water and food, she'd need both if she was going to survive.

She raided the hatches at the back of the cockpit, finding Hassan's stash of emergency rations in a rucksack along with some bottles. A brief taste confirmed they contained water. She found a few other things too; a gun, a pair of knives and a portable radio transmitter. She stored the items carefully and slung the rucksack across her back.

The ship jolted a third time and a shuddering mechanical groan echoed through the superstructure around her, the cockpit floor tilted. Sand gushed towards her, knocking her back against the rear bulkhead.

She struggled to free herself. The sand was incredibly fine. She could feel it pulling at her, as if she was wading through treacle. She stretched and grasped hold of one of the brace bars and pulled herself upwards, her forearms trembling with the effort. The sand reluctantly let go with a puckering slurp. She gingerly made her way forwards and upwards, avoiding the rising tide.

She heard a sharp slithering from behind her, more sand slipped in. The ship creaked again and then started moving backwards. Salomé braced herself as best she could as the ship tilted up and careened backwards down the sand dune.

The ship came to a shuddering halt at the base. Sand blasted up around her, filling the cockpit with a stinging confusion of dust and powder. She squinted, her eyes watering.

More sand was rushing in, rapidly changing from a trickle to a surge.

If I don't get out I'll be buried alive ... no one will ever know ...

Sweat chilled her. She pulled herself upwards, ignoring the pain in her eyes and the dryness in her throat. The ship continued to slide backwards underneath her, frustrating her efforts to escape the flow. Above her the shattered gap where the cockpit windows had once been was already half blocked. She scrambled forwards, almost swimming in the soft silty material.

CHAPTER NINE

She reached the threshold just as the sand was about to submerge the cockpit. She lunged forward desperately, catching the edge of the window frame and forcing her way through, cutting herself on the exposed metal. She scrabbled frantically through the gap, ignoring the burning sting of cuts on her arms and legs. The sand gave one final attempt at restraining her before finally letting go. She scrambled onto the upper hull, gasping for breath, panting but exultant to have survived.

She was given little respite. A gust of wind blew her off her feet. She slipped, thumping down on the hull and immediately slid to one side. She twisted as she fell, sliding inexorably towards the rear of the ship.

She struggled to find something, anything, to hold onto, but the surface of the hull was slick with no protrusions. She could only slow her slide, not arrest it.

An aerial flashed into her vision. She flung her arm out towards it. It cut into her hands, but she managed to hold on, her body coming to a halt with a painful jerk. She felt her feet slip over the starboard edge of the ship. She managed to wrestle her arm around the aerial.

She hung there for precious seconds, gasping for breath.

She felt movement and heard a creak. She watched with horror as the aerial bent, buckled and finally cracked under her weight.

Then she was plummeting through the air. She hit the ground, rolling down the side of the dune before coming to a halt at the bottom.

She lay there on her back for a moment, fighting to catch her breath in the thin air. The fall had happened in a curious slow motion, the gravity wasn't strong – fortunate for her.

Not far away the ship gave a final groan and came to rest, half submerged in the sand. She'd escaped. She was still alive.

She rolled over and got to her feet, clawing her way slowly and painfully back up the dune. Her feet sank in the fine sand. Stumbling forward she eventually reached the summit and stopped, looking around her.

Hassan's ship was almost unrecognisable. The main hull was mostly intact save the shattered cockpit, but it was scorched and burnt, particularly at the front. In some places entire panels were missing. The wide wing sections she remembered seeing at the spaceport were completely gone, ripped off by the look of the twisted and tortured metal remnants. Looking beyond the wreck she could see a wide track carved through the sand dunes, peppered with blackened and mangled debris stretching back for hundreds of metres.

She turned around, looking in the opposite direction.

Nothing had changed. As far as she could see, the dunes rolled endlessly. The mountains were the only thing to break the monotony. They were clearer now and she could see snow atop their peaks. She sat down, pulling a bottle of water out and taking a gulp, rinsing it around her mouth and spitting it out to remove the sand. She considered taking another but knew she had to ration herself, there was no telling how long she might need to make it last.

Always assuming there is some water on this planet … if there isn't …

She pushed those thoughts away. One thing at a time.

She pulled the radio out of the backpack and switched it on, bracing herself for disappointment.

It seemed unlikely there would be anything on this remote world.

The radio scanned up and down its frequency ranges. Crashes and crackles of static were all she could hear. She sighed, it was too much to hope that there would be anything here. Perhaps she'd have better luck in the mountains.

A beep and then a pulsing sound.

Salomé looked at the radio. It had picked up something; a regular beacon of some kind. She tapped at the device's small screen and squinted, shielding the view from the bright light of the star with her hand.

Transponder Beacon Detected. Range 35.2 kilometres.

Salomé remembered Hassan talking about transponders, something to do with identification.

Another ship?

She switched the radio onto wideband and pressed the transmit button. 'Hello? Can anyone hear me? I've crashed and need help. Is anyone there?'

There was no answer, just the slow and steady pulse of the beacon. She sighed.

With a little experimentation she was able to triangulate the direction of the beacon. It was located in the mountains directly in front of her.

'Thirty-five kilometres,' she said to herself. 'Guess I'm walking.'

She stowed the radio and slung the backpack across her shoulders once more, before trudging away across the dunes without a backward glance.

CHAPTER NINE

* * *

Hassan jerked his head up as the door to the hold clicked and opened. He gasped, the short intake of breath rasping through his dry throat. He couldn't stop his body trembling. His stomach twisted and felt as if it would jump up through his neck.

Octavia was back. Her two guards following behind.

She ignored him for a moment, focusing her attention on the bounty hunter. 'Take him to my cabin,' she instructed. 'I will deal with him later.'

Hassan watched as the bounty hunter was released from the bulkhead and roughly shoved out of the hold, both guards went with him. The door slid shut with a dull thunk.

Alone!

The sweet smell of her perfume wafted past. In any other environment it would have been enticing, exciting even. Here it was laced with the stench of dread.

Octavia walked across to him. He could see every detail of her face. The age lines, the twist of her lips, subtle make up, expertly applied. Eyes that burned with fierce intention, anticipation …

She looked at him for a long moment. 'Have you decided?' she asked.

Hassan tried to answer, but his voice failed him. He managed a shuddering shake of his head.

Octavia sighed, pulling the dagger from her waistband. 'That's not good enough, little boy. You must choose.'

Hassan swallowed, trying to get a little saliva to lubricate his mouth.

'An eye, a finger, a toe …' Octavia said, moved closer until she was almost touching him. He felt her hand grasp between his legs, '… your manhood perhaps.'

Hassan jolted and bucked against the bulkhead, a muffled squeak escaping him. Octavia laughed.

'Determine what you will give me.' Her tone grew more intense, louder and insistent. 'Tell me. It's right and proper that you choose your fate.'

He turned away, clenching his eyes shut, trying to fend off the hysteria rising in him. He couldn't stop an involuntary whimper of fear.

'No?'

He heard movement, a faint rustle of clothing ...

Utter agony shut down his thoughts, almost causing him to black out. He jolted in his restraints, screaming in shock, pain and surprise. He heard his own shriek echo back from the bulkhead walls. Dizziness and nausea surged around him, pushing all other considerations aside. His hand was on fire. He looked up and saw the dagger embedded in his palm. She'd pinned him to the bulkhead. It was nothing like he'd ever felt before. Tearing, searing, liquid pain that coursed into his arm and grew in waves, each crescendo greater than the last.

He felt hot blood running down his arm. Another eruption of pain spurted through him as Octavia twisted the dagger and pulled it back out. Another yell was wrenched from him. He hung there, feeling his legs giving way in shock. That placed more pressure on his wrists, releasing another torrent of pain. He screamed again, jolting back up. He felt a hot wetness in his trousers and felt a moment of embarrassment and shame.

'There are many nerves in the hands,' Octavia said, her voice even and level. He struggled to take in what she was saying. 'As good a place as any to start.'

* * *

Salomé struggled across the empty landscape. Within minutes of setting out a few things were very obvious to her. First the gravity was lower than she was used to; walking at a normal pace was almost impossible. She found the best compromise was to lope along in a series of slow strides, bouncing from one foot to the other.

Harder to bear was the dryness of the air. Her throat was parched almost as soon as she set out and she realised she was going to rapidly lose water. She ripped part of her flight overalls and improvised a simple face mask. That helped, but made another problem worse. The air was thin and she found herself gasping, labouring for breath. It forced her to stop every few hundred metres.

She'd walked for hours and the star was slowly dropping towards the horizon ahead. Before long it would set behind the mountains. Still there was no sign of vegetation or animals, not even insect life. One of her bottles of water was empty and she'd need to start on another before long. At the rate

CHAPTER NINE

she was going, she'd make the mountains with time enough to search for the signal, but if there was nothing useful there …

She angrily pushed the thought away, concentrating on placing one foot in front of the other.

Keep walking.

The dunes had given way to more rocky terrain, which was easier to navigate, but harder on her legs. She ached all over. As the star flickered and disappeared behind the mountains she decided the time had come for a rest. She found a small rocky outcrop and sat down with a sigh, rubbing at her legs to ease the strain.

After a drink she took out the radio again and checked it. The signal was still there, beeping away reassuringly.

Transponder Beacon Detected. Range 12.7 kilometres.

Again she tried the wideband comms.

'Hello. Can anyone hear me? If you can hear me, please answer?'

She fancied that she heard a faint clicking, but when she leant in close she could only discern a faint whisper of static.

She'd make it come the morning. It was too dangerous to continue walking in the night without some kind of illumination. She might fall down some unseen chasm or pit. She needed a rest too. She left the radio on, its faint light comforting in the growing darkness.

Above her the stars were already beginning to shine. She could see the darkness of the terminator sweeping across as the sky faded to black. A stiff breeze began to blow and she felt goose pimples across her exposed skin. The temperature was falling fast. She huddled into the outcrop, shielding herself as best she could.

She made herself a frugal meal from her rations by the light of the radio, then switched it off and eased herself down. As the last vestiges of light faded around her, the wind dropped. The stars were clear and bright, just as dazzling as they'd been from the cockpit of Hassan's ship.

She looked up forlornly, wondering if, amongst the myriads of distant worlds out there, there might be one, just one, she could call home. Somewhere out there was the Frontier too, was she any closer to this mysterious edge of space? She had no idea how far she'd come or even where she was.

Perhaps this is the Frontier?

That dark and sombre man. He'd stabbed her through the heart with a sword. She could see his face clearly now. Salomé ran her hand over the faint scar on her chest. There was more, another woman, a woman with blonde hair. Her pretty face was splattered with blood, her sightless eyes bereft of life, her face forever locked in an expression of shock and terror. A face familiar, so familiar, accompanied by a strong taint of regret and remorse.

Salomé swallowed. Had she caused this strange calamity to befall them all? If only her memory …

Guns firing. Delicately wrought decorations shattering in slow motion. Ducking to avoid the debris, then running, running in fear of her life, fingers clutching. A hand, the blonde-haired woman's hand …

Blood, a door slamming, peppered with bullet holes. Smoke …

And then darkness until she found herself on Hassan's ship, sick, confused and angry. Hassan, what had happened to him? That sombre man would have caught him. She felt a moment's regret at what she'd done but then the expression on her face hardened. He'd surely planned to use her, either as a travelling companion or a cheap deckhand until he found out who she really was and sold her to the highest bidder. Yes, she'd panicked, but he'd been a fool.

The sombre man's face formed in her mind again. Tall, stern and austere, his image struck quivering fear into her, an instinctive response to the latent aggression and finely controlled rage she sensed. A brutal killer lurked under the calm and measured exterior, she was sure of it.

Words came into her mind, shocking and unbelievable. She railed against them for a moment before realising they were her own; trusting, accommodating, even friendly.

I'm in debt to your guidance, wise old man. Will you always guide me?

She shook her head, she couldn't have said such a thing! And yet she knew it was true, her very core attested to it. The memory was sound and whole. She held a sword herself, an honourable bow and a smile of satisfaction.

She felt the memories start to fade.

'No … remember, just remember …' She clenched her eyes closed, but it was futile. The images slipped away once more and she was left in the darkness of the desert, bereft, alone.

CHAPTER NINE

A trickle of sand cascaded into her lap. She frowned in surprise, struggling to bring her thoughts back to the present. She looked up to see what had caused it.

A pair of rough and calloused feet. A grunt of surprise. Something whistling through the air.

Too late to avoid.

The stars spun into a whirling darkness.

* * *

Hassan tried to stand up, but his legs refused to steady, the pain blanked his mind each time he tried to control it. He could feel his arm shaking uncontrollably. He saw Octavia turn the dagger in her hand, its blade slick with blood. His blood …

'Do you feel a sense of justice?' she asked. 'Do you understand how you have wronged me? If I allowed the likes of you to steal from me and escape without retribution …'

He couldn't answer. He couldn't cope. Terror and panic overwhelmed him. He couldn't stop the tears, his resolve crumbling into dust. His body wouldn't obey his commands. He couldn't act, he could barely think. There was nothing but a desperate wish for it to be over, coupled with horror and a growing realisation that he alone was responsible for his predicament. He had decided to steal from her. Such a stupid, idiotic move. He could see that now. What had he been thinking? That she'd overlook his little heist because it was small? He knew her reputation, he knew how far her influence spread and she was going to make sure he understood that. She was going to kill him, but she was going to take her time.

Should have listened to Sushil …

'There are many points on the human body which can sustain a deep wound without damaging internal organs …'

He looked up in dread. Her face was set with a faint smile as she saw his expression.

'I see you are beginning to appreciate what you've done,' she said. 'This is good. We should all endeavour to learn.'

Octavia swung the dagger towards him. He watched helplessly as she drove the dagger into his shoulder near the collar bone. He felt the blade scrape his bone.

Then there was nothing but the screaming. Lights flickered at the edges of his vision, a redness closed in on him. Pain streamed through his body like an electric current, burning and stinging its way across his chest. Once again he lurched in his restraints, his hand lending its own refreshed burst of fire to the mix. Conscious thought was obliterated. His legs gave way completely and he hung by his wrists and his impaled shoulder. Incinerating pain lanced across him as his flesh tore under his own weight, crashing through his mind and overwhelming him.

He heard an unearthly shriek and dimly recognised it as his own before the blackness swallowed him.

* * *

Salomé woke. Her first sensation was biting cold. She moved feebly, trying to raise her head.

That was a mistake. Her neck pulsed with pain. Something had hit her.

The memory flooded back. There had been a dark figure. A bare foot, a man's foot; calloused and hairy … then nothing.

The faint sound of dripping water reached her ears.

She was freezing and shivering uncontrollably. She looked around. She was in a simple cell, featureless apart from a tiny hole cut in the roof through which a narrow beam of light speared the gloom. Three walls were bare, the same unforgiving rock as the floor. The fourth contained a small gated doorway, with a crudely made set of bars set on rusty hinges. Beyond that a narrow corridor led away, rapidly fading into darkness.

Casting around the room she saw little else save a pair of indentations in the stone floor. One was filled with water, the other with some unidentified white mulch. On the opposite side of the room was a hole in the floor from which a foul smell was wafting. She tried to move, only then finding that her hands were bound behind her back. She found herself dressed in a simple dirty white frock, tied at the waist with a rough piece of rope. Of her other clothes, even her boots, there was no sign.

CHAPTER NINE

The radio?

No, that was gone too.

Tears of frustration flashed in her eyes and she howled with rage, jolting spasmodically in sheer fury against the cords that held her. It did little to reduce her ire, but increased the pain in her wrists. After a moment she stopped, trying to focus her churning mind.

She rolled onto her side, slowly and painfully looping her arms under her legs. After a brief rest she got to her knees and crawled away, gasping with the effort. Her legs and arms were cramping, stiff and sore, the bonds around her wrists tight and secure. Her head pounded from the exertion.

She investigated the two bowl-like indentations. The water was obvious enough. The white mulch was some kind of crushed vegetable. It tasted bland, but food was food. She bent down and ravenously ate it, scraping every last morsel out as best she could.

She looked into the water, catching a faint reflection of herself in its surface. Her hair was a sodden black mess, wild and unkempt, she could make out a nasty congealed cut on her forehead and a face streaked with the crusty remains of blood, sweat and sand. It brought memories back into her mind …

Dark hair. Something bad about dark hair.

She shouldn't have dark hair, it was wrong.

A man, berating her for having dark hair. A long corridor, a palace, a throne. She was looking up at him, arguing … words …

Your very presence distresses me.

The memory faded. She grasped at it, trying to hold on, but it slipped away; ephemeral.

Frustration welled up. She was alone, imprisoned in this dank dungeon. She didn't know where she was or even who she was. Angry, she staggered across to the bars, ramming against them with her shoulder; the gate rattled, but remained locked in place.

'Let me out! Is there anyone there? I demand you let me out!'

She strained at the bars, exerting what little leverage she could muster. All ended in the same way, the bars were immovable; too strong for her. She sank slowly downwards, falling against the wall, headache throbbing. The bonds were cutting into her wrists. Tears came, scalding down her cheeks, shock and reaction mixing with despair, bewilderment and loneliness. Would this nightmare never end? The image of the sombre man in the trench coat came back to her. He'd tried to kill her again, but then he'd bizarrely intervened to prevent her capture? Why? Who was he?

Now she was lost again. Caught and molested by some other person or persons intent on doing her harm. She had no one, no family, no friends, no memory, not even a real name.

Save perhaps one. The sombre man had called her … Kahina. Was that her real name or something else? She spoke it out loud, whispering it like a mantra over and over again, trying to force memories to surface. Vague familiarity echoed in her mind, accompanied by a sense of disdain, dislike and humiliation. It didn't feel like a name she should be proud of.

Sobs wracked her, uncontrolled and unbidden.

How long she stayed like that she didn't know, but something roused her from her desolation. A noise; a soft low thrum that echoed down the corridor and reverberated off the stony walls. It was eerie and mesmerising. The hairs on the back of her neck rose and a chill ran down her spine. She scrambled to her feet, looking into the dark depths of the corridor.

Nothing moved; nothing that she could see.

The sound changed. It was almost imperceptible at first, but she could sense it was growing in volume, becoming more distinctive. She could distinguish different timbres, notes rising and falling in a bewitching harmony of sounds both bass and treble. It sounded almost as if …

With rising clarity she could make it out. Voices; calling in unison to a slow measured beat. A strange, intimidating and somehow tragic chant; punctuated by the sound of footsteps. After listening for a while she heard the central theme repeat every six beats with a sharp tap, other voices weaving more complex refrains on top of the rhythmic undercurrent.

She backed away to the rear of the cell as the chant continued to rise in volume. Orange light flickered and she could make out a dim wall at the far end of the corridor. Flickering shadows, hideously elongated, cast themselves across the wall.

They were coming closer.

A flaming torch came into view, the sudden brightness forcing her to squint and blink. Men, dressed in austere robes very much like the one she wore,

CHAPTER NINE

walked slowly but inexorably down the corridor, their dark eyes shining in the torchlight. Each looked remarkably similar, with hair cut down to bristle atop their heads.

They looked straight ahead as if mesmerised. Each bore a torch in one arm and a wooden staff in the other. On the sixth beat of their strange refrain, the staff was dropped in perfect synchronisation onto the stone floor with a loud crack. They walked towards her with almost mechanical precision, two abreast. Salomé counted ten of them.

She watched as they advanced down the corridor towards her, stopping immediately outside the barred doorway. The staffs came down with a final thud and their voices ceased.

Their bodies were stock still, immobile, their eyes never wavering. Long seconds passed in total silence save for the crackling torches. Salomé couldn't even hear them breathing.

'Who …'

The moment she spoke one of the men at the front turned to look at her. His mouth opened wide and an ear-splitting tone issued forth. It wasn't a cry or a yell, but a pure note, higher and louder than she could have imagined it was possible for a man to generate. It hammered round the cell at a deafening volume, forcing her to stagger back in pain, her ears ringing.

As abruptly as he'd started, the man stopped.

Salomé cautiously looked at him and opened her mouth. 'Are …'

The tone again, even more powerful than before. 'All right! I'll be quiet. Just stop!'

The man stopped and looked at her. Salomé looked back at him, not daring to utter a sound.

Satisfied, the man produced a heavy looking series of keys from within his robe and unlocked the gate. In unison the men stepped back a pace.

The gate swung back with a squeak of rust and old metal. He entered the cell and grabbed her by her wrists, pushing her towards the exit. She resisted and considered trying to fight him off, but the odds were ridiculous. She decided it would be better to save her strength.

A coarse hemp bag was pulled over her head and tightened with a noose. She yelled her protest, but there was nothing she could do. A rough shove in the back and a yank on her neck propelled her forwards. A second squeak and a clunking rattle told her they had locked the gate behind her.

She heard a deep hum from a pair of the men furthest away. Then the next pair hummed a harmony, as did the next two pairs.

Another yank on her neck started her walking forwards. She tried to resist but that just gained her a painful thump in the back. She heard two men beside her thud their staffs and then began a strange chant.

To her surprise she could understand them. They sung words on a single note, with a simple rise or fall to mark the end of a sentence as they marched on.

'You are to be taken to the assembly. You have trespassed and defiled a holy land in defiance of statute and law. You will be judged and sentenced by the Elders according to scripture. You will submit to just punishment for your heinous deeds. Your life is now in the custody of the Brotherhood of Resonance.'

Chapter Ten

Dalk had been led to Octavia's cabin. He was still handcuffed and the guards shackled him to a bulkhead. One left, the other remained, watching him warily.

'I'd tell the truth sooner rather than later,' the guard advised. 'She always gets what she wants.'

'Perhaps I'd rather die,' Dalk returned.

'Maybe you would.' The guard grinned. 'But she won't let you off that easily. That girl we caught? She lasted two days after her arm was ripped off. Sewn up the veins and arteries, no painkillers.'

'A charming mistress. Attention to detail too. It's most commendable.'

'Domina likes screams and blood,' the guard said coldly. 'She doesn't want you dying too quick.'

'I'll do my best not to get stains on the carpet.'

The guard scowled, annoyed.

'You'll think different before too long, bounty hunter. You'll be begging for death.'

'I'll take that under advisement.'

The guard stepped back. Dalk looked around the sumptuous cabin. He could see artworks and decorations from a dozen worlds. He knew Octavia had money beyond count and that her influence spread far and wide. She could have pretty much bought anyone at whim, so why her interest in Kahina?

Octavia had gone to extraordinary lengths to capture her. She'd been supplying arms to the Reclamists of course, tacitly helping the Federation as Dalk had planned, but he hadn't expected her to intercept Kahina's convoy and attempt to snatch the girl. What was the purpose in that? Ransom? No, she'd accused him of that. She wanted Kahina herself, for a reason compelling enough to make her attack the convoy, recruit a series of bounty hunters and then follow him across several star systems to personally try to recover the girl once more.

Why?

Dalk had seriously underestimated Octavia's commitment, assuming she was concerned simply with the loss of face resulting from Hassan's ill-advised heist. There was something else. Kahina was somehow vital to Octavia's plans.

Yet where was Kahina? Octavia didn't have her by her own admission. Somehow Kahina must have jumped out in Hassan's damaged ship. If Octavia had been unable to track her that implied a mis-jump, probably more by luck than judgement. If she'd survived that experience she could be anywhere. Literally anywhere. Hassan had said she was acting erratically, her memory only partially restored after her 'death'. If she wasn't marooned in the depths of space, she would be easy pickings for anybody looking to take advantage. He had to find her before she was lost to him forever.

Hassan's terrified face came to mind. The callow youth was out of his depth. Dalk shook his head at the mind-numbing stupidity of trying to swindle Octavia Quinton. What was the boy thinking? A desperate, ridiculous move. The boy had stumbled into something far bigger than he'd realised. Dalk felt regret for making the situation worse, but knew his involvement had made little difference. From the moment the boy had stolen from Octavia he'd marked himself. Octavia was never going to relent, her reputation wouldn't allow it. The boy should have run further and faster, he might have been safe in the heart of the Empire or the Alliance.

A foolish mistake. Did he deserve to die for it? Probably. Dalk sighed. If he could save him he would. If there was anything left to save.

The doors to the cabin snapped open. Dalk looked around seeing Octavia walk in. She dismissed the guard with a brief wave of her hand. He left and the doors snapped closed behind him. Octavia turned, a coy smile on her face.

'Your companion is most deliciously responsive,' she said. 'Perhaps I should be thanking you for delivering him into my hands. Retribution is so satisfying.'

'I live to serve,' Dalk replied.

'Do you indeed, Dalk Torgen?' She smiled at his brief look of surprise. 'Yes, I know who you are now. It took some time, I commend you on your thoroughness. It took a significant effort to discover your true identity. I see we have had dealings before now. Only you were called Solanac then.'

'I like a little variety.'

'Bounty hunter, revolutionary, Imperial servant and, if I'm not mistaken, a Military Commander for the Independents. You do get around, do you not?'

CHAPTER TEN

Dalk grew serious. 'What do you want with me, Quinton?'

'Octavia, I insist.'

'Octavia, then …'

'I want to know what you're about,' she said, simply. 'You served the Imperials yet your allegiance was with the Independents. You supported the Reclamists whilst claiming to be an Imperial, yet you arranged for the Loren girl to be spirited away whilst claiming to support the Reclamists, undermining their revolution. Quite a cocktail of identities. The Federation and the Empire are thrown into turmoil. No one has the upper hand. But where does your allegiance truly lie?'

Dalk didn't respond.

Octavia moved closer to him. Her voice grew soft and low.

'Torturing you would be tedious,' she mused. 'I know you're capable of resisting and I have no desire to end your life. Drugs I have, but they would leave you permanently crippled. That seems such a waste.'

'What do you suggest?'

Octavia smiled and backed away. 'You are doubtless curious as to why I am pursuing your Imperial girl. You've gone to great lengths to protect her. I am prepared to tell you why I need her. Perhaps our reasons are not too dissimilar. We might find an accommodation.'

'And just carry on as if nothing had happened?'

'You have not wronged me, Dalk,' she said, looking round at him. 'Not yet. In fact, we've worked well together for many years. I want that girl and I will have her. You could help me in that. If I understood your intentions …'

'Why should I trust you?'

'Because I can kill you right here and now. It would be a quick merciful death for you as befits your standing, but death nonetheless. Would you rather die? I will find her anyway and your plans will die with you. I'm offering a truce. Just help me find the girl.'

'Perhaps you will simply kill me when you have what you want.'

'A risk you'll have to take. I am many things, but I am not a liar. I will not kill you if you co-operate. You're more valuable alive than dead.'

Octavia folded her arms and smiled, waiting.

Dalk considered his options and then cast a glance above his head towards his shackled wrists. Octavia leant in close. Dalk smelt her perfume and a brief twinge of excitement coursed through him. She was a strangely desirable woman.

'Trust,' she whispered in his ear, 'the anticipation, the danger. Exciting, don't you think? History turns on moments such as these. Consider carefully.'

Dalk felt the shackles release. He could overpower her; he might never get a better opportunity …

The moment passed. Octavia stepped back, regarding him with a satisfied expression.

'Choice made,' she said, smiling. She turned to a nearby elegantly curved table where a crystal decanter filled with a mauve liquid sat surrounded by a series of tumblers.

'A drink? A toast to possibilities.'

Dalk made his way across to her, watching her carefully. She poured them both a drink and sipped hers as she handed a tumbler to him. She held out her glass in invitation.

He clinked his against hers. 'To possibilities,' he echoed.

* * *

Salomé was exhausted, dripping with sweat. It was hot. Too hot. She couldn't tell how long she'd been forced to walk. It had felt like interminable hours. Her feet were burning and sore, unused to walking barefoot. Within minutes of leaving the cell she could tell she was being led above ground. She heard the wind blowing around her.

They'd been leading her along by means of the noose, yanking at it every so often in order to adjust her direction. At times she'd felt the path go steeply upwards. She must be in the mountains. Were these people responsible for the beacon? Was it a lure? Some kind of snare to trap the unwary?

She staggered and would have fallen had she not been caught by someone behind her.

She was pulled ungracefully to one side and forced to kneel. Sounds of the men walking around her reached her ears. Hands fumbled at her neck and then the hood was pulled off.

CHAPTER TEN

Intense light assaulted her eyes, making her flinch and blink rapidly, a delicious cooling breeze swept across her. Her head was jerked roughly back and a leather flask was rammed into her mouth. Water splashed, she nearly choked, but desperately tried to swallow as much as she could.

After a couple of gulps the flask was pulled away. She gasped for breath, looking around her.

The men were arranged in a circle, with her at the centre. As she watched, the one with the flask settled down to join his companions. They faced outwards with their backs to her, kneeling in a similar fashion, staffs in their left hands. A low humming tone came from each of them.

They had arrived in a clearing, surrounded by a border of scraggy looking vegetation.

So there is some plant life after all.

She'd been unlucky to have crashed in the desert.

To her right the ground dropped away precipitately, they were at the edge of a steep escarpment. The star seemed to be in about the same place as she remembered when she set out from Hassan's ship. A day had passed, but how long was a day on this world?

Her gaze travelled around. Ahead she could see the path snake up around rocky outcrops. They were climbing out of a valley up the side of a mountain. Salomé could see the mountain range reaching into the distance, snow-capped and forbidding peaks jutting upwards into a clear magenta sky. They were the same mountains she'd seen from the desert. Was the beacon nearby?

High above she could make out some kind of dwelling, set against the sheer edge of the mountain. It had the look of a domed temple, carved from the rock itself. It might have been impressive once, but it gave a strong impression of neglect and age. The path headed in that direction. Was that her destination?

The heat overcame her and she swayed, falling to one side. Dimly she felt the men get to their feet and try to rouse her, but she was too far gone. She slipped into blissful unconsciousness, only vaguely aware of being hoisted up.

The next thing that roused her was a constant swaying and a sharp burning pain in her shoulders, wrists and ankles. They'd pulled the hood back over her head. She tried to move only to find she was now tied hand and foot. They'd bound her to a pole, slung like an animal ready for slaughter and they were carrying her between them. The clack of their staffs echoed off the mountain walls, a rhythmic beat that pounded onwards, ever up the mountainside.

She tried to count, but her mind could barely focus. A hundred steps easily, perhaps thousands …

The clack stopped. She felt hands brush across hers, the sound of a knife cutting. She fell to the ground with a thump, the breath was knocked out of her. She was hauled up and pulled along by her arms, her feet dragging behind her. Everything darkened abruptly and she felt cool. She must have been dragged into shadow.

A deep sonorous voice chanted a question.

'The Elders greet you. What is this that you see fit to bring it before the assembly?'

She heard one of the men reply in the same manner.

'A trespasser from the void. Found walking the barrens.' There was a brief pause.

'Let them be unveiled.'

Salomé felt her head jerked up and the hood was pulled away. She looked directly into the eyes of another of the men, superficially similar to the ones she had seen before, but wearing an ornate headpiece made of woven green threads of plant material. Two others sat beside him on a stone dais, similarly but less ostentatiously dressed. All three held staffs of wood about a metre and a half long.

She was standing in the shade of a courtyard, hewn from the solid rock, bordered by rough pillars that supported the enormous weight above. The floor was dusty and uneven, marked with dark stains. She could see crudely-made baskets arranged around the walls, containing meagre supplies of vegetables. There was water too, in a stone trough. She blinked, squinting, trying to see clearly.

Other detritus littered the floor. With growing horror Salomé made out gnawed bones, the remnants of ribcages and, arranged in a stack, a collection of discoloured skulls. Some were whole, others cracked and broken. She jolted back in shock, taking in the gaze of those empty eye sockets with a short yelp of fear.

The man recoiled in surprise. 'A woman.'

CHAPTER TEN

'She carried things forbidden,' one of the men beside her added, lowering her rucksack from off his back and tipping the contents onto the ground. The water bottles, rations, her tatty overalls and the radio fell out, bouncing in the low gravity, before lying still at the leader's feet.

The radio.

Salomé struggled forward, but was pulled back sharply.

'Tech.' The leader spat vehemently with an expression of supreme distaste.

'Tech is forbidden, void dweller!' he sang at her. 'Why do you bring this abomination to us? Tech is evil, tech is despair, tech is death!' The men around her took up the chant.

'Tech is evil, tech is despair, tech is death!'

'I didn't bring it to you ...' Salomé began. She found herself reviving in the cool air of the courtyard.

At the sound of her voice the zealots around her yelled, their leader clasping his hands to his ears in apparent shock.

'She is uncouth,' he sang, his voice shrill.

'I crashed in the desert!' she shouted, not heeding them. 'I have no quarrel with you, let me go.'

At an unseen signal something smashed into the back of her knees. Her legs crumpled and she found herself on her knees in the dirt. As she looked up the leader had stepped up to her.

His hand closed around her neck and lifted her up. She could see the white of his eyes, yellowed and bloodshot.

'Your crime is heinous, void dweller. You will be sacrificed for the good of the brotherhood.' He raised his head and sang to his companions. 'Prepare a pyre! Her crime becomes a blessing!'

Memories flooded her mind again; the sombre man, his hand at her neck, hurting her in exactly the same way as he stabbed her with his sword.

Rage suffused her, how dare these primitives treat her like this? The leader's staff resolved in her vision. She stared at it, imagining her fingers closing around it, hefting it. Movements, familiar and practiced, swirled in her consciousness. She knew how to use it! Blocks, strikes, parries, thrusts ... somehow she knew.

No more submission. She grabbed at it.

A deft twist and it was hers. Her first move was an abrupt upwards blow to the leader's outstretched arm. He yelled in surprise, released her and backpedalled away. Salomé instinctively brought the staff around, smashing one of her escorts in the neck and another in the leg, before stepping away.

More yells. A frenzy of movement. Her vision clouded with furious red.

The zealots came at her. She raged back, a spinning dervish of lethal uncontrolled fury. Bones shattered, wrists broke, skulls cracked. Yells turned to screams of fear. Her movements were precise and controlled with no compassion; relentless, determined, brutal and callous. The bodies of her victims fell at her feet.

She heard a strange, piercing high-pitched wail; a screeching, rending noise of wrath and indignation. Startled, she realised it came from her. Her vision cleared. She saw her own hands, bloodied, cut and bruised, the bodies of half a dozen men writhing painfully at her feet. The others were backing away in fear, chanting at a low ebb.

'Let me go,' she managed, spitting blood from her mouth. 'Step aside.' The zealots continued to retreat but made no other move.

She sensed movement behind her. Cursing, she spun around only to receive a dizzying blow to the face. She staggered back, half-blinded by pain. She lost her balance and heard running foot falls. She felt herself wrestled roughly to the ground, the sharp dirt grinding into the skin of her face as a hand pressed her head hard into the ground. She felt a knee in her back and her arms were pulled up behind her and quickly secured. Someone grabbed her by the hair.

She screamed as she was yanked to her feet, the pain intolerable.

The leader's face loomed in her view. It was cut and bleeding, his left eye already swollen half shut.

'Tech is evil, tech is despair, tech is death!' he chanted, mere inches from her face.

Salomé dimly heard the others repeat the refrain. Her head was yanked to one side. The leader stepped that way. Salomé saw the radio, still lying on the ground. The leader raised his staff.

Without the radio ...

'Don't!' Salomé yelled, struggling forwards, feeling her arms pulled painfully back as the zealots held her tight.

CHAPTER TEN

The staff came down, smashing the radio to smithereens. The power pack crackled and sparked for a moment.

'Tech is evil, tech is despair, tech is death!'

Tears welled up in her eyes. She tried to rise, but the strength that had consumed her was gone. She struggled helplessly. Without the radio she had no chance. They might as well have just killed her outright.

The leader turned to face her. 'Death to the void dweller!'

It took her a moment to realise he'd spoken the words rather than chanted them. Somehow that chilled her. She looked up into his crazed eyes. Madness; pure and unreasoning madness.

He readied his staff, raising it above his head, preparing a lethal killing blow. Salomé stared dully at it, resigned to the inevitable.

No hope, no answers ...

The leader's chest burst into flame. He screamed in horror and pain. The staff was flung aside as he fell backwards. The zealots beside her shouted in alarm. Salomé turned to see a bright beam of light flash towards her. It hit another of the zealots and his clothing caught fire too, he ran screaming.

The others ran, shrieking their fear and fury.

She staggered and turned around, her hands still tied behind her back. She looked across the courtyard, seeing a figure emerge from behind one of the columns. She stepped back in surprise.

A man stood there, dressed in a tatty grey smock, matched with a makeshift wide-brimmed hat tied by string under his chin. A neatly cropped salt and pepper moustache and beard framed a swarthy face counterpointed by a bright pair of eyes that studied her intently. The man held some kind of gun. As she watched a beam of intense light flashed out and caught another of the zealots.

'Presto, presto! We have little time,' he said, beckoning urgently to her. His voice had the most peculiar accent.

'Who are you?' Salomé demanded, staggering towards him. He was short and squat, she found herself looking down on him.

'Later, later. We need to be leaving before they return. Scare now, not last for long.' The man produced a knife and cut the rope around her wrist.

'There, free. Come, follow me, signorina.'

'Wait, how can I?'

'Trust me? Stay here if you wish.' The man turned and vaulted onto the wall of the courtyard, jabbing a thumb in the direction of the vanished zealots. 'They will kill you. Then they eat you.' He hummed for a moment. 'Maybe they do it the other way around. Hard to tell. They like women. More fat, less gristle, quicker to cook.'

Salomé stared at him. 'Cook me?' She looked around at the skulls and bones. 'Oh god …' She felt bile rise in her throat and swallowed, trying to clamp down on it.

'Your broadcast,' he explained. 'You crashed, yes? Picked up your radio sig.' He squinted at her confused look. 'Come in disguise, point gun, bang bang, rescue bella signorina, comprendere?'

Zealots reappeared on the opposite side of the courtyard, yelling out their horrible chants. They had stones in their hands.

The man raised the gun again and the zealots stopped. 'Get ready to run,' he whispered to her.

The zealots advanced a step, their leader raising a hand clenched around a stone.

'Come no closer,' the man called, aiming his gun again. The zealots exchanged looks and then inched forward again. 'I will not hesitate.'

One of the zealots raised his arm, poised to throw his stone. The man pulled the trigger of his gun.

Instead of a beam of radiation the gun emitted a spluttering hum that died abruptly. 'Cheap Federation junk …'

The man adjusted something on the gun and tried again, but with an even more lacklustre result. The zealots mumbled under their breath and advanced towards them.

'Ciao, miei amici!' the man said, throwing the gun at them. Salomé saw him drop over the edge of the courtyard and disappear. The zealots turned their attention to her. Salomé hesitated for a brief moment before jumping and leaping after him.

'Wait for me!'

The man turned, gestured and grabbed her hand before racing away downhill. He jumped and Salomé found herself hurtling through the air, the ground dropping away below her.

CHAPTER TEN

Gravity! Like flying …

A stone whistled past her ear as they hit the ground again several metres forward.

Salomé realised they had dropped onto the far side of the mountain. Other peaks were ahead of them, but the ground dropped rapidly away below. The sparse vegetation quickly gave way to thicker cactus-like undergrowth.

Tall enough to hide in?

The man pushed onwards, fighting his way through the thickening vegetation. They fled, hearing the hollering of the zealots behind them. More stones flew, landing close by and tumbling into the undergrowth.

Salomé struggled to keep up. She felt what little stamina she had left ebb away. The man could certainly move.

They crashed on through the vegetation. Sharp thorns scratched at Salomé's legs, but she paid no attention. The voices behind grew louder. She spared a backwards glance, but couldn't see through the dry plants.

'Can you swim, signorina?'

She looked back around. 'Swim? No! Why?'

'Good time to learn,' the man turned, pulling her close alongside. The vegetation abruptly ended and they raced out over a drop. Salomé screamed as she plummeted through the air, arms windmilling, trying to stay upright as she fell. The water wasn't far below, but the current was running in a curious slow motion, with cold surging melt water from the higher peaks. They both splashed into the torrent and were swept downstream.

She bobbed back to the surface, gasping in the sudden chill, struggling uselessly in the current. The water felt like syrup, the droplets from their splash still cascading down around them in slow motion. She caught a brief glimpse of the zealots standing atop the rise from which they had jumped, gesturing angrily towards her before they were swept out of sight behind a bend in the river.

* * *

Octavia placed her glass on the ornate table between herself and Dalk before letting out a deep breath. 'You are a man of surprises,' she said, running her finger around her mouth as she looked at him. 'Nostalgia and whimsy? You?'

'I've seen more than my share of death and destruction,' Dalk returned. 'All I want …'

'The dream of the Frontier?' she teased. 'That old cliché? Heading out in quest of a new world to call your own? How dreary. You'll need to go further than you think. That system of yours isn't even on the Frontier now. Times change, the new hyperdrives for instance …'

'Happiness can be found in many forms.' Dalk finished his drink and replaced his glass beside hers. 'Power, status, money. Is it strange that some of us simply desire to be left alone?'

'You think you'll ever be left alone on that moon?'

'The Tantalum rush won't last forever, five years at most. The mines provide a source of wealth that should be used to construct basic infrastructure, allowing the colonists to build an agrarian society.'

'So you'll be adding farmer Dalk to your list of personas?'

'They still need a leader, someone to ensure …'

Octavia grinned. 'So it is power you want.'

'Only to manage things to ensure they are carried out properly.'

'Power is power.' Octavia licked her lips. 'And now I understand why you need this girl. She is the last surviving heir, isn't she? You plan to reinstate her, reclaim the moon for the Imperials?'

Dalk didn't respond.

Octavia licked her lips. 'So … it's more subtle than that. That's just a step on the way. You want an independent world free from interference.' She paused, considering. 'You're going to get her to cede power to you. What if she doesn't want to?'

'She's no politician.' Dalk shrugged. 'She's the third daughter of a hated senator. She has no real ability or desire for such things. I trained her only so that she might survive the coup.'

Octavia nodded. 'So her usefulness to you lasts only as long as she retains the ability to discharge her duties and transfer power to you.'

'She will see things my way. Once her memory is correctly restored, she will come to rely on me as her trusted advisor once more. I will take the tedium of administration from her. With a little gentle persuasion she will be only too glad to hand over the reins.'

CHAPTER TEN

'You're so generous,' Octavia replied. 'And how will you stop the Imperials from interdicting your little moon and inserting a new Senator?'

'Imperials are the most literal of people,' Dalk replied. 'Kahina will, in a surprise move, revoke the Imperial claim to the system, perhaps in a fit of remorse for the deaths she and her people have been responsible for. If that does not convince, I might broker a deal with local privateers, an exclusive deal for cheap access to the Tantalum in exchange for protection from hostile intervention. Do you know anyone who might be interested in that?'

Octavia smiled. 'I do. A man named Solanac suggested the very same thing to me not so long ago.'

'And then, after a discretionary interval, perhaps some other calamity may befall poor Kahina Tijani Loren,' Dalk said, suggestively.

'Once you have control, you will no longer need her.'

'Perhaps she will take a trip back to her Imperial cousins. As you know, space travel remains fraught with danger …'

'Who knows what dastardly villains lurk in the darkness between worlds.'

'And one such villain might be tempted to put their own plans into play.'

Octavia sat back. 'You're asking me to wait, Dalk. I'm not a patient woman.'

'The girl will be yours, Octavia. I only need her to cede power to me. Once that is done, I will arrange for her to be delivered. The greater wealth of the moon will be yours in exchange for defence. I just need some time.'

'Three months, no longer.' Octavia's voice was firm. Dalk made to protest but she held up her hand. 'I will wait no longer, Dalk.'

Dalk nodded. He paused for a moment and then resumed the conversation. 'And you will do what with her?'

Octavia inclined her head. 'Concern for your charge, Dalk? Do you feel guilt at manipulating a young woman's life?'

'Curiosity,' Dalk replied. 'And no, I feel no guilt. She is an Imperial. They are consumed with their arrogance and overinflated sense of self-worth, they talk endlessly of honour and yet integrity is not something they understand. Flamboyancy is piled upon barely concealed deceit. They court one another with false pleasure, barely concealing their lies and traitorous intentions. They are hollow and empty, bereft of humanity and decentness. I despise them all.'

Octavia nodded in appreciation at the venom in his voice. 'The taciturn bounty hunter has emotions after all. Why, Dalk, you should become an orator for the Federation.'

Dalk's mouth curled with distaste. 'With their obsession with money and facile celebrity? Cramming every moment of their lives with technological distraction? Education dumbed down, all opinions provided by advertising sponsored media? Despite their haughty claims to have banished slavery they fail to notice that the vast majority of their sleepwalking populace are wage slaves to the giant corporations. They're more corrupt than the Imperials. I think not. And you still haven't told me why you want her.'

Octavia stood up and poured herself another drink. Dalk declined when she gestured to him.

She settled down in her chair again, crossing her legs. 'I just want her.'

Dalk's eyes narrowed. 'She's just a girl, barely a grown woman. A youth …'

'And they say youth is wasted on the young,' Octavia replied, her eyes bright with anticipation. 'Yet who wouldn't jump at the chance to revisit their youth with the wisdom of age? Let's just say her youthfulness will not be wasted.'

Dalk's eyes widened.

'The pod? I'm not sure that's even possible …'

'She, one of so very few, is genetically compatible. My specialists have assured me it can be done. They know they have to be certain, I'm not very tolerant of failure.'

'Or betrayal and theft it would seem.'

Octavia raised her head. 'The boy? Would you have me let him go?'

'He might know something about where the girl went. He revived her.'

Octavia paused for a long moment.

'I will consider it. He might come in useful.'

'Do we have a deal then?'

'Your moon, defence from the Imperials?'

'A fresh young girl delivered into your hands.' They shook hands.

* * *

Salomé struggled up a small sandy bank, pulling herself free of the muddy river. She collapsed just out of the water, exhausted and shivering. Belatedly

CHAPTER TEN

she realised she wasn't alone. The man staggered up beside her. He'd grabbed her the moment she'd surfaced in the river, his arm locking around her neck and pulling her to shore.

'Come, signorina,' he said. 'Can't stop here. Too open. They will follow.'

With a heavy sigh, she pulled herself upwards. Her legs were shaky and unsteady. The icy water had made her cuts and bruises sting sharply. The sun above was hot and the air humid. She stretched out, letting the warmth sooth her.

'Who were they?'

'Lunatico, fanatico,' the man replied, walking onwards. 'How you say? Mad. Crazy. Give them no thought. You are more important. What is your name?'

'Salomé,' she said, uncertainly.

'Salomé?' The man smiled and nodded, humming a tune to himself. 'Do you dance?'

Salomé frowned. 'Do I dance?'

'Salomé, was famous dancer in legend. Driving men wild with desire.' He winked at her. 'A good name, no?'

'It's ...' Salomé decided she'd better not reveal any more for now. 'And who are you?'

The man stretched to his full height; he was still shorter than her, but almost twice as wide. He had a heavy muscular build. He tipped his hat and bowed.

'My name?' he began grandly. 'I am Luciano Prestigio Giovanni.' There was much emphasis and flourish on the 'Prestigio'.

'Luchi ...'

He winced at her pronunciation. 'But ... you may call me Luko.'

'Luko.'

'Close enough. Come, we must keep moving.' He looked around, scanning the river behind them.

'Where are we going?'

'Back to my ship.'

'You have a ship?' Salomé said in delight. 'Truly?'

'Yes, signorina. Is not far. I have food, water and shelter too. But we must make haste. Come.'

He set off through the undergrowth. Salomé followed him, walking quickly to keep up. It was thick and damp down by the river bank. A mix of fern-like plants grew around them, some far taller than they were, providing ample shelter from the burning heat of the star above.

'You said you heard my radio?' Salomé asked.

Luko nodded. 'Yes. Heard your call. Tried to reach you before the fanaticos. Sorry I was late.'

Salomé frowned. 'Wait … why are you still here? If you have a ship …'

Luko grinned. 'Ah, yes. A puzzle, no? Perhaps you will be able to help.'

They reached a gulley in the forest of ferns, with a sharp cliff running above them. A narrow crack in the wall allowed them into a rough passageway. Luko squeezed inside. Salomé followed him.

Luko pulled a small device out of his pocket. Salomé recognised it as a 'glo'. Light flickered and they could see in the gloom. A fissure in the rock led onwards, barely wide enough for people to pass through.

'The fanatico think these caves have ghosts,' Luko chuckled to himself. 'But, it is I who haunts them.'

'Who are these fanaticos?'

'Long time ago, this planet … it was a religious enclave. They came to escape science, escape technology, build a new society. Sometime centuries gone.' Luko waved his arms expansively. 'The planet is off limits, it is forbidden to trade here.'

'So what happened?'

Luko laughed. 'Life without technology? Is rubbish, signorina. Something went wrong. Bad storm, maybe climate shift. Not sure. In a few years they start to fight, only the strongest and maddest survive, preying on each other and anyone else unlucky to land here, rest is history. All that is left is crazy monks and their singing. Fanatico, yes?'

They carefully proceeded onwards. It was cool and damp, refreshing after the stifling heat outside. The fissure slowly widened into a passageway, interrupted by glistening rocks, moulded and shaped into strange, almost organic shapes.

'Careful, signorina. Mind your head.'

Salomé ducked under the low roof and sidestepped a stalactite. As she walked around the corridor it widened into a cavern. Overhead, green-tinged light flickered down from cracks and holes in the vegetation cover. The cavern

CHAPTER TEN

must have been some kind of small crater before the forest subdued and covered it. A perfect hiding place.

'Ah, mia bellezza!'

Ahead of her, dominating the centre of the cavern, a ship stood on a tricycle undercarriage. It was unlike anything she'd ever seen before. It was stocky and wide, its hull composed of huge interlocking parts; a great series of flat triangular panels. There was not a single curve in evidence, it made even Hassan's decrepit vessel look modern and svelte. From this angle she got a brief impression that she was looking at the disembodied head of a fierce snake.

Some kind of mechanism jutted out from the forward part of the ship, she guessed it was a weapon of some kind. Above that a cockpit canopy could be seen, grimy and stained. The whole ship was covered with algae, mildew and moss. It looked both sinister and forlorn all at once, more like a solemn monument than an actual working ship. It was abundantly clear that it hadn't flown for years. A relic of a time long past.

'That's your ship?' she asked, uncertainly.

Luko smiled, gazing on the vessel fondly. 'My *Bella Principessa*.'

'What kind of ship is it?' she asked, wrinkling her nose at the dank smell around her. Luko looked round at her in astonishment. 'You not know?'

Salomé shook her head. 'Should I?'

Luko looked dismayed. 'The most famous ship in space? No?'

Salomé looked unimpressed. 'That ... that thing is famous?'

Luko spluttered. 'Oh, now you hurt me, signorina. Do you not see? Look beyond the mess, see her elegant lines. Dual Ziemann energy deflection shields, Irrikon thruspace drive, Kruger lightfast engines. This ... this is a Cobra and not just your ordinary Faulcon de Lacy Cobra!'

Salomé stepped back in surprise at the growing indignation on Luko's face.

'This ... this, young lady ... this ... is a hand built Cowell and MgRath Campaign model-from thirty-one twenty!'

Salomé raised her eyebrows innocently and spared the old ship another glance. 'Oh ...'

Cobra ... wasn't that what that old lady said she had flown?

'Does it work?' she asked.

Luko grimaced and paused, before looking around guiltily.

'I have a friend who has a saying ...' Luko frowned for a moment, trying to recall, 'ah yes ... the hamster is dead but the wheel is still spinning.'

'What? You mean it's broken?'

'Needs parts ...'

'You led me out here and it doesn't even work?'

'The ship is good, signorina. I fix all damage, but hyperdrive is ... how you say? Caput. Why you think I stuck here? I not come for vacation, you know.'

'Then ...'

'Pirates. Fighting, attack me in space,' Luko said. 'I fight back. Kill them all. But damaged you see. Set down for repairs. Hyperdrive no working. No parts, can't fix. No traders come this way. Planet is forbidden, remember.'

'You got marooned? For how long?'

Luko held up his hand and flexed his fingers and thumb four times.

'Twenty years?' Salomé gasped. 'You've been stuck here for twenty years?'

Luko nodded.

'Twenty years, signorina. Is a long time to wait, no?' He looked wistfully up at his dilapidated ship. 'The Cobra ... has not flown in all that time.'

'You've been on your own since then?'

'I saw a few other ships come down. A crash. Prospectors, pirates. Crews always were caught and eaten. I was not fast enough to save them. This time ...'

'Eaten?' Salomé's face paled. 'By those ...'

'Don't worry. We safe now. I have set a perimeter. If they enter the cavern ... zap!'

Salomé nodded in relief.

'So, big question. Your ship. Any good?'

Salomé looked forlorn. 'It was wrecked too. It's smashed, there's no way it will fly again.'

Luko shook his head. 'Just need spare parts. Does it have hyperdrive? What ship?'

Salomé nodded. 'Yes, yes it does. I don't know. It's small.'

'Show me.' Luko gestured to the sand. Salomé drew a rough picture of Hassan's ship with a fingertip.

'Eagle?' Luko queried.

CHAPTER TEN

Salomé nodded. She remembered Hassan identifying the ship as an Eagle. 'A Mark 1, I think.'

'Mmm. Maybe ok,' Luko answered, with a small shrug of his shoulders. 'Is an older ship, this is good. I will fire the drives. Leave tomorrow, find your ship and we pray for luck yes? Get off this dirtball. Come, you need medicine, then some food and rest.'

He led her down towards the antique ship.

* * *

Hassan came to, drawing a deep shuddering breath. Pain lanced across his body, but it was somehow numbed compared to before. He could just determine he was still hanging by his wrists, but his vision was blurred, sweat stung his eyes. He caught sight of his legs and feet below; rivulets of blood had dried and caked across them. His blood. The smell registered in his nostrils.

It was the opening of the door to the cell that had roused him. He couldn't raise his head, his neck was too stiff, but he recognised the sharp, clicking footsteps. She was back. His body trembled in response. He tried to say something, but his voice only managed a faint rasp.

'Still alive,' Octavia said from somewhere close by. 'It takes skill to inflict painful wounds without cutting major organs.'

He felt her finger grasp his chin. His neck twisted painfully as she pulled his head up and looked into his eyes.

'Time for remorse is over,' she said. 'You are purged of your sins, sweet little boy.'

He managed to look into her eyes, seeing her smile at the slim glimmer of hope that she saw. 'Your bounty hunter friend tells me you might be useful,' she said. 'That you might assist us with locating your passenger. You remember the girl? Yes, I see you do.'

Hassan swallowed, managing a tiny nod.

'Good,' Octavia continued. 'Good. Do you think you can help us?'

Hassan nodded again, still trying to get his voice to respond. He ran his tongue around the inside of his mouth.

'And if I release you will you co-operate with me? Work with me to locate her and hand her over safely into my hands?' Octavia paced around him, running her hand across his smeared and sweat-stained hair.

'Yes ...'

'I see. You'd betray her just like that? An innocent woman? Abducted against her will and handed over to a notorious villain like me?'

Hassan swallowed, unsure how to answer.

Octavia finished pacing and now stood in front of him again.

'I think you'll say anything just to save your own worthless life,' Octavia said, her voice calm and quiet.

To his horror she reached forward. He felt her fingers push into the rip in his shoulder. Fresh agony shocked through him. His body jerked feebly, his only sound a keening gasp of torment.

'You know nothing about her.' Octavia's voice grew angry. 'She outwitted you herself. She escaped you.'

He felt her fingers pull back; the burst of pain dragged a sharp yell from him.

'You're incompetent, a coward and a fool. Life on the frontier is not for the likes of you.'

A flash of metal. The dagger. A sharp movement close to his face. His neck ... his throat. He could feel the cold edge of the dagger. A quick slice was all it would take ...

Sushil ...

A rapid burst of thought fired through his tortured mind.

'Wait ...' he rasped. 'The transponder, I can decode it. You can track my ship ... I have the code. You can find her!'

The dagger pressed harder for a moment. Hassan felt hot blood run down his neck. The pressure relented.

'You will find her, you will hand her over,' Octavia said. 'Understood?'

Hassan nodded.

'It's your life or hers. If she is not mine ... I will finish what I have started, have no doubt about that.'

* * *

CHAPTER TEN

Luko had seen to the cuts on Salomé's wrists and face with some basic first aid and then insisted that she lie down for a while. Salomé surprised herself by accepting without much protest, falling gratefully into a bunk and drifting off to sleep almost immediately. Luko had a gentle but persuasive manner and she was utterly exhausted.

By the time she awoke it was dark outside the ship. The hold of the Cobra was far more expansive that that of the Eagle, providing plenty of room to walk about. Inside, the vessel was clean and smart, if rather old fashioned. There were no automatic doors between rooms, each area was secured with a manual hatch that had to be spun open and closed by hand.

She walked down the docking ramp to see a pair of chairs arranged at a small table. Luko was sitting in one, holding a glass of wine and sipping from it, all the while contemplating the dimly lit cavern around the ship.

It was a surprisingly lavish spread of food and beverages.

'Ah, signorina. Well rested I hope?' he said, greeting her with his habitual smile.

'Much better, thank you.'

Salomé recognised Imperial delicacies and fine wines. When she queried it, Luko simply shrugged and explained that he'd been carrying a cargo of luxuries and food stuffs when he'd been attacked and had been living off them ever since. They were all refrigerated, packed and stored aboard his ship.

'Help yourself,' he said. 'Just be careful, some of these are rich in the stomach.'

Salomé quickly loaded a plate and began eating, she was ravenous. She couldn't remember the last time she'd had a proper meal.

'Where did you get them from?' she said, in a brief pause between mouthfuls.

'I was a trader,' Luko told her. 'I go one place, buy cheap. Go somewhere else, sell at good price. Look for bargains and angles. Is not a bad life.' He grimaced. 'Other than pirates.'

'You said they attacked you,' Salomé said.

'They want my cargo, signorina. Take, sell. Not do the hard work. Traders have to be smart, with the big guns. Yes?'

Salomé looked up at the dark hulk of the Cobra. 'And does this have big guns?'

Luko grinned and raised a glass. 'The *Bella Principessa*? Has an ass of solid iron.'

Salomé looked blank and raised her eyebrows in a question as he sipped his wine.

'She is tough, she can fight,' Luko said with a wink.

'Oh.'

Luko studied her for a moment. 'So, your story, signorina. You no trader. Why you here?'

Salomé sighed. 'A long story.'

Luko laughed and raised his glass towards her. 'We have molto time.'

Salomé related the tale of how she'd woken on Hassan's ship, unable to recall who she was and where she'd been. How they'd encountered the sinister man on Ferenchia. The battle in space and how she'd escaped, crashed and been captured.

Luko listened throughout without interrupting, fascinated by her account. When she finished he pursed his lips for a moment.

'You don't know who you are?'

'No.'

'Imperial girl for sure. Your speech is strong. You call yourself Salomé, but is not your real name?'

Salomé shook her head.

'You want to find out?'

Salomé looked at him and frowned in confusion. 'But how could I do that?'

Luko smiled. 'A trader's best weapon is not his guns, signorina.' He tapped the side of his nose with his finger. 'Knowledge. Far more powerful. Come, let's see what we can find.'

He pulled out a small black box and tossed it on the table. Immediately a holofac image appeared.

'Too far out to call for help, but we still get the wideband news,' he said. He waved his fingers at the holofac and selected the galactic chart. Salomé saw the now familiar group of systems appear in the air between them.

'The ambush,' Luko asked. 'Where did it happen?'

Salomé pointed towards a group of star systems. 'Somewhere here, so Hassan said.'

'You've come a long way,' Luko acknowledged.

'So where are we?' she asked.

CHAPTER TEN

Luko smiled. 'This place?' He gestured to a faint system on the edge of the map. 'No real name. Is called, ah, LTT 8740.'

He pulled up a set of newsfeeds. Dozens of entries scrolled up in the air, fading away as they reached the top.

'No good, too much,' Luko said. 'We need to narrow it down.'

Salomé had a thought. 'Can you search for a name?'

'Of course, but what name?'

She leant forward and summoned up a keyboard on the table; she tapped out the name the trench-coated man had called at her.

Kahina.

'Search for that,' she instructed.

'Kahina?' Luko asked.

Salomé felt a wave of dread pass through her as he said the name. She shivered, feeling suddenly cold in the dampness of the cavern. Luko regarded her with a frown.

'This name, is not a good name for you?'

Salomé shrugged. 'I don't know, it feels sad ... no, it scares me ...'

Luko gestured for the search and the newsfeeds coalesced around a single system. Salomé read the name.

'The Prism system,' she whispered. It felt familiar, accompanied by a rush of anticipation and anxiety. A tightness grew in her chest.

Luko went to expand the information, but Salomé caught his arm. 'Wait,' she said.

'Signorina, you don't want to know?'

'What if I don't like what I learn?' she asked. Luko smiled.

'A good question,' he said, 'a very good question. Maybe you ask who you want to be?'

Salomé sighed. 'I don't know who I am, how can I know what I want to be?'

'Ask yourself what makes you happy.'

'Happy?' Salomé laughed. 'Don't be ridiculous. In the last few days, I've been stabbed, burnt, beaten and kicked. Kidnapped, stolen and abused. Hauled up a mountain. I nearly died of thirst and then almost drowned. I've been shot at, just escaped dying in a crash and that's before you even start on the loss of my ...' She glared at Luko's amused look. 'What?'

'But you kept going? Why? Why you not just give up? Eh?'

Salomé frowned. 'I don't know … I guess …'

'You love the adventure!' Luko grinned at her, clenching his fist. 'You pit yourself against the universe and still you win. Is fun, yes?'

'Adventure? Fun?' Salomé leant back. 'It was a nightmare. It still is! Here I am, stuck only the Emperor knows where with you and your stupid broken down ship …'

'Just think of the stories you will tell to your grandchildren.'

'Grandchildren?' Salomé replied, angrily. 'I won't have any …'

'Oh, signorina … surely every woman …'

'I'd rather travel to the edge of space than settle down to breed some popinjay's useless offspring.'

'Ah!'

Luko pointed a finger at her triumphantly. Salomé glared back at him.

'The edge of space,' Luko repeated, his eyes bright with triumph. 'There it is. Your heart's desire. Exploring, amongst the stars. The bliss of travel without pressure. The Frontier is calling you.'

'Don't be ridiculous. I want no such thing.'

Luko's face retained its irritating but knowing grin.

'Yes. Yes you do. I see it in your eyes. This look … I know this look. The Frontier has cast its spell … sooner or later …'

A vision of space swam across her mind. The view from the cockpit of Hassan's ship, how it had taken her breath away with myriad distant stars. The view across the city; lit by sunlight as they descended to land. The atmosphere fading from azure to black as they launched, leaving mundane planetside folks behind. Just a handful of worlds she had seen so far, each so different from the next. New worlds, an almost infinite number of places she had never seen. Yet out there, too many to count, let alone visit.

Explore the Frontier.

'Beyond the Frontier,' Luko whispered. 'Who knows what is there? Worlds, civilisations … possibilities. Only the bravest venture into the unknown, far beyond the core worlds, seeking … who knows what you might find?'

Salomé felt her heart stir at his words. It resonated with something deep inside her; a wanderlust.

CHAPTER TEN

To go out there, searching.
She shook her head.
'Maybe,' she said, 'but I must know who I am, otherwise ...'
Luko sighed. 'Truth is a dangerous thing, perhaps you not want to remember?'
'I must know, Luko.'
'This name, Kahina. It makes you feel bad. Maybe best to leave it where it lies?'
Salomé shook her head. 'No.'
Luko nodded reluctantly pulled the newsfeeds out and expanded them across the display. There were dozens of articles. They centred around one of the moons in the system. As it zoomed out Salomé saw the name 'Chione'.
'Chee on?' Luko asked, puzzling over it. 'Never heard of it.'
'Kee-own-nee,' Salomé corrected without thinking and then realised what she'd done. 'I knew this place. There were coloured stars in the sky, a warm sun sparkling on a blue sea, an eclipse casting a warm red shadow, it happened every day, it was a wonderful sight.'
'Sounds a most beautiful place. We are on the right track it would seem,' Luko said and opened the most prominent item associated with the moon. It was more than a week old.

In a dramatic political coup, revolutionary forces have usurped the control of Chione, a habitable moon in the Prism system. Chione, which boasts little save a Tantalum mining operation, was home to the Loren Lineage, an Imperial family originally from Haoria. Reports escaping from the world indicate that Senator Algreb Loren was assassinated by the revolutionaries. This group, calling themselves 'Reclamists', insist that they have a prior claim to the moon and are asserting rights that were taken from them by the Imperials. The capital, Leeson City, has been left in ruins as a result of the conflict.

Many pundits have speculated that the Federation bankrolled the revolutionary forces in order to destabilise the area. Federation and Imperial forces are known to be massing in the surrounding systems and a confrontation seems inevitable. The fate of the rest of the Loren family is unconfirmed officially, but it is understood that the Senator's wife, and his three daughters: Corine, Tala and Kahina, were also killed in the coup.

With the Senator and his family gone, ownership of the system remains unclear, with the Reclamists asserting their intention to uphold their claim. Pirate activity in the system is now rife and traders are advised to stay well clear of the area until the situation resolves itself. Dana Mayfield, reporting for the Imperial Herald.

'Are there any pictures?' Salomé demanded.

There were none connected with the news article itself, but a quick search revealed some holos of the Loren family.

Salomé gasped as a striking blonde-haired man appeared. Her hand went to her mouth in shock, stifling a small shriek. The image fired memories. She knew him …

You remain a disappointment to me.

Luko observed her reaction and read from the text. 'Senator Algreb Loren. A powerful man, yes?'

Salomé nodded. More images. Two women with blonde hair.

You must look the part for the wedding, no?

Salomé had seen one of them before. But not like this, not beautiful, elegant and sophisticated, but with a blood splattered face, dead, eyes unseeing.

How can I possibly know this? It's as if …

The final image appeared on the holofac.

Salomé stared in disbelief. The image was small and a little blurred. The woman in the image stood next to the two other sisters, her simple straight dark hair standing out in marked contrast with the elegant blonde curls of the others. The woman was dressed in a fine Imperial gown, decked with jewellery, carrying herself with an air of smug authority. Her expression was haughty and dismissive.

Memories assaulted her mind, snapshots of fleeting recall abruptly snapped into place in her consciousness. A barrage of images, sounds and reconstructed sequences blistered through her head.

She cried out in pain, almost overwhelmed before the sensation passed.

I can remember!

Luko did a doubletake, looking at Salomé and then back at the holofac a couple of times to check for himself.

'Is you, signorina!'

CHAPTER TEN

Salomé read the name from the image caption.

My name!

'Lady Kahina Tijani Loren, third daughter of Senator Algreb Loren of Chione. Deceased.' She looked up at Luko.

'You look very well for one who is dead,' he said with a chuckle. 'A Senator's daughter, eh?'

She didn't respond for a moment. 'These … these Reclamists,' she spluttered. 'I remember now … They destroyed my home, they assassinated my family.' Anger flooded her voice. 'They tried to murder me!'

'Signorina …'

Anger chilled and froze, replaced by an icy determination. Luko leant back away from the ferocity etched on her face.

'They stole my future. That moon is mine by right. I want it back.'

Her fists clenched and her body and voice shook. 'They will pay for this.' She had a name now too, her memory complete.

'Starting with a murderous traitor.' Her eyes narrowed. 'Dalk Torgen.'

Chapter Eleven

Hassan woke and found himself staring up into bright lights. He was horizontal, immobile. Within moments of waking he could feel pain burning through his shoulder, hand and neck. His body trembled with the memory, but he was able to retain control this time. He raised his arm, he could see his hand had been bandaged. It was by no means a professional job, but somebody had tried to take care of him.

'Did what I could.'

Hassan turned and looked across, seeing the bounty hunter watching him from a bunk on the opposite side of a room. The room itself was a simple cabin.

'She …'

'Decided not to kill you. We both have a use, so it would seem. My name is Dalk, by the way.'

'Hassan.'

Dalk leant in closer.

'We can get out of this alive. Just play along and do what you're told. We're not important in Octavia's grand scheme, she wants something else …'

'The girl,' Hassan croaked, trying to lubricate his mouth with his tongue.

Dalk nodded. 'Yes, the girl.'

Hassan frowned and then winced with pain. 'What's so important about her anyway?'

Dalk smiled. 'That depends on who you talk to.'

'You said she was the daughter of a Senator.'

'She is and she's heir to his estate. Her family suffered a coup by a rebellion, bankrolled by the Federation. Our mutual friend Octavia supplied the arms. The whole Imperial family was wiped out, she's the only survivor. The Imperials allowed it to happen to safely get rid of an unwanted Senator in a politically acceptable fashion; they planned to restore her to power so she was smuggled out …'

Hassan gulped.

'The convoy I attacked?'

'Yes, she was aboard. You caused no end of trouble,' Dalk replied. 'Octavia confounded the Imperial plan and you confounded hers.'

'I never meant to steal the girl. I just ...'

'What you meant to do is irrelevant. Kahina is missing. Octavia wants her and will stop at nothing to get hold of her.'

'Why? What use is she to her?'

Dalk hesitated. 'The usual. Ransom, money, influence. She's a Senator's daughter after all. Quite a prize for a pirate. She'll fetch a healthy sum regardless of whether she ends up returning to the Empire or as an object of ridicule in the Federation.'

'Octavia maintains her strength in this sector,' Hassan mused.

Dalk straightened. 'Whatever happens afterwards, it is more important that the girl is first reinstated to her position. In her absence the moon her family governed has since fallen into anarchy, Federation and Imperial fleets stand poised above it, both wishing to avoid a direct confrontation, but knowing it is inevitable unless the situation resolves. Her presence as a legal heir is the only thing that can do that.'

'Wait. You mean ... a war?' Hassan gasped.

'A war,' Dalk confirmed.

'Randomius ...'

'We must find her and quickly.'

Hassan thought it through for a moment. 'So why is a bounty hunter so interested in keeping the peace?'

Dalk sat back and regarded him. 'I would have thought by now you'd have learnt your lesson. Don't poke your nose where it's not welcome. It'll only bring you grief.'

* * *

Daylight shone through the vines overhead, lighting the cavern with a green tinge. Luko had primed the ship's drives ready for flight. He spent some time scrubbing moss and mildew from the accessible parts of the ship before reluctantly stopping for breakfast.

CHAPTER ELEVEN

Kahina had been busy too. She'd raided the ship for clothing, finding a simple but elegant dress in the supplies of luxuries aboard. She'd been a little surprised that it contained a series of clips that she had to wrap around her legs. It felt clingy and awkward to her. It was only after a little thought that she realised a traditional dress might be rather revealing in zero gravity. Clearly a clever tailor had thought through the problem of wearing something elegant aboard a free falling spacecraft. Whoever he or she was, Kahina was grateful.

She'd been able to get clean too. Her body was stiff from the injuries she'd suffered over the last few days, but she'd regained her strength. With her memories intact she was possessed of a steely determination, her face set and her mouth taut. A Senator's daughter once again.

Luko watched as she approached, giving her an appraising look.

'Bella signorina,' he said with a wink. 'Now you look like an Imperial princess.'

He saw her frown. 'I am not a princess. I am a lady, the daughter of a Senator. We do not have such outmoded titles.'

Luko sighed and then tried again. 'You still wish to return to your home and fight these … revolutionaries?'

This time he got a full on stare of disapproval. 'They killed my family and stole my home. Would you not do the same?'

'Signorina, you are very brave,' Luko said with an exaggerated shrug. 'But how you do this? One woman against an army? Is not good plan.'

She raised her head proudly. 'My father had a fleet of ships at his disposal.' She waved at the old ship behind him. 'Dozens of vessels, not like these insignificant little craft. Real warships. They are mine to command. Think of that. My people will rally to my call.'

Luko paused for a moment, deciding to probe a little further.

'These are same people who let you be captured? Great care they took of you!'

'They don't know I am alive. When they do it will be different. I must return to them. Then you will see.'

Luko shook his head. 'Happiness is not found in vengeance, signorina.'

Now she portrayed an arrogant air. 'It is our way. You wouldn't understand.'

Luko nodded and rolled his eyes. 'Ah … Imperial honour. This I know well.' He fixed her with a look. 'But is it your way, signorina? Hmmm? Remember your heart's desire.'

'That was just your supercilious nonsense,' she snapped. He noticed she dropped eye contact at the same time. 'A moment of weakness. You took advantage, just like the rest of them.' She looked back at him. 'What was your plan, trader Luko? Take me to the edge of space and sell me again like everyone else has tried to do?'

'Signorina, I mean you no harm. I wish only to see you do what you …'

'I will not be abused, cajoled, intimidated or coerced anymore.' Her voice was shrill. 'I will return to my people, to the Empire, to my home. Reclaim what is mine.'

Luko nodded disapprovingly. He looked away and then glanced back at her. She returned his gaze with an angry glare.

'So it seems,' he said thoughtfully. 'You will start a war to do this?'

'If necessary.' She nodded. 'My home was taken by force, I will use force to take it back.'

'Thousands will die,' Luko said, keeping his gaze steady and his voice measured. 'What of those that fight? Do you not care for them? Battles are not glorious stories you read in tales. Cold, lonely, brutal things they are. Best avoided. No one gains.'

She faced him, hand on hips. 'You think I should just leave them to it? My family's titles, honour and estates? Their power, their money?'

'Signorina, I have seen more battles lost than battles won. If you are happy to send thousands to their deaths to avenge your loss … I think you should ask what kind of leader you will be. Trust me, this is not what you want.'

'Don't you dare tell me what I want! What would you know of high society? Armies fight battles. That is what they are for.'

Luko grimaced and shook his head. 'Armies keep the peace.'

'Enough. You will take me back to my home. That's my price.' She turned away, waving her hand dismissively.

Luko looked surprised. 'Price, signorina?'

She turned back. 'You can fix your ship from the wreckage of mine, I will show you where it is; in return you must take me back to the Prism system.'

'Maybe I think I have already paid you back by saving you from Fanaticos. No?'

'You'd be wrong.'

CHAPTER ELEVEN

Luko laughed at her determined look.

'Is long way,' he said doubtfully. 'Navigation is treacherous.'

'That's where I need to go.' Her direct stare was back. 'Or we can stay here and rot away with your Fanaticos.'

Luko shrugged.

'Maybe it is better for the galaxy for you to stay here,' he said. 'Perhaps this is fate, hmmm? No war.'

She laughed. 'You'd stay here? I don't believe you.'

Luko looked at her. 'I am a man of principle. I will not help you start a war.'

'Your principles will do you little good if I kill you and steal your ship,' she replied. He saw her posture stiffen. 'Do not doubt me. I've done it before.'

Luko eyed her stance and her posture. He could tell it wasn't an idle threat. Where ever it was she came from, she had the air of a proficient fighter about her. 'I do not doubt you, signorina.'

'I'll make sure you're rewarded. My people will pay you handsomely for my safe return. More than enough to fix up your ship and get you back doing whatever it is you do.'

Luko grinned. 'Ah, now you appeal to my greed. Molto credits, yes?'

'Whatever you want,' she said.

Luko paced around for a moment, looking at his ship and the dank cavern in which it languished.

'I take you safely home,' he eventually said with a sigh, 'but I not fight your war.'

'Agreed,' she said immediately. 'But you should know, trader Luko … happiness is not found in money either.'

Luko smiled. 'Perhaps not, signorina. But better to be miserable in comfort than die a lonely painful death, eh?'

'I will not die.'

'We all die, signorina. The lucky ones get to choose how and when …'

She interrupted him. 'A deal, trader Luko?'

She held out her hand. Luko held her gaze for a moment. 'Promise me one thing.'

She eyed him suspiciously. 'I will not be …'

Luko held up his hands in a gesture of peace.

'Just listen,' he said softly. 'A momento ... listen to Salomé. She is ...'

'Salomé is dead.' She stepped back, eyes flashing. 'She never even existed.' She took off her ID bracelet and threw it at him. 'I am Lady Kahina Tijani Loren of Chione. Do we have a deal or not?'

Luko watched her for a long moment. He sighed. 'A deal, signorina Kahina. Back to the Empire we go.'

She turned on her heel and strode into the docking bay of the Cobra. Luko watched her go. He picked up the ID bracelet and tossed it in his hand before following her inside.

* * *

Kahina found her way to the cockpit. It was a far bigger space than the tiny version aboard the Eagle. She was able to sit alongside Luko as they both settled in and looked out of the large canopy that stretched across the forward hull. Luko triggered a control and a blast of something under high pressure cleared the mildew from the windows.

Luko set to work on more controls, flicking switches and twisting levers. Kahina looked around in surprise. The flight mechanisms were from a different era. Where the Eagle had been tatty and well used, the Cobra was polished and neat, but every control seemed like an antique. There were none of the familiar holofac displays; all of the instrumentation was far more primitive. She even spotted an ancient mechanical timepiece bolted low down on the console, its face pockmarked with age, marking out time in twenty-four hour segments by the means of two ornate pointers of different lengths.

The entire cockpit was dark hued, with each panel picked out with polished brass highlighting. A bewildering array of physical screens, dials and gauges festooned the cockpit in front of her. Luko finished a sequence of adjustments and a rising reverberation sounded through the vessel. Gauges quivered and rose from their stops, accompanied by an intensifying clamour of various mechanical sounds signalling a growing readiness for take-off.

Kahina grabbed the arms of her co-pilot's flight chair.

It's an antique, it belongs in a museum.

'Thrusters good,' Luko announced.

CHAPTER ELEVEN

Kahina watched as he examined the gauges, tapping one that failed to respond. She saw the needle quiver and settle down. 'Shields are charging. Main power. Hold secure. Ah … my *Bella Principessa*, you are ready to fly once more?'

She saw him trigger another control and the ship trembled, rising unsteadily underneath them. Clouds of smoke blasted out from around the vessel as it slowly rose. Kahina winced at the reverberation echoing through the ancient craft.

'Is it supposed to be this noisy?' she yelled.

'Just feel the power,' Luko replied, with a wide grin. 'She is a good ship.'

He pulled the control yoke in front of him and the old ship tore upwards on a plume of burning fire. Kahina was crushed into her flight chair, pinned by the acceleration. The ship smashed through the vegetation covering the cavern leaving it smoking and charred by the thrust from its take-off jets.

Luko let out a yell of exhilaration. 'She lives!'

He pushed the yoke and the Cobra accelerated forward. Kahina felt the pressure return in a different direction and saw the mountains recede rapidly on the rear viewing screens. She caught her breath.

It can certainly move …

'That way,' she pointed, gesturing across the desert landscape.

Luko banked the *Bella Principessa* in the direction she indicated. Between them an oblong scanner lit up, green and divided into quadrants. A blip appeared ahead, just off centre. She was pleased with herself, her directions had been good.

'I have it,' Luko said with a nod.

They covered the distance it had taken Kahina painful hours to walk in mere seconds. Luko circled around the shattered wreckage of the Eagle once to get a good view before settling the *Bella Principessa* alongside, carefully checking that the ground would support the weight of the ship before shutting down the thrusters.

* * *

A Federal corvette appeared in the depths of the Mithra system accompanied by a series of fighter escorts. Turning sharply the ships adjusted course, proceeding onwards at flank speed, drives roaring, plumes of exhaust plasma leaving a sparkling wake in the darkness.

Their destination was obvious. The planets in the system were millions of kilometres away, but ahead, shining brightly in the glow of twin stars, a series of large vessels could be seen arranged in a delta formation, holding station in the depths of the system.

A Federation fleet.

One large vessel dominated the assembly. Farragut-class battlecruisers were vessels on a scale that almost defied comprehension. It was unusual to see one of these enormous craft at any time; their presence signalled a significant wide-scale operation was being planned. The vast ship was accompanied by a flotilla of smaller vessels; frigates formed a protective escort, their hulls bristling with anti-fighter weaponry. Smaller, but more numerous, were the corvettes, accompanied by formations of single-pilot fighters that were escorting supply vessels to and from the fleet. Not yet fuelled and prepped, it was clear that the fleet was being readied for a major engagement.

Commissioner Tenim Neseva surveyed the approaching fleet from the bridge of his own corvette, the *Manucacamonton*. Jenu stood beside him, eyeing the mass of ships with a worried and awed expression on her face.

'I've never seen such a fleet,' she whispered.

Tenim nodded. 'Something this big hasn't happened in this sector since the Thargoid incursions of fifty years ago. The military are absolutely loving it. A chance to play with their big guns, strut about in immaculate uniforms, shout orders and justify the enormous cost of keeping all of this running. They can't wait to have a face-off with the Imperials. The odd minor skirmish is all very well, but ...'

'You think they're trigger happy? They want a conflict?'

'Do they want a fight?' Tenim chuckled. 'Of course they do. See that battlecruiser? It's never been in a proper fire-fight, neither it nor its captain. They actually don't know how they'll fare against their foes. On specs it's a close run thing, but in a real-life engagement? Nobody knows. They'd love nothing better than to get stuck into a proper battle and find out.'

'And what about the Imperials?'

'They've got something similar according to reconnaissance. Their fleet is

CHAPTER ELEVEN

positioned at Haoria. Before long we'll all be ready to jump into the Prism system. That's when things will get interesting.'

'A battle?' Jenu said with distaste.

Tenim shook his head. 'Don't worry, my dear. That's why we're here. Unfortunately for our military friends, wisdom and cool thinking will prevail over raw untempered lust for gore and glory. Our friend, Ambassador Cuthrick and I will negotiate a face saving truce for all involved.'

'Our … our friend?' Jenu stammered. 'He's the one who sanctioned the invasion of Chione!'

Tenim sighed. 'My dear, you need to appreciate the bigger picture. Chione was never ours in the first place and now the system is in the clutches of a notorious frontier's woman …'

'As you arranged.'

'My dear, a little more discreet please. I had nothing to do with it.'

'Nothing that could be proved.'

Tenim gave her an impatient look. 'Regardless, it's lawless and uncouth. It's high time that the boundaries of civilisation engulf this little system and push the lawlessness out to the edge where it belongs. The Imperials care little for the system itself; access to the Tantalum is all that matters. We're in the same position.'

'But, surely we want the moon?'

Tenim shrugged. 'Why? It's of no specific value, its strategic location is poor, the surface mostly water bound. There's nothing else of value in the system. It will be an administrative overhead for whoever controls it. We will deny that of course and then grudgingly give it up with great remorse, playing our part in keeping the peace.'

'Oh …'

'As long as appropriate rights to the Tantalum are secured and agreed, both sides will be happy with an arrangement one way or the other.'

'So you want to remove Octavia and her pirates.'

'We all do. She's been an excellent tool in frustrating Imperial ambition in the system until this point, but we're now ready to come to terms. This fleet is merely an announcement to the Imperials that it's time for that discussion to commence.'

'And what of the Loren girl?'

Tenim paused. 'Something of a wildcard in the game, it makes things interesting. Octavia will use her to attempt to start a conflict. The Imperials will use her to strengthen their bargaining position. Yet no one has mentioned her at all. Our own spies have been unable to locate her. Perhaps she's already dead. We'll have to deal with her as and when she appears. Fret not. What can a single girl possibly do?'

* * *

Luko had boarded the wreckage of the *Talon* and raided it for parts. It hadn't taken him long to find what he required. He responded to Kahina's questioning look with a brief thumbs up. The *Talon's* hyperdrive system was salvageable and had the spares Luko needed to fix the *Bella Principessa*.

It took him a while to pull the modules from the smashed ship. Kahina watched for a while, idly wondering what the collection of complex bits and pieces strewn across the cargo bay actually did. Luko had busied himself with removing the damaged equivalents from his own ship. Kahina left him to it, he seemed like he knew what he was doing, but it was clear it wouldn't be finished quickly.

She was occupied by her own thoughts.

Luko and his foolish prattling on about hopes and desires. He was clearly a fool and a dreamer. No wonder he'd got stuck on this desolate planet. By contrast, she was the daughter of a Senator, with responsibilities and duty to uphold. The last of her line, with an esteemed place in Imperial society to enjoy. Thousands of citizens to pledge their allegiance to her, an entire moon to rule …

She caught her breath, feeling her heart pounding with excitement.

Luko was right on one count though, reclaiming Chione wasn't going to be easy. She might have the rights to the moon, morally and legally, but taking them back was another thing entirely. The news reports said that Federation and Imperial fleets were massing in opposing systems. She'd read enough of her father's messages to know that such events were commonplace, if not on the scale of this one. They always ended in a face-saving climb down by both sides after days of aggressive posturing, a safety valve to prevent an all-out war.

CHAPTER ELEVEN

But they had all assumed the Loren family was no more. As a survivor, she changed the game. The Federation, if they truly had instigated the rebellion, would want her dead – she could expose their treachery. Rage flashed within her. Ultimately they were responsible for the death of her family, supporting these treacherous Reclamists. She remembered Vargo's furious face, the brutal execution of her parents and the bullets that slashed the life from her sisters.

There will be no mercy for you.

The Empire? Avoiding an expensive conflict would surely be uppermost in their minds, but how would they react to her survival? It would give them an excuse to further their ambitions in this sector, securing the mining rights for the Empire. They would be duty bound to defend her honour once they knew she was alive. Her father's fleet was now hers. Who was the man in charge? Ah, yes, Fleet Admiral Brice, she'd met him once. He knew his duty. The power was at her fingertips.

Her hands trembled with anticipation.

She remembered her father boasting about the Imperial fleet he commanded. She remembered a holofac of an enormous vessel, as big as a city … it was hers now. Hers! And Luko thought she'd be happy settling for a flux-stained piece of junk and heading out into the empty void? The fool.

And Dalk?

She repressed a tremble when she thought of him. She'd trusted him, believed in him. He'd trained her to fight, to understand the politics, to be ready. Ready for what? He'd betrayed her father to the Reclamists. He'd run her through with his sword. She could recall it clearly now, it was a killing blow; practiced, swift and deadly.

What had he said as blackness closed in about her?

It's better this way.

She'd woken on Hassan's ship. Restored to health. He'd said he'd attacked an Imperial ship on the orders of the black market dealer, the woman Hassan had been terrified of – what was her name?

Quinton. Octavia Quinton.

So why was she on that ship? Why go to the trouble of taking her body from Chione? Somebody needed her alive, that was clear enough. But why? Was it Dalk? Why arrange for her family to be killed and then save her in this bizarre fashion? Was it Octavia? What possible interest could a Senator's daughter be to a black market dealer? Ransom? That made no sense. There was no one left alive to pay it. No other Senator would care.

And yet ...

Dreams of space, travel and freedom crossed her mind once more. She didn't have to do this, she could leave it all behind, be the mysterious and vulnerable Salomé. Find a different way. No one would ever know. Just find a ship, a little money and head out into the void.

She shook her head to clear it. She was Lady Kahina Loren, heir to the Loren fortune, a member of high Imperial society, not some space-addled star-struck fool grubbing a trashy existence on the fringes of civilisation.

The plans had to be exposed, the hidden agendas revealed. She could think of only one way to do it. She would force the situation herself. No more secrets, no more deception. It would be plain, it would be simple.

She climbed up through the living quarters of the Cobra and into the cockpit, closing the bulkhead hatch behind her and sitting herself comfortably in the co-pilot's flight seat. She spotted her ID bracelet on the console. Luko must have picked it up and taken it in.

She reached forward and picked it up, turning it around in her hands for a few moments before clipping it around her wrist and composing herself. She activated the communication system, recording a message.

She was quite finished by the time Luko joined her an hour later. She was still sitting quietly, looking out as the stars flickered in the darkening sky. Luko activated the drives and the *Bella Principessa* roared upwards through the atmosphere and out into the void.

'You still wish to do this?' he asked, as the last wisps of atmosphere fell behind them.

Kahina touched the controls, gently banking the ship around in a slow turn. She gestured to the stars ahead, singling one out for particular attention. It was faint, but burned steadily in the darkness.

'See that star there?' she replied. 'It's mine. It belongs to me. I want it back. Does that answer your question?'

Luko shook his head and settled down beside her in the adjacent chair. 'Is your funeral, signorina.'

CHAPTER ELEVEN

Luko adjusted the controls and began the sequence to spool up the jump subsystems. Kahina watched in satisfaction as the desolate world receded far behind them. Once they were in range of a station with a transmission relay she could execute her plan.

A series of beeps indicated the hyperdrive was ready. Luko glanced across at her again. 'All green. So, signorina,' he said, 'to the Empire we go.'

Light flashed, space folded. The *Bella Principessa* disappeared into witchspace.

* * *

The Imperial cruiser *Atticus* held station scant light years from the massing Federation fleet. A 'Majestic-class' Interdictor, it was the Federation cruiser's equal in size, another behemoth of space. In design, spectacle and sheer presence, it overwhelmed its counterpart completely. Unlike the Federation ship, the Imperial vessel was more than a vehicle of war. Internally much of the ship was appointed with opulence enough to rival the embassies of the major Imperial worlds. A major part of the vessel, centred round the most prestigious areas, spun to provide its occupants with the luxury of artificial gravity. Within this area were staterooms, reception suites, function rooms all furnished with lavishness that redefined the boundaries of excess.

Lounging amidst this profligacy, two patrons of the Empire awaited the arrival of the ambassador and the admiral of the great ship.

'Your first time aboard?' Gerrun asked.

His companion looked distinctly ill at ease.

'If nature had intended man to travel through the implacable void it would have furnished us with stronger stomachs,' Zyair complained. His face was grey. He clutched at the arm of his chaise longue as if scared he would be thrown off it.

'Far better to be here in the carousel rather than the weightless sections,' Gerrun reassured him. 'You'll adjust soon enough.'

'I don't want to adjust. Life on a planet suits me far better. A stable planet, mind. Like the one our erstwhile Senator promised we would enjoy, or have you forgotten that?'

'I have not forgotten. I'd simply refrain from criticising him aboard this vessel. Fleet Admiral Brice ...'

'... was the Senator's right-hand man. You think I don't recall? I assume you haven't forgotten that he was the one who dropped the bombs on the original colonists?'

'Illegal occupiers, I believe you mean.'

'I know what I mean. He had no qualms about that, did he?' Gerrun leant forward.

'My friend, what is it that concerns you so?'

Zyair matched his move, leaning in close, his voice dropping to a whisper.

'Only this, Patron Gerrun. That man is a butcher, a maniac at the helm of one of the most powerful vessels our glorious Empire has ever sent forth. We stand across from a fleet of Federation vessels, captained by equally inflexible military men, bedecked and beweaponed in ships of pure unalloyed destructive power – and you ask what concerns me?'

'Ambassador Cuthrick will negotiate a truce with the Federation. Their commissioner has no interest in a conflict either.'

'You underestimate the military inclination to violence. We've had relative peace for decades, yet each confrontation results in greater escalation. More ships are deployed, more hands on triggers. One single mistake, a flash point ... that's all it will take, my dear Gerrun. Mark my words.'

'You do paint a depressing picture,' Gerrun replied. 'Surely some credit must go to the military; they have kept the peace you refer to.'

Zyair was spared from answering by the approach of Ambassador Cuthrick. As always he was accompanied by his pair of aides. Gerrun and Zyair came to their feet as they approached, exchanging customary bows. As was appropriate, Gerrun and Zyair bowed lower than the ambassador, whilst the aides bowed lowest of all, lowering themselves upon one knee as etiquette demanded.

'Ambassador.'

'Patrons.' Cuthrick's voice was as smooth and melodious as ever.

'What news?' Gerrun demanded.

'The Federation fleet continues to mass as we anticipated,' Cuthrick said. 'A strength at least equal to ours.'

'War mongering dogs,' Zyair said.

CHAPTER ELEVEN

Cuthrick held up his hands in a gesture of peace. 'My counterpart, Commissioner Neseva has just rendezvoused with them. He will mollify matters on the Federation side.'

'Can we trust him?' Zyair demanded.

Cuthrick considered the matter. 'Trust is a powerful word, dear Patron. Commissioner Neseva certainly desires that we collectively avoid a war. I would say that we can depend upon him. Certainly he is more of an ally to the cause of peace than are our own military personnel.'

'It was ever thus with military minds,' Gerrun agreed.

'And Dalk?' Zyair demanded. 'Where is he? And where is that dratted Loren girl?'

'Where indeed?' Cuthrick replied.

* * *

The *Keimola Gateway* was an old station, in a system of little note in the grand scheme of things. A cluster of ships hung close by, either parked or abandoned. The station slowly spun in the darkness, lights trailing in slow circles around a rectangular docking bay. It was a curiously simple design. At first glance one might mistake it for a cube, but each corner was sliced away as if by some astronomical scythe. It was a dodecahedron, forever rolling on a central axis of symmetry. A classic Coriolis.

Approaching it slowly was an old fashioned ship, its stained and tarnished hull also a series of simple interlocking geometric shapes, navigation lights blinking purposefully in the darkness. The dim light of cockpit illumination could be seen filtering from the upper hull.

With a flicker of reaction control systems, the ship began to roll to starboard, matching the rotation of the station and aligning itself smoothly with the gaping docking bay. Drives, once white hot with power, cooled to a dull red. The ship slowed with brief bursts of retro-fire from forward thrusters.

Aboard the *Bella Principessa*, Kahina watched as Luko finished the adjustments to their approach. She'd watched in surprise as Luko lined everything up manually throughout. She couldn't fault his ability, they were heading dead centre into the docking bay, their rotation perfectly aligned.

'No computers?' she queried.

Luko gave her a disparaging look. 'Flight assist? Pah. Can't dock your ship yourself? Not deserve to be in space. Relax, signorina.'

Kahina watched as the enormous bulk of the station swam towards them, she strained her neck to look upwards at the towering forward face with the stars spinning behind it. It made her dizzy, so she looked forward again. The docking bay expanded towards them, swallowing the Cobra like a maw. Luko touched the retros again and the ship coasted into the bay, coming to a graceful halt. She briefly saw a circular corridor with a matching docking bay at the far end; the space inside contained many other ships.

Enormous mechanical arms secured their vessel, dragging it down to the floor of the bay before clamping into place. The Cobra was ushered forward into an appropriately sized receptacle. A brief clunk signalled they were secure.

Luko powered down the ship.

'Refuel, restore and recuperate,' he said. 'A few more jumps …'

'… and I'll be home,' Kahina finished for him.

Luko nodded and got tentatively to his feet, letting his magnetic boots clamp to the floor. 'I will see to ship,' he said. 'You wish to see the station, yes?'

Kahina nodded.

'Grab your ID. No stealing my ship and making away?'

'We made a deal, didn't we?'

Luko nodded, gave her a cautious look and descended from the cockpit. Kahina followed him, feeling the faint grip of artificial gravity tugging at her as she descended through the Cobra's decks. It still made her feel queasy, but experience had allowed her to anticipate and acclimatise to the sensation. Luko was busy opening up the portside airlock.

She placed her hand on her ID bracelet and spun it around on her wrist.

With this I'm just Salomé. But not for much longer.

The internal airlock door swung inwards, presenting them both with a narrow corridor, lit intermittently by faint green lights. They made their way clumsily down its length, moving slowly in the low gravity.

At the far end was a similar hatchway. Luko operated the controls and the hatch opened, allowing them into a small square room. A sign flashed on in front of them in red, buzzing for attention.

CHAPTER ELEVEN

DeCom.

Kahina sighed, remembering the irritating procedure from before. This time it was short however, the light flickered to green almost immediately and a door before them slid open.

Beyond was a much larger space. Kahina blinked in surprise, unprepared for the view that awaited beyond.

The ceiling was transparent.

They had emerged just below the central axis of the station. Their ship, presumably along with hundreds of others, was parked in a small purpose-made bay. From these bays, all routes led to this central complex, a cylinder within the station itself whereby ships could be seen moving through an empty central space, some arriving and slowing to dock, others leaving. It was a most peculiar sight. The floor curved sharply up to her right and left, meeting itself some few hundred metres above her head. She looked up and could see people walking around on the ceiling.

No, it's still the floor, even up there!

A ship passed between them and her, slowly moving along the central chamber, its drives glowing faintly as it left on its way to who knew where.

At the far end of the space Kahina could just make out a rectangular docking slit, the equal of the one they had come through. Beyond it was inky blackness.

Space and the void ...

Only when looking forwards and back was some semblance of normality retained. With a mental effort, Kahina could imagine she was walking though some strange gently curving furrow in the ground. People milled around her, oblivious to the peculiarity. Perhaps it was no more extraordinary to them than a walk across a street in a planetside city.

Luko caught her astonished expression. 'You get used to it. Come.'

He led her to the side of the space, where a cluster of people were already waiting. As they approached, a door opened, revealing the interior of some kind of transport device. Along with many others Kahina and Luko filed in. There were seats, which surprised her; what purpose did they serve in the minimal gravity? Everyone seemed keen to take one, so Kahina did so too, seating herself slowly beside Luko.

'Hold on,' he advised.

Kahina did as instructed, clamping her hands around the conveniently placed grab handles alongside.

Across from her sat a family group, what she assumed were two parents and two young boys judging by the family likeness. Kahina studied them for a moment. The man had greying hair and a stern face, but it softened into a grin as he engaged in some game of words with the youngest boy. Kahina saw the laughter lines around his face. The young boy laughed out loud. Next to him the woman was talking seriously with the older son, her long brown wavy hair half hiding her face. The older son seemed to be complaining about something. The woman gently raised a finger and gave him a look. The son subsided and pulled a face. The woman laughed.

Family ...

Kahina sighed loudly. The man looked up at her briefly, a faint frown crossing his face. Kahina looked back at him, his face had a vague familiarity about it, but there was no way she could have met him before.

With a brief tone the transport lurched. Kahina grabbed the handles tighter, fighting against the unexpected sensation of being pulled upwards out of her seat. It was some kind of lift, taking them 'down' towards the outside edge of the station. The sensation faded, replaced by a rapidly increasing feeling of weight and a curious sense of being pushed back in her chair. She noticed the family on the other side seemed to have the opposite problem, they were leaning forwards in their seats.

With another tone the lift came to a halt. The moment it did so, Kahina could see people tapping their shoes, disengaging the magnetic clamps. They stood up, impatiently waiting for the doors to open. Gravity felt normal! The moment the doors opened, everyone surged out, including the family group, leaving Kahina and Luko behind.

Luko helped her to her feet. She caught her breath. How strange to feel heavy again. 'Ok?' he asked.

She nodded.

They emerged from the lift. Kahina blinked in surprise.

Noise. The combined chatter, shouting and bustle of hundreds of people milling around about her. The lower levels of the station were crammed full of people, pushing in one direction or another. Small bots flew overhead,

CHAPTER ELEVEN

some carrying out errands for their owners, others dragging holofac advertisements behind them. One passed close over her head, making her duck instinctively. Somebody nearby giggled at her. She looked, catching a faint glimpse of the machine as it whirred away, blaring an irritating but catchy tune as it did so.

Priest's perfect protopolpys! Tuttle's tasty therapsabladders! Just five credits, all you can eat! Last real food before witchspace ...

Huge holofac images glowed around her, full height holograms of bizarre looking clothing, ships, food, and here and there surprisingly erotic forms of entertainment that left her gaping in surprise. It was gauche and unsophisticated; it would never have been allowed on an Imperial world. They seemed to be in a huge shopping precinct. Shops haphazardly framed a street that ran straight in both directions.

No, not straight.

It gently curved up to her right and left, rising up like a cliff. Her mouth dropped open with a gasp of surprise.

The lift they had just arrived in had descended down a vast columnar support which ran from the central axis of the station down to here, near the outside. She could see two others, each arranged a quarter of the way around the inside of the station. She guessed there was a fourth, hidden from her view. The 'street' circumnavigated the inside of this self-contained world, meeting itself high above her head, behind the central hub. She'd been 'up' there just a moment ago. Buildings jutted upwards from the ground towards the axis all around her. Above she could distinguish side 'streets', departing the main route and allowing access into other parts of the station. There was even one green area, about a third of the way around the circumference from her position, framing what was clearly a lake.

She swallowed. It looked totally ridiculous. Untold millions of litres of water just hanging there on the wall, poised to fall ...

But from there I'm hanging in the air too!

Kahina staggered backwards, trying to make sense of it all. She was jostled impatiently by people trying to get past.

'You look like tourist,' Luko scolded, pulling her behind him and to one side, out of the never-ending stream of people. 'Golden rule. Never look up. Yes?'

Kahina took a deep breath and nodded. Keeping her eyes at 'ground' level definitely helped.

'I need to get parts,' Luko said. 'You want to come with me or look around?'

Kahina looked around her, still fascinated. 'I'll look …'

'Docking Bay 42 if you get lost, yes?' Luko said, looking seriously at her. 'And don't buy anything. They see you coming a light year away. Tourist prices, bad.'

Kahina frowned, but conceded the point. 'Sure?' he queried.

Kahina nodded. 'See you soon.'

Luko disappeared into the crowd. Kahina turned and headed in the other direction. She traversed the crowd, finding that people on the other side of the street were generally heading in the direction she was going. One thing reassured her, it was impossible to get lost. A quick glance overhead told her exactly where she was. She'd easily be able to find her way back to the lift.

She looked around her for a specific sign, not seeing it immediately in the crowded mix of banners and adverts. Above, transports came and went, she instinctively moved aside as an aircar with police markings slowly traversed the area, before moving onwards.

There, a comms station.

That was what she needed. She moved onwards, past a busy crowd of people clustered around one stall. She negotiated her way past, trying to get through as politely as possible. Something was grabbing their attention. She idly looked across.

She caught sight of a rather shabby looking man, with long almost mane-like hair and wild protruding eyes, standing on a series of packing crates. They were all marked *SS Hesperus* in hastily painted text. He held something in his hand; it looked like a small round mound of fur. She caught his voice, hawking his wares.

'Are you looking for a cute and fluffy companion for those long interstellar journeys perchance? I have some rare, exotic and adorable creatures from the far flung corners of the galaxy aboard that would give you much care and affection in the dark and lonely void …'

Whatever the creatures were they seemed popular. Folk were waving credit vouchers and ID bracelets at him. She could see kids cradling the things

CHAPTER ELEVEN

excitedly in their hands. Some of them made little whistling noises. One had eyes she could see, huge soulful eyes with big brown irises. They were adorably cute, perhaps she could get one.

A man pushed past with a rough laugh. 'Look at that 'stard with his Trumbles. Get one of those on your ship and you can kiss your cargo goodbye, teeth like razors, eat anything. And they sell 'em to kids!'

Perhaps not.

She spotted the family she'd seen in the lift on the far side of the Trumble seller. Both boys clearly had their minds set on owning one of the furry creatures. The father shook his head. The youngest child pouted. She heard him even over the sound of the crowd.

'Oh … disappointment!'

She moved on. The comm station wasn't busy compared to the other stalls and shops. It seemed like most folk were after food, drink and entertainment. There were a series of holofac cubicles. With a quick look around her she stepped inside one, allowing the door to close behind her. She settled into the single chair contained within.

She touched the communication system, waiting for it to link up and negotiate with the station's systems. A few moments later a young man's face appeared.

'Station five comms. How can I help?'

'I need a message sent to the Imperial Herald and the Imperial Citizen,' Kahina said.

'News report, general enquiries or job application?'

Kahina smiled. 'Oh, news. Definitely, news.'

'Standby.' The man looked aside. Kahina could see him calling up a holofac display and gesturing with his hand. 'Direct message or pre-rec?'

'Pre-rec.'

'File please.'

Kahina tapped commands into her own console and tapped her bracelet against it, sending a file across the link.

'That will take about half an hour to reach them, ok?'

'That's fine.'

'Charge is fifteen credits. ID please.'

Kahina placed her ID bracelet on the console. It flickered briefly as it was interrogated. 'That's on its way. Anything else I can do for you?'

Kahina smiled at him. 'Oh no, I think that's more than enough. But thank you anyway.' The man nodded and she closed down the link. She relaxed back in her chair for a moment. There was no turning back now.

Chapter Twelve

The *Manucacamonton* slowed as it approached the enormous Federation battlecruiser. The ship was a dramatic sight at close range. Jenu's overall impression was of an enormous double-bladed sword. The ship's centre line was bisected by a large division, empty and open to space. She could see ships flitting in and out of it and could make out deck upon deck of lights, still tiny even from this distance.

The bridge of the vessel was located near the stern, overlooking the docking area. Dotted around the hull were the telltale blisters of ballistic turrets, missile defences, laser barrage guns, plasma emplacements and doubtless many other weapons devised by those who had designed the vessel.

The ship had little aesthetic appeal, it was built to intimidate, to frighten, to ensure power could be demonstrated easily and deployed swiftly. The arrival of a ship such as this could cow an entire system into submission. Jenu could understand why, her overriding impression was of brooding malevolence.

Communications barked, sharp and efficient, over the comms system. Shields were carefully lowered for the approach, docking clearance was granted and terse instructions given to their fighter escort. Jenu watched as their ship nestled up against the internal flanks of the battlecruiser. With a faint rumble they came to a halt.

Tenim turned, his magnetic boots disengaging and reclamping to the corrugated floor of the bridge. He signalled to Jenu. She gave the battlecruiser one last glance and turned to follow him.

They were met by the captain and his first officer on the other side of the airlock. Both stood ram-rod straight, clean shaven, chins jutting forward. Their uniform was dark and functional, their rank indicated by small emblems on cuffs and collars. As Tenim and Jenu stepped out both snapped a salute in perfect unison.

'Commissioner Neseva.'

'Permission to come aboard, Captain?'

'Permission granted, Commissioner. Welcome aboard the *Xajorkith*.'

Tenim nodded and looked back at Jenu, rolling his eyes with amusement. He looked back at the officers.

'At ease, gentlemen.'

Both men eased their stance, just perceptibly. 'Might I introduce my aide, Jenu Merrington.'

Both officers gave her a peremptory nod. The captain extended his hand. Jenu took it and was rewarded with a firm shake.

'Ms Merrington. My vessel is at your disposal.'

'Most kind,' Jenu replied.

'We've had a long trip, Captain,' Tenim began, 'perhaps we might …'

'Quarters have been prepared, Commissioner,' the captain answered. 'However, we've received a transmission we think you ought to see immediately. It has a direct bearing on our current situation.'

Tenim frowned. 'From the Imperials?'

The captain and the first officer exchanged a look before the captain replied. 'Not exactly, Commissioner.'

Tenim raised an eyebrow.

'Then you'd better show us. Have someone deal with our effects.'

The captain signalled to some nearby deckhands and they scurried off. The captain gestured along the internal corridor that ran the length of the docking area.

Tenim and Jenu were led towards the rear of the vessel. Jenu was quickly disorientated by the sheer internal size of the ship, particularly once they were led away from the areas where external windows allowed a view into space. The interior was drab, grey and functional. Each section of the vessel was sealed off from the next by a series of blast doors, requiring tedious stepping over raised bulkheads to venture into the next section. At least the doors were open, though she assumed they would be closed in the heat of battle. It seemed curiously low tech. Jenu assumed it was a precaution against breaches to the hull. This was a military vessel after all, not a pleasure cruiser.

They arrived in a comms centre. The captain dismissed the operatives inside and closed the door behind them. The first officer busied himself with activating the display units.

A large holofac emitter in the middle of the room began to glow and then

CHAPTER TWELVE

the image of a young woman appeared. She was simply clothed, in a plain but smart dress, a single necklace around her neck. Her hair was dark, cut at the shoulders and neatly brushed. Her face bore the marks of bruises and cuts. Behind her the bulkhead of an old ship could be vaguely made out.

Jenu gasped and Tenim straightened in surprise. There was no mistaking her identity.

The woman turned to look at whatever recording device had been used to create the holofac and began speaking in resolute and assured tones. She was clearly angry, her eyes flashing with emotion and zeal. Tenim and Jenu watched in disbelief and growing alarm as her words filled the room.

'Fellow citizens of the Empire. I am Lady Kahina Tijani Loren …'

The message was direct, challenging and determined. She concluded with an ultimatum, leaning forward aggressively. Then the holofac transmission ended.

Tenim looked at Jenu.

'We did wonder when she'd appear again. She appears to have adopted her own position.'

'She can't mean it?' Jenu said.

'She looked like she meant it to me,' Tenim said thoughtfully. 'Misguided and naïve perhaps, but definitely sincere.' He turned to the captain. 'When did this arrive?'

The captain checked his chronometer. 'Approximately twenty minutes ago, Commissioner. It was wideband, sent out by one of the Imperial newsfeeds. It will be propagating across the systems as we speak.'

'Could it be jammed?'

The first officer shook his head. 'Impossible, Commissioner, the independent networks will already have it by now.'

Tenim nodded.

'Well then. Captain, your priorities have changed.' The captain snapped to attention.

'Bring the fleet to a state of battle readiness,' Tenim instructed. 'We must be prepared to jump to the Prism system as fast as is practically possible. A blockade, if you please.'

The captain nodded, his eyes glowing with excitement. 'It will be done, Commissioner.'

'One further thing, Captain.'

'Commissioner?'

'If you identify the ship that wretched girl is on and it happens to suffer an unfortunate accident …'

'Understood, Commissioner.'

The captain signalled to his first officer and both departed quickly, striding purposefully out of the room.

Jenu turned to Tenim.

'Jump to the Prism system? I thought we were just going to stand off on opposing star systems. The Imperials will be forced to respond if we go in. All those ships in the same system? It will start a war!'

Tenim sighed. 'I'm afraid that is almost inevitable now, my dear. Imperial honour will demand a response to the girl's directive.'

'But …'

Tenim held up a hand. 'No buts, my dear. I'm afraid the Loren girl has pulled the trigger. We must move quickly now … before the hammer falls.'

* * *

Gerrun poured himself a Zaqueesoan Evil Juice and downed a generous portion, savouring the sensation as it warmed the back of his throat and eased its way down into his stomach. Zyair continued to quiz the ambassador.

'Have you heard from Dalk?'

Cuthrick shrugged. 'Alas, Patron Dalk appears to have failed in his mission. We can only assume the girl is lost to us, thus we will have to negotiate harder with the Federation from an inferior position. Fear not, patrons. We will reclaim Chione. The Federation only wants access to resources. We will negotiate a truce. It will present some legal difficulty, but another Senator will be encouraged to adopt this troublesome system and you can henceforth alter your allegiance with no loss of prestige. Your skills and knowledge will no doubt be a key asset.'

'The rebels … these vulgar Reclamists?' Zyair asked.

'They will be … resettled,' Cuthrick said. 'One of the key points of negotiation. We will have to repair the damage they have inflicted. We will offer to do this,

CHAPTER TWELVE

in exchange for ownership and leave the rebels to Federation jurisdiction and law. They encouraged them, it will be their problem to manage. The fleets will disband and we can all return to a semblance of normality.'

'Disband the fleet, you say?'

The three dignitaries looked up as another man approached, striding purposefully to them with no preamble or further acknowledgement. Grey haired, with an erect military bearing, his uniform, ornately festooned with rank and decoration, immediately gave him away.

'Fleet Admiral Brice,' Cuthrick acknowledged, with an incline of his head. Gerrun and Zyair bowed. The two silent aides almost prostrated themselves.

'The fleet will not disband, we have orders.'

Cuthrick raised his head very slightly.

'Orders, Fleet Admiral?' he enquired, a trace of confusion in his voice. 'Perhaps I misunderstand military protocol. I was under the impression that only I had the appropriate jurisdiction …'

'I answer first to the Loren family,' Brice replied. 'I served the Senator …'

'The Senator is dead,' Zyair said, before quickly continuing. 'Most distressing of course. His family too, may their glorious memories never fade …'

Brice interrupted with an air of smug assurance. 'Not entirely accurate.' Zyair looked at Gerrun, who quickly shook his head.

'I'm afraid I don't understand,' Cuthrick said.

'Orders. In the name of the Senator.' Brice gestured and a portable holofac transmitter flared into life.

Zyair's eyes widened as he recognised the subject of the recording. 'His daughter …'

The young woman was unmistakeable. The Imperials watched; Admiral Brice with smug satisfaction, the Patrons and the ambassador with horror and dismay.

'Fellow citizens of the Empire. I am Lady Kahina Tijani Loren …'

The recording played out, much to Cuthrick, Gerrun and Zyair's alarm. 'Are you sure it's really her?' Cuthrick asked.

'Bio-trace came along with the transmission,' Brice answered. 'The Federation are trying to deny it of course …'

'You can't be thinking of carrying this out?' Zyair said, breaking the shocked silence.

Brice smiled. 'I am a loyal servant of the Senator and his family. I swore a vow of allegiance to the Loren dynasty. I will not break it now, like others have done.'

He looked at Gerrun and Zyair, who refused to meet his gaze.

'Most honourable indeed,' Cuthrick said. 'But the wider consequences, we risk …'

Brice turned on him. 'They murdered my Senator. They have treated a lady of the Empire with disgrace. Look at her, wretched and dishevelled. I will not live to see her dishonoured, not on my watch. I will scatter these Reclamists to the ends of space and restore the family I serve to its rightful place. In the Emperor's glorious name!'

'We risk a war, man!'

Brice spun around, his voice cold and threatening.

'And if anyone attempts to stop me, Federation or otherwise …' Brice looked at each of them in turn. 'I will destroy them too.'

Brice turned away and hit a nearby intercom.

'Bridge, this is the admiral. Set condition prime throughout the ship. No further external comms, bring all ships and weapons to a state of full readiness. We jump to the Prism system within the hour …'

'Aye sir,' came the immediate response.

'Fleet Admiral, no …' Cuthrick moved towards him.

Brice ignored the remonstration and talked into the intercom, a satisfied smile on his face. 'You have your orders.'

He punched the intercom off and strode away without a backward glance.

* * *

Deep in the Prism system Daedalion continued moving in its orbit as it had for aeons uncounted, as it would continue to do long after current events were lost in the depths of time. Its shadow eclipsed the warm moon of Chione, casting a chill across the Imperial Palace on the island of New Ithaca.

Vargo, the leader of the Reclamists, watched as the stars sprang into the sky, his expression dour and unmoved despite the spectacular display of celestial

CHAPTER TWELVE

mechanics that graced the moon every single day. He wasn't looking at the backdrop, but at a heavily muscled man before him who had just stepped out of a transport that had landed in the gardens of the palace.

The man's face was flushed, though whether from exertion or anger was impossible to tell. 'Mitchell?' Vargo queried.

'Had to come in person,' Mitchell said. 'Revolt.'

'Put them down,' Vargo said dismissively. 'They are only Imperial minions. Just deal ...'

'We've tried that. Hundreds were slain, thousands ... but they won't stop. The mines are overrun, the transports aren't running ... they just keep chanting.'

Vargo frowned. 'Chanting? Chanting what?'

Mitchell held out a holofac. It illuminated with a hologram of a surging crowd, waving ragged clothing and angrily pushing forwards past the recorder. They were shouting something, but the meaning was unclear, a name perhaps.

'What?' Vargo yelled.

Mitchell altered the holofac to play a different recording.

'This came through two hours ago, it was wideband, all the major newsfeeds are covering it. Everyone has seen it. It's her ... she's coming back.'

Vargo stared. It was a woman, dressed in a simple gown, addressing the recorder directly ... a woman he'd seen killed.

Executed in front of my eyes!

Run through with a sword; her eyes glazing over; blood.

She was dead ... so how?

He listened intently as she spoke, rage clenching his hands into fists.

'The bitch ... how? Dalk ... double-crossed us ...' Vargo staggered back against the threshold of the palace, seeing his plans crumple into dust.

'Federation and Imperial fleets are already coming. They're going to blockade the system within hours. It's war.'

Vargo raised his head, determination setting his eyes ablaze.

'Call in everyone, abandon the mines, torch it all. Then get back here with everything we have. She wants her moon back? There'll be nothing worth saving when I'm finished with it.'

Around them the light brightened sharply. Chione moved out of the shadow of Daedalion, the stars and darkness were banished. Another day had begun.

*　*　*

Hassan, limping and supported by Dalk, was roughly ushered onto the bridge of Octavia's *Anaconda*. Octavia was already there. As she saw them she strode across aggressively.

'Perhaps you trained your girl too well, Patron Dalk,' she sneered. 'Your protégé has taken matters into her own hands.'

Dalk frowned. 'What do you mean?'

Octavia threw a holofac transceiver to him.

'I can't do justice to it myself. She can explain, in her own words.'

Hassan looked confused. 'You've found her?'

Octavia looked furiously at him. 'No, foolish boy, I have not found her! She has made herself known. We received a sector wide transmission. It's on the damn news!'

Dalk thumbed the holofac and an image formed. It was Kahina, dressed in a simple but elegant gown, standing on the bridge of some vessel. He could make out a half-healed cut on her forehead. She looked bruised and battered, but there was no mistaking her determination. The ship behind her wasn't Hassan's Eagle, it was something bigger.

She's regained her memory! But without tutoring, without guidance … No, Kahina! Don't …

The holofac played. Kahina spoke to the recorder in measured tones to start with, factual and to the point.

'Fellow citizens of the Empire. I am Lady Kahina Tijani Loren. I am the daughter of Senator Algreb Loren of Chione, late of the Prism system. My father, along with the rest of my family, was first betrayed and then brutally murdered by revolutionaries calling themselves "Reclamists". They are slyly backed by the Federation. My home has fallen into their clutches and is beset by pirates and the uncouth. These contemptible revolutionaries sought to kill me too, but I have eluded them. It was reported I too had been killed, yet I am alive; they have failed in their ambition.

CHAPTER TWELVE

'Chione belonged to my father by Imperial decree. It was an outpost of the Empire, wrenched from our grasp by the Federation dogs. The occupation is both unlawful and repulsive. With my father's death, rights fall to me, his only living heir. I have been intolerably wronged.

'I will reclaim my world, taken from me by force. I return now to the Empire. I ask you to help me, assist me in defending my honour from those who have no respect for the glory of our grand Imperium. Let me restore what was taken.'

Kahina's voice rose in volume and tempo. Her eyes flashed with anger and zeal.

'I will not be stopped, I will not be slowed. I will take vengeance for the death of my father, a faithful son of the Empire. Together we can restore Chione to Imperial grandeur, frustrating those who would plot against me. I would have these Reclamists brought low. Stand with me, rise up and defend me.

'I am Lady Kahina Tijani Loren of Chione. By my express command this galactic date I require the armies loyal to my father, duty bound by honour and oaths of loyalty to the Loren family, commanded by Fleet Admiral Brice Laurval ... to invade and hold the Prism system for my pleasure. I will return!'

The holofac faded and shut itself down.

Hassan and Dalk exchanged a horrified glance, before both looking towards Octavia.

She stood stock still, staring at the silent holofac before turning to face the two men, her mouth twisted venomously.

'We go to find her now. Pray for success, gentlemen.' She straightened, pointing a trembling finger towards them both. 'You understand the cost of failure.'

* * *

Tenim viewed the latest holofac comunique with dismay.

'Trouble?' Jenu asked, watching the expression on his face.

'Events, my dear. Events.' Tenim sighed deeply. 'Vargo has lost control of the moon. The slaves have overrun the Reclamist movement. They've even seized the space station ...'

'*Hiram's Anchorage*,' Jenu added.

Tenim nodded. 'I fear that his little insurgency is at an end. Vargo and his cronies are holed up in the Imperial Palace awaiting their fate.'

'Then we've lost?'

Tenim smiled. 'A setback, no more. Vargo and his foolish ideas of revolution were never more than an aside. It is the Loren girl that concerns us now. If she successfully returns to the Prism system we will be at a serious disadvantage. Cuthrick will be insufferable.'

'How are we going to stop her? Nobody even knows where she is.'

'We know where she was when she made her transmission and we know where she is headed. I'd imagine that a talented bounty hunter would have little trouble tracking her down.' Tenim paused. 'Should such a ghastly thing be arranged, of course.'

Jenu raised her eyebrows and gave Tenim a knowing look.

*　*　*

The *Bella Principessa* slipped its orbital berth above the planet and began to manoeuvre for the hyperspace jump point. Serviced, refuelled and checked over by technicians it had been restored to full operation. Kahina had fretted a little at the delay, but Luko had informed her that travelling through the systems between their current location and the Empire meant traversing some dangerous parts of space. Most of the worlds hereabout were independent systems; law enforcement was patchy and occasionally non-existent. Flying through with an undependable ship was not recommended.

Twenty years of standing in a damp cavern hadn't done the on board systems much good. Three energy conduits had been replaced, along with the induction coils for the forward weapons. A myriad of other components had been adjusted and checked. Luko had looked longingly at some new drive system upgrades that were on offer, but that would have taken days to install. Kahina had refused point blank.

Kahina watched the other ships come and go around them. It was busier now, traffic seemed to have increased in the few short hours they'd stopped over at the small station. There was a bewildering array of vessels. She spotted a familiar looking Eagle amongst the mix, but the others were unfamiliar, their

CHAPTER TWELVE

blocky and angular lines looking gauche and coarse to her Imperial aesthetic taste.

Luko pointed out some of the interesting ones.

'Type 7 Freighter,' he gestured. 'Slow, ugly as my fat aunt, but if you want stuff moved cheap – nothing better. Sidewinders in the escort too. Nasty little ships, punch above their weight. Always they fly in packs. Watch out for them.'

Kahina watched the formation drift past, wondering where they were going. 'Now …' Luko said appraisingly, 'this more like it. See that? Is a Vulture.'

Another ship cruised past. It was squat and sharply pointed like an arrowhead, with four flanged wing extensions. It looked purposeful and tough. Kahina saw the holofac overlay identify it as the *Raeben*.

'Always flown by folks with bad tempers,' Luko said. 'Pilots always frowning, never smile. Pretty good in a fight, not sharp in turns so they say.'

'Have you fought one?' Kahina asked.

Luko smiled. 'Not yet. Would be a good match for the *Bella Principessa*.' He patted the console ahead of him. 'Cobra is faster, but armour … not so much. Would be an interesting fight.'

'Are you one of these Elite people?'

'Elite?' Luko laughed. 'No, signorina. Not many pilots are Elite. Takes skill, courage and much time … they ruthless too.' He frowned at her. 'What do you know about the Elite?'

Kahina shrugged. 'Not much. I met an old lady who said she was Elite …'

'Pah. Hardly anyone is Elite. Everyone claims they are above average, but mostly harmless is the truth.'

'Mostly harmless?'

Luko grinned. 'Rookie on second flight.'

'Oh …'

A group of four dark hulled and even more dart-like ships blasted past at a high speed. Kahina only got a brief view of them before they dropped astern.

'Vipers,' Luko said. 'Policia mostly. Don't mess with a Viper.'

'They look pretty brutal,' she said.

'Designed to fight, nothing else,' Luko said, with a grimace. 'Small, fast and deadly. Kill pilot? Ship keeps coming. Kill ship? Missile on your tail. Kill missile? The other Viper you not see … it kills you. Don't mess with a Viper.'

'Could you fight them?'

Luko smiled. 'Signorina, never start a fight you can't win. Even the best pilots know when to run.'

The other ships disappeared behind them and another vessel drew her attention. This one was smooth and elegant, with a curving bow and a smooth modern look. She could just make out the name emblazoned on the bow, *Piekna Flecistka*.

Luko smiled. 'And here is someone with money ...'

Kahina admired the clean lines of the vessel, the hull was painted white and it sparkled brightly in the light of the star.

'Expensive?'

'Molto. Is a Dolphin yacht. Very nice, very swish.' Luko gestured expansively 'I am big man, molto credits. I wish to show off, out of my way. I more important than you, I not care what you think, I cannot fly for ...'

Kahina laughed. 'Why, my dear Luko, I do believe you're jealous!' Luko shrugged and muttered something under his breath.

'And what does your choice of ship say about you?' Kahina asked, with a wry smile. Luko tapped the console of the Cobra fondly.

'Ah ... the pilot of a classic Cobra?' Luko pulled his tunic tighter around him. 'Here is a man of taste and discretion. A man who loves elegant design; sophisticated and suave. A man not swayed by fashion.'

'Oh really? Looks like an old piece of junk to me.'

Luko looked hurt. 'You're cruel, signorina, but perhaps you not wrong. She is old, but ... how you say? Reliable, dependable, simple. You can trust an original Cobra. It will never let you down.'

'Other than when the hyperdrive system dies and maroons you on a barren rock for twenty years.'

Luko looked at her quizzical expression.

'Cheap Federation parts,' he said with distaste. 'I say this for your Empire, better quality. Damned expensive, but better.'

'Glad you approve, citizen.'

'I do not approve,' Luko said, growing serious. 'Your Empire is oppressive. You have slavery and servitude. This is not right.'

'Slavery is a safety net for society,' Kahina replied, the answer coming easily

CHAPTER TWELVE

to her. 'It ensures nobody can starve or fall into poverty. What would you have? That or the squalor the poor live in inside the Federation after the corporations have sucked the life out of them? Our way is far better.'

Luko smiled, but shook his head. 'The daughter of a Senator …'

'Slaves are well treated, it is the law. Honour demands it.'

'Maybe in the core,' Luko answered her. 'Try the outlying systems. Life as a slave? Desperate, brutal and short. You ever talk to the slaves on your precious little moon?'

'I gave instructions to those at the palace, they were well treated.'

'And those who worked in your mines? Slaves do not revolt for no reason, signorina. They were treated not so well, eh?'

'Slaves will always demand more than they deserve. Federation propaganda, nothing more.'

'Is not. I have seen. It is Imperial short-sightedness.'

She glared at him. 'I hope you can fly better than you grasp politics.'

Kahina noticed that Luko had been watching the instruments with a frown on his face. 'I think I …' his voice tailed off.

'What is it?' she asked. Luko shrugged.

'Not sure.' Luko waved his hand. 'Ah … probably nothing.'

On the astrogation scanner one of the markers had stopped moving relative to their position; something was pacing them. As she watched, Kahina saw it inch a little closer.

Kahina looked over her shoulder through the rear cockpit windows. She could see a ship a few kilometres back. She squinted; it looked like the ship she'd seen earlier, the *Raeben*.

'Do we warn him to stay back?'

Luko shook his head. Kahina realised that Luko had been watching the ship and had been studying it curiously. She felt suddenly cold.

Something wasn't right. Kahina had no idea what it was. Something was not going according to routine.

An audio communication sounded.

'*Bella Principessa*, this is SysCon. You are cleared for hyperspace transit, proceed when ready.'

'Ack, SysCon.'

Luko closed the link and looked across at Kahina. 'Here we go. Hang on to your seat.'

The rising hum of the hyperspace generators resonated through the ship. As it reached a crescendo, space flickered before them, the stars rushing past in a blur of motion. The hum dropped and faded away rapidly.

Kahina blinked. She still found it hard to believe she was now several light years from where she had been moments before. She wasn't sure she'd ever really grasp it …

Red lights, a warning sound from the console. Kahina remembered the sound.

Threat warning.

She looked at the console. There was a target, portside aft, glowing red on the display. It was in exactly the same position as the *Raeben* had been, but rapidly closing.

'They can't be thinking of attacking us …'

'The hell they can't!'

A voice crackled on the wideband transmitter. Kahina recognised the sharp and grating tones of a Federation accent.

'Cobra *Bella Principessa*. Stand down. Prepare to be boarded or destroyed. I only want your passenger.'

Luko looked across at her. 'I would say your secret is … not so secret, signorina.' Kahina swallowed.

So fast. But how?

Luko's hands were flying across the controls. Kahina briefly saw messages on the console, weapons priming, shields raising, drives readied for maximum bursts of power. Holofac targeting reticules appeared before their vision in the cockpit windows. The *Bella Principessa* surged forward, rotating on its centre axis and then coming about in a wide arc.

Actinic light flashed around the ship. Kahina remembered the glowing discharge of the shields.

Warning! Rear shields at 76%.

A bright beam of light flashed close by. The *Bella Principessa's* shields flared again in response. Luko triggered the forward weapons and the bass vibrato thrum buzzed through the ship. Kahina recalled it from before, but it was far

CHAPTER TWELVE

more intense this time, she could almost sense the vast power being discharged into the void.

Ahead now, the *Raeben* was still closing, bright beams of light marking the emission of its forward weapons. The *Bella Principessa's* shields flared again. Luko returned fire.

Warning! Forward shields at 45%.

Kahina jolted as an abrupt warning siren shrieked nearby.

Incoming Missile!

She gasped as she saw something detach from the lower hull of the *Raeben*. A bright halo of flame surrounded it and it surged forward, closing the distance between the two ships with terrifying rapidity. She tensed in her chair, grasping the armrests and bracing her feet.

Luko's hand moved to a supplementary control. Kahina watched him pause for a moment and then press it. A pulse of energy rang out; the *Bella Principessa* rang like a gong. The missile was close now, just a few seconds to impact. She prepared herself for the inevitable explosion, there was no way they could avoid it …

A bright cascade of light splashed across the cockpit, forcing her to shield her eyes. The missile was gone, replaced by a cloud of smoke and debris that flashed past them as the *Bella Principessa* surged onwards. The *Raeben* changed course rapidly, pulling up in an abrupt climb.

'Sbaglio!' Luko had a fierce grin on his face.

Luko nudged his ship into pursuit triggering his weapons again. Kahina saw a line of sparking fire burn down the exposed lower hull of the *Raeben*. Shields flared, flickered and collapsed. A blackened stain was the result. The weapons fire stopped.

Warning! Forward weapons, thermal overload.

The *Raeben* turned, trailing smoke and flame before the hull sealed itself. Luko turned his ship into pursuit. Kahina felt the spin and tried to ignore the whirling star field outside, concentrating on the ship before them.

A red targeting reticule appeared in space, Luko adjusted course and pulled a separate trigger on the control yoke. A mechanical clunk echoed through the ship. Kahina watched as one of their own missiles rushed forwards, trailing a plume of flame. She watched as it arced towards their assailant.

A glowing translucent sphere formed around the *Raeben* and then abruptly expanded, fading as it did so. The missile struck the sphere moments before it would have hit the other ship. Kahina watched in dismay as it broke up and exploded. The *Raeben* was unharmed.

The ships continued to duel, trading fire, spiralling around each other in the darkness. Kahina clamped down on nausea that rose up within her, she couldn't afford to be sick, not here … not now. Luko seemed immune to it.

Maybe you get used to it!

Her head was jolted left and right, her body crushed one way and then the other. Luko didn't fly straight for more than a moment. Just as she tried to draw breath, another stomach lurching manoeuvre would commence. She tasted bile in her throat and on her tongue. She clenched her eyes shut, forcing herself to breathe, trying to avoid vomiting. If she could only anticipate …

Just let it be over, please.

The *Raeben* abruptly shut down its drive, a flare of light glowing across its bow. Kahina watched in surprise as it rapidly slowed. The *Bella Principessa* roared past, unable to match the change in velocity.

'Dannazioni!' Luko yelled. Kahina watched as he flung the controls hard over. The *Bella Principessa* spun rapidly and then dived away, desperately trying to regain the initiative. Light crashed about them again. Warnings flickered on the console.

Warning! Rear shields failed!

Now there was another sound, a fearful mix of rending, tearing followed by a scream of tortured metal. Hot smoke filtered into the cockpit and sparks flew. Kahina didn't see what happened next; there was an echoing thump and the *Bella Principessa* whirled out of control.

She was flung back in her chair and then wrenched abruptly forward before being slung left and then right. The pattern repeated itself. She screamed with the disorientation. The stars were just streaks of light outside, spiralling at random.

'Luko!'

She managed to turn her head and look across. Her heart thumped painfully in her chest and she felt sweat chill across her in sudden panic. Luko was slumped in his seat, blood rushing from a wound on his forehead where he'd

CHAPTER TWELVE

been bashed against his seat. His hands had fallen from the controls, which were crashing from one side to the other without direction. The *Bella Principessa* was completely out of control. The ship groaned and screeched around her.

Instinctively she grabbed the controls ahead of her. They were an identical copy of the primary systems Luko had been using. They were stiff, jolting in her hands as she tried to wrestle the ship back to her command.

Warning! Rear shields failed!

Kahina glanced at the scanner. The *Raeben* was still behind them. She didn't know why it hadn't finished them off. Maybe the uncontrolled spin had bought them a little time. Regardless, with no shields, it would doubtless make short work of them on the next hit. She had to do something …

Panic gripped her.

I don't know how to fight!

She'd no grasp of space combat, she was going to die the moment that ship out there adjusted its course.

The *Bella Principessa* danced under her direction, spinning around and then arcing back on itself.

Kahina had an idea, an idea borne of desperation; she didn't know whether it would work. She was no fighter pilot, no combateer, it was crazy …

… it was the only thing she could think of.

She pulled her ship around and aimed directly at the other vessel, pushing the throttles forward to their stops. The *Bella Principessa* stuttered forward unevenly; they must have taken some damage. Kahina adjusted the course as the ship tried to yaw sideways, keeping the *Raeben* dead ahead.

Laser fire flashed out. Shields crashed into life once more, deflecting the deadly ephemeral barrage.

Warning! Forward shields at 15%.

The range continued to close. The *Raeben* didn't veer off. They were only seconds away from impact. Kahina tensed her arms, fighting the overwhelming desire to pull back on the controls to avoid a deadly collision. The other ship loomed frighteningly in the cockpit windows. She grabbed another control in a fierce grip. A series of tones followed by an imperious buzzing signalled that the targeting systems had locked onto the *Raeben* …

Missile: Target locked.

In that last split second the *Raeben* jinked aside, firing up its drives in an attempt to evade the *Bella Principessa* as it barrelled in at full speed on an insane trajectory. As it did so, Kahina grasped the second trigger.

The missile roared away at point blank range.

No chance to react.

There was a flash and a heavy thump from below. The *Bella Principessa* jolted, dragging the controls from her hands. Flames and debris spun briefly past the cockpit windows before disappearing into the darkness.

Kahina craned her neck around to see what had happened. She looked out of the rear windows.

Flame, debris and drifting smoke. The scanner was a crackle of static and confusion.

All she could see was empty space, the stars slowly coming to a halt after the wild gyrations of the battle. She held her breath.

The *Raeben* abruptly appeared, terrifyingly close. She stifled a scream of surprise.

But the other ship was drifting. She watched the hull slide past, a sparking, flaming mess of torn panels and ruined components. It spun past, slowly growing smaller. She watched for a moment, seeing the navigation lights on the exterior flicker and grow dark.

I killed it.

* * *

'She'll be aiming direct for the Prism system,' Dalk said, looking across to Hassan. 'You've got the triangulation points?'

Hassan, sitting alongside him amongst the consoles on the bridge of Octavia's ship, gestured across with an outstretched hand. A holofac display drifted between the two men.

'Best I can do,' Hassan replied. 'Timings of the transmissions of her message and the various relay points means she has to be somewhere around here.'

Dalk studied the display. They'd narrowed it down to three systems.

'Then we've got time. She's a little further out than we are. Time enough to get there before her, the Federation, and the Imperials if we move fast enough.'

CHAPTER TWELVE

'Any ideas on how she's doing it?'

'Must have help,' Dalk replied. 'Recognise the background from her video?'

Hassan looked at Kahina's holofac transmission. The bulkhead behind her was dark for the most part, but a few telltale lights and a couple of obscure control panels were visible.

'It's old whatever it is. Krait?'

Dalk shook his head.

'What you're looking at there is a classic old school Cobra Mark 3. Cowell and MgRath vintage.'

Hassan's nose wrinkled. 'A Cobra that old? Lucky it's still flying …'

'Don't underestimate it,' Dalk replied. 'One of the toughest little ships money can buy. Built them properly back in the day and it's easy to keep them competitive too, one of the best modular chassis designs.'

'No match for this ship.'

Dalk rubbed his chin. 'Depends who's flying it.'

Octavia arrived behind them.

'I hope you have located her.'

'Close enough,' Dalk replied. 'She's nearby, but we won't find her before she reaches home if we try to follow. Our best bet is to get there before her.'

'I'm assuming you have a plan?'

Dalk nodded. 'If she's planning to take the moon she'll need to secure the station first. She'll probably try to sneak aboard incognito. The Reclamists still hold it, but it's mostly crewed by slaves that may or may not decide to throw their lot in with her. She'll have to convince them to help her. That's our chance to grab her.'

'Why should the slaves help us?'

Dalk grinned. 'You forget, Octavia. I am the voice of reason, a Patron of the Empire. The slaves will respect me, answer to me. I can turn their loyalty. But we must reach the station before she does.'

'Which station is it?'

'There's only one. *Hiram's Anchorage*. It's in low orbit around the moon, Chione. It's heavily fortified, neither the Federation or Imperial fleets will be able to approach until it stands down. Otherwise it's just a processing …'

'I don't care what it is,' Octavia snapped. She turned and barked instructions. 'Helmsman! Prism system, Chione moon. Best possible speed and more.'

The crew of the *Retribution* jumped to their tasks. Octavia turned back to Dalk and Hassan. 'And what of the girl?'

'I can deal with Kahina,' Dalk replied. 'She will need my help to take back her world. Yours too.' He nodded at Octavia.

'I will expect to be compensated,' Octavia replied, with a faint grin.

'You will be,' Dalk said. 'I will arrange for Kahina to provide … appropriate payment.'

'We have a deal.'

'The Imperials will pay a high price for her safe return,' Hassan added. 'Perhaps they can be persuaded to contribute …'

Octavia briefly looked at Dalk. 'I'm sure they will.'

Hassan looked at the satisfied grin on Octavia's face and the grim expression on Dalk's.

They've got another thing coming if they believe that girl will just comply with their plan! And I've got to find a way to make sure she does …

* * *

Luko woke abruptly, lurching upwards. He felt a hand on his chest, pushing him back down. 'Easy.'

He opened his eyes and found Kahina looking down at him. 'The Vulture!' His eyes were wide with panic.

'Shhhh. It's dead.'

He looked at her. 'Dead? How?'

She smiled faintly and shrugged. 'I killed it.'

Luko tried to sit up, but a surge of pain blasted across his forehead. He winced. He felt Kahina push him back down.

'Ahhh …'

'Hold still, you hit your head pretty hard.' Her voice took on a sterner tone. He took a deep breath and then looked around. He was in his cabin, buckled into his couch.

'Help me up,' he said.

'Are you sure?'

'Signorina, we may not be alone. Best to check, yes?'

CHAPTER TWELVE

He saw her nod and she unstrapped the buckles before helping him back up to the cockpit. He adjusted a few of the controls and then brought the ship about. The remains of the *Raeben* spun slowly before them, it was clear it was completely wrecked.

Luko studied it for a few brief moments and then turned to Kahina with a smile, raising his hands in appraisal.

'We have some damage but … bravissimo, signorina. How you do this?'

He saw her look out of the cockpit windows. 'Missile. Same trick he used, a little closer.'

Luko nodded. 'You make a pretty good fighter, yes? Instinct very good.'

She smiled and looked away, a trace of colour blushing into her cheeks. 'It just happened.'

'Exactimo. You knew. This is good. Fast on the trigger I think.'

'Yeah, I tend to shoot first …'

Luko grinned. 'It is your style, yes? Just choose your next target carefully, signorina.' He checked the scanners, relieved to see nothing else present.

'Who was on that ship?'

Luko gestured for the scanner information, there was little to go on. As he expected, there was no transponder code.

'My guess? Was bounty hunter.'

'After me?'

Luko nodded. 'Federation agent perhaps? How they find us so fast? Is a puzzle.' The girl looked distinctly uncomfortable. He watched her with narrowed eyes. 'Signorina?'

She was refusing eye contact, picking at her clothing with her fingers. 'I sent a message.'

'A message? When? To who?'

'Back on the station, I sent a message to my people.'

Luko turned on her, his voice rising. 'Saying what?'

'I sent instructions to my people to take back my home.'

'You sent it crypto on narrowband, yes? Please say you did.'

Kahina didn't reply.

'Not wideband public?'

'News.' Kahina's voice was small.

'The news!' Luko held his head in his hands.

'I didn't have a choice!' Kahina returned. 'Other comms would have been jammed. I needed to make sure they received it. I needed to reclaim my home before the Federation usurps it. You weren't going to help me, were you? They had to know I was alive, so they can take the system back – otherwise it would be lost forever.'

'And now everyone knows. Bounty hunters everywhere! Everyone try to kill you – kill me too! What you thinking?'

'I didn't think …'

'This I agree!' Luko was furious. 'You start your crazy war. I not want to be involved. Just take you home – this was deal. Not fight your battle.'

'I'm not asking you to fight in my battle.'

'Really?' He glared at her. 'What you call this?' He gestured to the wrecked ship outside. 'You expect to fly back to your home without a fight?'

'I killed that ship, not you!'

Luko stopped. She was right. He was in her debt. He sank back in the pilot's seat. 'You save my life. Now I owe you, this is what you say?'

'Something like that.'

Luko eyed her for a moment, before flipping on the astrogation console and calling up the newsfeeds.

'Then let us see what you have done, yes?'

Kahina watched. This time it was no simple news article. The holofac lit up with a woman, clearly a reporter from one of the Imperial news channels. She spoke in tense excited tones.

'… And in a dramatic turn of events, a woman claiming to be Lady Kahina Tijani Loren, the exiled and supposedly dead daughter of the late Senator Algreb Loren of the Prism system, has broadcast a declaration of war on the self-styled Reclamists who deposed her father. Demanding in no uncertain terms that Imperial forces loyal to her family invade the system, Kahina also points the finger of blame for the assassination of her family squarely at the Federation, alleging that they did indeed bankroll the Reclamists as many have speculated.

'Speaking in strident tones, on a pre-recorded message broadcast wideband from an unknown location, she instructs Imperial forces to re-assert her family's claim to their home world by use of force.

CHAPTER TWELVE

'The Imperials, who have confirmed her identity, have moved swiftly in an attempt to blockade the system. The Federation claims the message has been faked and that the Imperials are trying to precipitate a conflict, but they are moving their own forces into the system in a state of high alert. Independent reports indicate that both fleets are prepared for an extended military encounter.

'If it really is the Senator's daughter, it's unclear how she escaped the assassination of her family. Her precise whereabouts are also unknown. Some reports have her in the outlying systems, others already with the Imperial armada positioning itself in the Prism system.

'Nearby systems are already fortifying their own installations fearing that an outbreak of war may spill over into their territories. So far, nothing further has been heard from Kahina. Her next move may well dictate the fate of the entire sector.'

The holofac transmission fizzled out. Luko looked across at her. 'You one crazy bitch, signorina.'

Chapter Thirteen

High above the azure blue curve of Chione hung the sombre mass of *Hiram's Anchorage*. Massive bulk freighters, kilometre-long buttresses of heavy duty frames stacked with endless rows of containers, drifted listlessly nearby, their systems shut down.

Few lights were shining from the station. The docking bays were closed and sealed off, with enormous blast doors secured over their entrances. Huge turrets slowly rotated on their gimbals, prepared to unleash fierce destructive firepower at any target that came into range.

A brief flicker of light twinkled in the darkness and a small point of light appeared in the distance. The turrets swung ponderously, their guidance systems tracking the approaching vessel, coldly calculating trajectories and firing solutions. Within moments dozens of weapons were poised to be unleashed against the invader.

Aboard the *Retribution* the threat warning indicators were flashing imminent doom. Dalk enjoyed a moment of perverse pleasure as he watched the faces of Octavia's crew blanch as they detected the multiple weapons' locks.

'Shit,' Hassan said from beside him, watching the station grow larger through the expansive bridge windows. 'The thing's a bloody fortress.'

'Mining operations are lucrative targets,' Dalk replied. 'You've got to be able to defend yourself.'

'Dalk, get down here.'

Octavia had gestured to him. Dalk walked down from the outer ring of the bridge to her chair, situated at the very centre of the room. Hassan followed behind him.

Octavia gestured at the screen.

'We'll be in firing range in thirty seconds, I suggest you get them to lower their shields.'

Dalk studied the approaching station with a practised eye.

'You'll need to do exactly what I say in that case.'

'This is my ship, bounty hunter.' Octavia's gaze was fierce and confrontational.

Dalk shrugged, backed up a step and swept his arm wide. 'Then be my guest.'

Octavia glared at him.

Fence with me on my home turf? You'll need my experience, you wait and see.

'Widebands comms to the station,' Octavia snapped.

'Already signalling us,' one of her crew replied. 'Shall I put it on?'

Dalk watched as Octavia signalled for the comms to be broadcast and then listened intently.

'Anaconda-class vessel *Retribution*. Alter course and avoid Chione *aegis*. You will be fired upon if you encroach a five-kilometre proximity zone.' The voice sounded business like, but young and high-pitched.

Octavia thumbed the transmit button on her chair.

'This is the Commander of the *Retribution*. I have urgent business aboard your station and demand you allow me to dock. Lower your shields.'

'Range seven kilometres,' Hassan whispered. The answer was swift.

'*Retribution*. Docking permission is denied.' The voice faltered and cracked. 'Alter course and avoid Chione *aegis*. You will be fired upon.'

Dalk smiled to himself.

So, now what are you going to do?

'Who the hell is this?' Octavia demanded.

This time there was another voice, also young, but sharp, arrogant and proud. '*Hiram's Anchorage* is held by Imperial forces loyal to the Senator's daughter, Lady Kahina Tijani Loren of Chione. You are identified as Commander Quinton, Allegiance Federation. Withdraw, Commander, or we will fire on you.'

'Six kilometres.'

One of the crew looked around as more targets appeared on the scanner. 'Domina, we have multiple targets exiting hyperspace. Identities are Federation!'

'The blockade arrives,' Dalk said, tapping his fingers on the arm of Octavia's chair. 'Time is of the essence …'

They could all see the ships, a neat arrangement of star-like points arrayed in a tidy delta formation. One was particularly bright. Hassan saw the scanner information scrolling up a nearby holofac … a Farragut class battlecruiser! There was no way they would get out from under the guns of something that big if it got into range.

Dalk saw Octavia was thinking it through rapidly, clearly coming to a similar conclusion.

CHAPTER THIRTEEN

Need me now, do you?

She gestured to Dalk. 'Do what he says. Hold our position!' She looked at him. 'No games, Dalk.'

Dalk grinned. 'No games. Give me the comm.'

'Five kilometres,' Hassan breathed. 'Talk about cutting it fine.'

Dalk stared at the now stationary bulk of *Hiram's Anchorage* for a long moment before activating the wideband transmitter.

'*Hiram's Anchorage*, this is Patron Dalk Torgen, erstwhile of Chione, servant to Senator Algreb Loren. As you can hear, I am aboard the *Retribution*. You will also have noticed the arrival of a Federation task force. They intend to blockade this system. If you wish the Empire to come to your assistance in your fight to reclaim this system …' Dalk paused for a moment, 'I suggest you lower your shields and allow us to dock.'

There was silence from the other end of the comm link.

'Patron Dalk Torgen?' someone stuttered amidst a crackle of static.

'Impedance growing on all channels,' one of the bridge crew called. 'They're jamming the comms.'

'*Hiram's Anchorage*,' Dalk continued. 'I will assist you in restoring Lady Kahina to her home and Chione to the Empire. Let me aboard before the Federation dogs arrive and destroy us all.'

More lights flickered across the scanners. Hassan watched the bridge crew react in growing alarm.

More target locks.

'Fighters inbound,' he whispered to Dalk. 'We've got about three minutes.'

Octavia gestured to her crew. 'Spool up the hyperdrive, this isn't going to work.'

'How … how do we know that you are Dalk?' a tremulous voice replied, 'and what are you doing on a Federation ship?'

'Switch on your holofac transmitter,' Dalk instructed.

The *Retribution*'s holofac viewer flickered and a group of dishevelled men and women could be seen clustered around a series of grim and tarnished control panels.

The slaves really did revolt and take back the station, extraordinary.

Dalk flipped a control for the holofac feed. His image was transmitted to the space station. 'You recognise me?' Dalk said.

The group nodded in unison.

'Now I'm guessing that none of you have much experience in repelling a Federation task force.' Dalk spoke forcefully and powerfully. 'In minutes they will deploy a highly trained Elite fighting unit. If they succeed in entering orbit space they will board the station, slaughter everyone on board, commandeer the station and then decimate our home. Imperial reinforcements are on their way, but have yet to arrive. We must hold the line until that time. Lower your shields, allow me to board and let me help you restore our world to its rightful owner – Lady Kahina, daughter of Algreb.'

The group looked at each other; faint snatches of whispers could be heard passing between them, their words unintelligible.

The wideband communications system buzzed.

'This is Federation Commissioner Tenim Neseva to all vessels and installations within the Prism system. Under Federal Statute I declare this system under interstellar martial law. All ships and installations will disarm, stand down and prepare for inspection. Any attempt to flee or undertake any hostile action will result in the application of deadly force …'

'*Hiram's Anchorage* – lower your shields.' Dalk raised his voice. 'You cannot deal with this, I can. Let me aboard!'

'I don't know … I just …' The folk aboard the space station were arguing. Dalk saw one of them push the first one aside.

'Shields are down. We'll trust you, Patron Dalk. Help us.'

Dalk bowed. 'At your service.'

'They're opening the gates,' Hassan said, blowing out his cheeks, watching as the barricades on the primary docking bay opened outwards.

Dalk turned to Octavia and gestured to the space station ahead, with a mocking deference. 'Your ship, Octavia.'

She raised an eyebrow at him and snapped an order at her crew. 'Not bad, bounty hunter, not bad.'

* * *

'I may not be a military expert, but it would seem the tactical situation is poor. I suggest an altercation is not in our best interests.'

CHAPTER THIRTEEN

Ambassador Cuthrick, flanked by his two aides and accompanied by Patrons Gerrun and Zyair, stood on the expansive bridge of the Imperial Interdictor *Atticus*. Before them, casting a bright blue glare through the vast bridge viewing windows, hung two glorious crescents, one larger than the other. The furthest was flicked with densely swirling patterns of cloud from which the occasional flicker of lightning could be seen, the closer one was calmer, with faint trails of cloud. Tiny lights could be seen shining from the darkened side.

Moments before, the Imperial fleet had arrived in the Prism system.

Situated between their position and the system were arrayed a bright multitude of tiny flicks of light, arranged around the Chione moon. The Federation fleet was already in position.

'Tactical breakdown,' Admiral Brice ordered, ignoring the presence of the politicians. He stood, leaning against a magnificently crafted silver handrail, arms outstretched before him and hands clasped firmly around it.

'Sir,' his first officer replied, 'we have the Federation battlecruiser *Xajorkith*, two destroyers, eight frigates and sixteen corvettes. All ships have shields engaged and weapons deployed. Braces of fighter-class vessels are patrolling the system. Capital-class ships are deployed between us and orbit space of the Chione moon. We're outgunned, sir.'

'We're too late,' Cuthrick observed. 'Let me negotiate with my counterpart and we can …' Cuthrick saw Brice purse his lips, but he continued to ignore the ambassador.

'You forget the defences of the mining facility,' Brice said, talking directly to his first officer. 'Sir?'

'We manoeuvre the Federation dogs back against it. They'll be caught in the crossfire and forced to defend two flanks.'

His first officer considered the tactic. 'We'll have to come in at flank speed in a highly elliptical path in order to achieve that. The station is in a low orbit. It will require some tight co-ordination.'

Brice looked at him. 'I'm sure you're more than up to the task.'

'Yes, sir.'

'Plot the course, Commander.'

Cuthrick tried again. 'Admiral, I really must protest …'

'Must you, Ambassador?' Brice turned slowly to face him.

'At least let me try to defuse the situation. A military confrontation will cause nothing but death and destruction not only to both fleets but to the moon itself.'

'The Federation have illegally invaded this system, disregarded our sovereignty and blockaded one of our own installations – and you want to negotiate?'

'They don't want a war.' Cuthrick's voice was uncharacteristically harsh. 'No sane man does.' Cuthrick studied the Admiral's face, it was haughty, dismissive, arrogant and self-assured.

'But they've started one – and I have my orders.'

Brice turned back and resumed his stance against the handrail, overlooking the frenetic activity across the bridge. 'Bring all weapons to bear, secure habitation zones and prep for zero-gravity. All decks, red alert.'

Cuthrick saw Zyair wince as a harsh klaxon blared across the bridge. The interior lighting faded to a dim background level.

'Entirely safe,' Zyair muttered to Gerrun. 'That's what you said about space travel. Routine! Not in the least bit arduous. Can I presume you didn't have a military firefight in mind when you convinced me to come on this ridiculous errand?'

'My dear friend, I can only apologise,' Gerrun replied. 'Events have ... rather overtaken me.'

'Have you at least been in a battle?'

'On rare occasions,' Gerrun answered. 'What should I expect?'

'Initially? Rather unpleasant nausea, a lot of shouting, light, noise and confusion. If things go well, a little vibration, a lurch here and there ...'

'And if things don't go well?'

Gerrun smiled. 'Oh, I shouldn't worry about that.'

'But that young fool said we were out-gunned. If we're overwhelmed ...'

'We will have little time to concern ourselves with the outcome,' Cuthrick added, with a deep sigh. 'The void is rather harsh. Death will be swift.'

'Death? What about escape pods and whatnot? Surely ...'

'And you've received training on how to use one, have you?' Gerrun said, with a faint tone of amusement. 'You can navigate successfully to a nearby starport?'

CHAPTER THIRTEEN

'Can't you?'

'Alas, no.'

Zyair's mouth dropped open. 'Is there nothing we can do?'

Gerrun gestured expansively with a shrug.

Cuthrick considered the matter. 'Perhaps we could beseech a random selection of deities for a miracle.'

* * *

A brief stopover for repairs, a short cut through a dark system and the *Bella Principessa* materialised in the Prism system. Kahina caught her breath as the bright light from the Prism star itself burst into the cockpit of the Cobra.

So close to the sun!

Most of the heat was filtered out, but she could still feel the radiance on her face. Luko was studying the cockpit instrumentation intently. He'd been doing something unusual with the hyperdrive mechanism on the final jump; whatever it was, it involved a lot of manual computations that had kept one of the on board computers busy for several minutes.

'Not bad, eh?' he said, looking across at her for approval.

'What did you do?'

'Jumped the old fashioned way,' he replied. 'Long ago they called it "faraway", you work it all out by hand. Too easy now, all automatic, lost all the charm.'

'So why bother?'

'We control precisely where we arrive. See? We can sneak up to your little moon. Come in from the sun and no one notice us.'

The *Bella Principessa* was hurtling onwards, the sun falling behind them, its glare fading away beyond the edge of the cockpit windows. As they rounded its limb they could see a bright planet ahead. Even from this distance it was clear it had rings. Kahina remembered its name; Mestra, the first planet. Bright against the blackness shone the three other stars that made up the Prism system; bright white, fierce blue and a fiery red. A nursery rhyme she remembered hearing the children at the palace chant came suddenly to mind, unbidden:

Prism owns the day so bright,
Diamond's white will guard the night,
Sapphire's blue, a royal hue,
Ruby's red is warm and true.

Above and to the right they could see another bright pair of dots. A planet and its moon.

Daedalion and Chione. Her heart thumped in her chest.

Home.

The sight of those bright sparks in the darkness drew a short gasp from her. A wave of relief mixed with anticipation and determination washed across her. It was hers, taken from her.

Not long now and it will be mine again.

Luko adjusted the course towards the planet and the moon, and then shut down the drives. 'We coast from here, signorina …'

The scanner pinged at them and a series of yellow markers appeared across the forward section of the display.

'… or maybe not.'

'What is it?' Kahina asked, seeing his puzzled frown as he rapidly assessed the situation.

'Ships. Molto ships!'

* * *

More sounds echoed through the bridge of the Imperial battleship. Cuthrick, Zyair and Gerrun looked up as the first officer returned.

'Sir.'

The three Imperials watched closely as Brice acknowledged him. 'Course ready?'

'Still plotting, sir. Something else. We have a new contact, azimuth seventy-two, altitude negative eight. It's coming in from the sun. Target designated as Beta One.'

'What is it?'

'Looks like a small ship, sir. Possibly civilian. Impossible to gauge from here. It's heading in-system though, straight towards the Chione moon. Active scanners only, looks like it's coasting.'

CHAPTER THIRTEEN

They saw Brice narrow his eyes. 'Why would a civilian vessel attempt to run a Federation blockade …' Brice looked up. 'Damnation. It's her. Plot an intercept course and deploy a fighter phalanx! I want that ship intercepted, defended and escorted. Double time!'

Gerrun leant over to Zyair.

'Remarkably quick, these deities, wouldn't you say?'

* * *

Kahina leaned across, looking at the display. It was covered in yellow markers now. As she watched, the wideband comms crackled into life.

'This is Federation Commissioner Tenim Neseva to all vessels and installations within the Prism system. Under Federal Statute I declare this system under interstellar martial law. All ships and installations will disarm, stand down and prepare for inspection. Any attempt to flee or undertake any hostile action will result in the application of deadly force.'

'The Federation is already here,' Kahina said in dismay. 'You've got to get me to the station. Quickly.'

'Signorina, that is a Federation task force. If we fire the drives they will detect us, if they haven't already.'

More markers appeared on the scanner. Pinpoints flashed in the darkness, more ships appearing from hyperspace. Luko aimed the passive scanners onto them.

'More company,' he said. 'Now the Imperials join the party.'

'Get me a scan of the lead ship. Can you identify it?'

Luko tweaked the settings of the scanner. 'Registered as the *Atticus*, does that help?'

Kahina nodded grimly. 'That belongs to Admiral Brice. He was in service to my father. That is my fleet.'

'Then they are on the wrong side of the moon. The Federation holds the approach.'

'Can you get past the Federation ships?'

Luko studied the scanner display, nervously chewing his fingertip before shaking his head. 'They see us soon. The sun only hide us for so long. Even with the drives off …'

'Then I've got to get a message to Admiral Brice.'

Luko shook his head. 'The Federation is jamming, you can try …'

Kahina opened up the holofac comm system and made a brief call. There was no acknowledgement from the Imperial fleet, but she could see ships turning and heading in their direction.

'Head for the station at full speed, everyone will see that, won't they?' she asked. Luko sighed. 'Oh yes, they will see it, ok.'

Kahina saw him reluctantly trigger the thrusters. With a rising rumble the Cobra surged ahead. On the rear-view display Kahina could see that they were trailing a bright plume of exhaust flux visible for hundreds of kilometres across space.

'We are now a big fat target …' Luko said. 'So much for a stealthy approach.'

'Just get us in range of the station.'

'Sir, a transmission,' an Imperial operative announced.

Brice turned, taking in the new information. A holofac appeared; it was laced with static, unstable and flickering, the audio barely discernible. He could just make out the face of a woman in the few brief moments of clarity.

'Boost the gain.'

'Already at maximum, sir.'

'… miral …. ice … eed … dezvous … rams … horage … laves … ill … elp me … fend … ship.'

Brice looked at the small vessel's trajectory plot. 'She's heading for the station. Covering fire! And protect that ship at all costs!'

* * *

'Captain?'

Tenim and Jenu stood on the bridge of the *Xajorkith* as the Imperial fleet arrived and began forming up.

'We have the upper hand,' the captain responded to Tenim's request for an update, 'a larger force and an advantageous position.'

'I'm glad to hear it,' Tenim replied. 'What about the station?'

'It is a formidable opponent,' the captain replied, 'but it cannot manoeuvre.

CHAPTER THIRTEEN

Our analysis shows it has only short to medium-range weaponry. It is no threat to this vessel, but we should be cautious with the rest of the fleet.'

Tenim looked out of the bridge windows to where the Imperial fleet was swiftly organising itself after the hyperspace jump.

'And what would you do if you were them?'

The captain studied the Imperial fleet for a few moments and then turned back to Tenim with a wry grin.

'I'd send in my ambassador.'

Tenim smiled in response. 'And if they decide diplomacy is not going to work?'

The captain frowned. 'They would try to take advantage of the station in some fashion. Some kind of pincer move would be my guess.'

A distinctive ping echoed through the bridge. The captain turned. Tenim followed his movements as he moved across to the navigation officer, leant over his console and discussed the new information.

'What is it?' Jenu whispered from beside him. 'New ship contact,' Tenim replied.

The navigation officer gestured and a holofac overlay appeared across the bridge windows, a cross-hair spinning around and highlighting a slowly moving point of light against the backdrop of space.

As Tenim and Jenu watched, the holofac system resolved the dot, magnifying it upwards until the blurred form of an old ship could be seen, trailing a bright glaring tail of blue energy.

'Incoming vessel, Commissioner,' the captain said, walking back to them. 'It's an old trading vessel, Cobra-class.'

'What is it doing?' Tenim asked.

'Heading straight for the station. It's in a hurry. Running flat out.' Tenim looked at the ship on the holofac for a moment.

'I believe our Imperial heiress is making her move,' Tenim mused, stroking his beard. 'Orders, Commissioner?'

'I believe I put this system under interstellar martial law, Captain,' Tenim replied. 'That vessel is violating that directive. Jam all communications, intercept it …'

The captain waited. Tenim lowered his hand. '… and blow it out of the stars.'

* * *

Kahina saw the targeting system light up with threat warnings once again. She was quite used to the sound. She knew what it meant. She instinctively pulled her flight harness tighter around her.

Luko was studying the instruments too.

'I am thinking you are not very popular in the Federation, signorina.'

'The feeling is mutual.'

On the scanner a series of red dots had broken off from the Federation armada and were rapidly closing the distance. A corresponding series of yellow dots were swarming from the Imperial fleet, but it was clear the Federation ships would arrive first.

'My ships will defend me,' Kahina said, watching the scanner. 'But we've got to give them more time.'

Luko widened the scanner radius until the Sun, the ringed planet Mestra and the other bodies in the system were visible. The different trajectories of the combative ships were plotted with estimated times of interception. They had only minutes before the ships would arrive.

'If you crazy, I be crazy too,' Luko said with a grin.

Kahina felt the sharp turn as he wrenched the *Bella Principessa* around onto a new course. 'What are you doing? We need to get to the station!'

Luko shook his head. 'We will not make it in time. We need … how you say … a diversion.' The *Bella Principessa* stopped turning. Luko had pushed the controls back to a neutral position.

Kahina looked out of the cockpit windows. The gas giant Mestra was dead ahead, its rings shining brightly in the light of the Prism sun.

'What are you doing?'

'Making sure we stay alive.'

* * *

Even at full thrust, the Cobra was no match in raw speed for either the Federation or Imperial fighters. The Federation craft were standard F63 Condors, small single man fighters, their sharp angular design a testament to

CHAPTER THIRTEEN

their purpose. With no jump drive and only short-range flight capability they did one thing and did it well. They were fast, they were nimble. They swarmed a target and despatched it. Their only relative weakness was a lack of armour and minimal shielding.

Their Imperial counterparts shared the same design brief, but Imperial aesthetics once more determined their overall appearance. Where the Federation ships were stubby and gaunt, the Imperial ships were outstretched, organic, but no less intimidating.

Both classes of ships had but a single purpose. Speed … and bringing their weapons to bear as soon as was practically possible.

The Federation wing Commander checked his squadron, seeing them automatically drop into a delta formation as they closed on the target. The range was dropping fast, despite the Cobra's sudden course change towards the gas giant.

'All ships, target is Cobra-class vessel ahead. Engage and destroy. Watch for Imperial interceptors, but do not engage. I repeat, do not engage Imperial fighters.'

'Imperial fighters coming in hot,' his wingman said. 'ETA thirty seconds.' The wing Commander adjusted his own scanners.

'All ships, lock missiles on target and fire at will. I repeat, fire at will.'

* * *

Kahina heard the threat warning again. The words *'Incoming Missile'* flashed on the console. She could see half a dozen marks streaking towards them. The gas giant was huge in the forward windows. Luko spun the Cobra around and changed course again, triggering the electronic countermeasure system. Kahina braced herself as the unpleasant experience of ship based combat started all over again.

On the scanner, all but two of the high speed trailing marks of the missiles flickered and vanished, dashed to oblivion by the *Bella Principessa's* electronic defences. The remaining two continued to close.

Kahina turned her attention away from the scanner and back to the cockpit windows, gasping in horror at the sight that confronted her.

Luko had steered his ship away from the approaching curve of Mestra, but was now aiming the ship directly into the ring system. Already small debris was flickering past the ship; bright streaks of fire marking the demise of dust and debris as it impacted against the ship's shields and instantly vaporised.

'What are you doing?' Her voice was high with alarm.

'We cannot outrun them, signorina.' By comparison, Luko's voice was calm and resigned. 'We must evade them.'

'But you can't fly a ship through the rings … that's impossible. You'll kill us!'

Luko grinned a mad man's grin. 'The word impossible, signorina, is found only in the dictionary of fools.'

Rocks and boulders started to hurtle past. Kahina instinctively ducked as one spiralled past close to the windows. A flash of light from the rear view signalled the demise of the remaining missiles, but Kahina could see the Federation fighters were now in range. Bright bursts of laser fire leapt from them. The *Bella Principessa's* shields flared in response. Rocks smashed around them as the incoming fire found innocent targets.

Luko didn't reduce speed, but guided his ship deeper into the rings, wrenching it around the bigger rocks. Kahina could see an unending field of rock stretching out into the remote distance, through which the light of the Prism star flickered uncertainly. She could see Luko had been doubly cunning; the Federation fighters had to contend with a difficult target, their sight and instruments blinded by the fierce starlight, amidst a tumbling menagerie of clashing rocks, ice and debris. All Luko had to do was not crash.

'Take the weapons,' Luko instructed tersely. 'Shoot at anything that gets in the way!'

Kahina grabbed the controls in front of her and placed her fingers around the trigger. Rocks hurtled past, she swallowed down on nausea as the ship gyrated. Tracer fire from the pursuing Federation ships continued to flail nearby, occasionally blistering off the rocks, shattering their surfaces and adding more debris to the maelstrom.

Kahina felt the ship lurch beneath her as Luko wrested it around a large boulder tumbling in their direction. As it cleared their path another was revealed, heading straight towards them. Kahina instinctively triggered the

CHAPTER THIRTEEN

weapons. The Cobra's forward weapon array burst forth, splashing liquid fire across the surface of the asteroid …

… which resisted the onslaught.

Kahina stared in horror as the surface of the rock rushed up to meet them; they would be dashed across it. She could see the craters, fine riles and fissures on the surface, growing larger with terrifying rapidity. Certain death, impacting on the surface.

She kept her finger on the trigger.

Like a crystal cut by an expert jeweller, the rock abruptly split along its length under the fury of the *Bella Principessa*'s weapons. Luko rotated the Cobra around its centre axis as the two halves moved slowly away. Kahina stared at rock walls as they shot past the cockpit windows.

Almost close enough to touch.

Harsh yellow light flickered from behind them. Two of the Federation fighters had not been so fortunate. Having not anticipated the trajectory of the shattered asteroid they had ploughed directly into its remains, their fragile hulls scattered to dust by the collision.

* * *

The Imperial cruiser *Atticus* turned slowly and began heading away from its previous position, adopting a course towards Mestra. Cutters and other warships adopted flanking positions alongside. Huge drive units, dozens of metres in diameter, glowed with the white heat of disrupted atoms. The glowing fury of harnessed power coursed through the ship.

Across a few hundred kilometres of space the Federation fleet was performing a similar manoeuvre. Both fleets were traversing the long sides of an isosceles triangle, it was inevitable that they would meet at the pinnacle.

Admiral Brice watched as the Federation battleship grew in the port bridge windows. He could see it was also running at flank speed. A race, in essence, even if the huge ships were ponderous in the extreme.

He toyed with the idea of sending the faster Cutters ahead, but it would have been foolhardy to leave his flagship unprotected with the Federation fleet so close. His counterpart in the Federation fleet seemed to be having similar thoughts. The Federation fleet remained in formation, moving only as quickly as the enormous Federation battleship.

'Firing range in five minutes,' his first officer reported, anticipating his next query. 'All port batteries primed, shields biased to port. We've lost contact with the fighters, sir. They reported the civilian ship had entered the rings.'

Brice nodded.

'Admiral,' Cuthrick interjected from behind, 'at least let me try to reach an accord with the Federation. This does not need to escalate into a war.'

Brice reviewed the telemetry on the various scanners and tactical displays around the bridge. He might as well give the wretched politicians a chance. It would make no difference to the outcome, but it would make life easier after the event. All possible avenues would have been explored.

'Very well, Ambassador. You shall have your chance. Be quick, you have … one minute and forty-five seconds before the situation will become academic.'

Cuthrick exchanged a look with Gerrun and Zyair. Brice shook his head in contempt as Zyair gestured urgently.

Cuthrick signalled for a holofac transmission.

* * *

'The Imperials are signalling,' The Federation captain reported. 'Ambassador Cuthrick for you, Commissioner.'

'Put him on.'

The captain signalled for the jamming to be relented. The bridge holofac system flickered into life and the form of the Imperial ambassador appeared before Tenim and Jenu. They could see his two aides and two other gentlemen, one extremely large and one painfully thin, dressed in the garb of Patrons.

'Ambassador Cuthrick,' Tenim acknowledged.

'Commissioner Neseva.' Cuthrick's voice was smooth and unruffled as ever. 'Apologies if I seem hasty and wish to dispense with our traditional pleasantries, the matter at hand …'

'Quite pressing,' Tenim agreed. 'Perhaps you didn't receive our previous transmission. We have declared interstellar martial law as per statute. I humbly

CHAPTER THIRTEEN

suggest you stand your fleet down. Your presence here is, sad to say, effectively illegal.'

'The application of Federal martial law in an Imperial system is,' Cuthrick lowered his head slightly, 'rather unorthodox, wouldn't you agree?'

'Not in the slightest,' Tenim replied. 'Agreed statute allows for either power to implement interstellar martial law when a system's government has dissolved and trade or the free passage of civilians is threatened. This system is rife with piracy and no stable government remains. In the absence of effective Imperial control ...'

'Our sincere apologies for our tardiness in resolving this matter,' Cuthrick said. 'As you are no doubt aware, we are now in a position to bolster the true government of this system. Might I suggest you stand your fleet down whilst we discuss the affair?'

'Nothing would please me more.' Tenim smiled grimly and then echoed the Ambassador's words for emphasis. 'But, as you are no doubt aware, we are bound by Federal law to enforce the application of interstellar martial law now that it has been officially declared. We have a ship blatantly contravening that regulation as we speak. Once that has been dealt with we will be more than happy to convene a discussion to that end.'

'A single ship justifies such a deployment, Commissioner?'

'A known criminal ambassador, masquerading as an Imperial Senator no less. A heinous crime.'

'Perhaps, given that crime, it might be more appropriate for us to deal with this individual? Masquerading as an Imperial Senator is a serious offence as you say. We would be happy to take this problem off your hands, so to speak, in the interests of interstellar peace and co-operation.'

'Your offer is most generous,' Tenim answered. 'However, we will secure the individual as per policy, once they have been processed after due procedure we will release them into your custody. We believe that is right and proper. Is that clear, or do you need further clarification?'

Cuthrick inclined his head slightly. 'Your intentions are very clear indeed, Commissioner.'

Below Tenim, one of the Federation scanner operatives turned in alarm, speaking rapidly to the captain.

'Sir, we have the Cobra-class vessel on scanners. It's emerged from the ring system. Our fighters have it surrounded. Imperial fighters attempting to divert ...'

There was flash of light in distant space, a small explosion flickered briefly from the rings.

Abruptly Ambassador Cuthrick leant forward, his image distorting as the holofac tried to re-render his face at close range.

'Commissioner! Admiral Brice will open fire. For all our sakes, desist ...'

From across the transmission came the faint sound of orders being barked. Tenim couldn't quite make out the words.

The transmission was abruptly cut off. The holofac flickered and died.

'Cut off at the source, sir,' the captain said in response to Tenim's questioning look. 'We're entering firing range.'

Another crew member looked up from her instruments. 'We've lost contact with our flight wing ...'

* * *

The remaining Federation fighters followed the Cobra as it rotated up and out of the rings. They could see its shields had taken a hammering, partly from their weapons fire and partly from being unable to avoid minor collisions with stray pieces of debris from the rings.

The Cobra tore upwards, trailing a plume of disrupted flux drive energy and a flaming collection of dislodged dust and rock. The Federation fighters followed close behind, like a pack of angry bees hunting a besieged albatross.

For a moment the old trading vessel hung there before the fighters. The wing commander had a moment to take in the familiar shape of its two main drives, the triangular outrigger thrusters on the wing tips.

Laser fire traced around it. Belatedly the Imperial fighters had located them. 'All ships, break and defend, break and defend ...'

He'd waited a moment too long. A stray shot penetrated the cockpit. There was no immediate explosion, just the harsh snap of venting atmosphere from the cockpit. His remlok immediately compensated, protecting him from the harsh vacuum of space.

CHAPTER THIRTEEN

Rocks still clouded his view. He saw the Cobra dance to one side to avoid one as it hurtled past.

He pulled his controls aside to follow. Red lights flashed on his console.

Warning: Portside manoeuvring jets failure!

He cursed. Damage from the laser or from some other hit? He wrestled the controls the other way.

Turn … turn! No …

A brief explosion lit up the darkness. The errant rock spun away, unaffected.

* * *

'Was it us?' Admiral Brice demanded.

'No, sir, the Federation fighter simply got in the way, a stray shot … it crashed into a rock.'

Brice shook his head and looked briefly at the Federation convoy, looming still closer in the windows.

'And the chances the Federation will see it that way?'

It was a rhetorical question. The pivot point had been reached. It was time to ensure he retained the advantage.

'Cancel that damned holofac transmission. All batteries, open fire!'

* * *

'They fired on us!' The second in command called, his voice attenuated by the poor quality communication to the Federation battleship. 'Wing lead is gone, I repeat gone. Imperial fighters took him out …'

Static crackled and obscured his voice.

'The 'stards fired on us …' the captain muttered before raising his voice. 'Weapons systems live, lock targets and open fire on the Imperials!'

The gunnery officer turned, looking directly at the captain. 'Sir, we have incoming!' The captain looked briefly at Tenim and then back to his crew.

'All hands, defensive fire! Change course relative ninety degrees to starboard, engage at will.'

ELITE: RECLAMATION

* * *

Along the portside flank of the Imperial vessels, flame jetted briefly into the void. Huge turrets launched ballistic ordnance along carefully plotted trajectories. Torpedoes, sleek elongated weapons of mass destruction, launched from their storage bays lodged along the lower hull of the vast ships. They streaked out, trailing plumes of vapour from their simple chemical engines.

The Federation fleet responded in kind. Space between the ships, empty for a moment, was promptly filled with criss-crossing metal, fire and hurtling debris.

Aboard all ships, smaller turrets tracked the incoming weapons and blasted out staccato bursts of defensive flak-fire. Brief explosions flashed in the darkness; a rain of fire and destruction connected the two fleets.

The fleets converged, ships breaking from formation to evade fire or gain a superior position. Beam weapons were triggered, scintillating rays of vicious directed energy, impaling smaller vessels, ripping shields away, burning through hulls and disgorging their internals into the void.

Ships died, the victims of unfortunate impacts to their main reactor cores, unleashing in seconds the stored energy necessary to power a vessel for months. Others heroically sacrificed themselves to prevent damage to a more valuable vessel. Still more, damaged or bereft of functioning weapons, resorted to high-speed ramming moves to inflict whatever damage they could.

Shields flashed and flickered, energy erupted and was deflected. Fighter vessels twisted around the larger ships, trading fire with each other. Minor victories were won, small defeats endured.

The fleets continued their melee.

Kahina caught sight of the battle as the *Bella Principessa* emerged from the rock field. She gasped in dismay as an Imperial cutter was impaled by a bright beam of intense fire from the *Xajorkith*. In horror she saw the cutter hang impotently for a moment, before its structure failed, separating into two major pieces which broke apart in opposite directions, shedding debris and fiery embers of disintegrating components through space. The *Bella Principessa* rocked briefly as Luko turned to avoid the wreckage.

How many people aboard that ship?

CHAPTER THIRTEEN

'You have your war, signorina,' Luko said darkly.

'Get me to the station,' she replied, her face ashen, but still firmly set.

All around them the firefight raged. The Federation ships unleashed a barrage of fire in their direction which the Imperial ships countered with their own, or simply intervened by positioning their own ships in a defensive posture. Fighters zipped and whirled around them, trading tracer fire in a deadly dance of death.

Luko guided the Cobra onwards, never triggering his own weapons, but threading a path through the bewildering tumult. He plotted a path that took them close to the Imperial battleship, hiding under the protection of its guns. As they raced across its hull, Kahina caught brief glimpses of the massive weapons protruding from the enormous ship. Muzzles flashed, turrets turned and tracked, parts of the hull glowed with heat and fire, explosions crackled around them as the Federation marksmen attempted to destroy their ship.

The *Bella Principessa* slipped along the flank of the *Atticus*, dodging through the flak-fire, drives flaring brightly, rolling this way and that, still driving directly for Chione.

* * *

'Covering fire!' Brice ordered.

The mighty guns aboard the *Atticus* thundered in concert as the Imperial ships converged to protect the tiny Cobra-class vessel as it weaved between them. The Federation ships were close now, pounding away with every piece of ordnance at their disposal.

'Shields failed in zones five through eight, sir! Damage to portside generators and drive one. We can't bring our main batteries to bear in this configuration!'

'Maintain position until the Cobra is under cover of the station,' Brice ordered, his face grim with determination. The Imperial fleet was being forced to hold a defensive line in order to protect the Cobra. It exposed them to the full fury of the Federation fleet, without being able to respond in kind. Already outnumbered, they would quickly be overwhelmed unless …

Another Imperial frigate flashed into oblivion nearby, its flaming hull spinning with the impact of a devastating Federation barrage. Brice watched in fury as it rolled aside, ablaze from stem to stern, turning in a last desperate move. It narrowly missed the *Atticus*, instead burning across space and crashing into the rear of the *Xajorkith*. Molten debris sprayed in all directions.

'Cobra is past the phalanx, sir! Still running at full throttle.'

Brice grimaced and clenched his fist. 'Form up, all ships! Concentrate fire on the Federation battlecruiser, rear quarter. Now we turn the tide!'

As one the Imperial ships turned, now free to unleash their own weapons to best effect. Beam weapons converged and struck out. The Federation battleship took the brunt of the incoming fire. Already weakened by the suicidal strike of the frigate, the shields along its flank failed momentarily. Missiles screamed inwards towards the rear of the mighty vessel, a coordinated strike on the damaged section.

The starboard drive, already damaged, exploded under the assault, ripping away a sizable chunk of the ship with it.

The *Xajorkith* lurched perceptibly and then slowly pulled away, one of its drives reduced to slag.

* * *

Tenim staggered as the *Xajorkith* lurched beneath him. From the tremors writhing through the deck he sensed they'd suffered a significant amount of damage. The consternation of the bridge crew confirmed it.

'Shields failing, sir!'

'Drive four is offline, power fluctuations …'

'Disengage and withdraw,' the captain shouted above the mayhem. 'Pull back! Signal all ships, disengage!'

'Captain, we need that ship!' Tenim demanded.

The captain shook his head. 'Commissioner, the ship is out of range, with the Imperial fleet interposed. We have significant damage, we must withdraw. If we remain in proximity …'

Tenim slammed his palm down against the bridge railing.

'Damn the girl,' he fumed. 'What is it going to take to rid us of her?'

Abruptly the battle was over. The Federation ships pulled back out of range,

CHAPTER THIRTEEN

re-establishing their formation, the frigates and corvettes forming a protective perimeter around the damaged battleship.

'Damage report?' the captain demanded.

'Drive four is gone, sir. We have significant damage astern but can still manoeuvre. Sixty-two per cent of our fleet remains intact and operable.'

'Tactical.'

The Federation crew studied the displays for long moments, calling up information on the opposing fleet statistics and positions.

'Imperial fleet came off worse,' the first officer said, 'but they are now between us and the moon with the additional firepower of the station.'

The captain nodded.

'Begin recovery operations for the damaged ships, I don't want any more hands lost.'

'We lost,' Jenu said, softly from beside Tenim. Tenim turned to look at her. Her face was pale and harrowed.

Tenim sighed deeply, but shook his head.

'Not quite, my dear, there is one more throw of the dice.'

Chapter Fourteen

The light from the explosions and weapons fire unexpectedly faded away. Luko glanced at the rear-view display seeing the Imperial ships converging behind them. The Federation ships were further back, effectively blocked.

A shield.

'I will say this for your Imperials,' he said appraisingly, 'they know their tactics.'

Kahina was looking forwards; the bulk of the station was close now. *Hiram's Anchorage* looked dark and forbidding from this angle, unlit by the sun and hiding in Chione's shadow.

She triggered the comm link.

'*Hiram's Anchorage*, this is Kahina Tijani Loren. I call to the slaves loyal to my father, Algreb Loren. Allow me to dock.'

The answer was prompt, but the voice sounded less than enthusiastic, almost worried, but it had a strong Imperial accent.

'Most honoured daughter of Algreb, Kahina. Please proceed to the main docking bay.' There was a pause. 'We will meet you in the habitation ring.'

Static crackled and the communication cut off. *Hiram's Anchorage* was close by. The *Bella Principessa* slowed as it approached.

Kahina looked at Luko, who was frowning. 'Something wrong?' she demanded.

'They your people,' he said mysteriously. 'You tell me.'

'I need their help.'

Luko nodded and turned the ship towards the gaping docking bay.

* * *

The massive blast doors sealed the docking bay from the outside. As they locked into place, the *Bella Principessa* was also being shepherded into position. Kahina and Luko left their ship behind and entered the airlock arrangement. It felt routine now. Kahina welcomed the feeling of weight as the lift mechanism dropped them into the habitation ring.

The doors snapped open and they both cautiously stepped out, weapons drawn. Luko had insisted they were armed.

Kahina cautiously looked across the habitation ring. It was strewn with debris, bits of ships, drive units, fuel scoop convertors, cargo bay extensions, shield generators and all sort of associated junk from ships both large and small. Around the ring was all manner of discarded machinery, all broken down, some half dismantled. There was no sign of life.

'They said they would meet us here,' she said, looking around the gently curving floor.

The entire habitation area was a mess, cargo pods and ship parts were spread around in a haphazard manner. The floor was covered with discarded consoles, conduits, bolts, ripped and torn sections of hull plating. Here and there were puddles of grease or leaked coolant, or other even less salubrious fluids. Kahina sidestepped them, trying to stay clear. Everything was grimy, covered in grease. Even the air felt polluted, with a strong whiff of unidentified fumes. The dim illumination showed the air was full of dust.

'There has been a fight,' Luko muttered.

Kahina could feel her palms getting sweaty. She closed her fingers tighter, she didn't want to drop her gun. It felt thick and heavy in her hand.

Luko stepped up beside her, walking backwards, his own gun pointing back the way they had come. There was no sign of anyone.

'Perhaps they are delayed ...' Luko offered.

'Until further notice, I'm afraid.'

The snapping sound of handheld weapons priming to fire reached their ears. Smartly attired guards appeared from behind the ruined consoles, packing crates, storage lockers and cargo canisters. Each held a gun on them. There were at least half a dozen they could see and doubtless many more they could not.

Kahina and Luko lowered their weapons; they were hopelessly out numbered. Two of the guards quickly disarmed them and hurried back out of the way.

The voice had come from ahead of Kahina. She squinted into the gloom as a figure walked towards her. The voice was lighter than she'd expected, the sound of sharply clicking heels echoed on the metallic floor. Kahina could see shiny boots sparkling in the darkness long before the figure strode into the light.

CHAPTER FOURTEEN

Each footstep was carefully placed in front of the next, a purposeful but stylish gait; hips swinging. It was a woman.

She stepped into the light. The woman had a tall imposing frame, an athletic build framed by a dramatic gown with gold highlights. Blonde hair framed a strong face with a pair of bright but fierce eyes.

The gown barely hid a trim but voluptuous figure. She wore a curiously bulky gun, loosely held in a belt at her side. Next to it Kahina could see a sabre buckled in a thin scabbard.

'Who is this?' Luko whispered.

Kahina shook her head briefly. 'I don't know.'

The woman strode up to her, staring directly into her eyes. She was considerably taller than Kahina. Kahina had to strain her neck to return her gaze.

The woman slowly walked around her, before returning to face Kahina again.

'It seems impossible that you don't know me,' the woman said. 'Yet I suppose we have never met ... whilst you were conscious anyway.'

Kahina frowned. 'Who are you?'

The woman ignored her. 'But I know you well, Kahina Loren. So young ...'

'Then it is rude to keep me at a disadvantage,' Kahina replied.

The woman smiled. 'Perhaps you have heard of me. My name is Octavia Quinton.'

Kahina's eyes widened in recognition. She heard Luko gasp beside her.

'Oh merda,' he muttered.

'And who are you?' Octavia asked, reluctantly turning her attention to him. Luko had to look up even more than Kahina.

'I? I am just a simple trader ...'

'Are you indeed?' Octavia slid her gaze away from him with disinterest, focusing back on Kahina. 'You've led us a merry dance across this sector, young lady.'

'My name is Kahina.'

'Kahina Loren.' Octavia laid a hand on Kahina's shoulder, possessively. 'Daughter of the late Senator Algreb Loren, third of three daughters, all sadly no longer with us.'

'Why should you take an interest in me?' Kahina stepped aside, shrugging Octavia's hand off her shoulder. She recalled a conversation with Hassan from days before. 'You wanted me, why?'

'I take an interest in all persons of influence in my territory,' Octavia replied easily, 'and I want you for what you can do for me. An Imperial Senator has influence that would benefit me greatly; favourable trade considerations and so on. There is much you might do on my behalf.'

'And why should I help you?'

'A mutually beneficial arrangement. You wish to reclaim your moon, I could help you with that.'

'What have you done with my slaves?' Kahina demanded.

Octavia chuckled. 'Your slaves? This system is mine, little one, for now at least.'

'It belonged to my father, the Senator. Now it belongs to me.'

'You are dead, don't you remember being killed?' Octavia toyed with her. 'Dispatched by the Reclamists. So tragic to lose your life so young.'

'I am not dead!'

'No, you're not.'

Kahina started at the sound of another voice. A shiver ran down her spine, sending the hairs on the back of her neck tingling with fear, anticipation and cold vengeance.

That voice.

A sword, a stance, a shadow. She swallowed and felt her sweat chill across her from head to foot.

A second figure emerged from the gloom, taller even than Octavia. Bald headed and dressed in a trademark dark trench coat unbuckled at the waist. Even Luko recoiled slightly.

Kahina gasped, her lip curling in rage. She spat out her next words.

'Dalk Torgen.'

* * *

Kahina lurched forward, but Luko grabbed her shoulder before she could be knocked back by the two guards who stepped towards her, guns raised.

'Let me go.'

CHAPTER FOURTEEN

'Now is not the time,' Luko whispered in her ear.

'He killed my family, he killed me.'

Rage clouded her vision, she wanted to grab Octavia's sword, pull it out and run Dalk through ... no, slice and rip his skin, batter him to a pulp and only then end his life when he begged for mercy. Blood, guts ... she would dismember him in front of his own eyes, slice him up piece by piece. She could almost feel her hand upon the sword hilt, turning, twisting ... striking.

His voice brought her back to the present with a jolt. 'I did not kill your family.'

'How dare you ...' Kahina struggled for words, '... even speak of them. I was there, you were one of the Reclamists! You murdered them. I saw it all.'

Dalk straightened and took a step towards her.

'Come no closer, traitor.' Kahina wrestled her shoulder out of Luko's grasp.

'Signorina, no.'

Dalk slowly drew his own sword and held it towards her, point first. She stared down the length of the ornate blade for a moment.

'Finishing what you started?' she asked, refusing to be cowed.

'You would not be standing there if I had intended for you to die,' Dalk answered. 'Think, Kahina. You were restored, brought back to life at huge expense. Yes, the plan went awry ...'

'You killed my family!' Kahina said, her voice almost a scream.

'They were already dead,' Dalk shouted back, cutting across her, his voice echoing around the empty desolate chamber.

Kahina shook her head. 'No. What madness is this?'

As she watched cautiously, Dalk lowered his sword and turned aside, striding a few paces away before turning back to her. His coat billowed outwards briefly with the move. 'Politics within the Empire had already turned against your father. His treatment of the slaves, the executions in the city piazza? These were the tipping point. I had already dealt with several Imperial assassins intent on ending his life.'

'You betrayed him. You didn't defend him ...'

'You're wrong. At first I did, but it became clear that the situation was untenable. Your father became mentally unfit to rule. The Reclamists became a threat because of his draconian policies of suppression – yes, his fault. His madness fanned their flames. The Empire determined he could not be allowed to remain in power, the Tantalum was too valuable. From that point his fate was sealed. It was simply a matter of how ... and when.'

'This is lies ...'

'Why do you think I trained you, Kahina?' She stepped back as Dalk raised his voice still further, advancing towards her. 'Why spend all that time with the least favoured daughter of a failing Senator? Why other than to prepare you for becoming the Senator of the Prism system? Your sisters were useless; facile and vacuous. You alone had the intellect, the resolve and the cunning. Your right could not be questioned. Your claim was legal and all parties would recognise it. There would be peace ...'

'Peace? You killed him, murdered him and my mother ... my sisters.' Kahina shook with the effort of forcing back tears. She refused to cry.

'Your father was advised of the danger to himself and his family. He ignored the warnings. I infiltrated the Reclamists ... became trusted by them, yes!' Dalk waved his arm. 'But only to protect the single member of the family who could possibly continue the line. I could not save your family, but I could save you!'

Can he possibly be telling the truth?

'You were one of them, you're no loyal Imperial,' she returned. 'You hated my father. You betrayed me. You ran me through with a sword!'

'An act, Kahina!'

'An act?' she cried out in incredulity.

'Yes, an act! The Reclamists had to be convinced of your death. It was the only way we could safely remove you from the system. You were to be restored and safely kept until conditions were right for your return. I arranged for the medical transport, the convoy and your evacuation. The Reclamists believed they had won.'

'I don't believe you.'

'Then why am I not killing you now?' Dalk placed his hands on his hips and regarded her. 'I want you to reclaim Chione. That was always my intention.'

Kahina's mouth twisted in a sneer. 'How can I trust you, Dalk Torgen? You scheme and lie! You put me through hell for your machinations. I was abandoned, alone and lost because of you.'

CHAPTER FOURTEEN

'No, that was my doing.' Octavia said, her voice gentle and reassuring after Dalk's directness and ferocity. She stepped forward to stand beside him. 'A juicy selection of technology such as that used by Dalk proved too tempting. It was I who decided to appropriate your ship.'

Kahina scowled at her and swiftly turned her attention back to Dalk.

Dalk gestured briefly with his right hand and another figure was pulled out of the shadows by two of the guards.

Kahina looked at him in surprise. It was the youth she'd stolen the ship from – Hassan. She felt a pang of guilt and shame. He was in a bad way, his face battered and bruised. His hands were crudely bandaged. She wondered what had happened to him after she'd abandoned him to Dalk. The guards shoved him forwards.

'Hassan?' Kahina asked. Hassan didn't say anything, but briefly looked up at her.

'You can blame him for your trials. He was the one who stole you and led us a merry chase across the sector. Octavia stole you from me, Hassan stole you from Octavia. You were brought back to consciousness in an improper fashion. Your memories damaged and fragmented. That was never the intention, none of it.'

'You played me, Dalk,' Kahina said. 'Played me like a piece in a game of chance.'

'And what was the alternative?' Dalk said, his voice uncharacteristically angry. 'Millions of people depend on Chione for their livelihoods. The Empire had already determined your father had to go. Other Senators were looking greedily at this system, dreaming up their own plans for expansion and annexation. Would you have let them take over?'

'They wouldn't dare annex …'

'Plans were already in motion. What would your life have been then, Kahina? Least favoured daughter of a disgraced Senator? Perhaps you'd just quietly disappear? Does life as a slave on Achenar appeal? Patron Gerrun has a taste for classy whores so it is said, perhaps you could apply? Or perhaps you'd enjoy being paraded through the Federation as an example of hubris and Imperial pride after a fall?'

Kahina shuddered.

'You think this was my plan alone?' Dalk continued. 'The Empire is interested in stability and commerce, Kahina. Remember your lessons, you know this! The fate of the Loren family line reached even to the echelons of the Duvals. Your father was dead from the moment he came to their attention. What could we Patrons do against such might? You were the only alternative. It was that or hand the Prism system to another family.'

'You schemed with the other Patrons? Gerrun and that ridiculous Zyair?'

'Yes we schemed! You're not a child, Kahina. You know how politics works. How else could we serve your family? The Empire had determined you were all to be removed. Your sisters were useless fripperies, nothing more. We could only save you. The Loren line would remain intact. And you … you would be Senator of the Prism system.'

Senator?

'Trust me, Kahina.'

Kahina laughed at him. 'You would have me trust you now? After what you have done? Murderer, traitor … liar!'

'All the Patrons are in agreement, Kahina. We will pledge our allegiance to you. You are the rightful heir to the Prism system. It is yours by right of inheritance. You are your father's daughter. We will ensure the Empire recognises this. You will be Senator.'

Kahina turned away, her head spinning. She couldn't take it all in. It was madness, surely? Dalk had actually tried to save her? Was it possible? She turned back on him angrily.

'As Senator I would have the right to execute whosoever I chose, Dalk,' she said. 'Perhaps I would warrant your death as my first act.'

Dalk looked at her. For a moment he said nothing, but then he knelt down on one knee and looked up at her. 'I swore an oath of allegiance to your family. My allegiance lies with you as your father's heir. I have done my best to ensure the continuation of your family line. If your trust in me is broken irreconcilably, I will accept my fate for the part I have played.'

Kahina held her breath for a moment, before letting it out, trying to slow the thoughts churning through her mind. 'Will you now …?'

She looked across at Octavia.

'And what do you want from all this?'

CHAPTER FOURTEEN

Octavia smiled. 'Dalk made me certain promises in exchange for supporting your claim to this system. I expect to have them honoured.' After a moment she added, 'Senator.'

'I see,' Kahina replied, 'and what did my oh so loyal servant promise you?'

'An exclusive contract on the Tantalum on behalf of Federation buyers.'

'You think I would sell my Tantalum to the Federation after what they tried to do?'

'You will need money to rebuild your home, Senator,' Octavia replied. 'The Federation has no interest in your little world, but they have interest in trading that one commodity. Money is money. Strike a deal and the money will flow to you. You'll be able to name your price. Create a legacy beyond the dreams of your father.'

'I will have no Federation dogs on my world,' Kahina said, coldly.

'You would never need to do so. I would handle that transaction for you. Only the money would come to you.'

'Minus a cut,' Kahina asked.

'I ask for only forty per cent, Senator.'

'You will settle for twenty.'

The guards around them made a show of checking their guns and adjusting their aim. 'Thirty-five,' Octavia replied, folding her arms in front of her.

The two women looked at each other for a long moment. A faint smile grew on Octavia's face.

Kahina looked around at the guards surrounding her. 'Thirty.'

Octavia nodded. 'As you wish, Senator.'

Kahina turned back to Dalk.

'You ask much, Dalk.'

Dalk climbed slowly to his feet, facing her in a formal fashion.

'You trusted me once. Trust me again. I live only to serve you, Kahina Tijani of the house of Loren.'

We'll see about that.

'I will test your allegiance then, Patron Dalk,' she said, her voice snide. 'Your first act of service to me as Senator of Chione.'

'Command me, Senator.'

Kahina's stare was intense.

'Kill the Reclamists, but hold Vargo for me. Bring me my father's sceptre. Reclaim my home.'

Dalk nodded.

'It shall be done.'

* * *

Dalk's plan was simple and straightforward. Vargo and his men were holed up in the Imperial Palace. It was heavily defended by ground to air defences, installed due to the paranoia of Kahina's father. Those defences had to be neutralised. Fortunately Kahina knew precisely where the main power generator was – buried in the mountainside on the west side of her island home. If that could be destroyed and the defences taken down, they could remove any remaining resistance with impunity.

Retribution, Octavia's Anaconda, had by far the most fearsome weaponry aboard. Its plasma accelerator would make short work of the power generator, assuming it could get close enough to use it. Flying such a big and heavy ship down through the atmosphere would be no mean feat; the bulky ship would lack manoeuvrability in the atmosphere, making it a big fat target. The other ships appropriated from *Hiram's Anchorage* would have to draw fire and clear a path.

Dalk had already surveyed the vessels moored aboard the station. They were a mixture of old Sidewinders and Adders, mostly fitted to Imperial specification. It made sense to leave the few Federation vessels alone in case of any ambiguity. Most were lightly armed, and there wasn't much time but to load them up with more than a few missiles and the other bits of portable ordnance available.

Dalk briefed the slaves aboard the station. A dozen or so were pilots, more used to the controls of liners and transports on behalf of their citizens. They were supplemented by the few pilots that could be spared from the Imperial task force, still uneasily standing off against the Federation fleet holding in high orbit. No communication attempts had been made between the two opposing

CHAPTER FOURTEEN

powers and no ship movements had been seen. The Federation appeared to be watching and waiting.

The smaller vessels would not engage the ground targets, their aim was simply to clear a path so that Octavia's Anaconda could make a run on the island in order to disable its defences.

Dalk initially suggested that Kahina remain aboard the station to await news of their anticipated victory, but she flatly refused.

'I will not stand by like a coward,' she replied, angrily rebuffing Dalk's suggestion.

'It's too dangerous. Your safety is paramount,' Dalk insisted. 'If we lose you, we lose everything.'

'I will not ask others to do what I am not prepared to do myself,' Kahina replied. 'I can fly.'

'She's pretty good, actually,' Hassan added.

Dalk glared at him. 'She's not qualified …'

'She might be safer with us,' Octavia added. 'If the Federation overruns the Imperial fleet she might be caught up here. At least on the moon …'

'She can ride with me,' Hassan said, casting a look towards Octavia. Dalk looked at their determined faces and sighed. He turned to Kahina.

'You will hang back from the main attack force, you will not engage other than to defend yourself and you'll take the best ship we can spare. Agreed?'

Kahina looked across at Octavia and Hassan. They all nodded.

Dalk strode away and looked out of the panoramic windows framing the observation room.

Chione lay before them, peaceful, blue and blissful.

'Where's your trader friend, anyway?' he said, turning around. 'Is he joining us? We could use another ship.'

'He's …' Kahina began uncertainly. 'I will speak to him.'

'We launch within the hour. Time is short.'

* * *

Octavia retreated aboard the *Retribution*, accompanied by her second in command. 'Is it done?' she snapped as she entered the bridge.

'Both devices fitted and tested. We'll be able to track them and ... deal with them should the need arise.'

Octavia nodded. 'Let's see if our young friend comes through for us. If not, the moment the opportunity presents itself we will snatch her and high tail it out. Keep the hyperdrive spooled at all times. Until that point we're Dalk's loyal followers. Clear?'

'Yes, Domina.'

'Good. Power up the ship. Let's go murder some revolutionaries.'

Her officer turned to begin his duties. Octavia left the bridge and proceeded to her quarters. She relaxed into one of her lounge chairs and fired up a holofac transmission. Various cryptographic exchanges took place before the holofac flared into life.

'Ms Quinton.'

Octavia smiled at the figure before her. She could just make out a woman behind him, standing just within range of the holofac receiver.

'Commissioner Neseva. How does the hour find you?'

'All the better for hearing from you, my dear. We are rather in the dark out here.'

Octavia nodded. 'Perhaps I can enlighten you. Our errant daughter of the Empire plans an assault on her home within the next few minutes. It seems likely she will succeed.'

'Why do you say that?'

'Because I'm helping her.'

'Ah ...' Tenim replied.

'I'd imagine this is not aligned with the fortunes of the Federation.'

'You imagine correctly. The question is ...'

'I will deal with her. I have taken steps to ensure she is appropriated, but further ... insurance ... would be welcome.'

'What did you have in mind?'

'We've placed a tracking device aboard her vessel. If it is activated, retrieve her. Here is the code.' Octavia flicked her fingers towards the display and a scatter of data appeared briefly. 'In case she evades me you will be able to secure her. Have ships ready to hyperspace on a moment's notice.'

'We will oblige.'

CHAPTER FOURTEEN

'She is mine, Commissioner. Do not think to take her yourself. I can ensure the Federation gains nothing from this system. Understand that well.'

'I understand you completely, Ms Quinton.' Tenim said, evenly. 'Rest assured, we want only to ensure that the Imperial woman does not return to a position of authority over this moon. We will then negotiate an equitable accord with the Imperials as we intended. Her disposition after that … I leave in your most capable hands.'

'Make sure you do.'

Octavia nodded brusquely and then closed the call.

* * *

Kahina stood beneath the shadow of the *Bella Principessa*. Luko was making some last minute checks to his ship, in preparation for leaving. Kahina glared at him for a long moment, rage boiling in her as he seemed unconcerned and continued to ignore her.

'So you're leaving.'

'You are right, signorina.' Luko did not make eye contact. 'Our deal is done. I got you safely home, no?'

'And that's it, is it? After all we went through, you're just going to leave?'

'I will not fight …'

'… my war? Your same old tired line?' Kahina scoffed at him. 'I fight for freedom, this is a worthy thing, freeing my home from oppression.'

'Do you?' Luko turned and looked directly at her. 'You plan to attack these rebels. No talk, no trying to find a peace? Pah. You want a war. More people will die, did you not see that battle you caused up there?' He gestured to the faint lights that marked the opposing fleets far beyond the overhead windows.

'The Federation interfered. They are the aggressors.'

'Always it is someone else. No, signorina! This is your fight, your war, these deaths are yours to account for. Stop this battle, talk to these rebels …'

'They will not negotiate; it's a waste of time. You've seen what they've done to my world. I need you, Luko, your tactics, your expertise …'

'Fighting is not the answer. You will do more damage. The Empire and the Federation are here – talk to them, find a solution …'

'It won't work.'

'How you know – 'til you try?'

'Because I know.'

Luko dismissed her with a wave. 'You are like all Imperials; vengeance, revenge, honour … this is not the way.'

Kahina's expression hardened. 'Then go. Go back and hide out there in your cosy traders' universe. Go on! Just remember how it feels next time a pirate snatches your cargo and leaves you penniless, adrift and alone. You'll want revenge then.'

Luko looked up and held her glance for a long moment, but no words came. He looked away, shaking his head.

She turned and stalked away, furious and dismayed. The ship next along in the bay had been earmarked for her. Hassan was outside, checking its systems.

'Is he joining us?'

'No,' Kahina said, biting down on rising fury.

'Shame, could have used that ship. He's a flyer and no mistake.'

'He's not coming. We'll do without him.'

Hassan considered the matter for a moment. Kahina was clearly furious. 'You ready?' he asked.

'Yes I am,' she replied forcefully. Hassan stepped back at her sharp tones. 'Are you?'

'Ship is prepped. Let's see if we can keep this one intact, eh?'

He tried to lighten the conversation, but Kahina's expression turned to one of guilt and regret.

'I am sorry about what happened before, it was not my intention to cause so much trouble, I had no idea …'

'… that I'd get tortured, stabbed, lose my ship and all my money? You're very good at making trouble.'

'You shouldn't have got involved!' Kahina shot back, her anger flaring.

'Easy, Sal … Kahina, save the firepower for your friends surface-side …' Hassan held up his hands. 'What happened to my ship, by the way?'

'It … crashed.'

Hassan snorted. 'Then if we get through all this in one piece and reinstate your Imperial backside to its rightful place … you owe me a ship … and not a piece of crap Eagle, something decent and modern.'

CHAPTER FOURTEEN

Kahina looked at him. 'You do this for me, I'll see you rewarded. Ship, money. I don't care what you want, you can have it. Deal?'

'A deal.'

Around them ships were firing up their drives, the sound echoing through the vast interior of the station. Kahina watched Luko's ship launch and head out of the docking bay. It turned away from Chione, heading out towards the stars.

She trembled, watching as it disappeared from view.

Is there no true loyalty in this universe?

It was time to go.

'You ready?' Hassan asked.

Kahina nodded. 'Let's take back my world.'

* * *

'I don't understand,' Jenu said, looking at the tactical display on the bridge of the Federation battlecruiser. It was showing a series of markers leaving the orbital space station. As she watched they formed up into a loose formation and began descending towards the moon.

'What don't you understand, my dear?' Tenim replied.

'We can't leave the Loren girl in the hands of Octavia Quinton. Surely once she's done with her she'll just sell the girl back to the Imperials? Then where will we be?'

'We have a deal with her,' Tenim replied. 'A matter of trust, surely.'

Jenu looked agog. 'You trust Octavia Quinton?'

'I trust her to do what I expect.'

'And what's that exactly?'

Tenim turned to her, his lips curving in a half smile. 'Wait and see.'

He stepped down towards the captain, who was overseeing the repair activities taking place. 'Captain? Ah … yes. I need a favour …'

* * *

Hassan adjusted the course of the ship they'd been assigned as it fell into position at the rear of the phalanx of vessels leaving *Hiram's Anchorage*. It was an Adder-class vessel, rather curiously named the *Black Monk*. It was a little more roomy than Hassan's old Eagle. An old design, it was famed for being tough and sturdy, if not the last word in offensive firepower.

'It handles well planetside,' he said. 'These old beasts have wing-folding mechs, less of a brick and more of a plane.'

The rest of the 'fleet' was centred around Octavia's Anaconda, the *Retribution*. It was by far the largest vessel. Dalk had chosen a rather scarred and battered looking Asp, an ex-military ship with a fearsome reputation for being resilient in a firefight. It was positioned above the *Retribution*.

The remaining ships were mostly a collection of old Sidewinders, a few Eagles and a squadron of Imperial fighters that had been spared from the Imperial fleet in orbit, still facing off against the Federation armada.

The holofac system crackled into life. Hassan saw an ornately dressed gentleman appear. He bowed his head as he caught sight of Kahina.

'Ambassador Cuthrick,' Kahina acknowledged.

'Lady Kahina. Are things in place?'

'We are ready, the attack will commence in moments.' Hassan thought her voice shook, but a determined look was set on her face.

'May fortune favour you. We will watch your back and prevent Federation interference. Take back your world. I look forward to greeting you as Senator of Chione.'

'It won't be long, Ambassador, thank you for your service.'

'Until we meet again, Lady Kahina.'

The holofac faded. Kahina looked across. Hassan saw her lick her lips and run a hand through her hair.

'Ready?' he asked.

'Ready,' she answered. 'Signal all ships. Begin the attack.'

* * *

The glowing blue curve of the moon flattened out rapidly below them. Atmospheric entry was the incinerating hell it had been before and then the

CHAPTER FOURTEEN

fleet dropped into the thickening atmosphere. It was a beautiful cloudless day with good visibility. Kahina knew precisely where they were, the shapes of the continents were intimately familiar, almost reassuring.

The fleet flew in over the Garian Sea, closing rapidly on the island of New Ithaca where the Imperial Palace was located. They were approaching from several hundred miles away, keeping the island below the horizon for now, hoping to make their detection more difficult for the defenders. Each ship streamed a thick trail of vapour behind it, roaring across the archipelago far beyond the speed of sound, a fierce rumble echoing off the water far below.

The ships flew lower still, descending until they were a scant few metres above the flickering blue surface of the sea, drawing plumes of water rushing into the air in their wake. They were approaching from the north, with the light of the Prism star behind them, its glare providing a little extra cover in the hope that it would confuse the targeting systems of the defence networks.

Dalk's voice crackled over the narrowband comms.

'Range fifty kilometres. Stand by for incoming. Engage and destroy hostile vessels but do not close on the island until the defences are neutralised.'

Kahina heard the acknowledgements crackle back across the link.

Streams of tracer fire flashed towards them, with shocking suddenness the air was rent with the black crashes of explosive fire. Turbulence buffeted the *Black Monk*. Hassan wrestled with the controls to keep the ship in the protective shadow of the *Retribution*. Fire flashed around them. Kahina saw one Sidewinder take a hit and explode nearby. Debris, trailing burning torrents of flame and smoke flashed past the windows and were gone.

Just as she was recovering from that, an Imperial fighter above and to the right was also hit, spiralling away out of control. She watched in dismay as it ploughed into the sea, shattering into pieces on impact in a splash of water. It fell behind and was gone.

More death ... is this truly worth this sacrifice? Am I doing the right thing?

The fleet responded. Missiles streaked forward, dropping out of their launch mechanisms and blasting forwards towards targets unseen. Kahina caught a brief view of the island of New Ithaca just appearing over the horizon when another brief command buzzed over the narrowband comms.

'Break and attack, all ships, break and attack.'

The *Black Monk* rose and turned. Kahina gasped, ships were everywhere, turning and twisting in the air, lasers and particle weapons flashing and discharging. She could make almost no sense of which ship was which, only the large *Retribution* was obvious, making its way directly towards the island.

It was clear the defenders saw it as the most significant threat. Ships targeted it immediately. Kahina saw its shields flare in response as weapons fire flickered along its flank, streaming backwards in a burning wake as the Anaconda ploughed onwards. She could just make out Dalk's ship targeting and destroying those vessels. It was a battle of attrition.

A jolt brought her attention to her immediate surroundings. The shields aboard the *Black Monk* flared. Hassan threw the controls over, sending the Adder into a loop and a sharp turn, hoping to evade whatever ship had decided to take a fancy to incinerating them.

The bright red beam of a laser passed close by, Hassan rolled the other way. Another jolt. A warning siren from the on board systems.

Shields failed!

'They've locked on to us,' Hassan snapped into the narrowband. 'Could use a little help here.'

The *Black Monk* dived towards the surface of the sea, heading straight downwards towards the scintillating blue surface. Kahina glanced at the rear-view monitor, briefly seeing two ships flicker across the displays.

'Two of them ...' she whispered.

The *Black Monk* jolted a third time and then the threat warning alarm sounded, buzzing furiously.

'Missile lock ...' Hassan wrenched the controls back and the *Black Monk* rose abruptly, crushing them painfully in their seats. The sea was close, rushing by below them, just metres away.

The horizon appeared, an explosion flashed from the rear view.

Hassan grinned. Kahina looked forward only to gasp in surprise. A ship was heading directly towards them, guns blazing.

A Sidewinder rocketed past with a roar, mere metres above them. More explosions followed. Hassan looked across at Kahina.

'Cutting it fine.'

Kahina gritted her teeth. 'It's a habit I wish to break.'

CHAPTER FOURTEEN

Octavia's voice was next to sound across the comms.

'We're almost in range of the palace defences. Flak-fire is intense. Ten seconds.'

'All ships, converge on the *Retribution* and draw fire.' Dalk's voice was firm and insistent.

Hassan adjusted the course of the *Black Monk*. They were now some distance behind the main fleet. The fleet was converging on the island; it seemed the defenders' ships had been beaten back, though streams of fire still erupted from the defensive emplacements on the hillside. Kahina feared the smaller ships wouldn't last long against the surface weapons at close range.

'Five seconds.'

Two more of the Sidewinders succumbed to the defensive fire, spiralling into destruction as the defences blasted another wave of flak into the sky. Dark clouds flashed past, rocking the *Black Monk*.

'We have range.'

A beam of intense white light burst from the *Retribution,* scouring the surface of the island. An intense flash followed causing all the pilots to shield their eyes from the glare. When they could see again, a colossal mushroom cloud of smoke and debris was rising from the mountains on the west side of the island.

The flak-fire abruptly ceased.

Kahina watched as the *Retribution* veered aside, climbing beyond the island and turning back towards them.

Cheers and yells of delight crashed across the communications channels; whoops and hollerings of success and achievement.

'She did it,' Kahina said in delight. 'She came through, we've won!'

Kahina watched as their companion ships headed down towards New Ithaca. The defences were gone, their approach was clear now.

Elated, she looked across to Hassan, her expression changing to confusion. He'd undone his seat harness and was stepping out of the flight chair.

'Hassan?'

He swung at her. Something connected with the back of her head. Blackness followed, deeper than the void.

* * *

Dalk saw the *Retribution* come about after the attack run. The defences were down, the ground assault could commence. Octavia's ship's formidable firepower had won the day for them.

He punched up the narrowband comms and opened a channel to the *Black Monk*.

'You're in the clear now, follow us in. Just keep an eye out for any small-scale ground to air defences.'

The *Black Monk* continued to fly straight and true, angling away from New Ithaca.

'Kahina, Hassan. Please respond.' Dalk scrutinised the scanner. Octavia's *Retribution* was rising up to meet the *Black Monk* on a parallel course.

Octavia.

Angrily he wrenched his Asp out of formation, cancelling the undercarriage deployment and accelerating as rapidly as he could towards the two errant ships.

* * *

Hassan secured himself back into the pilot's chair. Kahina was slumped beside him, stunned into unconsciousness by the blow he'd dealt her with the butt of his Cowell '55. Sweat formed on his forehead despite the cool air aboard the ship; his hands were clenched on the controls, knuckles showing white against his skin.

'Sorry lady,' he muttered. 'But it's me or you.'

The narrowband comms buzzed again, but he didn't acknowledge it. Octavia's vessel was before him, the cargo bay gaping wide. He steered the *Black Monk* towards it as fast as he dared.

Laser fire splashed across the cockpit. The shields on the *Retribution* flared in response, easily deflecting the blast. Hassan could see Dalk's Asp attempting to intercept them.

Turret guns aboard the *Retribution* swung around and began to discharge in ugly, heavy thumps. The laser fire ceased. Hassan had no time to see what had become of the bounty hunter's vessel. The bulk of the *Retribution* swelled

CHAPTER FOURTEEN

before him and then he was inside, hitting the retros in a hasty attempt to stop the *Black Monk* from smashing into the rear wall of the cargo bay.

'I'm aboard!' he yelled into the comms, engaging the magnetic clamps to ensure the *Black Monk* was secured. 'Get out of here!'

The response was immediate. The floor tilted up under him and a fierce acceleration gripped him. The *Retribution* was blasting up out of the atmosphere.

'Good work, little boy.' Octavia's tones sounded across the cockpit. 'I trust you have my prize with you.'

'She's here. I had to knock her out, but she's here,' Hassan stammered. 'Our deal. I got you the girl. You'll let me go, no questions, no bounty, no retribution?'

'Consider your debt paid,' Octavia replied slowly, her voice warm with satisfaction.

'I want this ship too,' Hassan added, in afterthought.

'Take it. All is right with the void.'

Chapter Fifteen

Sickness and nausea. Feelings that were all too familiar to her. Pain and a dull ache across the back of her head. Consciousness returned and her surroundings began to register.

'She's awake,' a soft and worried voice said from nearby. She couldn't place it. A man's voice she didn't recognise.

Motion, a whirl of grey and harsh lights. She blinked, feeling her arms being pulled and then restrained.

Hassan?

'Bring her to me.'

That voice she did know. Dread flooded through her, making her body shake. She felt herself propelled forwards against her will. She struggled but she had no purchase – weightless! She blinked, trying to focus her eyes. She heard the click of magboots on metallic hull plates before her vision cleared.

Octavia Quinton stood before her, looking down with an intensely satisfied expression suffusing her sharp features. Kahina felt herself pulled upright. She was dimly aware that she was being held by two men. To Octavia's left-hand side was a smaller man, dressed in some kind of medical gown.

A Doctor. Why?

The Doctor was standing in front of a large flat device, secured at waist height. Kahina's eyes widened as she recognised the pod she'd been put in after Dalk had 'killed' her.

What is that doing here?

'Welcome, Kahina Loren,' Octavia said. 'Do not attempt to flee. I would not have you damaged further, not now. Not after all the trouble I have taken to ensure your presence.'

Octavia stroked a finger across Kahina's cheek. Kahina twisted away angrily, tensing against the men that held her. It was useless, they tightened their grip. She could barely move.

Octavia laughed. 'So much spirit. You will serve me well.'

'I won't serve you. I am destined to be a Senator! You dare abduct me within range of my people?'

'Your people can not help you,' Octavia replied. 'Your young friend saw to that.'

Hassan was wrenched into her line of sight. He was also secured by two guards. Kahina glared at him, jostling against her restraints furiously once more.

'You …. utter 'stard. Why?'

'Don't be too hard on him,' Octavia said, drawing her attention. 'It was your life or his. Not a difficult choice to make.'

'My fleet will hunt you down,' Kahina said.

Octavia shook her head. 'They are not the power in this sector … I am.'

Kahina struggled again.

'What do you want of me?'

'Just do as she says,' Hassan said. 'It's a ransom demand, they'll pay and you'll be back with your people before …'

'Ransomed?' Octavia asked, smoothly interrupting. 'Whatever gave you that idea?' She smiled cruelly, stepping across between the pair of them.

Kahina saw alarm grow on Hassan's face.

What have you done, Hassan?

'You said you were going to ransom her back to the Imperials,' he said, his voice tight and high.

'Oh, you're far too trusting, little boy,' Octavia sneered. 'Money and power I have more than I could ever use. Time, that's the one thing that eludes me. The one thing our lovely Imperial beauty here can give me.'

'Time?' Kahina demanded. 'What are you talking about?'

'I am taking your body, girl.'

'What?' Kahina jolted back in horror.

'This pod that Dalk so kindly furnished me with – it can save and restore a mind. Your Imperial scientists are so clever, so many secrets. I am old, my body is tired and worn. Yours is young and fresh. Your mind will be emptied. I will transfer my own self into …'

Kahina gasped in terror, tussling against the two men. Their grip on her arms became so fierce she cried out. Octavia continued, regardless.

'… yours. It will be mine until such time as it is worn out and old. Then, perhaps I will return it to you.'

CHAPTER FIFTEEN

'No!' Kahina screamed and twisted wildly, kicking her legs and wrenching her torso in a desperate attempt to free herself.

'Subdue her,' Octavia said, gesturing to the Doctor. He moved forward gingerly, grabbing Kahina's arm and trying to hold it steady. Kahina continued to writhe desperately, cursing and howling profanities.

'This wasn't the deal, you said you'd let her go!' Hassan said, pulling forwards. His own guards pulled him back.

The sleeve of Kahina's dress was yanked up and a patch was placed on her arm. A faint hiss sounded from it. Kahina jerked spasmodically and then went limp, her voice slurring.

Octavia turned on Hassan, he saw her hand go to the hilt of her sword. 'I've spared your life, boy, given you a way out. Be glad I'm not disembowelling you on the spot. It's what you deserve.'

Hassan watched as the Doctor backed away from Kahina and her pair of guards. He turned to the pod, waving his hands over it. Holofac displays shimmered and changed. The top cracked open, the lid lifting and folding back. Hassan could just see the interior, brightly lit and filled with a faint mist which slowly rolled out, spreading in all directions in the zero-G. He remembered how he'd first found Kahina in the hold of his ship.

'It is ready, Domina,' the Doctor announced.

Octavia nodded and gestured to the guards. 'Secure her.'

Hassan stared helplessly as Kahina's limp body was dragged forward, faint mutterings of protest still just audible. Somehow she managed to raise her head and look at him.

'Please, Hassan, don't let … don't leave me …' Her tone was heavy with fading hope and desperation, her face bereft and disconsolate as the drug continued to take hold.

He held her gaze for a moment. Shame and a crushing sense of worthlessness saturated his thoughts.

I've killed her … worse, a living death, her mind put aside and her body stolen … you're such a shit, Hassan.

He saw her face crumple into despair. He couldn't bear to look and turned his head aside.

'Too cowardly to face the results of your actions, little boy?' Octavia sneered.

'Go, you useless flux-stain. At least this girl has the courage to face her end with grace and dignity.' She signalled to the guards. 'Get him off my ship.'

* * *

Hassan was forced back into the cargo bay of the *Retribution*. The guards shoved him forwards and then closed the airlock behind him. The old Adder, the *Black Monk*, stood before him. He could take it, run for the Frontier, get as far from here as possible. Run until dozens of light years were behind him. Run where no one could find him, run to where not a single soul had heard of this accursed system and the name of the daughter of an Imperial Senator.

Kahina's desperate visage flashed across his mind. He staggered forward and fell against the landing struts of the Adder, his magboots snapping and clicking underfoot. Would he ever be able to shift that image from his consciousness? She was an innocent, he'd handed her over to save his own skin. He'd said he wasn't a pirate, just the one heist he'd promised himself, but now he'd pedalled flesh, worse than a slave trader, no conscience, no morals.

Is that who I really am?

Hide and start again – somewhere else. Far from here … it was the only choice. There was nothing he could do against Octavia. How could he face down someone with the power she had? Even Luko had abandoned Kahina, was this any different? Lone wolf, every man for himself. That was the way of the void; the way of the Frontier.

Her desperate face, haunting me for the rest of my life?

He punched out at the landing strut in sheer frustration, his tortured mind locked in regret, shame, remorse and burning anger. He punched again and again, until his knuckles ripped and tore. Small droplets of blood splashed outwards, drifting slowly away. The landing strut clanked dully with the impact. Some wires were dislodged from above him and hung down impotently, a faint red glow flickering from above. He lowered himself down to the floor, head in hands and sobs coming to him unbidden.

'… Kahina … I'm …'

He shuddered into hysterics, unable to continue.

Wires?

CHAPTER FIFTEEN

The pain in his hand lanced through his thoughts, bringing a measure of sanity back to him.

He looked up, staring at the wires hanging down above his head. They were unfamiliar. There shouldn't be anything there. Frowning, he clambered back to his feet to get a better look.

Something had been lodged into the undercarriage compartment, a device. Faint red lights flickered from it.

Hassan's eyes widened as he recognised it.

A bomb! And some kind of homing device! The bitch is going to kill me anyway!

* * *

Octavia watched as Kahina was wrestled forward and hoisted into the pod. The girl still struggled, despite the heavy dose of sedative that had been administered to her. She had spirit; that was plain to see. In some ways it was a shame her mind had to go to waste, but her body was all that really mattered.

Octavia ran her eyes hungrily up and down the girl's lithe form, enjoying how the simple dress she wore flattered her physique and curves. To be young again; firm skin, muscle tone, to be fit and healthy, without the need for drugs, stimulants or prosthetics. She would look after this body and when the time eventually came, another would be procured. With this technology she could continue to expand her grasp on systems, utilise the wisdom and experience of multiple life-times. The possibilities were endless.

'His ship is away.'

Octavia looked up at her second in command. He held a portable holofac projector in his hand.

The image of the old Adder could be seen receding on it.

'So the coward runs,' she replied, with a shake of her head. 'Trigger the bomb. Destroy him.' The man nodded, gesturing to the holofac display. Octavia resumed her study of Kahina. The Doctor had strapped her in place within the pod, placing a small tab on her forehead. Now unable to move, the girl's face was locked in a frozen tableau of terror.

It will soon pass, girl, this isn't death ... you might even call it merciful.

Octavia smiled to herself as the pod closed.

The deck lurched underneath her, jolting with sufficient force to dislodge her magboots. She was thrown through the air, colliding painfully with the roof of the medi-lab. The lights flickered and failed, smothering her in whirling darkness. She collided with another part of the room, a burst of pain in her arm and shoulder. The ship was spinning as if at random. Dazed, she tried to grab onto something, anything, to halt her trajectory and save herself from further injury.

Emergency lights flashed on, bathing the room in a subdued red illumination. She managed to get hold of a table, bolted to the floor, but from her perspective hanging from the wall. Inertia threw her this way and that as she tried to avoid being sent spinning once more.

She caught sight of her second in command, his body rotating sickeningly in the air, his arms and legs flaccid, blood spurting intermittently in a bright streaming arc from a wound in his head. The holofac transmitter spun past as well, bouncing off the walls and floating away. The Doctor's body was nearby, also floating aimlessly, cannoning into the walls without restraint. Only the girl seemed unaffected, safely secured in her pod.

What ... what happened?

The door to the medi-lab snapped open and she made out a figure standing in the entrance, magboots firmly locked on the floor, standing at right angles to her frame of reference. Light flickered from damaged circuitry in the background, briefly illuminating his features.

The boy! But his ship was supposed to be ...

Her realisation was cut shot. Hassan raised a gun towards her and pulled the trigger. She saw the muzzle flash, the dull thump of bullets streaking across towards her ...

Pain, screaming.

Vengeance.

* * *

Hassan holstered his gun and checked his magboots. So far, so good. Disconnecting the bomb and leaving it next to the internal engine access ways from the cargo bay before launching his Adder on autopilot had clearly been something Octavia hadn't anticipated.

CHAPTER FIFTEEN

On seeing his Adder gone she'd triggered the bomb, succeeding only in blowing out one of her own drives and sending her ship in a brain-jarring uncontrolled spin through space. Unprepared, dozens of the crew were injured or incapacitated.

Shooting Octavia was just the icing on the cake. He could hardly believe it; one of his plans had worked.

He made his way across to the pod, struggling through the debris floating around in the room, moving this way and that as the ship's erratic movements took their toll. He reached the pod, hastily calling up the holofac displays and gesturing for the 'open' sequence. The top rolled back, revealing Kahina's imprisoned form. He pulled back the securing harnesses.

'Are you ok?' he asked.

Her face was a mask of disbelief and fear, then she recognised him. Her features softened for a moment before anger returned.

'You ... 'stard!' her voice was slurred, but intelligible. She raised an arm and tried to slap his face. He caught it easily.

'Not now. Let's get you out of here.'

He pulled her up, her body soft and limp in his grasp, clamping her alongside him as the ship continued to whirl around them. Debris in the room continued to fly in random directions. The Doctor's body rotated past. Hassan pushed it away and they reached the doorway. She trailed behind him awkwardly, her feet unsecured by magboots.

'What happened?' Kahina gasped.

'Bomb,' Hassan answered.

'Bomb?'

'Just hold on to me,' Hassan said, hoisting her onto his shoulders. 'As tight as you can.'

She managed to wrap her arms and legs around him and he stomped down the dimly lit corridor, bracing himself against the walls to ward off the uncertain movements of the ship.

A jolt threw them to one side and the sickening motion slowed. Somebody on the bridge was trying to get the ship under control. Time was running out. Hassan hastened onwards, arriving at a bulkhead door. He spun it open and stumbled through. Inside was a small enclosed area with a series of hatches. He felt Kahina move her head to see better, felt her body heat on his neck.

'Where?' Her voice was clearer now, more alert.

'Escape pod,' Hassan answered, 'Grab onto something whilst I prep it.'

Kahina let go of him and pushed herself towards the wall, grabbing an exposed handle and bracing herself against it. Hassan opened one of the pods and looked inside briefly.

Two man pods. Thank Randomius for that.

He activated the on board avionics and listened while they hummed into readiness. Holofac displays flickered and stabilised. The pod was ready to fly.

'Here,' he called, stretching out towards Kahina. She shook her head.

'No. I don't trust …'

'We don't have time for this.'

'You sold me out.'

'Yeah. Bad call. You can shoot me later … but I'm trying to rescue you …' he raised his voice, 'so get in the damn pod!'

Voices sounded from the corridor behind them. Urgent cries of anger. Orders were barked.

Kahina looked around in alarm and fear.

'Or you can stay here and get your mind wiped. Your choice, lady!'

Kahina launched herself across to him. He caught her in mid-air and pushed her into the pod. 'Buckle in. The acceleration is supposed to be pretty bad.'

'There! The escape pods!' Voices sounded from the corridor they'd just left. Octavia's guards. The guards were close now, shadows flickered around the entrance to the pod control room.

Hassan threw himself feet first into the pod and pulled the hatchway closed behind him. He hit the small couch inside with a thump, grabbing frantically at the securing straps floating around him.

The pod sealed with a hiss.

Kahina had tied herself into a couch on the opposite side. She looked across at him. 'Ready?' he asked.

She didn't answer, but simply closed her eyes and braced herself.

The pod eject controls were simple, designed to be used in an emergency. A single red button marked 'ESC'.

Hassan hit it.

There was a clunk, a jolt and then something crashed into the back of him,

CHAPTER FIFTEEN

crushing him into the couch. A massive weight slammed across his chest, cutting off his breath. Panic rose. He couldn't move, couldn't even turn his head. It felt as if his eyes were being squeezed out of his skull.

Witchin' hell … that's …

The pressure was relentless.

He dimly heard Kahina's scream of pain before he passed out.

* * *

Pain and an incendiary rage.

Octavia's unique physiology couldn't be overcome by a few bullet wounds. She was injured certainly, but it only slowed her down.

She reached the bridge, barking instructions at her crew to stabilise the ship. They reacted in fear at her presence, already demoralised by the damage to the ship. She was splattered in blood, her left arm hanging useless by her side. Her crew gasped, their faces pale.

To her they were all expendable in pursuit of her dream.

'Where's that escape pod?' she growled. 'Find it and bring it aboard!'

The holofac systems were flickering with the damage the ship had suffered, but the astrogation scanners were still tracking with sufficient detail. The pod could be seen, its tiny drive units thrusting at full power.

'Intercept course laid in,' one of the crew responded.

The *Retribution* jolted unevenly as the ship got under way. Octavia could see the damage that had been inflicted. One of the drives was completely offline, auxiliary thrusters were compensating for the off-axis thrust of the other, the ship 'crabbing' unevenly forward.

Even half-crippled, a small escape pod was no match for the bigger ship. Octavia watched as the pod appeared on the forward viewer. The holofac overlay swirled across it, a targeting reticule providing range and intercept time. It wouldn't be long.

The pod was running on a curving trajectory, its initial burst of acceleration exhausted. Octavia could see it was attempting to rendezvous with the *Black Monk*, which was still cruising alongside on its autopilot.

'No …' Octavia said. 'Weapons, take out that Adder. Now!'

* * *

In the hold of Octavia's ship a small device completed a predetermined countdown. It was not artificially intelligent, it had no concept of its role in the events that were taking place around it. Electronic components dutifully executed instructions as dictated by the commands of their programmer.

A homing signal began transmitting.

* * *

'Hassan!'

Hassan blinked and shook his head. *Space, whirling stars, a ship.* 'Hassan!'

Kahina was yelling at him. He stared outwards, struggling to assemble his thoughts. That acceleration …

The *Black Monk*, not far away; ahead in the viewer. 'Can we get aboard?' Kahina asked.

Hassan nodded. Quickly he reached forward, overriding the escape pod controls. If Octavia's ship was still operational their escape pod was a sitting duck. No shields, no armour. A single round of autocannon fire would splash them into the void.

The escape pod banked around, locking onto the Adder's trajectory. The *Black Monk* flew straight and true. All Hassan had to do was fly into the cargo bay.

A stream of coruscating energy flashed across space between them, lighting the cockpit with a fierce blue glow. Hassan yelled in surprise as the pod bucked and jolted. Space was filled with spinning debris, burning gas and trails of smoke. Kahina shrieked in dismay beside him.

The *Black Monk* was gone. 'Shit!'

Hassan wrenched his head around and looked behind him.

It was the *Retribution*, closing fast from their starboard side. As he watched, grappling cables snaked out towards the escape pod. Another jolt signalled they were caught once more.

A holofac display flashed into life. Hassan and Kahina watched as Octavia's form coalesced before them. Her face streaked with blood.

'I thought …'

CHAPTER FIFTEEN

'... you'd killed me? You have no idea what agonies I will put you through now, little boy.' The display flickered and faded. The escape pod jolted as the *Retribution* reeled them in.

'No ...' Kahina said, 'no ... I won't ... don't let her take me!'

* * *

The distinct tones of a homing signal sounded across the bridge of the Federation battlecruiser. 'We have the signal,' the captain said. 'It's the code that privateer woman gave us.'

'Right on cue,' Tenim said.

He and Jenu stood on the bridge of the Federation battlecruiser, trying to determine the outcome of the battle on the moon from their remote viewpoint. The Federation scanners had picked up the profile of Octavia's *Retribution* the moment it had left the atmosphere of the moon. Some kind of battle had taken place, but it was difficult to determine precisely what was happening.

'What is she doing?' Jenu asked.

'Struggling to reclaim her prize,' Tenim replied. 'She's hoping to sneak off with the Loren girl and thus undertake whatever nefarious notion she has in mind. I imagine the girl is putting up a fight. It looks as if her plans have gone awry.' He turned to the captain. 'At your convenience.'

Jenu looked across the bridge as the captain signalled to the gunnery officer. 'What are you doing?' she whispered.

'Insurance, as agreed,' Tenim said.

'For Octavia?'

'Of course not. For the Federation, naturally.'

'Ready, Commissioner,' the captain reported. 'Missiles locked on the tracking signal source and Octavia's vessel.'

'You're going to shoot it down?' Jenu asked. 'But the girl's aboard that ship she's snagged!'

Tenim nodded. 'The girl's ship is tagged as fugitive, as is Octavia's. Legally we're in the clear. No more Imperial claim. A neat and tidy solution. Launch when ready, Captain.'

The captain turned and signalled to his gunnery officer. 'Fire.'

* * *

Octavia's contemplation was cut short as threat warning indicators flashed across monitors and the on board klaxon shrieked imminent doom.

'Incoming missiles, Domina!'

Octavia stared at the displays in disbelief. 'From where?'

'Federation fleet, Domina. Two locked on us, two pinging for the tracking device.'

Tenim! How dare you fire on me.

Rage surged through her mind, lighting her brain with fury. The Federation cared nothing for the Imperial girl, particularly if her death could be painted as an unfortunate accident. They'd have their negotiating position. Tenim would be rid of her too.

The ringing tones of the ECM defence systems echoed through the bridge. The missiles came on regardless. Octavia was not surprised to see them unaffected. Tenim would have used the most sophisticated weapons at his disposal.

She saw her helm officer plot an evasive high-G course.

'Belay that! Divert all remaining power to shields, defensive fire …'

'But, Domina!'

'Hold our course, damn you … I will not lose my prize!'

The Helmsman took another look at the incoming missiles, his trembling hand hovering over the commit confirmation for the course change.

He lowered his hand.

It was the last thing he did. Octavia's Lance and Fermann Widowmaker blew the back of his head right off. Some of the crew screamed at the unexpectedly loud noise that battered the bridge. Blood, bone, skin and hair splashed outwards, unhindered by gravity, splashing in all directions, heedless of whether it hit crew, controls or instruments.

Octavia leapt forward through the flying gore, obsessive desire in her eyes, a howl of wrath in her throat, angrily pulling what remained of him out of his seat and throwing his body out of the way, her crew scattering as they tried to avoid her.

The *Retribution* lurched briefly as the course took hold and then was abruptly cancelled. The ship continued running in a straight line.

CHAPTER FIFTEEN

Belatedly the turret weapons on the upper hull began spraying flak-fire towards the missiles. Explosions rippled briefly in the vacuum. The missiles ducked and weaved on their approach, easily evading the protective curtain the *Retribution* was trying to establish.

The first missile erupted against the starboard shields, a scintillating flash of energy, its fury dissipated and hurled back in the direction of attack. The second roared in a moment later adding its combined assault on the beleaguered barricades of the ship. The shields were ripped asunder; their generators overloading and burning out under the deadly barrage. The hull took an element of the impact but remained sound.

The final pair of missiles seemed to pause in their inbound flight, adjusting their course to track the source of the elusive tracking signal.

* * *

Hassan had tried everything to break the hold of the grappling hooks, thrusting the escape pod from one side to another, but it was to no avail. They were caught and they were being reeled in. There were no weapons aboard, there was nothing else they could do. The vast bulk of Octavia's vessel grew in the cockpit windows. Explosions flashed violently, but the ship remained.

Kahina watched it with terror, Hassan with growing fear.

'There must be something ...' Her voice sounded small and faint.

'There's nothing,' Hassan replied, 'nothing. We've no weapons, nothing.'

'I won't wake up a burnt out old woman ...' Kahina was close to hysteria, her voice wavering. 'I won't ... you can kill me first ... don't let her take me ...'

Hassan cast about the narrow cockpit for anything he could use, but the interior was deliberately sparse, even the controls were simple. Basic navigation computers, minimal holofac systems, a distress transmitter, food and rations, emergency canopy blast bolts ...

His heart thudded in his chest.

Blow the canopy, a few seconds of pain and we'll both be beyond Octavia's reach forever.

He could end it now. Kahina would never know; it would be a kindness. Better death than torture or aging in an instant of perceived time.

You were right, Sushil, someone always ends up getting hurt ...

He gestured at the comm interface, pulling up the canopy blast commands. *Warning! Ejection codes required. This process cannot be aborted. Confirm!*

'What are you doing?' Kahina asked. 'Emergency canopy blast ... what does that mean?' He looked at her. 'I can stop her from getting hold of us. Eject us into the void.'

Kahina stared at him, puzzlement cracking into realisation and terror before falling into acceptance.

She reached out and grabbed his hand.

'I'm sorry ...' His voice cracked. Words seemed woefully inadequate.

'You came back for me,' she said, favouring him with a faint smile. 'It's enough. Now ... before it's too late ...'

His fingers moved towards the display. A brief gesture was all it would take ...

A shadow passed across the cockpit. Hassan turned and looked up as the dark panels of another ship flew alongside at close range.

'What?'

Drives roared, a ship was chasing down the pod. He cursed and then blinked. The ship was familiar. A flat low profile, twin exhaust outlets framed with outrigger thrusters, a glare of actinic thruster flux ... a Cobra.

'Signorina, hope I can be of service ...' A jaunty voice with a thick accent crackled across the narrowband comms.

Hassan watched in disbelief as the Cobra spun around its centre axis, weapons blazing. The cables securing their escape pod to the *Retribution* were shattered, snaking and flailing away into the darkness.

Hassan watched, bemused as their tiny vessel spiralled free from its captivity. He wrestled the controls back to an even keel and then found himself laughing, a giddy sense of unexpected relief washing over him.

'It's Luko! He came back!' Kahina was screaming from beside him. Ahead the Cobra was banking around, lining up to scoop their pod to safety.

More missiles surged out of the darkness, seeking targets. Hassan and Kahina stared, watching them.

'Come on, do it ... do it,' Hassan murmured.

The missiles locked on, turning onto a new course. He punched up the holofac in glee.

CHAPTER FIFTEEN

* * *

Octavia, still clinging to the navigation console, watched in disbelief as the holofac flickered into life. She recognised Hassan, he was looking at her with contempt.

'Octavia.'

'What do you want, little boy? I will show no mercy now.'

'Justice must be served. Wrong acts cannot go unpunished. Don't you agree?'

'What are you talking about?' she snarled. 'This changes nothing, your friend will die under my guns. I will still have you and the girl.'

'No ...' Hassan was shaking his head. 'It's payback time.'

She laughed. 'You really are the most contemptible fool.'

'I found your transponder,' Hassan interrupted conversationally. 'I might be a coward but I'm no fool. I wasn't going to fall for the same trick twice. So I bolted it back into your cargo bay. Even I figured the Federation would double-cross you. First thing they teach you in Alliance space, never trust the Feds. Who's the fool now?'

Octavia's eyes widened in horror.

The tracking device was aboard the Adder, it should have been destroyed ...

The threat warning indicators lit up again as the missiles established their target lock ... on her ship.

'You've got about five seconds,' Hassan said, watching his own instruments for a moment before giving her a last look, 'then order will be restored and all will be right with the void.'

'Not possible ...'

The missiles turned, shrieking in towards the stricken *Retribution*.

'Die, you sadistic bitch ...'

No shields, no defences, no hope.

Impact. Flame. The rushing sound of escaping air. Blackness. Void.

The explosion was dramatic, a ball of fire hundreds of metres in diameter flared brightly in the darkness above the moon of Chione. It was visible from the surface of the moon, a bright spark of fire in the twilight sky.

A moment later it guttered, bereft of sustaining oxygen, revealing the ripped and tattered debris that had, a moment before, been the Anaconda-class vessel

Retribution. A vessel no more, it was nothing but a tumbling menagerie of whirling, twisting, sparking blackened wreckage slowly dispersing through space.

Tenim and Jenu saw the flash, but the detail was invisible at their range. The Tactical display was flickering, confused by the myriad of contacts in the wake of the explosion.

'And that, my dear, is how you wrap up the situation in one fell swoop,' Tenim said smugly. Jenu nodded, still looking at the displays, trying to make sense of them.

Tenim turned, signalling to the captain.

'Get me the Imperial ambassador, I believe it's time to open final negotiations for this wretched backwater of a system …'

* * *

Hassan clambered up out of his harness, clamping his magboots to the floor of the pod. Luko had scooped them aboard and the pod was secured in the Cobra's expansive cargo bay, locked in place between the familiar cargo canisters. He turned to Kahina, who was struggling up beside him.

'Hassan! I … are you ok? Is …'

'I'm fine …'

She pulled him into an embrace and he felt a warm kiss upon his cheek. 'You saved me.'

'Only just,' he managed to reply, feeling his face flush. 'Looks like I had some help.' He felt her floating away and pulled her back down. 'Wooah, there. Grab some boots before …'

Footsteps sounded from behind them, clicking on the Cobra's amidships companion way. Kahina released Hassan and turned herself around, seeing Luko standing at the top of the ramp.

'Signorina …'

She stared at him for a long moment, seeing worry, disgrace and uncertainty etched on his face. Kahina looked away, grabbing herself a pair of magboots and clipping them on to her feet. Standing up she smoothed down her dress and then stepped out of the pod, facing him.

CHAPTER FIFTEEN

'So you came back then?' she called out, her voice sharp.

Luko grimaced. 'You make my life molto difficult, signorina. Guilt and shame, this I do not need.'

Kahina walked towards Luko. He stepped towards her. Hassan watched as they eyed each other for a long moment.

'You are my friend,' Luko said, sombrely. 'I could not abandon you at your time of need.'

Kahina paused and then hugged him close.

'Luko ...'

His arms went gently around her, slowly tightening into an embrace. 'Come. That ship is destroyed, we should get back to your moon.'

Kahina nodded. 'I need to send a message first, quickly!'

* * *

The holofac system lit up within moments. The Imperial ambassador appeared to be standing just across from Tenim.

'Commissioner,' Ambassador Cuthrick announced with the customary incline of his head. 'I trust you weren't unduly inconvenienced by our little altercation earlier?'

'Not in the slightest,' Tenim replied, 'an interesting exercise, I must compliment your military staff for the efficacy of their training and deployment.'

'I'll be sure to pass along your compliments,' Cuthrick said. 'Your own staff conducted themselves with masterful aplomb. How might I aid you at this time?'

Tenim stretched to his full height. 'You have my commiserations on the unfortunate death of your Imperial heir. It appears she was aboard that pirate vessel, a most unfortunate outcome. Our condolences to the Empire. A tragic loss.'

Cuthrick bowed. 'Tragic indeed.'

Jenu saw a readout flicker on the scanners. She frowned, seeing the uncertain outline of a ship in the debris field.

'Uh, Tenim ...'

Tenim glared at her angrily before responding to the holofac image of the ambassador.

'Of course, with her demise and the downfall of the rebellion, the moon now lies without jurisdiction. In light of its previously established status as an Imperial system we would be happy to rescind our declaration of martial law …'

'I'm gratified to hear that, Commissioner.'

'… upon receipt of certain assurances and commitments.'

'And what commitments are you seeking, pray tell?' Cuthrick asked innocently.

'Why, assurances over the well-being of the populace, naturally,' Tenim replied with an exaggerated show of concern. 'After the agonies of destruction wrought over the last few weeks, surely they deserve a time of peace?'

'I couldn't agree more, Commissioner.'

Jenu watched as the debris field on the scanners continued to disperse. There was another signal present. A ship remained, turning and thrusting back towards the moon.

'Tenim …'

'Not now,' Tenim whispered impatiently out of the corner of his mouth before smiling back at Cuthrick.

'That is good to hear,' he said, responding to the ambassador. 'A viable economy and a stable political outlook would do much to promote peace and prosperity.'

'A wise course of action. I concur completely.'

'We'd be prepared to do our piece in securing a lasting harmony,' Tenim said. 'Our trade boards and guilds will keep pirates and outlaws at bay across the various shipping lanes, establish routes and stabilise the market.'

'Most impressive. And what would you ask for such unprompted generosity?'

'A mere consideration,' Tenim answered smoothly. 'Some advantageous trade terms regarding exports of certain commodities. We can discuss the tedious details at our leisure.'

Cuthrick raised his head a little and then nodded.

'It's a very generous offer,' he began, 'but alas, I'm forced to decline.'

Tenim was taken aback. 'Decline?'

Cuthrick smiled. 'Indeed. I'm afraid I have been given a directive which is, shall we say, rather at odds with your wishes.'

CHAPTER FIFTEEN

'A directive from whom?'

'A moment please.'

Cuthrick made a show of reaching for a communique nearby. Something had been printed out for him. He picked it up and studied it for a moment and then looked towards Tenim.

'Please accept my apologies in advance. The text is, whilst direct and unambiguous, somewhat uncouth and vulgar.'

Tenim looked around at Jenu, who pointed to the scanner readouts. 'A ship fleeing the scene. The Imperial girl.'

Tenim's face clouded with anger. 'What? She can't be …'

Cuthrick cleared his throat. Tenim looked at him.

'We received this from one Kahina Tijani Loren, acting Senator of Chione. The message reads … Federation dogs … I imagine that means you and your much esteemed colleagues.' Cuthrick looked pained. 'I do apologise for the tone, it's rather undiplomatic. The youth of today you understand …'

Tenim glowered, unable to respond. Cuthrick continued.

'Your deplorable attempt on my life has failed. I survive and claim this system as my own. Leave immediately or I will … oh dear, I really do regret the timbre of this message, so impolite … ensure no Federation scum escape alive.'

Cuthrick looked up and carefully folded the paper away, placing it within his robes. His wan smile was firmly in place.

'I do suggest you comply,' Cuthrick said. 'Senators can be so very determined.'

'You would let this young upstart determine your policy …' Tenim spluttered.

Cuthrick smiled. 'It would be unfortunate if we had to reveal that a Federation official sanctioned a murder attempt on an Imperial Senator. The political damage might be irreversible.'

'I …'

'Missiles, Commissioner?' Cuthrick clicked his tongue. 'Rather gauche, don't you think?'

'You wouldn't …'

'Not if you and your fleet depart this Imperial system immediately.' Cuthrick's voice had just the faintest of hard edges.

Tenim's fists clenched. He licked his lips and took a deep breath, letting it out with a long sigh. He forced a smile.

'Until next time, Ambassador.' Cuthrick inclined his head.
'A pleasure as always, Commissioner.'

Chapter Sixteen

Luko landed the *Bella Principessa* amidst the gardens of the Imperial Palace. There was little left of them. The lawns were burnt and churned, with some significant craters where errant weapons had discharged. Trees were smouldering stumps, the ornate fountains and statues that had marked a gravelled path from the cliffs to the palace entrance were nothing more than scattered rubble.

Kahina walked down the Cobra's cargo bay ramp, surveying the wreckage, flanked by Hassan and Luko. Kahina could see Dalk standing before the palace. As he caught sight of her he quickly began walking towards them.

Kahina walked forward, with Hassan and Luko behind.

Dalk met her halfway. She saw he had a sword buckled at his waist. It was hers, the one she had trained with in the rooms below the palace. It seemed so long ago.

'You're safe?' Dalk asked, his face a mask of worry.

'I survived. Hassan and Luko saved me.'

Dalk looked at the two traders with incredulity. 'They did?'

'Don't look so surprised,' Hassan said. 'We're not as dumb as we look.'

'But what happened?' Dalk demanded.

'Octavia tried to kidnap me,' Kahina explained, breathlessly. 'Blackmailed Hassan, fortunately he had an attack of conscience.'

'She'd planted a bomb and a transponder on my ship,' Hassan added. 'But I swapped them out.'

'Damaged her ship, we only just got out …' Kahina continued.

'… and the Feds finished her off,' Hassan finished. 'Luko turned up just in the nick of time.' Luko acknowledged Dalk's look with a brief nod.

'I knew we couldn't trust her,' Dalk admitted. 'But I didn't anticipate she'd try to abduct you right out of the air. What did she intend?'

'Who's to say?' Hassan asked, giving Dalk a quick glance.

'Enough of her,' Kahina said. 'She's dead and gone. New Ithaca. Is my home secure?'

'The Island is ours and we've captured the few surviving Reclamists,' Dalk said. 'The Federation fleet is departing and the Imperial representatives are already on their way down. The moon is yours.'

Kahina nodded and swallowed. 'And Vargo?'

'We have him,' he announced. 'Inside.'

Kahina pursed her lips.

'Time for this to be ended then. Bring him out.'

Dalk bowed and retreated into the palace. A moment later a man was hauled out, stumbling between two Imperial guards. Dalk walked behind, a gun trained on the captured man.

It was Vargo. He was pulled roughly forwards. His clothing was dusty, frayed, burnt in places, his body bloodied and stained. One of his eyes was missing, a gory socket was all that remained. He collapsed to his knees as Dalk's guards released him.

'Leader of the Reclaimists. The last of them,' Dalk announced. Kahina looked at him with disgust, stepping towards him.

'My sword,' she demanded.

Dalk handed her the ornate scabbard he'd been carrying for her. Kahina accepted it and then drew the blade, holding it aloft.

'Perhaps you remember me, Vargo,' she said. 'I had this sword then too, but now the odds are in my favour.'

'Imperial flux-stain ...'

Dalk struck him down and he fell, spread-eagled on the floor. 'Enough, Dalk,' Kahina said. 'Give it up, Vargo. Surrender to me.'

Vargo slowly and painfully raised his head, looking at her. 'You think you've won, Imperial slut? You think you have your world back?"

His voice choked off in a fit of coughing, only belatedly did Kahina realise he was laughing. 'Chione is mine now,' she replied. 'Your Federation friends have deserted you, their fleet is already leaving. You've lost.'

'Your Imperial control will fail. Empires fall, little girl, remember that. You won't last long.'

'Long enough.'

'I'd watch him if I were you,' Vargo smirked, gesturing vaguely towards Dalk. 'He's betrayed us both.'

CHAPTER SIXTEEN

'Dalk was always acting in my interests,' Kahina countered.

'Playing you for the fool you are ... Chione will never be yours. He'll turn on you like he turned on me.'

Vargo smiled at the look of doubt that passed across her face. In that moment he lurched forward, a dagger somehow appearing in his right hand. Kahina deftly sidestepped the blow, expertly turning her sword in a practiced cutting move.

Vargo fell onto his back, gasping in astonishment. His throat was cut.

Kahina stepped over his convulsing body, looking towards the smoking remains of the Imperial Palace.

'Clean up this mess,' she instructed.

* * *

Kahina walked on into the palace, entering through the remains of the once beautiful flamewood doors. Their bright steel bindings were twisted and cracked, the colonnade above shattered and fractured. She walked onwards, through the grand foyer and up to the dark panelled doors that led into the reception hall. They too were scarred and timeworn, their immaculate veneer and thick polish cut and scraped, but they still held firm.

She'd stood here before, not so long ago, awaiting her father's pleasure. A father who had never cared for her, but just used her, exploiting her for his own ends. A rule ended in ignominy.

Now it is my turn to rule.

She pushed the doors aside and walked forward into the shattered remnants of the reception hall. It reeked of smoke and weapons fire. The beautiful mosaic flooring was ruined, smashed and churned to rubble. Here and there tattered fragments of the once beautiful tapestries lay burnt and frayed.

Part of the ceiling had fallen in, with daylight shining through the gap, a column of light with motes of dust dancing within. Doors were broken, columns riddled with bullet holes. The grand staircase she remembered fleeing up with her sister had caught fire and was still smouldering away. Statues, urns, works of art were all defaced, crushed and shattered beyond repair.

Only her father's throne atop its dais had remained virtually unscathed. She shivered, remembering how she had abased herself before her father, how he'd insulted her.

Unconsciously, she ran a hand through her thick dark hair.

He'd tried to arrange that marriage and she'd cruelly inflicted the match upon her sister. How clever she thought she'd been. All dust now. All dead. Reclaiming her home wouldn't bring any of them back. This was all there was – a ruin, a shadow of its former glory, a faint echo of a life that might have been.

'A little work needed I think.'

She was startled out of her reverie by the voice and glanced around to see Luko looking at her. He'd been standing in the shadows of the columns that ran along the side of the reception hall. He walked across to her, his footsteps causing new swathes of dust to float in slowly swirling clouds. She didn't know what to say.

'Is all yours now,' Luko said. 'These rebels are dead, the Empire is at your back. You have all the power at your command. Now, all you must do is take the sceptre of a Senator.'

He gestured to her father's sceptre which had been placed carefully atop the throne, awaiting someone to heft it.

'All I must do ...' she said, softly.

'Are you proud of what you've done?' Luko's voice was sharp.

'I took back what was mine,' Kahina snapped at him. 'Things are as they should have been.'

'And this is what you wanted, signorina?' Luko looked around the ruin that had once been her home. 'A burning moon, a ruined world, a broken home? It was worth all those deaths, yes?'

Kahina fought back tears. It was her world by right. It belonged to her. That people had fought and died because of that fact wasn't her fault. She had never asked to be a pawn in the game played out by Dalk, Octavia, the patrons, the Empire and the Federation. She had been swept up against her will – stabbed, killed, ill-treated, burnt, punched, kicked. She'd almost had her body stolen. She was owed, wasn't she? Hadn't she lost enough already? Her family brutally murdered, her home destroyed, a sword thrust through her chest. Agony and pain she had endured ... and for what?

Why so harsh, Luko?

CHAPTER SIXTEEN

'You wouldn't understand.' Tears came now, burning on her cheeks. She couldn't tell if it was rage, frustration or sorrow.

'I understand more than you know.'

'You're just a simple trader,' she snapped. 'What would you know about matters of high politics?'

Luko stiffened and pursed his lips. 'I know when to stop. That time is now, signorina.'

'This world belongs to my family.'

Luko raised his voice above hers. 'You cannot own a world, signorina. What are we? We are mere creatures. We are born, we live, we die. We have such short years. This world has been here since before humans even were. Will be here long after we are forgotten. We do not own anything.'

'Spare me your crude philosophy.'

'Then listen to this, young woman,' Luko said severely. 'You have molto power. What you have done … has already killed thousands. What you do next may kill thousands more. Decide for them, not for you.'

'What would you have me do?' Kahina said, glaring at him.

Luko tilted his head slightly. 'I? I am just a simple trader. I know nothing of high politics.' Her face fell as he turned away.

'Luko … I'm sorry … please … don't go.'

He strode away, ignoring her. Her rage flared.

'Stop! I command you to return!'

Luko stopped and then slowly turned around to look at her. 'I am not your subject, signorina. I am a free man. You do not command me.' He gestured abruptly with his hand. 'You are home and you have won.' He looked at the ruins around them and then back at her, bowing in a ridiculous fashion. 'Enjoy your victory, glorious Senator.'

Kahina watched him go, trembling with fury. She turned on her heel, face set with determination, reaching out for the sceptre on her father's throne. Her fingers almost touched it, but she pulled back just inches away, her hand quivering.

'It is mine,' she cried, clenching her eyes shut and stretching forward again.

It was in vain. Her strength left her and she collapsed at the foot of the throne, her cries of anguish echoing in the empty desolation.

That was how Dalk found her. 'Senator!'

Kahina looked up, her face tear streaked and stained with dust. 'I am no Senator, Dalk. I cannot even take the sceptre.'

'My lady …' Dalk helped her to her feet, 'you are tired and worn out, you should rest …'

'No. Luko was right. This isn't what I wanted.'

'Kahina, we have fought hard and won. Your victory is at hand.'

'Rule a world, Dalk? I am my father's daughter. Look at what I have wrought. Death, destruction, pain and ruin. Maybe the Lorens are not fit to rule, perhaps I should have died.'

'You are distraught … exhausted!'

'I cannot bear this!' Kahina said, sobbing once more. 'Years of rule, endless politics, scheming and plotting. I should never have come back. I wish I'd stayed away.' Her voice cracked. 'What should I do, Dalk? What would you do?'

'It's not my place, Senator.'

'But?' She looked up, faint hope in her eyes.

Dalk frowned, rubbing his chin and stepping around her for a moment.

'Perhaps … you might consider ceding your power to another. Someone who valued peace above all, someone who served your interests in all things. Retain the title and the ultimate authority, but leave the tedium behind.'

She looked up at him.

'Yes! You are right,' she said, with a nod, encouraging him to continue. 'But whom?'

'They would have to serve as your advisor in these matters, take the minutiae of administration from you,' Dalk replied, thoughtfully. 'Your wishes carried out to best effect, your father's legacy honoured, your own established. Dependable and trustworthy, naturally. Skill, tact and a deft touch, one acclimatised to the necessary subtleties of the role. Someone upon whom you could utterly rely.'

'You would see this done for me?'

Dalk bowed low. 'I served your father, now I serve you. Such an undertaking would be an honour beyond all honours.'

'And how can this be accomplished? Is it even legal?'

CHAPTER SIXTEEN

Dalk looked thoughtful for a moment. 'It is not entirely without precedent. Power has been ceded to officials and dignitaries in the past. There is paperwork of course, but a formal ceremony is traditionally used …'

'Arrange it,' Kahina said, abruptly. 'I want everyone there. Those who supported me, those who fought for me, Luko and Hassan too, even those noxious Patrons, the ambassador … and, of course, you Dalk.'

'It shall be done, Senator.'

'I am most grateful.'

Dalk bowed again. 'With your permission, Senator?'

Kahina nodded and Dalk withdrew, striding quickly out of the hall.

* * *

'She's going to cede power to him?' Hassan yelled. 'Dalk? I wouldn't trust him much more than Octavia. That whole pod business was his idea. He could have been in league with Octavia for all we know. He's a power broker, maybe this was what he wanted all along.'

Luko sat back in his chair. The pair of traders was ensconced aboard the *Bella Principessa*, watching the sun glisten over the bay.

'The choice is hers, my young friend.'

'After all this, she really thinks Dalk has her best interests at heart?'

Luko shrugged. 'She is no fool, but … ah … I have not the mind for these political games. Perhaps she is right.'

'You know it's not right.'

Luko sighed and licked his lips before nodding.

'Yes. She makes a mistake, I think. I do not trust this … Dalk. But his hold over her is strong. He is her mentor. What we think … she not care. She trusts him.'

Hassan looked out over the bay.

'We'll find out soon enough, I guess.'

* * *

Kahina strode majestically back into the reception hall a mere two days later. It had been hurriedly cleaned and repaired. It was not perfect, but it now retained a semblance of its former glory. Dignitaries and representatives from nearby Imperial worlds had arrived to see her take office, their entourages accompanying them. She recognised Senators from the nearby worlds, their Patrons, important citizens from across the local parts of the Empire.

And hats of course, bigger and more flamboyant than ever.

She was dressed in a flowing azure gown, not so ostentatious as many, but she wore her father's gold chain of the Senate and had the family's priceless sword in a bright-steel scabbard at her side. A shimmering tiara completed her adornment, perched on her immaculately prepared hair, contrasting strikingly with her dark locks.

She saw that many of the other women, so often blonde, had dyed their hair a deep black. It was the latest fashion, so they'd fawningly informed her. She had nodded in conceited delight.

As she approached the dais she saw Luko and Hassan standing side by side, looking at her with wide eyes. Imperial pageantry was clearly something new to their eyes. Luko held her gaze for a moment, watching her closely. She returned the stare for a long moment, before moving on.

Ambassador Cuthrick awaited her, with Patrons Zyair and Gerrun flanking him. Patron Dalk stood slightly to one side. They were also decked in appropriately lavish outfits, procured from some of the best tailors the Empire could deploy at such short notice. All wore ceremonial swords as custom dictated.

Dalk held in his hands the sceptre of Chione, the sign of her father's office. All four bowed as she approached. She bowed in return and then stood before them in an attitude of deference.

It was only appropriate. For now, she was just Lady Kahina, an Imperial citizen. Dalk stepped forward.

'Through great trial, misfortune and danger has our most revered young citizen arrived at this unique moment. Throughout she has been a beacon, a shining star in the firmament of the Empire, upholding our interests in all things, defeating our opponents, scattering those who would do us harm. She has triumphed over adversity, tragedy and disaster, always seeking to defend

CHAPTER SIXTEEN

her people, her home … her world. We welcome home Lady Kahina Tijani, daughter of Algreb of the house of Loren.'

Applause rocked the hall, with cheers intermixed alongside. Dalk waited for it to subside.

'Kneel, Lady Kahina, daughter of Algreb.'

Kahina knelt at the foot of the throne. Dalk took the Sceptre, raised it before the assembly and then instructed her to reach out and take it.

As she did so a rumble of approval echoed around the hall.

'Arise, Senator Kahina Tijani Loren of Chione, in the Prism system.'

She climbed daintily to her feet as the four men bowed low before her. She walked past them and took her seat on the dais, hoisting the sceptre before her and looking around at her subjects.

Rapturous applause followed. She waited for long moments until it began to subside and then held a hand aloft.

'Many died to see our world restored to Imperial jurisdiction,' she said, her voice clear and direct, resonating around the hall. 'We have confounded rebels, pushed back the wretched Federation and reclaimed our rights. This I did not achieve alone, but by the sacrifice of many and I would have them remembered and recalled to mind at this time.'

Silence fell and heads were bowed in reverence.

Kahina got to her feet, placing the sceptre carefully on the throne behind her.

'Further to this, my first act as Senator will be to grant executive powers to those that have served me well, to ensure a peaceful future for all my subjects.'

A muted whispering sped around the hall. Kahina watched as heads nodded and turned to each other in hushed conversation.

'Ambassador Cuthrick, Patrons Dalk, Zyair and Gerrun. You will hereby witness these actions as right and proper before this assembly.'

All four men stepped before her, bowed and then acknowledged her in unison. 'We will, Senator.'

As one, they knelt before her.

Kahina stood tall, smiling down on the men abased beneath her. She drew her ceremonial sword, holding it hilt down for a moment before lowering the blade.

'I, Senator Kahina Tijani Loren, daughter of Algreb, hereby cede all authority, powers both legal and temporal accorded to me upon the death of my father to my faithful servant ...'

Dalk held his breath for a moment, bowing his head to accept the touch of the flat blade upon his scalp.

At last ...

All his plans had come to fruition, all the schemes, all the intrigue, all the battles and fights. Finally, Chione would belong once more to those from whom it had been stolen all those years ago. Even Octavia has been removed from the equation. He could rebuild, oust the Federation, oust the Empire, be free once more ...

Kahina took her own breath and then announced her choice in tones of ringing clarity. '... Ambassador Cuthrick Delaney.'

There was an audible gasp from around the room, with the notable exception of the ambassador. Dalk looked up at Kahina, a burning rage igniting within him. He saw her face full of glee, her head tilted up, smugly looking down at him. At the haughty expression on her face, his rage flamed brightly.

'How dare you ...' he began, 'you promised.'

Kahina fixed him with a glare, though a smile played across her lips. 'You asked me to cede power to one who valued peace above all, one who served my interests in all things.'

'That one is me, girl,' Dalk growled.

'You?' Kahina replied innocently. 'You who murdered me? Abducted me? Used me to further your own ends?' She abruptly brought the sword around, the tip just under his chin. 'Exactly how have you served me, traitor Dalk?'

Still kneeling, Gerrun muttered to Zyair. 'She has a point.' Zyair nodded, his eyes watching the sword. 'A very sharp one.'

Dalk glared at Kahina, trembling with the effort of remaining in control. 'Chione is mine.'

'Chione was never yours,' Kahina retorted. 'Is that what this world needs? More death, more war, more fighting over resources? How many have already died? Not even the Federation makes that mistake. You don't want peace, Dalk. You'll stop at nothing, will you? Power and control; that's what you desire.'

'You know nothing of what I desire, little girl.' Dalk wrestled his thoughts back into line. There were other ways he could deal with this upstart

CHAPTER SIXTEEN

child. 'This is my world, taken from me by Imperial aggression. Have you forgotten the destruction wrought by your precious Imperial fleet? Bombs dropped by command of your, oh so honourable Fleet Admiral? Authorised by your very own beloved father? You are the daughter of a disgraced genocidal Senator. You aren't fit to rule. Return Chione to one who is, its rightful owner.'

'I give Chione to those who will serve its best interests,' Kahina replied. 'There will be no more war, no evictions, no …'

'You defy me? I taught you, schooled you, tutored you, you'd be nothing without …'

'And I'm in debt to your guidance, Dalk,' she replied. 'Are you displeased that I have become the leader you always thought I could be? Or would you rather me not know my own will?'

'Chione is mine!' Dalk roared.

'You lost Chione the moment you schemed, Dalk,' Kahina said softly. 'What is it you're supposed to stand for? Freedom? Self-determination? Freedom from corruption? That's what you said you valued, but you'd happily see me abused to put you where you could enjoy your so-called rights.' Her voice grew angry. 'I know what you had planned with Octavia. My body at her whim, a living death! You've forgotten the meaning of what you fought for. All you have is vengeance for those that wronged you, but they're all gone, Dalk! Dead and buried. Tragic yes, but the conflict stops here and now. Today we will make amends for all who suffered. Survivors from all sides will be catered for. Chione will welcome all.'

He shook his head. 'You are a naïve fool …'

'Times change, Dalk. Time for Chione to move on too. Let's put the past behind us and look to the future. There is always a role for those with ability.'

Kahina lowered the sword a touch and then stepped back. She held her other hand towards him, palm open.

'I would still have you serve me, Dalk. Let's rebuild this moon for all concerned. Join me in this. I will forgive you for past wrongs.'

Dalk bowed his head. He could acquiesce, rebuild his plans, influence and cajole. It would take time … His rage boiled over. The girl would stand in his way at every stage, with the power of the Imperial regime behind her.

Dalk heard Gerrun mutter some instruction to the Imperial guards stationed alongside. He heard their footsteps as they moved slowly forwards. Dalk sensed them out of the corner of his eye. Kahina had no intention of honouring him with a position, she would quietly dispose of him once she'd put that toady Cuthrick in position.

Damn her!

With a quick reflex move he batted Kahina's sword away and backpedalled to his feet. Before she could advance on him he'd drawn his own sword. He straightened to his full height and regarded her with a cold stare. Gerrun, Zyair and Cuthrick retreated clumsily away from him.

'You will cede power to me or I will kill you,' Dalk roared.

'Dalk, relent,' Cuthrick said, raising his voice. 'Guards, subdue him!'

Kahina held up her hand.

'No,' she said, equally firmly. 'He is mine. Back away.'

'Senator …' Cuthrick's voice was tight with worry.

'Do as I say! Back away!'

Cuthrick, Zyair and Gerrun climbed to their feet and stepped back. Dalk watched as she turned her attention back to him. 'My father wronged you, Dalk, in that you speak the truth. I will not deny you the chance to slake your thirst for vengeance. Either way, this conflict stops here.'

'Kahina … no!' Hassan called. Dalk saw Luko pull the youth back. Luko's face was bright with approval and satisfaction.

'She does this for her people,' Luko said. 'Is an honourable thing …'

'… but he'll kill her!' Hassan cried.

Dalk warily watched as Kahina stepped down from the dais and advanced towards him, dropping into a guarded stance, holding her sword before her.

'Come then, Dalk,' she said. 'I'll answer for the crimes of my father. You'll answer for your crimes against me, my family and the slaves who have died for the sake of your intrigue. Let's see who has the greater wrath.'

'I will kill you,' Dalk said. She seemed assured, too assured. 'If you stand in your father's place, expect no mercy.'

A smile touched the edges of her lips. 'I have reason enough to hate you too. Perhaps you remember? I warned you I'd have you one day, old man.'

Dalk circled her, never taking his eyes off her, conscious of the echo of

CHAPTER SIXTEEN

a conservation held but a few short weeks before. Friends then; mortal enemies now.

'But not this day, Imperial girl. This day will see the end of you and your execrable family.'

'And where will you go, old man?' she sneered, still sidestepping around, keeping him directly ahead. 'You're a traitor to the Empire, you'll be wanted by the Federation. Octavia is dead, the traders will never trust you. You played a dangerous game … and you lost. Kill me and you've achieved nothing, you'll never leave this hall alive. Why not work with me rather than against me? Chione belongs to me, you know this. It is legally binding.'

'At least I'll have the satisfaction of ridding the universe of the last accursed flux-stained offspring of the Loren family. I should have known better than to cultivate you.'

'Regret the time spent training me? An Imperial lady at your beck and call?'

Dalk growled. 'Imperial trash! And you're no lady, your father was right. You are worthless, deformed …'

Kahina's face hardened and a muscle in her cheek twitched. Her hand tightened on the hilt of her sword. The tip raised.

'Choice made then, Dalk. Come and get me, old man.'

Dalk swung at her, a blur of flashing swinging metal. Kahina parried three times in rapid succession and jumped back, sword still held towards him.

'Is that the best you can do?' she jeered.

'I haven't even started,' he replied, readying another attack. This time it was more measured; a combination of thrusts and twists, aiming to disarm her. She responded with deft strokes, turning the blade aside each time. Back and forth they fought, sparks flying from their swinging weapons. Kahina kicked out and sent Dalk stumbling backwards. He turned quickly and they circled back to guard positions, warily watching each other.

She's fast! Too fast. She was faking during her lessons with me! The conniving…

'I learnt my lessons better than you knew,' she said, a smile touching her lips as she read the confused expression on his face. 'Perhaps you've forgotten how astute a student I was. Did you think you were my only tutor? Prepare to reap what you have sown. I am the voices of my family and every slave you sent to death to pay the price for your failed reclamation.'

'My voice speaks for those your father murdered,' Dalk returned. 'I will extract revenge from you for their suffering. You will feel every death, every cut a sweet morsel until you lie gutted; your body unrecognisable. You won't come back from death this time, I promise you that.'

'Thus speaks traitor Dalk,' Kahina said. 'You have no honour left, no loyalty, nothing but selfish ambition and wrath. I pity you!'

Dalk howled out of sheer frustration and launched himself towards her. He swung his sword in great sweeping arcs, consumed by rage. Kahina parried and blocked, but was sent stumbling back, trying desperately to defend herself.

'This is my world! This is my home! It is mine!'

Dalk's rage burst its carefully woven bounds of restraint. His sword crashed down upon the maddening girl time and again. She dodged, ducked and wove out of the way. He pursued her relentlessly, enraged by every blow that failed to land on her. Sparks flashed and spiralled away from the whirling blades.

Dalk saw a brief moment of advantage and let loose a punch. Kahina saw it coming and stepped aside, but she was a moment too late. The blow did little actual harm, but it unbalanced her. Dalk was ready with a thrust.

His blade sliced across her left arm, just above the elbow. Blood flowed. Kahina yelped in surprise and backed away. A gasp of horror was drawn from the onlookers.

'First blood to me,' Dalk gasped with the exertion. 'Relent. Cede to me and I will spare you … safe passage back … to the Empire.'

Kahina shook her head, also trying to catch her breath. 'If my death … saves my world from further torment … I go willingly.'

'Then let me speed your demise,' Dalk growled, stabbing forwards once more.

Kahina parried and turned his blade back on him. He sidestepped the return swing and then came at her again, cutting down at her with powerful strokes, forcing her to defend and back away. It was clear she was tiring. Their blades crossed, bring them close together.

'I don't want to kill you,' he said.

'Nor I you,' she returned, her voice catching.

'Then give me what I want. End this madness.'

'The madness is yours …'

CHAPTER SIXTEEN

He pushed her backwards. She stumbled and fell, rolling aside as his blade swept down, clanging against the marble flooring. He struck at her in fury, frustrated at not being able to land a killing bow. She scrambled away and regained her feet, expertly deflecting his attacks, ducking a swipe at her neck she was unable to block in time.

She jumped back onto the dais. He could see she was sweating fiercely, her hair dank against her forehead. Dalk pursued her up to Algreb's throne. She dropped her guard for a moment, Dalk seized the opportunity and stabbed forward.

She sidestepped the blow and brought the pommel of her sword down on his elbow, bringing her knee up at the same time. A wet crunch preceded a shattering shock of agony. He yelled in pain and surprise. Before he could recover, the flat of her sword smashed into his head, cracking his nose. Blood spurted from his face. He dropped his sword, but lashed out with his fist, connecting hard with her shoulder. Her sword clattered down beside her as she fell backwards, rolling down onto the marble floor. He heard her land and cry out in pain.

Dalk staggered forward. She'd broken his elbow with that move, his sword arm was useless, blood was gushing from his ruined nose. He gritted his teeth against the pain and turned to face her as she got unsteadily to her feet. She was off balance, shaking her head.

'A cheap trick,' he spat.

'You taught me never to stop fighting until I could fight no more,' she answered. 'Blame yourself if I listened.'

They faced each other again. She was sweating and breathing hard. Blood was flowing freely down her arm. He glared at her, humiliated, finding it impossible to believe he had yet to defeat this upstart, this interloper, this Imperial ... girl. He who had taken down the fighting-forces of the Empire and the Federation. An Elite pilot, a warrior. She looked exhausted, ready to submit. She was a worthy opponent; perhaps he had trained her too well. No matter, her time was near. He smiled, she had put everything into that last move and had nothing more to give.

She didn't move as he approached, but dropped her guard slightly. Her shoulders drooped as she raised her arms to guard herself. She staggered slightly to one side, shaking her head. He feinted and then punched with his good arm.

She wasn't there. For a moment he caught a glimpse of her face, her eyes bright and sharp.

She'd summoned up some reserve of strength, he'd been tricked. He realised a moment too late.

She grabbed his outstretched arm, pushed it up and twisted his wrist into a vicious lock. She brought her elbow crashing into his kidneys. As he doubled over she brought up her fist backwards and sideways. She hit him straight between the eyes. The pain was excruciating, he felt shattered fragments of his nose burst through his skin. He went down heavily, flat on his back, winded and gasping.

He made to get up, but the sword point was back at his throat. 'Enough,' she said. 'Give it up, Dalk.'

She stood over him, blood oozing from the wound on her arm, he could see it dripping down to her wrist. He hoped it hurt like hell.

'You can't even finish me …' His eyes caught hers.

Steely determination, regret, anger and remorse.

She backed away just a little, repositioning the sword. 'I don't want to kill you …'

His lips curled in anger, ignoring her words and wrestling himself upwards to attack her once more.

Sadness in her eyes …

Pain speared through him. A groan escaped his throat. He looked down to see the sword embedded in his chest. His legs collapsed under him, an intense burning fire cascading through his torso.

'… but I will.' Her voice was soft.

She'd stabbed him through the heart. Neat, precise and clean. He gasped, unable to comprehend his own mortality. He reached forward, grabbing her wrist in a crushing grip.

'No …' he managed to utter. 'This circle is truly broken now.'

His strength failed him and he fell back against the cold marble floor.

She knelt down, positioning herself next to him. In shock he looked up as she bent over him.

CHAPTER SIXTEEN

He could see tears in her eyes. As he watched they trickled unashamedly down her cheeks. 'You were right,' she said sadly. 'It is better this way.'

Darkness swept in, eclipsing his life, his dreams and his aspirations. All were smothered in a veil of inky nothingness.

* * *

Luko watched as the landscape around him emerged from the shadow of Daedalion. The faintly glimmering stars were banished as the sky brightened to a glorious azure once more, the daily eclipse was over. The sun light sparkled on the bay as the dark shadow of the planet swept away to the west.

Behind him, the ruined palace still stood, a shadow of its original glory, burnt and blackened from the battle. He stood, enjoying the warmth upon his face, his eyes closed for a moment.

He heard footsteps, light and even, crunching on the broken pathway nearby. They stopped next to him.

'Ah, signorina. You were right, this is a beautiful place.'

'It is.' Her voice was soft and thoughtful.

Luko looked across at her, squinting in the brightness. 'You are very brave, but you took a big risk.'

She returned his glance. 'I had to stop him, stop everything. Like you said, there should be no more death.'

Luko nodded. 'You did trust him, no?'

'I wanted to believe him. He did save me, that much was true. He just forgot what he was fighting for. He was a good man once.'

'Too much power is never good for anyone.'

Kahina sighed. 'It was the right thing to do, wasn't it?'

'Your precious moon is once more an outpost of your glorious empire. Trade will flow again, people will be safe. This is good, yes?'

Kahina nodded. 'Ambassador Cuthrick will ensure peace and prosperity, I'm sure.'

Luko nodded. 'He seems … ok. A good man, for an Imperial.'

He grinned at her sharp look, but she didn't respond to the jibe. 'I owe you an apology.'

Luko looked at her in surprise. 'Signorina?'

'You knew, didn't you? You knew I didn't want this obligation. To be a Senator ...'

Luko smiled. 'I wondered. The weight of such responsibility? Not good for one so young I think. You had a dream and you gave it up for duty. I not like to see anyone miss their heart's desire. Very sad.'

'I should have listened to you.'

'Ah ...' Luko said, shaking his head. 'Not be so hard on yourself. The young never listen to the old, this is the way of things. Experience?' He winked. 'Something you get ... just after you need it.'

'Perhaps I could have stopped this.'

Luko shrugged. 'Perhaps. But with politics there is always war. War is not the battle. War is greed, war is fear. Is not your fault. We ... just people passing through history. We step on the stage, we say our lines, we step off.'

'I don't want to be on the stage anymore.'

Luko looked at her. 'Somehow I think we have not heard the last of you, signorina.'

Kahina smiled. 'Perhaps.'

Luko nodded. 'To be happy, that is what we all really want. Some of us ... we think this is money or power, or riches. But this is not true. What we want is to be content. This is all. See a dream come true, yes?'

'I hear you.' Kahina changed the subject. 'So what next? Where will your dreams take you, trader Luko?'

Luko sucked in his breath and then let it out with an exaggerated sigh. 'Ah, somewhere quiet I think. Good food, good company, no more stress. A holiday perhaps. The universe deserves to see a little more of Luciano Prestigio Giovanni, no?'

Kahina laughed. 'You'll be bored inside a week.'

Luko looked across at her with a more serious expression. 'You not wrong. Somewhere with people. I have been alone too long.'

'That I can understand.'

'Or perhaps I will just enjoying being on a planet ... that I can leave whenever I wish.'

Kahina laughed. 'Make sure you keep some spares aboard.'

CHAPTER SIXTEEN

'And what of you, little signorina? You reclaimed your moon then you give it all way. Crazy, no?'

She looked up at the blue sky.

'I'm going to do what you suggested.'

'And what is that?'

'I'm going to listen to Salomé.'

Luko frowned for a moment, before a wide smile grew on his face. He placed an arm around her shoulders and gave them a squeeze. Kahina relaxed into his embrace.

'Keep listening. She was a good girl. She will not lead you astray.' Tears sprang into Kahina's eyes.

'I will miss you.'

'I miss you too, signorina.'

He released her and she stepped back. After a moment she took the Imperial tiara from her head.

'Here,' she said, handing it to him and wrapping his hands about it. 'Something to remember me by. She won't need it, will she?'

Luko took it solemnly. 'Good luck, Salomé.'

AD 3301
Epilogue

Two figures were crouched over a small desk. The room around them was featureless; gunmetal grey walls surrounded them on all sides, the only illumination provided by a glowing holofac projector.

'We've got to be quick.'

It was Salomé. She typed commands into the system, the projector responding with a query interface.

'You going to tell me what precisely you're looking for?' Hassan looked over her shoulder, his features cast in silhouette by the faint glow.

'Something I promised myself I'd look up when I had a chance.'

'This is a secure Imperial data bank. If we get caught ...'

'And I had to pay a lot of money to get an access code.' Salomé continued to type furiously. Information flickered into view around them.

'Jeez, this is old stuff,' Hassan said looking at the data. 'Galcop? I scanned them in grad school back home. Gramps used to talk about the Old Worlds, that's more than a hundred years ago. What are you looking for?'

Salomé flicked her fingers and a piece of search text moved across the holofac projection. The words *Formidine Rift* glowed briefly. Her hair flopped forward, so she pushed it back behind her ear.

There was little response to the query, a few phrases, a couple of vague trajectory plots. The system indicated it was still searching.

Salomé gestured impatiently. 'It's got to be here. She said something about plotting a course from Reorte to ... ah, there it is!'

'Somebody has a sense of humour,' Hassan said, scanning the text. 'The friendliest place this side of Riedquat? Nice choice ...'

'Riedquat? Where's that? You know it?'

Hassan scoffed. 'Not from personal experience. It's a hell-hole. An anarchy system for centuries. Totally lawless. No sane trader would go near it.'

The search completed. A single holofac photo was returned, accompanied by a short video.

The photo was of a fifty-something woman, dressed in an old fashioned one piece traders' outfit. She was quite petite, with a pale face framed by simply brushed brown hair, parted in the middle into two neat folds on either side of her head. There were no earrings or adornments of any kind. She looked pretty, but very ordinary save for a pair of deep brown eyes.

'It's her, decades ago …' Salomé reached forward to start the video playing.

'Who is she?' Hassan queried.

'Just this old woman I met, looks like she was telling the truth after all.'

The video played.

'If you're listening to this it means you're smart enough to have bypassed Galcop, Federation and Imperial security.' The woman on the video smiled. 'Not bad, but it's nothing compared to what's coming. I'm guessing you'll be pressed for time so I'll be quick. You'll find the coordinates at the end of this message. You'll need a tough ship and a good pilot. It's a long way, so make sure you're prepped, no one will be around to help you out. Once you reach the rift you're going to have to plot a way across. There are no stars for dozens of light years and the dark systems haven't been mapped, so take your time, watch your six.' The woman leaned in closer to the recording device. 'What's there? Wish I could tell you, but they edited my memory pretty good, took me long enough to stitch this lot back together. Whatever it is, it's something that Galcop, the Imps and the Feds don't want us to see. Good luck, and … right on, Commander.'

The holofac faded, leaving them with just the text. Salomé looked at Hassan with a mischievous grin.

'Shall we?'

* * *

The suns had set and twilight was upon the world. Heading home after a long day in the field, Sushil heard a distant double thunderclap from the clear sky above him. He pulled on the reins of his herg and the grumpy animal plodded gratefully to a halt, flapping the blood flushed cooling membranes behind its head. It snorted as he dismounted, looking upwards in surprise.

Amongst the stars he could see a vapour trail high in the atmosphere and

EPILOGUE

a sun-like orb of brightness moving slowly across the sky. As he watched, the light faded and a vessel could be seen, turning in the sky to slow its approach. It was coming towards him. He watched in dismay as it closed. The shape of the ship gave away its origins. There was no mistaking it.

Imperials!

What were they doing here? He'd heard the stories of how they'd invade a world, take it over and subdue the settlers. Was this an invasion?

The ship approached. A breeze arose around him. The herg stirred uneasily behind him, trumpeting through its twin nasal passages. The ship swept in like a gigantic predatory reptile from times long lost, turning gracefully, undercarriage unlocking and folding out in a smooth ballet of design, flourish and technology.

It was a sleek yet intimidating ship. It was immediately obvious to him that it was a new vessel. The hull gleamed with burnished duralium, no scars of battle marked its striking paintwork, radiation had yet to taint its exterior. Hull lights twinkled and flashed, accentuating the flowing curves and sweeping design of the ship. It was elegant, sophisticated, more than just a ship; it was a thing of beauty, a dream of spaceflight rendered into art.

It was also vast. Sushil had never seen a ship of this size up close. It had to be almost a hundred metres long. It was also a warship; a variety of weapons jutted from the twin engine nacelles, missiles lurked, half hidden in the lower hull, poised to fly. He briefly caught sight of an elegantly illuminated hull plate bearing the vessel's name as it swept over him.

Seven Veils.

He ducked instinctively as the ground trembled under his feet.

The vessel slowed, descending into the empty fallow field where Hassan's *Talon* had once stood. With a gentleness that belied its size it settled to the ground with barely a whisper of fading drives. Lights flashed on beneath its hull, illuminating the ground around it with a bright blue-white glow.

Sushil watched as a ramp lowered from the mid-section, unfolding and expanding in another engineering tour de force.

Sushil tied his herg to a tree and walked across to the ship. Better that he found out what they wanted. There was no thought of resistance; this ship could probably subdue their planet on its own.

Imperials here? A long way from the Empire.

He walked so he was standing just before it, subdued and intimidated by its bulk yet marvelling at the complexity and ostentatiousness of its design. Shadows flickered at the top of the ramp. Bright lights lit the interior; he couldn't see clearly. A figure ... no two figures. One walking forwards towards him, arms outstretched.

'Kick-ass and blinged enough for you, Sush?'

Sushil gaped.

Hassan stood before him, but this was not the younger brother he remembered. He was dressed in a smart well-heeled and immaculately tailored outfit, a few steps short of a uniform. His hair was neatly trimmed, styled and clipped. He stood tall, shoulders back. A man, no longer the troubled and insecure youth Sushil had waved away scant months before.

'Hassan?'

'Told you I'd got a plan.'

'No shit ... this your ship? I mean ... you serious? This ...'

'She's quite a sight isn't she? An Imperial Courier.'

'But how did you afford ...'

'Let's just say somebody owed me a ship.' Hassan turned aside for a moment, gesturing to the other figure who had remained at the top of the ramp in the glare of the lights.

Sushil watched as the figure stepped down the ramp. By the gait and poise it was clearly a woman, her features obscured by the glare. She was a little taller than Hassan.

She stepped in front of the lights and Sushil got a clear look at her. Her face was striking, a shade away from beautiful, with grey eyes set against dark black hair. She was dressed in an elegant but simple gown, in a fetching shade of dark green. Her arms were bare, and her right arm bore a thin recently healed scar several inches long.

'I think he got the better side of the deal, personally,' the woman said. Sushil couldn't help but frown at her strong Imperial accent.

'Sushil, this is ... Salomé.'

'And you must be Hassan's sensible older brother.' She extended her hand to him. Sushil took it, bemused.

EPILOGUE

He stuttered, strangely intimidated by the woman. 'Er ... you're ...'

'Travelling together,' Hassan added, under his breath.

'Ah ...' Sushil managed to answer, releasing her hand. 'Salomé?'

She raised her head and said quietly, 'Just Salomé.'

A story there, clearly. I wonder what it is ...

'But you're back, man!' Sushil exclaimed, looking back at his brother. 'I mean ... look at you! Did you do it? What happened to you out there? Did your plan actually work?'

Hassan was about to answer, but Salomé interrupted. 'Would it surprise you to learn that it was a complete disaster from beginning to end?'

Sushil stared at her for a moment before laughing. 'She's got you pegged, little brother.' Hassan nodded in agreement.

'Let's just say things didn't quite work out how I expected,' Hassan said, 'but it was one hell of a ride.'

'So why you shipping out with my little brother?' Sushil asked Salomé. 'He's trouble, you know ...'

Salomé smiled. 'I know. I've dealt with far worse, believe me.'

'You here for long?' Sushil asked.

Hassan shook his head. 'Just a brief stop,' he said. 'Heading out to the edge.'

Sushil shook his head. 'That same old crazy dream of yours?' He looked at Salomé. 'You too?' She nodded. 'You'll look after him, right?'

'I'll do my best to keep him in one piece,' she answered.

'Where you going, anyway?'

Hassan pointed up to the stars above them. 'Just out there, Sush. Past the core worlds, past the outlying civilisations, over the edge of the maps and the known routes. We've got a little quest in mind. Who knows what we'll find.'

The girl stepped forward, out away from the ship, running her hand through her dark hair as a cool breeze ruffled it. She looked upwards, a strange wistful expression on her upturned features, her eyes dancing with the reflection of the uncounted stars above.

Sushil watched the same rapt expression grow on his brother's face as they both stared upwards into the darkening sky. Both his brother and the mysterious woman stood contemplating the vast unending universe arrayed above their heads.

Whatever it is, they've got it bad.

Myriad stars pricked the darkness of space. Not far away from here was the border, the boundary, the limit of known space; the edge over which only those who couldn't resist the siren song of adventure dared to go; those to which 'dangerous' was just a substitute for exhilaration.

They call it the Frontier.

About the Author

Drew Wagar is a British science fiction and fantasy author. He lives in Kent with his wife, two sons, a dog and a cat. His favourite colour is dark green. Everything else is subject to change without notice.

You can reach Drew as follows:

Drew's Website: http://www.drewwagar.com

Facebook: http://www.facebook.com/drewwagarwriter

Twitter: http://www.twitter.com/drewwagar

Other books available in the Elite: Dangerous series

Elite: And Here The Wheel by John Harper
Elite: Mostly Harmless by Kate Russell
Elite: Tales From The Frontier by 15 authors from around the world
All of the above published by Fantastic Books Publishing

Elite: Wanted by Gavin Deas
Elite: Nemorensis by Simon Spurrier
Elite: Docking is Difficult by Gideon Defoe
Published by Gollancz

Out of the Darkness by T.James

An excerpt from 'The Shadeward Saga', an upcoming SF series by Drew Wagar

Lacaille

The Lacaille system, officially 'Lacaille 9352, Red Dwarf Class M2V' in the stellar catalogue, was not a primary colonisation target. Red dwarf stars were considered generally poor candidates and the system was relegated to the lower end of the league table. The only reason it was considered at all was that, at a distance of just over ten light years, it was reachable by ships powered by the new atomic pulse engines, a factor that eventually became critical.

It had been known for some time that there were several planets in the system. Esurio, along with four unremarkable gas giants and a series of rocky dwarf worlds, had already been catalogued and studied in some detail by Sol based orbiting telescopes and, more recently, by high speed atomic space-probes. The returning data was greeted with initial enthusiasm.

Esurio lay within Lacaille's 'goldilocks zone', close enough to support liquid water, and far enough out to prevent it evaporating away. Around a more familiar star the planet would have been considered the ideal target, a close parallel of the home-world. A red dwarf would naturally mean that metals would be in short supply, but that could be countered by technology. It might support a simple agrarian culture.

Further analysis quickly dashed those hopes.

Lacaille's peculiar properties made the colonisation of Esurio problematic for many reasons. The star was extremely faint and cool, with the planet in an alarmingly close orbit. Conditions on the surface ranged from the extreme to the astonishing. Tidally locked to its parent star; one side of the planet always faced the glow of ruddy sunlight; the other was forever shrouded in eternal night.

An everlasting hurricane raged on the sub-stellar pole, fed by ferocious evaporation from the surface due to the intense heat. At the terminator, kilometre high cliffs of eternal ice and glaciers that dwarfed anything ever seen before marked the transition onto the darkside. Images showed a narrow temperate zone between the two extremes.

Lacaille's brightness dropped precipately as sun spots periodically blotched its

surface, far bigger than the tiny motes that affected the star humans called 'the Sun', causing dramatic temperature drops. At other times the star flared brightly, a runaway fusion reaction brightening the star in moments and swamping its planets in dangerous ultra-violet radiation and excessive heat.

There was no evidence of any intelligent life, yet there was something there; sensors confirmed the tell-tale presence of oxygen and methane in the atmosphere. Air pressure was higher than the home-world despite lower gravity. None of the probes had the resolution to peer down to the surface during their brief encounters as they flashed through the system on a one way journey. The planet's magnetic field was weak as expected, the planet slowly losing its atmosphere under the fierce glare of Lacaille.

With long term viability uncertain and the rigours to be endured by any prospective colonists considered insurmountable, Esurio was marked as 'non-viable' and overlooked in favour of more conventional spheres by the committees of the home-world.

That was, until those same committees were awakened to the knowledge that before long they would have no home-world.

The resultant programme was rushed, with provisions and equipment pared to the absolute minimum. The timescales allowed no other outcome. The known issues were immense and intractable, but they were overcome, though often by controversial and experimental means.

After much sacrifice and difficulty, Esurio was colonised. Only the brave and hardy survived.

Prologue
Round 2287, Ninth Pass

Rain cascaded down in sheets, cold dark and heavy despite the eternal sun, whipped into frenzy by a fierce and fickle wind. It blew one way and then another with unrelenting strength, battering the slate grey rocks that formed the steep flank of the mountain. Lightning flickered in the grey gloom, giving a brief view of stark and craggy outcrops, and terrifying drops into shadowed chasms. Thunder rolled not far behind, hammering the rocks and echoing around the unseen valleys. Smaller debris was dislodged, tumbling down and scattering across a muddy and treacherous narrow track that cut through the landscape like a thin sinuous snake. On one side a steep rocky bluff, on the other a drop back down into the valley far below.

Toiling up this path at a charge were two heavy set creatures steaming with exertion, yoked to a battered wooden carriage, illuminated by dimly flickering torches which guttered in the screaming wind, threatening to be extinguished but somehow just managing to stay alight. Two black feathered arrows were stuck in the wooden frame on the rear of the carriage, the wood splintered around them.

Atop the carriage, two men draped in thick oil skins hung on for dear life as the carriage jolted from rock to pothole and back again. One cracked a whip, driving the beasts onwards at a reckless speed. The other turned to look behind them, squinting through the rain.

He chose an unfortunate moment. Arrows whistled out of the gloom. One passed between the two men, the second stuck the man in the chest, throwing him back against his companion. With a screech he fell head first from the carriage and was crushed under the rear wheel as the carriage plunged ahead. The carriage jolted, the wheel coming back down onto the track with an abrupt shock. Spokes splintered, the wheel turned once and then came apart. The carriage canted over, crashing onto its side close to the edge of the path, sliding to a stop above an invisible drop into the darkness.

A baby's cry rang out in the darkness. It came from inside the carriage.

The remaining man, dazed and battered but otherwise uninjured, desperately climbed back to open the side door. The carriage shifted as the panicking beasts, still yoked to the carriage, tried to regain their feet and escape. The carriage was dragged perilously closer to the edge. He pulled out a knife, cut the traces and the beasts roared, quickly fleeing into the rain and disappearing.

He pulled open the door. A woman half clambered out, her face white with fear, but set with determination. For a moment they argued, but then she lifted out a pair of babies swaddled in fine linen and handed them to the man, pushing him away, gesturing for him to run. Her shouts were swept away by the wind. A brief embrace followed and then he ran. Lightning crackled and the following clap of thunder made him duck instinctively.

He clambered up the rocky slopes adjacent to the crashed carriage, seeking to put as much distance between him and it as possible. Barely audible shouts brought his attention around. He ducked down behind a boulder and peered over the top. One of the babies in his arms whimpered and he gently tried to keep it quiet, holding a trembling finger to his lips.

Far below, the woman in the carriage had managed to somehow clamber down. It was clear she had been injured in the crash, her ankle twisted or broken. She had limped a short distance, but was now facing back down the path; the direction the carriage had driven.

She stood silent, the wind snatching her sodden dark hair around her face. Run….

More of the beasts charged into the flickering light from the torches aboard the upturned carriage. They bore four riders, thin figures dressed in lightweight mail, armed with swords and with bows slung across their backs. Their heads were covered by capes, their faces hidden. They stopped and dismounted, striding forward in a line. One gestured to the woman with a gloved hand. She took a backward step, shaking her head.

The leader's gesture came again, imperious, demanding, yet the woman's face was set and determined.

The woman cried out plaintively and hobbled towards the carriage, giving it a sharp push. The leader unslung the bow, notched an arrow, drew and fired.

No!

The carriage slipped on the edge, overbalanced and then rolled into the chasm. The shattering crash of it breaking apart on the rocks below reverberated back to the onlookers. Lightning flickered and a boom of thunder masked out what little sound was left to hear.

The man was unable to watch, slumping behind the boulder as the woman sank to her knees and fell to one side, an arrow protruding from her chest. He crouched, huddled over his charges, shuddering in despair and grief.

The leader of the warriors strode forward and pulled the woman up by the throat. A brief interrogation followed, the woman defiant even as her life drained away. The leader threw her to the ground in disgust, leaving her convulsing and doubling up before finally lying still. The leader's cape fell back revealing a strong female face, with blonde hair, shaved on the left side over the ear, and grown long on the other. A simple metallic band was set across her forehead. Her face was a mask of frustration.

The concealed man risked a glance and saw they were looking over the edge of the chasm, down into the unseen depths. Lightning flashed again, with a thunderous boom smashing down around them. Dangerously large rocks rumbled past the man, one bounced over his head as he ducked low just in time. They fell onto the path, passing perilously close to the warriors.

A brief angry debate amongst the four warriors was quickly brought to a conclusion. They unceremoniously picked up the dead woman's body and flung it into the chasm before jumping aboard their beasts and turning about, heading back the way they had come, quickly vanishing into the storm.

The man was left upon the darkened mountainside, the pair of babies huddled securely in the folds of his clothing. Panic overwhelmed his grief and he ran.

The storm continued, showing no signs of abating.

Chapter One
Daine, Capital of Drayden Round 2305, Fourth Pass

The creature landed on the branch of the shade and folded its three pairs of wings. Its body, almost a hand in length, shone iridescent in the warm light of Lacaille, flickering from cyan to magenta and back again as it turned. Caught in its mouthparts was the struggling form of a smaller black insect.

Kiri watched, fascinated, as the flit rapidly and efficiently consumed the unfortunate narg, enjoying the swift and fierce dismemberment of the prey, seeing its legs twitch impotently as it died accompanied by a faint, but delicious, squelching and cracking sound. Flits were a rare sight in these parts, usually found only in the shadeward. The weather had been somewhat cooler of late, encouraging the pretty creatures into the shade forests around the city.

She carefully lowered a brace of marsips to the ground. They were small but tasty rodents that she'd caught earlier. She approached cautiously, moving slowly to stay as quiet as possible. As she crept amongst the tall straight trunks of the shades she dislodged streams of condensation from the thin curtain like filaments that hung down from the branches around her; she brushed it out of her eyes. Sunlight filtered through in bright red majestic beams of light from the canopy overhead. Far above the outstretched cups of the shades fought for dominance against each other, each one struggling for position; a silent, desperate and eternal battle to secure precious light and water. A faint mist hovered between their trunks.

Kiri turned, put her finger to her lips and beckoned to her companion, who likewise lowered a series of strung up marsips to the ground and crept forward.

Hunting in the forests of Daine was illegal, but all the onlies did it. It was the only way to supplement their food supply. Stealing from traders in the city brought you quickly to the attention of the guards. It had to be done sparingly.

They dared not go too far into the forest. Stranger creatures lived within and there were other hazards too. It wasn't just the animals you had to concern yourself with. There were many traps for the unwary. Sand and bogs featured aplenty and, according to some of the more wild accounts, there were even plants that took a fancy to flesh.

The flit seemed unconcerned with their stealthy approach, quickly finishing its meal. Nothing was wasted; even the extremities of the narg were consumed. The flit turned and seemed to be looking at them. Kiri wondered how she appeared to the gaze of those three tiny faceted eyes, set like sapphires in the creature's angular head. Small wonder flits were admired when their eyes looked like jewels. Kiri was entranced. Funny how all the animals had three eyes and her kind had only two…

Without making a sound she managed to get within a few hands of the creature and paused there, bracing herself against a shade trunk, watching it.

'Isn't it pretty,' her companion whispered in delight. 'I've never seen one so close.'

Tia had been Kiri's companion for many rounds. Kiri had found her after her parents had died in one of the plagues that occasionally beset their lands. Just a child, Kiri had looked after her, teaching her how to survive in a city that neither wanted nor acknowledged their existence. Onlies; unseen, scraping a living via theft and cunning.

Kiri smiled briefly, admiring the beautiful delicate creature.

The flit remained unmoved for a moment before Kiri saw its antenna rise up as if sensing something. A moment later she too heard a noise. People somewhere close. Annoyed, she looked over her shoulder, searching amongst the trunks. She couldn't see anyone, but voices were getting louder. She cursed under her breath.

The flit extended its wings, one pair at a time. The fore wings low, the centre pair held horizontal with the final rear pair held high. It was poised, ready to fly.

'No, don't go…' Kiri whispered.

Voices were loud, accompanied by the crashing sounds of clumsy footsteps trampling vegetation underfoot. Guffaws and giggles shattered the quiet of the forest. The flit's wings disappeared in a flurry of movement and it spiralled upwards, disappearing into the canopy. Kiri turned in anger as a group of three boys stumbled into the small clearing. It was a group of three brothers from the city. She'd seen them before.

'Watch your shadow, you snuts!' she called out.

In their haste, the boys hadn't noticed Kiri and Tia until almost walking straight into them. The younger two stumbled back against the shades in fright at her sharp glare. The other boy was bigger, stronger and less intimidated. Kiri could see he was carrying a wooden sword, his hand resting protectively on the hilt. It was no toy, but a practice weapon, properly weighted and balanced. Tia caught sight of the sword and sidled behind Kiri, holding her arm nervously.

'What you doing here, slums?' he said, sizing them up, spying the sets of dead marsips on the ground. 'Hunting again? 'Gainst the law, as you've been told before.'

'Look to your own shade,' Kiri retorted. 'Might ask you the same thing. We were here first.'

'You can't order us about,' one of the smaller ones said impulsively. 'You're not a priestess.'

'Not yet,' Kiri fired back. 'But I will be. And then when you displease me I'll drag you to the temple, cut out your heart and eat it in front of you. Slash! Squish! Yum!'

She mimed stabbing the small boy with a knife, licking it and then wiping her mouth with the back of her hand. Kiri laughed as the boy cringed in fear and yelped. The bigger boy pushed in front of him, defensively.

'You won't be a priestess,' he sneered. 'You've got no line. Got to be noble, everyone knows that.'

'Don't need one,' Kiri retorted, facing off against him. She was a head shorter than the chunkier boy, still awaiting the growth spurt she knew was due. Kiri felt Tia's warning tug on her arm.

'Kiri, let's go, we can find other food...' the smaller girl pleaded. Kiri pulled herself free.

I'll be scorched before I give up my prey on account of this snut...

She stared fiercely up into Choso's blue eyes, ignoring the short blonde hair, muscular arms and stocky torso before her. Tia backed away, leaving Kiri facing Choso alone.

Kiri could tell Choso wasn't used to the onlies standing up against him.

She'd seen him intimidate others. It wasn't going to work on her, even if his father was captain of the temple guard.

He'd never cornered her before; the other onlies always fled like marsips at the first sign of trouble. Not her. She defied and taunted the family children, letting them chase her down streets to get caught in ingenious traps, piles of refuse cunningly rigged to fall down or into a pack of starving rabid carns.

She saw Choso run his eyes over her thin and lanky frame, topped by an unruly matted crop of black hair tied up on her head with a dirty cord. He grimaced at her grimy skin and tatty mix of stolen clothing, only then meeting the gaze of her fierce hazel eyes.

Kiri had been chased around the city, always skulking, stealing food brazenly from the traders. She knew Choso's father had been tasked with clearing the streets of her and the rest of the illegal youngsters. Most of the time it appeared he'd largely succeeded. She, and others like her, raided the city during the sleeping. Where they went other-times had always been a secret. Not any longer. Life was going to get even harder now Choso knew where they hid.

'Be thinking you can fight your way in then, slum girl?' Choso laughed, poking her with an outstretched finger. He walked around her and she stood still defensively, looking at him as he paced. 'You wouldn't last a spell in the arena.'

'I could beat you now, city mulch,' Kiri snapped back, spinning around to face him.

Choso pushed her hard and she stumbled backwards, losing her footing. Before she could react he'd grabbed her tunic at the scruff of the neck and hauled her back to her feet, roughly pushing her up against the smooth trunk of the nearest shade, her feet dangling in the air. The impact hurt her back. The sword was in his other hand, pointing at her face. She grabbed at the arm holding her, unable to move it, struggling against his superior strength. He lowered her to the ground, but kept the sword at her face.

Kiri heard Tia screech in fear. The other two brothers laughed. 'Learn her, Choso!' one shouted. Choso grinned cruelly in response.

'I'm thinking you need to know your place, slum,' he said, jabbing her cheek with the point of his sword and jolting her against the shade. It might have only been a wooden sword, but it hurt like fury. She rubbed her check, seeing blood on her fingers. She could feel it dripping down her cheek and neck.

Her eyes narrowed.

'I do,' she whispered under her breath. Choso frowned, leaning in closer to hear her, wrinkling his nose at the odour rising from her dirty clothes.

She brought her knee up as hard as she could, driving it into Choso's unprotected crotch. He screamed in agony, letting her go and dropping his sword. As he leant forward Kiri punched him directly in the throat, with a short sharp yell. Choso's cries were choked off and he fell to his knees. Kiri nonchalantly pushed him over with an outstretched foot. She backed away, standing next to Tia.

'Told you.'

Chose was trying to gasp out some words, she couldn't make them out. His brothers were at his side, trying to help him up. Choso struggled to make himself heard, howling out his pain and indignation. Kiri caught his eyes as he managed to look up with murderous intent, his face suffused with anger, bright red and sweating, desperately trying to regain his feet.

He croaked out something. His brothers didn't understand and leant in closer. Kiri caught the next words.

'Get them,' Choso panted out, furiously impotent.

Kiri looked around at Tia. The small girl was quaking with fear, her eyes wide. Kiri motioned with her eyes. Tia nodded.

Kiri turned her attention back to the boys. The next youngest brother picked up the sword and stepped towards her. Kiri warily circled back. The boy swung clumsily at her head and she ducked, the wooden sword striking the bark of a shade with a dull thud, showering her in splinters. Kiri jumped aside, only to be blocked by the other brother. He swung a punch at her which she narrowly avoided. Then there was a gap between them.

It took us a long spell to catch those marsips…

'Now!' she yelled to Tia. The other girl disappeared into the undergrowth as fast as the marsips they'd been pursuing.

She ran too, following in the direction Tia had fled.

They had a head start and both were good runners, you didn't last long as an only if you couldn't run. Unfortunately, the boys behind her were equally fast, and after gaining a little of a head start Kiri could sense she wasn't outrunning them. She lurched between the shade trunks looking for the easiest way forward, legs pounding with exertion, outstretched branches whipping painfully past her.

She heard an abrupt shriek ahead. Before she could stop she ran too quickly up a rise, onto a damp outcrop, lost her footing and slid down the other side, smearing herself in mud and winding herself as she hit the bottom, rolling onto her front. Tia was already sprawled in the mud before her. She saw the two brothers reach the top of the rise and make the same mistake. They came crashing down alongside her.

Kiri jumped unsteadily to her feet, struggling for breath. Tia seemed to have been badly winded by the fall, she'd only managed to get to her knees, gasping for breath. Kiri spied a sturdy branch on the ground and grabbed it, brandishing it in front of her, stepping between Tia and their pursuers. The two brothers circled her warily, preventing her from leaving. Both were now grinning at her predicament. Choso appeared at the top of the bank and awkwardly swung himself down, still gasping in pain.

'You're proper droughted now,' he said with a grimace, grabbing the wooden sword from the brother to his right. Kiri watched as he swung it experimentally. He seemed to know what he was doing. The sword whistled as it passed through the air.

The other two brothers circled behind her. Kiri raised her branch in defence, sidestepping and trying to keep them away from Tia.

'Tia!' she hissed, from between clenched teeth, unable to spare a glance down at her companion. All she could hear was the poor girl gasping and wheezing. Maybe she was hurt.

Kiri had no idea whether Choso had received any real training in the use of a sword, but she was painfully aware she had none whatsoever. She'd heard tell that a barbarian from Drem in the shadeward had once knocked the head of a slave clean off with nothing but a wooden sword. It wouldn't do to underestimate it. She kept her eyes focused on the tip as Choso waved it about.

She saw his eyes flicker from right to left and sensed rather than felt the two brothers closing in on her. Quickly as a flash she spun, dealing both of them a sharp whack to the head with her branch. Both yelled and fell backwards.

Choso's yell brought her attention back and she raised her branch in defence just quick enough to block a blow to her torso that would have easily broken a rib. Her arms trembled as she deflected the impact, the branch vibrating painfully in her hands. Choso turned and swung his sword down on her, aiming for her head. Again she blocked it. Choso twisted the sword in a peculiar way and Kiri found the branch wrenched from her hands. It splattered into the mud a few hand lengths away.

Choso didn't hesitate. He stabbed forward at Kiri's unprotected chest, aiming to skewer her neatly through the heart. Kiri threw up her hands defensively, but it was too late.

'No!'

Kiri felt herself jolted aside, away from the deadly thrust of Choso's sword. Choso yelled, driving the sword forward. Kiri fell into the mud, rolling, trying to turn her head to see. She heard sharp impact, a gasp that turned into a horrid gurgle.

Eyes, widening in horror and pain, caught her own in realisation. Hands that spasmed uncontrollably, knees that buckled. Redness, stillness. Too much redness…

A pounding in her ears. Rage and anger at the merciless of the world.

Choso pulled his sword back abruptly. Tia fell backwards to the ground, lying on her back, staring in to the forest canopy. Kiri ran to her, heedless of the danger.

'Tia!'

The girl's face was pale, her breath bubbling red in her mouth. Blood trickled out. She choked trying to say something, her body convulsing. Her hands flailed around for a moment before Kiri grasped them tightly. There was blood everywhere. Tia's eyes looked into Kiri's in terror before their gaze suddenly froze, looking past Kiri, sightless and empty.

Her body was abruptly still. Kiri found she was shaking and unable to stop herself.

How long she was immobile she wasn't sure, but the cracking of a twig on the ground nearby brought her back to the present. She looked up, seeing Choso slowly stepping towards her, his sword stained with blood. Tia's blood.

'I didn't mean to...' Choso stammered. 'I was only trying to scare you...'

Kiri's face was suffused with rage. She looked up furiously.

'Murderer!' Tears streaked her face, burning hot.

She let go of Tia's hands, hating the way her arms dropped lifelessly into the mud. She caught sight of her branch and grabbed it, brandishing it in front of her and stalking towards Choso, her thoughts only of revenge.

Choso backed away from the incensed expression on her face, but she closed with him. 'Enough, slum! Or... or I'll do the same to you!' he stammered.

Kiri was oblivious. She swung viciously at Choso. He only just managed to deflect the blow. Kiri attacked again, swinging wildly with the branch, screaming out her injustice on the figure of hate before her. She beat him down, her strength mindless and irresistible. Choso stumbled back losing his footing. She raised the branch, aiming a blow at his head, aiming to kill if she could.

Pain flashed up her calf. In her rage she'd forgotten the other two brothers. One had grabbed another branch and struck at her with it. Her leg gave way, sprawling her back into the mud. The three boys moved to surround her.

'Hit her again!' Choso shouted. 'Kill her!'

The brother who had struck backed away, shaking his head. 'I ain't doing it. Not killin'.'

Choso cursed at him. 'If she tells what we've done, you think it will go well with us? Murdering an' all? Kill her! No one need know, no one cares about these slums...'

'I ain't doing it,' the brother repeated and then stepped back again.

Kiri spared Tia's forlorn and lifeless body another glance, summoning what little resolve remained to her. She sprang to her feet, pushed past the undecided brother and fled again, staggering away in shock, trying to force her mind to work.

She heard Choso's yell of anger, and could hear them crashing through the undergrowth behind, hounding her, yelling curses as they tried to overtake. She couldn't run as well as before, a large bruise had already broken out on the leg where she'd been hit and it stung like a narg bite. There was no way she could be stealthy either, no way she could stop them from following. They were gaining, like a pack of carns chasing down a wounded herg.

Ahead the forest was thinning; she was nearly back to the suburbs. She leapt over a series of low bushes and burst out onto the dry and dusty lane that led around the city, blinking in the bright sunlight after the gloom of the forest. In front of her was the exposed side of a house, serving as a natural wall to the road. She skidded to a halt, almost falling as she stopped close to the wall and quickly considered her options.

She didn't have long to think. Choso and one brother emerged to her right, with the other brother coming out on her left, blocking the lane. She quickly looked in both directions. She'd not be able to get past, and they'd grab hold of her if she tried to run back to the forest. She'd have no chance in a close-quarters fist-fight with them, and they weren't going to let her go after what had happened…

Tia… oh, Tia…

Redness swamped her vision again. The horrible sound of the sword echoed through her mind; the blood was still slick on her fingers, she could smell it in her nostrils. Tia's body impaled, sliding to the ground…

Kiri shook her head.

Concentrate! They're going to kill you next!

Choso began patting the blade of the sword against his other palm and stalked towards her slowly.

'Enough of your furling, slum,' he said, his voice menacing. 'Gonna beat you like the carn you are.'

'Better a carn than a dung herg like you, murdering snut!' she replied bitterly, looked up and jumped.

The wall was higher than an average adult, but she caught the top of it with one hand, swinging precariously for a moment before securing her opposite elbow and levering herself up, her bare calloused feet clawing for grip against the sandy rocks of the wall. The rough rock cut at her hands and feet but it was nothing she wasn't used to. Choso and his brothers rushed forward to grab her, but she slipped out of reach, standing up on the wall and tip-toeing along it, taunting them with curses, still holding her branch.

From the wall the tiled roof of the house led up and away from the road. The brothers began to throw pebbles and stones at her, so she scrambled up the roof, delicately treading along the stone guttering to get out of their range.

It was a large house, with a series of verandas that overlooked the forest behind her. She was able to jump up to the next one and continued climbing until she reached the highest level. Behind the house was a series of similar buildings. It wouldn't be hard for her to quickly find a place to hide.

Choso cursed and she heard him climbing the wall behind her. She watched as he slipped back a couple of times before he managed to get to the top, accompanied by the cheers of encouragement from his brothers. Quickly he began to head towards her. Kiri deftly made her way around the edge of the veranda she was on and came to a point above the street on the other side.

For a moment she gasped. Before her the city rose, houses first, increasingly more ornate as they approached the centre, marked by rising plumes of smoke from chimneys. Beyond that the grander buildings of the city courts could be seen, spires and towers reaching for the sky, some clad in precious metals, sparkling in the warm light of Lacaille.

Her eyes were drawn to the centre immediately. Beyond the houses and the spires was a vast pyramid, smooth sided and austere compared with the more baroque architecture around it, built of smooth redstone. It dominated the view, contrasting sharply with the lighter stone of the other buildings. Kiri had heard that the interior was paved in metal, but found it hard to believe such a wonder could really be true. Metal was just too precious…

Around it was a large piazza, cleared and empty now. Kiri had skulked around it during the celebration days, seeing the priestesses parade in their fancy gowns and pageantry. It was there that the arena was set up, and women from all around Drayden would come to fight to gain a place alongside the priestesses. Most failed of course, you could never tell who was going to win. Sometimes the most unlikely entrants made it through. Some of the challenges were strange and unusual.

One day… I'll get my chance.

A sound from behind her brought her back to her immediate problems. Choso had gained the roof. She looked forward and down, ignoring the dazzling view.

It was only then she realised she'd miscalculated. The road had dropped away on the far side of the house, leaving her with a drop that sent her reeling backwards when she peered over the edge.

There was no way down. The next house was smaller than it had appeared and on the opposite side of the road. It was too far to jump.

Choso appeared around the edge of the roof, smiling cruelly at having cornered her. She watched as he slowly made his own way along the guttering, clearly conscious of the long fall below. He had to continually bend down to steady himself with one hand as he slowly moved towards her. His body was in almost complete silhouette, framed against the huge ruddy orb of Lacaille hanging in the sky behind him.

Kiri looked about desperately for another way to escape, but the only route was back the way she had come, a route now guarded by the furious bulk of Choso, still moving towards her. She turned and raised the branch in her hand, her eyes widened. She was suddenly conscious of her heart beating fast in her chest accompanied by a buzzing in her ears.

She heard the scuttering sound of feet in the dust far below and realised the other two brothers had found their way around the wall and were looking up at the altercation from below. Moments later taunts and abuse were hurled in her direction along with encouragement for Choso.

Choso took a couple of practise swings with his sword, all the time adjusting his balance on the sloping roof. Kiri braced herself.

'Gonna end you now, slum,' Choso said, licking his lips, a grin twisting his features. Below, the brothers continued to yell enthusiastically to him.

Kiri spat at him and stabbed out with her branch. Choso parried the blow and turned it back on her, twisting his sword down, around and up in what was now obviously a practised move. The branch was wrenched from her hand a second time. It clattered across the tiles and dropped over the edge, landing with a faint thud on the ground below. Kiri stepped back, almost losing her footing as she reached the edge of the guttering, her heel exposed above the drop. A tile cracked and pieces of debris dropped into the street behind her.

Kiri tensed, waiting to see what Choso was going to try next, concentrating on his shoulders; you could always see the strike coming if you paid attention. She saw a flicker of movement and leapt up the sloping roof. Choso had tried to chop at her legs, but she evaded the blow, the sword slamming into the tiled roof below her. Kiri landed further up and scrambled for a moment, one hand on the apex of the roof. Choso growled in fury and moved below her, ready to stab upwards. Now she was worse off, helpless as he approached. He was going to gut her right there.

Kiri tried to prise her way upwards, aiming to gain the other side and escape Choso that way. Her feet struggled for grip on the smooth tiles. She couldn't get any purchase. Choso laughed and readied a blow. She felt sweat drip down her face and her stomach clench. Kiri focused her attention on her precarious grip, staring at the curved tile grasped in her hand as if it were the only thing that existed in her world. Her fingers were slipping.

No! Hold on... don't...

She heard the sword swish through the air. A strange feeling rippled through her, a crisp metallic tang she could almost taste.

There was a loud crack. Kiri felt the side of her body slam into the tiles as her feet completely lost grip. She stared in astonishment as the tile she had been holding shattered into fragments for no apparent reason. A moment later there was a sickening sliding sensation as the tiles underneath her gave way, cascading rapidly down the roof. She scrabbled desperately for grip, hurtling down and yelling out in fear. She cannoned into Choso and knocked them both over the edge amidst a cloud of dust, broken tiles, dirt and fluffs of greening. She heard a yell as she flung out her hands, feeling her palms rip and tear as she tried to slow her descent. There was a heavy thump from somewhere below her.

Kiri blinked, trying to clear her eyes. For a moment she could see nothing but swirling dust which burned her eyes. The urge to rub them was intense, but she knew she didn't dare move. There was no sound but an unpleasant creaking from above her and the faint showering of dust and debris. For a moment she held still, her eyes stinging, feeling dust and dirt cascade around her.

A brief glance confirmed she was hanging by the guttering at least fifty hands above the ground below. She blinked rapidly, trying to clear her eyes. They watered, blurring her vision. She shook her head, feeling the fluid dripping down her cheeks. She looked up to see blood dripping down her outstretched arms from lacerations in her palms. The pain was intense, making her wince, but she clung on desperately. She looked down, trying to find something to brace her feet against; unfortunately the guttering overhung the wall of the house by some margin and her feet couldn't reach anything.

The guttering creaked again and shifted a finger's length, jolting her downwards and showering her with dust again. She looked up and saw the guttering breaking free from its supports. She struggled in vain for a moment and then felt herself falling, yelling out as she did so.

She braced against the certain death she knew was coming, screaming out her defiance. The breath was knocked out of her on impact, but it was not the hard abrupt end she had expected. She hit something soft, heard a grunt and then found herself on the ground dazed and winded, but most definitely alive.

'Caught the slum!' somebody said above her. A crowd of people were around her, pushing and shoving. She was wrestled roughly to her feet and pushed forward. A crowd had gathered; they must have been drawn to the ruckus. Ahead she could see they were clustered around something on the ground. Before she could see what it was she was pushed forward with enough force to throw her to the ground again, falling head first on to the stony ground.

She raised her head to see blank eyes, already cloudy, staring sightlessly at her. It was Choso, lying on his back in the dirt. His mouth was open, a look of profound astonishment frozen on his face. A pool of murky dark red blood was oozing out from somewhere behind his head. Kiri had only a moment to grasp what had happened.

'Snuttin' dirty slum!'

She was unprepared for the kick that came out of nowhere into her stomach. She rolled onto her side, curling up in agony. Another kick caught her from behind in the kidneys, throwing her over in the opposite direction. She felt rather than heard a rib crack in her chest as further blows rained down upon her. One caught her in the head. She saw a brief burst of flickering lights before blackness claimed her vision.

'Not here!' someone yelled. 'Take her out on the lane and throw her body in the woods…'

Kiri dimly felt her ankles being grabbed and then she felt herself being carelessly hauled across the rough ground, the sharp edges of stones cutting into her back and arms. It seemed to last a lifetime, but she couldn't even cry out, the pain in her chest too extreme for her to anything more than gasp for breath. The world spun away from her again.

A jolt in her arms and a heavy thud brought her back to consciousness. She drew a shuddering breath, but the pain was intense, her muscles spasming and causing her to shake uncontrollably. She tried to move but couldn't get her body to respond. The taste of blood was on her lips. One eye was already swollen shut, but she managed to open the other one.

For a moment she could make no sense of what she was seeing. All she could make out were... shoes. It took her a moment to realise she was still surrounded by a crowd of people. With faint amusement she recognised the wall behind them. She had climbed it just a few minutes before. Dimly she saw a hand reach down, her vision blackening around the edges. She recognised the colour of the tunic on the arm, one of Choso's brothers. The hand grasped a smooth round rock from the edge of the lane and lifted it slowly out of her line of sight. She whimpered feebly.

I'll see you in the after soon, Tia...

Nothing happened for a long moment. Then she heard another cracking sound. Pain registered in her leg, but it was nothing compared to the agony already burning through her. She heard the sound of more stones being picked up, a rough scraping noise from all around her. Mutterings of assent and approval followed, quickly growing into a roar, like carns baying for blood.

Kiri's consciousness faded away as the next stone struck her supine body. There was a vague feeling of frustration, but it was swamped by a sudden wrathful anger that surged through her. Her last thought burnt through her mind.

I don't want to die!

She felt the strange tang once again, metallic, almost like the blood she could taste in her mouth, but oh so powerful! It was intoxicating, crackling through her whole self. She heard a yell and then exclamations of surprise, pain and fear. Next came the sound of feet scuffling and folks moving rapidly backwards in apparent alarm.

'Hold!'

The cry was imperious, firm and stern. More words followed, but Kiri could not understand them. Their impact was immediate. The crowd became silent and rapidly dispersed. She saw feet running, raising a cloud of dust. She tried to turn her head to see, but found she couldn't move.

Deliberate footsteps sounded, moving swiftly towards her prone form. She felt a hand push back the bloodied hair from her face and then fingers placed against her neck. For the third time she felt the peculiar tang tingle through her, less intense this time, almost comforting.

Are you still alive, can you hear me…?

Kiri felt as if a strange musical voice had said the words inside her head; it was accompanied by a sense of astonishment, anger and abject concern.

'It's her,' the voice said, quietly. 'Did you see what she did…?'

'A slum girl?' the second voice interrupted doubtfully, carrying an air of distaste. 'We can't afford to lose any of them, you know that. She must be one of…'

'Is she alive?'

'Barely. Be quick. Help me get her to the infirmary, before it's too late.'

Kiri felt herself gently hoisted into the air. Her body cradled in strong but delicate arms. Her broken ribs grated painfully and she yelped in pain.

'Uhh. She's filthy and rank! Disgusting!'

'Stop complaining and hurry.'

Kiri's vision was almost a complete blur, but she caught sight of a startling cyan and magenta gown, shining in the sunlight.

Just like the flit…

Her working eye focussed briefly, seeing a sparkling pendant shaped like a tall elongated triangle. Her gaze travelled upwards to see a beautiful but ghostly pale face, a simple tiara perched on a high forehead with immaculate dark hair brushed to the right side with a distinctive silver streak.

A Priestess…!

Blackness abruptly engulfed her and sound faded into utter silence.

Printed in Great Britain
by Amazon